D0973338

Dear Reader,

We've brought back two best-loved Nora Roberts classics. Both feature architects, sexy and skilled, who break down walls—both physical and emotional—as they fall in love with strong, passionate women.

Confirmed bachelor Nathan Powell had his life mapped out—until he discovered author Jackie "Jack" MacNamara living in his house. This mismatched couple are like oil and water, but there's absolutely no doubt who will be *Loving Jack*.

Some men make your pulse hammer, your heart rise and fall. Abra Wilson found that architect Cody Johnson was just such a man. Though he was utterly distracting, Cody was the kind of charmer Abra refused to fall for. But her *Best Laid Plans* go awry when Cody has other ideas…

Happy reading!

The Editors
Silhouette Books

NORA ROBERTS

The HEART *of the* HOME

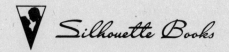

Silhouette Books

SILHOUETTE™

The Heart of the Home

ISBN-13: 978-1-335-14579-6

Recycling programs for this product may not exist in your area.

Copyright © 2020 by Harlequin Books S.A.

Loving Jack
First published in 1988. This edition published in 2020.
Copyright © 1988 by Nora Roberts

Best Laid Plans
First published in 1989. This edition published in 2020.
Copyright © 1989 by Nora Roberts

This edition published by arrangement with Harlequin Books S.A.

For questions and comments about the quality of this book, please contact us at CustomerService@Harlequin.com.

Silhouette
22 Adelaide St. West, 40th Floor
Toronto, Ontario M5H 4E3, Canada
www.Harlequin.com

Printed in U.S.A.

CONTENTS

LOVING JACK

To Kasey Michaels,
because Jackie is a heroine she'll understand.

Chapter 1

The minute Jackie saw the house, she was in love. Of course, she acknowledged, she did fall in love easily. It wasn't that she was easily impressed, she was just open, wide-open, to emotions—her own and everyone else's.

The house had a lot of emotion in it, she felt, and not all of it serene. That was good. Total serenity would have been all right for a day or two, but boredom would have closed in. She preferred the contrasts here, the strong angles and arrogant juts of the corners, softened occasionally by curving windows and unexpectedly charming archways.

The white-painted walls glittered in the sunlight, set off by stark ebony trim. Though she didn't believe the world was black-and-white, the house made the statement that the two opposing forces could live together in harmony.

The windows were wide, welcoming the view from both east and west, while skylights let in generous slices of sun. Flowers grew in profusion in the side garden and in terra-

cotta pots along the terraces. She enjoyed the bold color
they added, the touch of the exotic and lush. They'd have
to be tended, of course—and religiously, if the heat continued and the rain didn't come. She didn't mind getting
dirty, though, especially if there was a reward at the end.

Through wide glass doors she looked out at the crystal-
line waters of a kidney-shaped tiled pool. That, too, would
require tending, but that, too, offered rewards. She could
already picture herself sitting beside it, watching the sun
set with the scent of flowers everywhere. Alone. That was
a small hitch, but one she was willing to accept.

Beyond the pool and the sloping slice of lawn was the Intracoastal Waterway. Its waters were dark, mysterious, but
even as she watched, a motorboat putted by. She discovered
she liked the sound of it. It meant there were people close
enough to make contact but not so close as to interfere.

The water roads reminded her of Venice and a particularly pleasant month she had spent there during her teens.
She'd ridden in gondolas and flirted with dark-eyed men.
Florida in the spring wasn't as romantic as Italy, but it
suited her just fine.

"I love it." She turned back to the wide, sun-washed
room. There were twin sofas the color of oatmeal on a
steel-blue carpet. The rest of the furniture was an elegant
ebony and leaned toward the masculine. Jackie approved
of its strength and style. She rarely wasted her time looking for flaws and was willing to accept them when they
jumped out at her. But in this house and everything about
it she saw perfection.

She beamed at the man standing casually in front of the
white marble fireplace. The hearth had been cleaned and
swept and was a home for a potted fern. The man's tropi-
cal-looking white pants and shirt might have been chosen

for precisely that pose. Knowing Frederick Q. MacNamara as she did, Jackie was sure it had been.

"When can I move in?"

Fred's smile lit up his round, boyish face. No one looking at it would have been reminded of a shark. "That's our Jack, always going on impulse." His body was rounded, too—not quite fat, but not really firm, either. Fred's favorite exercise was hailing—cabs or waiters. He moved toward her with a languid grace that had once been feigned but was now second nature. "You haven't even seen the second floor."

"I'll see it when I unpack."

"Jack, I want you to be sure." He patted her cheek—older, more experienced cousin to young scatterbrain. She didn't take offense. "I'd hate for you to regret this in a day or two. After all, you're proposing to live in this house by yourself for three months."

"I've got to live somewhere." She gestured, palm out, with a hand as slim and delicate as the rest of her. Gold and colored stones glittered on four fingers, a sign of her love of the pretty. "If I'm going to be serious about writing, I should be alone. Since I don't think I'd care for a garret, why shouldn't it be here?"

She paused a moment. It never paid to be too casual with Fred, cousin or not. Not that she didn't like him. Jackie had always had a soft spot for Fred, though she knew he had a habit of skimming off the top and dealing from the bottom.

"You're sure it's all right for you to sublet it to me?"

"Perfectly." His voice was as smooth as his face. Whatever wrinkles Fred had were carefully camouflaged. "The owner only uses it as a winter home, and then only sporadically. He prefers having someone in residence rather than leaving it empty. I told Nathan I'd take care of things until November, but then this business in San Diego came up, and it can't be put off. You know how it is, darling."

Jackie knew exactly how it was. With Fred, "sudden business" usually meant he was avoiding either a jealous husband or the law. Despite his unprepossessing looks, he had constant problems with the former, and not even a prepossessing family name could always protect him from the latter.

She should have been warier, but Jackie wasn't always wise, and the house—the look, the feel, of it—had already blinded her.

"If the owner wants it occupied, I'm happy to accommodate him. Let me sign on the dotted line, Fred. I want to unpack and spend a couple of hours in the pool."

"If you're sure." He was already drawing a paper from his pocket. "I don't want a scene later—like the time you bought my Porsche."

"You failed to tell me the transmission was held together with Krazy Glue."

"Let the buyer beware," Fred said mildly, and handed her a monogrammed silver pen.

She had a quick flash of trepidation. This was cousin Fred, after all. Fred of the easy deal and the can't-miss investment. Then a bird flew into the garden and began to sing cheerily, and Jackie took it as an omen. She signed the lease in a bold, flowing hand before drawing out her checkbook.

"A thousand a month for three months?"

"Plus five hundred damage deposit," Fred added.

"Right." She supposed she was lucky dear cousin Fred wasn't charging her a commission. "Are you leaving me a number, an address or something so I can get in touch with the owner if necessary?"

Fred looked blank for a moment, then beamed at her. It was that MacNamara smile, charming and guileless. "I've already told him about the turnover. Don't worry about a thing, sweetie. He'll be in touch with you."

"Fine." She wasn't going to worry about details. It was spring, and she had a new house, a new project. New beginnings were the best thing in the world. "I'll take care of everything." She touched a large Chinese urn. She'd begin by putting fresh flowers in it. "Will you be staying tonight, Fred?"

The check was already stashed in the inside pocket of his jacket. He resisted the urge to add a loving pat. "I'd love to hang around, indulge in some family gossip, but since we've got everything squared away, I should catch a flight to the Coast. You'll need to get to the market pretty soon, Jack. There're some essentials in the kitchen, but not much else." As he spoke, he started across the room toward a pile of baggage. It never occurred to him to offer to take his cousin's bags upstairs for her, or for her to ask him to. "Keys are there on the table. Enjoy yourself."

"I will." When he hefted his cases, she walked over to open the door for him. She'd meant her invitation to spend the night sincerely, and she was just as sincerely glad he'd refused. "Thanks, Fred. I really appreciate this."

"My pleasure, darling." He leaned down to exchange a kiss with her. Jackie got a whiff of his expensive cologne. "Give my love to the family when you talk to them."

"I will. Safe trip, Fred." She watched him walk out to a long, lean convertible. It was white, like his suit. After stowing his cases, Fred scooted behind the wheel and sent her a lazy salute. Then she was alone.

Jackie turned back to the room and hugged herself. She was alone, and on her own. She'd been there before, of course. She was twenty-five, after all, and had taken solo trips and vacations, had her own apartment and her own life. But each time she started out with something new it was a fresh adventure.

As of this day…was it March 25, 26? She shook her head. It didn't matter. As of this day, she was beginning a new career. Jacqueline R. MacNamara, novelist.

It had a nice ring, she thought. The first thing she was going to do was unpack her new typewriter and begin chapter one. With a laugh, she grabbed the typewriter case and her heaviest suitcase and started upstairs.

It didn't take long to acclimate herself, to the South, to the house, to her new routine. She rose early, enjoying the morning quiet with juice and a piece of toast—or flat cola and cold pizza, if that was handier. Her typing improved with practice, and by the end of the third day her machine was humming nicely. She would break in the afternoon to have a dip in the pool, lie in the sun and think about the next scene, or plot twist.

She tanned easily and quickly. It was a gift Jackie attributed to the Italian great-grandmother who had breached the MacNamara's obsessively Irish ranks. The color pleased her, and most of the time she remembered the face creams and moisturizers that her mother had always touted. "Good skin and bone structure make a beauty, Jacqueline. Not style or fashion or clever makeup," she'd often declared.

Well, Jackie had the skin and bone structure, though even her mother had to admit she would never be a true beauty. She was pretty enough, in a piquant, healthy sort of way. But her face was triangular rather than oval, her mouth wide rather than bowed. Her eyes were just a shade too big, and they were brown. The Italian again. She hadn't inherited the sea green or sky blue that dominated the rest of her family. Her hair was brown, as well. During her teens she'd experimented with rinses and streaks, often to her mother's embarrassment, but had finally settled for what God had given her. She'd even come to like it, and the fact that it curled on its own meant she didn't have to spend precious time in salons. She kept it short, and its natural fullness and curl made a halo around her face.

She was glad of its length now, because of her afternoon dips. It only took a few shakes and a little finger-combing to make it spring back to its casual style.

She took each morning as it came, diving headfirst into writing after she woke, then into the pool each afternoon. After a quick forage for lunch, she went back to her machine and worked until evening. She might play in the garden then, or sit and watch the boats or read on the terrace. If the day had been particularly productive, she would treat herself to the whirlpool, letting the bubbling water and the sultry heat of the glass enclosure make her pleasantly tired.

She locked the house for the owner's benefit rather than for her own safety. Each night Jackie slipped into bed in the room she'd chosen with perfect peace of mind and the tingling excitement of what the next morning would bring.

Whenever her thoughts turned to Fred, she smiled. Maybe the family was wrong about Fred after all. It was true that more than once he'd taken some gullible relative for a ride down a one-way street and left him—or her— at a dead end. But he'd certainly done her a good turn when he'd suggested the house in Florida. On the evening of the third day, Jackie lowered herself into the churning waters of the spa and thought about sending cousin Fred some flowers.

She owed him one.

* * *

He was dead tired, and happy as hell to be home at last. The final leg of the journey had seemed interminable. Being on American soil again after six months hadn't been enough. When Nathan had landed in New York, the first real flood of impatience had struck. He was home, yet not home. For the first time in months he had allowed himself to think of his own house, his own bed. His own private sacrosanct space.

Then there had been an hour's delay that had left him roaming the airport and almost grinding his teeth. Even once he'd been airborne he hadn't been able to stop checking and rechecking his watch to see how much longer he had to hang in the sky.

The airport in Fort Lauderdale still wasn't home. He'd spent a cold, hard winter in Germany and he'd had enough of the charm of snow and icicles. The warm, moist air and the sight of palms only served to annoy him, because he wasn't quite there yet.

He'd arranged to have his car delivered to the airport, and when he'd finally eased himself into the familiar interior he'd felt like himself again. The hours of flying from Frankfurt to New York no longer mattered. The delays and impatience were forgotten. He was behind the wheel, and twenty minutes from pulling into his own driveway. When he went to bed that night it would be between his own sheets. Freshly laundered and turned back by Mrs. Grange, who Fred MacNamara had assured him would have the house ready for his arrival.

Nathan felt a little twist of guilt about Fred. He knew he'd hustled the man along to get him up and out of the house before his arrival, but after six months of intense work in Germany he wasn't in the mood for a houseguest.

He'd have to be sure to get in touch with Fred and thank him for keeping an eye on things. It was an arrangement that had solved a multitude of problems with little fuss. As far as Nathan was concerned, the less fuss the better. He definitely owed Frank MacNamara a very large thank-you.

In a few days, Nathan thought as he slipped his key into the lock. After he'd slept for twenty hours and indulged in some good, old-fashioned sloth.

Nathan pushed open the door, hit the lights and just looked. Home. It was so incredibly good to be home, in the house he'd designed and built, among things chosen for his own taste and comfort.

Home. It was exactly as he—no, it wasn't exactly as he'd left it, he realized quickly. Because his eyes were gritty with fatigue, he rubbed them as he studied the room. His room.

Who had moved the Ming over to the window and stuck irises in it? And why was the Meissen bowl on the table instead of the shelf? He frowned. He was a meticulous man, and he could see a dozen small things out of place.

He'd have to speak to Mrs. Grange about it, but he wasn't going to let a few annoyances spoil his pleasure at being home.

It was tempting to go straight to the kitchen and pour himself something long and cold, but he believed in doing first things first. Hefting his cases, he walked upstairs, relishing each moment of quiet and solitude.

He flipped on the lights in his bedroom and stopped short. Very slowly, he lowered the suitcases and walked to the bed. It wasn't turned down, but made up haphazardly. His dresser, the Chippendale he'd picked up at Sotheby's five years before, was crowded with pots and bottles. There was a definite scent here, not only from the baby roses that had been stuck in the Waterford—which belonged in the dining room cabinet—but a scent of woman. Powder, lotion and oil. Neither strong nor rich, but light and intrusive. His eyes narrowed when he saw the swatch of color on the spread. Nathan picked up the thin, almost microscopic bikini panties.

Mrs. Grange? The very idea was laughable. The sturdy Mrs. Grange wouldn't be able to fit one leg inside that little number. If Fred had had a guest... Nathan turned the panties over under the light. He supposed he could tolerate Fred having had a companion, but not in his room. And why in hell weren't her things packed and gone?

He got an image. It might have been the architect in him that enabled him to take a blank page or an empty lot and fill it completely in his mind. He saw a tall, slim woman, sexy, a little loud and bold. Ready to party. A redhead, probably, with lots of teeth and a rowdy turn of mind. That was fine for Fred, but the agreement had been that the house was to be empty and back in order on Nathan's return.

He gave the bottles on his dresser one last glance. He'd have Mrs. Grange dispose of them. Without thinking, he stuffed the thin piece of nylon in his pocket and strode out to see what else wasn't as it should be.

Jackie, her eyes shut and her head resting on the crimson edge of the spa, sang to herself. It had been a particularly good day. The tale was spinning out of her head and onto the page so quickly it was almost scary. She was glad she'd picked the West for her setting, old Arizona, desolate, tough, dusty and full of grit. That was just the right backdrop for her hard-bitten hero and her primly naive heroine.

They were already bumping along the rocky road to romance, though she didn't think even they knew it yet. She loved being able to put herself back in the 1800s, feeling the heat, smelling the sweat. And of course there was danger and adventure at every step. Her convent-raised heroine was having a devil of a time, but she was coping. Strong. Jackie couldn't have written about a weak-minded woman if she'd had to.

And her hero. Just thinking about him made her smile. She could see him perfectly, just as if he'd popped out of her imagination into the tub with her. That dark black hair, thick, glinting red in the sun when he removed his hat. Long enough that a woman could get a handful of it. The body lean and hard from riding, brown from the sun, scarred from the trouble he never walked away from.

You could see that in his face, a lean, bony face that was often shadowed by the beard he didn't bother to shave. He had a mouth that could smile and make a woman's heart pump fast. Or it could tighten and send shivers of fear up a man's spine. And his eyes. Oh, his eyes were a wonder. Slate gray and fringed by long, dark lashes, crinkled at the corners from squinting into the Arizona sun. Flat and hard when he pulled the trigger, hot and passionate when he took a woman.

Every woman in Arizona was in love with Jake Redman. And Jackie was pleased to be a little in love with him herself. Didn't that make him real? she thought as the bubbles swirled around her. If she could see him so clearly, and feel for him this intensely, didn't it mean she was doing the job right? He wasn't a good man, not through and through. It would be up to the heroine to mine the gold from him, and accept the rough stones along with it. And boy, was he going to give Miss Sarah Conway a run for her money. Jackie could hardly wait to sit down with them so that they could show her what happened next. If she concentrated hard enough, she could almost hear him speak to her.

"What in the hell are you doing?"

Still dreaming, Jackie opened her eyes and looked into the face of her imagination. Jake? she thought, wondering if the hot water had soaked into her brain. Jake didn't wear suits and ties, but she recognized the look that meant he was about to draw and fire. Her mouth fell open and she stared.

His hair was shorter, but not by much, and the shadow of beard was there. She pressed her fingers to her eyes and got chlorine in them, then blinked them open. He was still there, a little closer now. The sound of the spa's motor seemed louder as it filled her head.

"Am I dreaming?"

Nathan's eyes narrowed. She wasn't the rowdy redhead he'd pictured, but a cute, doe-eyed brunette. Either way, she didn't belong in his house. "What you're doing is trespassing. Now who the hell are you?"

The voice. Good grief, even the voice was right. Jackie shook her head and struggled to get a grip on herself. This was the twentieth century, and no matter how real her characters seemed on paper, they didn't come to life in five-hundred-dollar suits. The simple fact was that she was alone with a stranger and in a very vulnerable position.

She wondered how much she remembered from her karate course, then took another look at the man's broad shoulders and decided it just wasn't going to be enough.

"Who are you?" The edge of fear gave her voice haughty, rounded tones her mother would have been proud of.

"You're the one who has questions to answer," he countered. "But I'm Nathan Powell."

"The architect? Oh, I've admired your work. I saw the Ridgeway Center in Chicago, and…" She started to scoot up, no longer afraid, but then she remembered she hadn't bothered to put on a suit and slumped back again. "You have a marvelous flair for combining aesthetics with practicality."

"Thanks. Now—"

"But what are you doing here?"

His eyes narrowed again, and for the second time Jackie saw something of her gunslinger in them. "That's my question. This is my house."

"Yours?" She rubbed the back of her wrist over her eyes as she tried to think. "You're Nathan? Fred's Nathan?" Relieved, she smiled again. "Well, that explains things."

A dimple appeared at the corner of her mouth when she smiled. Nathan noticed it, then ignored it. He was a fastidious man, and fastidious men didn't come home to find strange women in their tubs. "Not to me. I'm going to repeat myself. Who the hell are you?"

"Oh. Sorry. I'm Jack." When his brow rose, she smiled again and extended a wet hand. "Jackie—Jacqueline MacNamara. Fred's cousin."

He glanced at her hand, and at the glitter of jewels on it, but didn't take it in his. He was afraid that if he did he might just haul her out onto the tiled floor. "And why, Miss MacNamara, are you sitting in my spa, and sleeping in my bed?"

"Is that your room? Sorry, Fred didn't say which I was to take, so I took the one I liked best. He's in San Diego, you know."

"I don't give a damn where he is." He'd always been a patient man. At least that was what he'd always believed. Right now, though, he was finding he had no patience at all. "What I want to know is why you're in my house."

"Oh, I sublet it from Fred. Didn't he get ahold of you?"

"You what?"

"You know, it's hard to talk with this motor running. Wait." She held up a hand before he could hit the off button. "I'm, ah...well, I wasn't expecting anyone, so I'm not exactly dressed for company. Would you mind?"

He glanced down automatically to where the water churned hot and fast at the subtle curve of her breast. Nathan set his teeth. "I'll be in the kitchen. Make it fast."

Jackie let out a long breath when she was alone. "I think Fred did it again," she muttered as she hauled herself out of the tub and dried off.

Nathan made himself a long gin and tonic, using a liberal hand with the gin. As far as homecomings went, this one left a lot to be desired. There might have been men who'd be pleasantly surprised to come home after an exhausting project and find naked women waiting in their sunrooms. Unfortunately, he just wasn't one of them. He took a deep drink as he leaned back against the counter. It was, he supposed, just a question of taking one step at a time—and the first would be disposing of Jacqueline MacNamara.

"Mr. Powell?"

He glanced over to see her step into the kitchen. She was still dripping a bit. Her legs were lightly tanned and long—very long, he noticed—skimmed at the thighs by a terry-cloth robe that was as boldly striped as Joseph's coat of many colors. Her hair curled damply around her face in a soggy halo, with a fringe of bangs that accented dark, wide eyes. She was smiling, and the dimple was back. He wasn't sure he liked that. When she smiled she looked as though she could sell you ten acres of Florida swampland.

"It appears we're going to have to discuss your cousin."

"Fred." Jackie nodded, still smiling, and slipped onto a rattan stool at the breakfast bar. She'd already decided she'd do best by being totally at ease and in control. If he thought she was nervous and unsure of her position... Well, she wasn't positive, but she had a very good idea she'd find herself standing outside the house, bag in hand. "He's quite a character, isn't he? How did you meet him?"

"Through a mutual friend." He grimaced a little, thinking he was going to have to talk with Justine, as well. "I had a project in Germany that was going to keep me out of the country for a few months. I needed someone to house-sit. He was recommended. As I knew his aunt—"

"Patricia—Patricia MacNamara's my mother."

"Adele Lindstrom."

"Oh, Aunt Adele. She's my mother's sister." It was more than a smile this time. Something wickedly amused flashed in Jackie's eyes. "She's a lovely woman."

There was something droll, a bit too droll, in the comment. Nathan chose to ignore it. "I worked with Adele briefly on a revitalization project in Chicago. Because of the connection, and the recommendation, I decided to have Fred look out for the house while I was away."

Jackie bit her bottom lip. It was her first sign of nerves, and though she didn't realize it, that small gesture cleared a great deal of ground for her. "He wasn't renting it from you?"

"Renting it? Of course not." She was twisting her rings, one at a time, around her fingers. Don't get involved, he warned himself. Tell her to pack up and move out. No explanations, no apologies. You can be in bed in ten minutes. Nathan felt rather than heard his own sigh. Not many people knew that Nathan Powell was a sucker. "Is that what he told you?"

"I suppose I'd better tell you the whole story. Could I have one of those?"

When she indicated his glass, he nearly snapped at her. Manners had been bred carefully into him, and he was irritated at his oversight, even though she was hardly a guest.

Without speaking, he poured and mixed another drink, then sat it in front of her. "I'd appreciate it if you could condense the whole story and just give me the highlights."

"Okay." She took a sip, bracing herself. "Fred called me last week. He'd heard through the family grapevine that I was looking for a place to stay for a few months. A nice quiet place where I could work. I'm a writer," she said with the audacious pride of one who believed it. When this brought no response, she drank again and continued. "Anyway, Fred said he had a place that might suit me. He told me he'd been renting this house... He described it," Jackie explained, "and I just couldn't wait to see it. It's a beautiful place, so thoughtfully designed. Now that I know who you are, I can see why—the strength and charm of the structure, the openness of the space. If I hadn't been so intent on what I was doing, I'd have recognized your style right away. I studied architecture for a couple of semesters at Columbia."

"That's fascinating, I'm sure... LaFont?"

"Yes, he's a wonderful old duck, isn't he? So pompous and sure of his own worth."

Nathan raised a brow. He'd studied with LaFont himself—a lifetime ago, it seemed—and was well aware that the old duck, as Jackie had termed him, only took on the most promising students. He opened his mouth again, then shut it. He wouldn't be drawn out. "Let's get back to your cousin, Miss MacNamara."

"Jackie," she said, flashing that smile again. "Well, if I hadn't been really anxious to get settled, I probably would have said thanks but no thanks. Fred's always got an angle. But I came down. I took one look at the place, and that was that. He said he had to leave for San Diego right away on business and that the owner—you—didn't want the house empty while you were away. I suppose you don't really just use it as a winter home sporadically, do you?"

"No." He drew a cigarette out of his pocket. He'd successfully cut down to ten a day, but these were extenuating circumstances. "I live here year-round, except when a project takes me away. The arrangement was for Fred to live here during my absence. I called two weeks ago to let him know when I'd be arriving. He was to contact Mrs. Grange and leave his forwarding address with her."

"Mrs. Grange?"

"The housekeeper."

"He didn't mention a housekeeper."

"Why doesn't that surprise me?" Nathan murmured, and finished off his drink. "That takes us to the point of your occupation."

Jackie drew a long breath. "I signed a lease. Three months. I wrote Fred a check for the rent, in advance, plus a damage deposit."

"That's unfortunate." He wouldn't feel sorry for her. He'd be damned if he would. "You didn't sign a lease with the owner."

"With your proxy. With whom I thought was your proxy," she amended. "Cousin Fred can be very smooth." He wasn't smiling, Jackie noted. Not even a glimmer. It was a pity he couldn't see the humor in the situation. "Look, Mr. Powell—Nathan—it's obvious Fred's pulled something on both of us, but there must be a way we can work it out. As far as the thirty-five hundred dollars goes—"

"Thirty-five hundred?" Nathan said. "You paid him thirty-five hundred dollars?"

"It seemed reasonable." She was tempted to pout because of his tone, but she didn't think it would help. "You do have a beautiful home, and there was the pool, and the sunroom. Anyway, with a bit of family pressure, I may be able to get some of it back. Sooner or later." She thought about the money a moment longer, then dismissed it. "But the real problem is how to handle this situation."

"Which is?"

"My being here, and your being here."

"That's easy." Nathan tapped out his cigarette. There was no reason, absolutely no reason, why he should feel guilty that she'd lost money. "I can recommend a couple of excellent hotels."

She smiled again. She was sure he could, but she had no intention of going to one. The dimple was still in place, but if Nathan had looked closely he would have seen that the soft brown eyes had hardened with determination.

"That would solve your part of the problem, but not mine. I do have a lease."

"You have a worthless piece of paper."

"Very possibly." She tapped her ringed fingers on the counter as she considered. "Did you ever study law? When I was at Harvard—"

"Harvard?"

"Very briefly." She brushed away the hallowed halls with the back of her hand. "I didn't really take to it, but I do think it might be difficult and, worse, annoying to toss me out on my ear." She swirled her drink and considered. "Of course, if you wanted to get a warrant and take it to court, dragging cousin Fred into it, you'd win eventually. I'm sure of that. In the meantime," she continued before he could find the right words, "I'm sure we can come up with a much more suitable solution for everyone. You must be exhausted." She changed her tone so smoothly he could only stare. "Why don't you go on up and get a good night's sleep? Everything's clearer on a good night's sleep, don't you think? We can hash through all this tomorrow."

"It's not a matter of hashing through anything, Miss MacNamara. It's a matter of your packing up your things." He shoved a hand into his pocket, and his fingers brushed the swatch of nylon. Gritting his teeth, he pulled it out. "These are yours?"

"Yes, thanks." Without a blush, Jackie accepted her underwear. "It's a little late to be calling the cops and explaining all of this to them. I imagine you could throw me out bodily, but you'd hate yourself for it."

She had him there. Nathan began to think she had a lot more in common with her cousin than a family name. He glanced at his watch and swore. It was already after midnight, and he didn't—quite—have the heart to dump her in the street. The worst of it was that he was nearly tired enough to see double and couldn't seem to come up with the right, or the most promising, arguments. So he'd let it ride—for the moment.

"I'll give you twenty-four hours, Miss MacNamara. That seems more than reasonable to me."

"I knew you were a reasonable man." She smiled at him again. "Why don't you go get some sleep? I'll lock up."

"You're in my bed."

"I beg your pardon?"

"Your things are in my room."

"Oh." Jackie scratched at her temple. "Well, I suppose if it was really important to you, I could haul everything out tonight."

"Never mind." Maybe it was all a nightmare. A hallucination. He'd wake up in the morning and discover everything was as it should be. "I'll take one of the guest rooms."

"That's a much better idea. You really do look tired. Sleep well."

He stared at her for nearly a full minute. When he was gone, Jackie laid her head down on the counter and began to giggle. Oh, she'd get Fred for this, make no mistake. But now, just now, it was the funniest thing that had happened to her in months.

Chapter 2

When Nathan woke, it was after ten East Coast time, but the nightmare wasn't over. He realized that as soon as he saw the muted striped paper on the wall of the guest room. He was in his own house, but he'd somehow found himself relegated to the position of guest.

His suitcases, open but still packed, sat on the mahogany chest under the garden window. He'd left his drapes undrawn, and sunlight poured in over the neatly folded shirts. Deliberately he turned away from them. He'd be damned if he'd unpack until he could do so in the privacy of his own room.

A man had a right to his own closet.

Jacqueline MacNamara had been correct about one thing. He felt better after a full night's sleep. His mind was clearer. Though it wasn't something he cared to dwell on, he went over everything that had happened from the time he'd unlocked his door until he'd fallen, facefirst, into the guest bed.

He realized he'd been a fool not to toss her out on her pert little ear the night before, but that could be rectified. And the sooner the better.

He showered, taking his shaving gear into the bathroom with him, but meticulously replacing everything in the kit when he was finished. Nothing was coming out until it could be placed in his own cabinets and drawers. After he'd dressed, in light cotton pants and shirt, he felt in charge again. If he couldn't deal with a dippy little number like the brunette snuggled in his bed, he was definitely slipping. Still, it wouldn't hurt to have a cup of coffee first.

He was halfway down the stairs when he smelled it. Coffee. Strong, fresh coffee. The aroma was so welcome he nearly smiled, but then he remembered who must have brewed it. Strengthening his resolve, he continued. Another scent wafted toward him. Bacon? Surely that was bacon. Obviously she was making herself right at home. He heard the music, as well—rock, something cheerful and bouncy and loud enough to be heard a room away.

No, the nightmare wasn't over, but it was going to end, and end quickly.

Nathan strode into the kitchen prepared to shoot straight from the hip.

"Good morning." Jackie greeted him with a smile that competed with the sunshine. As a concession to him, she turned the radio down, but not off. "I wasn't sure how long you'd sleep, but I didn't think you were the type to stay in bed through the morning, so I started breakfast. I hope you like blueberry pancakes. I slipped out early and bought the berries. They're fresh." Before he could speak, she popped one into his mouth. "Have a seat. I'll get your coffee."

"Miss MacNamara—"

"Jackie, please. Cream?"

"Black. We left things a bit up in the air last night, but we've got to settle this business now."

"Absolutely. I hope you like your bacon crisp." She set a platter on the counter, where a place was already set with his good china and a damask napkin. She noticed that he'd shaved. With the shadow of beard gone, he didn't look quite as much like her Jake—except around the eyes. It wouldn't be wise, she decided, to underestimate him.

"I've given it a lot of thought, Nathan, and I think I've come up with the ideal solution." She poured batter onto the griddle and adjusted the flame. "Did you sleep well?"

"Fine." At least he'd felt fine when he'd awakened. Now he reached for the coffee almost defensively. She was like a sunbeam that had intruded when all he'd really wanted to do was draw the shades and take a nap.

"My mother's fond of saying you always sleep best at home, but it's never mattered to me. I can sleep anywhere. Would you like the paper?"

"No." He sipped the coffee, stared at it, then sipped again. Maybe it was his imagination, but it was the best cup of coffee he'd ever tasted.

"I buy the beans from a little shop in town," she said, answering his unspoken question as she flipped the pancakes with an expert hand. "I don't drink it often myself. That's why I think it's important to have a really good cup. Ready for these?" Before he could answer, she took his plate and stacked pancakes on it. "You've a wonderful view from right here." Jackie poured a second cup of coffee and sat beside him. "It makes eating an event."

Nathan found himself reaching for the syrup. It wouldn't

hurt to eat first. He could still toss her out later. "How long have you been here?"

"Just a few days. Fred's always had an excellent sense of timing. How are your pancakes?"

It seemed only fair to give her her due. "They're wonderful. Aren't you eating?"

"I sort of sampled as I went along." But that didn't stop her from plucking another slice of bacon. She nibbled, approved, then smiled at him. "Do you cook?"

"Only if the package comes with instructions."

Jackie felt the first thrill of victory. "I'm really a very good cook."

"Studied at the Cordon Bleu, I imagine."

"Only for six months," she said, grinning at him. "But I did learn most of the basics. From there I decided to go my own way, experiment, you know? Cooking should be as much of an adventure as anything else."

To Nathan, cooking was drudgery that usually ended in failure. He only grunted.

"Your Mrs. Grange," Jackie began conversationally. "Is she supposed to come in every day, do the cleaning and the cooking?"

"Once a week." The pancakes were absolutely fabulous. He'd grown accustomed to hotel food, and as excellent as it had been, it couldn't compete with this. He began to relax as he studied the view. She was right, it was great, and he couldn't remember ever having enjoyed breakfast more. "She cleans, does the weekly marketing, and usually fixes a casserole or something." Nathan took another forkful, then stopped himself before he could again be seduced by the flavor. "Why?"

"It all has to do with our little dilemma."

"Your dilemma."

"Whatever. I wonder, are you a fair man, Nathan? Your buildings certainly show a sense of style and order, but I can't really tell if you have a sense of fair play." She lifted the coffeepot. "Let me top that off for you."

He was losing his appetite rapidly. "What are you getting at?"

"I'm out thirty-five hundred." Jackie munched on the bacon. "Now, I'm not going to try to make you think that the loss is going to have me on the street corner selling pencils, but it's not really the amount. It's the principle. You believe in principles, don't you?"

Cautious, he gave a noncommittal shrug.

"I paid, in good faith, for a place to live and to work for three months."

"I'm sure your family retains excellent lawyers. Why don't you sue your cousin?"

"The MacNamaras don't solve family problems that way. Oh, I'll settle up with him—when he least expects it."

There was a look in her eyes that made Nathan think she would do just that, and beautifully. He had to fight back a surge of admiration. "I'll wish you the best of luck here, but your family problems don't involve me."

"They do when it's your house in the middle of it. Do you want some more?"

"No. Thanks," he added belatedly. "Miss—Jackie—I'm going to be perfectly frank with you." He settled back, prepared to be both reasonable and firm. If he'd known her better, Nathan would have felt his first qualms when she turned her big brown eyes on him with a look of complete cooperation. "My work in Germany was difficult and tiring. I have a couple of months of free time coming, which I intend to spend here, alone, doing as little as possible."

"What were you building?"

"What?"

"In Germany. What were you building?"

"An entertainment complex, but that isn't really relevant. I'm sorry if it seems insensitive, but I don't feel responsible for your situation."

"It doesn't seem insensitive at all." Jackie patted his hand, then poured him more coffee. "Why should you, after all? An entertainment complex. It sounds fascinating, and I'd really love to hear all about it later, but the thing is, Nathan—" she paused as she topped off her own cup "—is that I kind of see us as two people in the same boat. We both expected to spend the next couple of months alone, pursuing our own projects, and Fred screwed up the works. Do you like Oriental food?"

He was losing ground. Nathan didn't know why, or when, the sand had started to shift beneath his feet, but there it was. Resting his elbows on the counter, he held his head in his hands. "What the hell does that have to do with anything?"

"It has to do with my idea, and I wanted to know what kind of food you liked, or particularly didn't like. Me, I'll eat anything, but most people have definite preferences." Jackie cupped her mug in both hands as she tucked her legs, lotus-style, under her on the stool. She was wearing shorts today, vivid blue ones with a flamingo emblem on one leg. Nathan studied the odd pink bird for a long time before he lifted his gaze to hers.

"Why don't you just tell me your idea while I still have a small part of my sanity?"

"The object is for both of us to have what we want—or as nearly as possible. It's a big house."

She lifted both brows as his eyes narrowed. That look, she thought again. That Jake look was hard to resist. Nathan's coming back when he did might have been the sort of odd bonus fate sometimes tossed out. Jackie was always ready to make the grab for it.

"I'm an excellent roommate. I could give you references from several people. I went to a variety of colleges, you see, so I lived with a variety of people. I can be neat if that's important, and I can be quiet and unobtrusive."

"I find that difficult to believe."

"No, really, especially when I'm immersed in my own project, like I am now. I write almost all day. This story's really the most important thing in my life right now. I'll have to tell you about it, but we'll save that."

"I'd appreciate it."

"You have a wonderfully subtle sense of humor, Nathan. Don't ever lose it. Anyhow, I'm a strong believer in atmosphere. You must be, too, being an architect."

"You're losing me again." He shoved the coffee aside. Too much stimulation, that must be it. Another cup and he might just start understanding her.

"The house," Jackie said patiently. Her eyes were the problem, Nathan decided. There was something about them that compelled you to look and listen when all you really wanted to do was hold your hands over your ears and run.

"What about the house?"

"There's something about it. The minute I set up here, everything just started flowing. With the story. If I moved, well, don't you think things might stop flowing just as quickly? I don't want to chance that. So I'm willing to make some compromises."

"You're willing to make some compromises," Nathan repeated slowly. "That's fascinating. You're living in my house, without my consent, but you're willing to make some compromises."

"It's only fair." There was that smile again, quick and brilliant. "You don't cook. I do." Jackie gestured with both hands as if to show the simplicity of it. "I'll prepare all of your meals, at my expense, for as long as I'm here."

It sounded reasonable. Why in the hell did it sound so reasonable when she said it? "That's very generous of you, but I don't want a cook, or a roommate."

"How do you know? You haven't had either yet."

"What I want," he began, careful to space his words and keep his tone even, "is privacy."

"Of course you do." She didn't touch him, but her tone was like a pat on the head. He nearly growled. "We'll make a pact right now. I'll respect your privacy and you'll respect mine. Nathan..." She leaned toward him, again covering his hand with hers in a move that was natural rather than calculated. "I know you've got absolutely no reason to do me any favors, but I'm really committed to this book. For reasons of my own, I've a great need to finish it, and I'm sure I can. Here."

"If you're trying to make me feel guilty because I'd be sabotaging the great American novel—"

"No, I'm not. I would have if I'd thought of it, but I didn't. I'm just asking you to give me a chance. A couple of weeks. If I drive you crazy, I'll leave."

"Jacqueline, I've known you about twelve hours, and you've already driven me crazy."

She was winning. There was just the slightest hint of it in his tone, but she caught it and pounced. "You ate all your pancakes."

Almost guiltily, Nathan looked down at his empty plate. "I've had nothing but airplane food for twenty-four hours."

"Wait until you taste my crepes. And my Belgian waffles." She caught her lower lip between her teeth. "Nathan, think of it. You won't have to open a single can as long as I'm around."

Involuntarily he thought of all the haphazard meals he'd prepared, and about the barely edible ones he brought into the house in foam containers. "I'll eat out."

"A fat lot of privacy you'd have sitting in crowded restaurants and competing for a waiter's attention. With my solution, you won't have to do anything but relax."

He hated restaurants. And God knew he'd had enough of them over the past year. The arrangement made perfect sense, at least while he was comfortably full of her blueberry pancakes.

"I want my room back."

"That goes without saying."

"And I don't like small talk in the morning."

"Completely uncivilized. I do want pool privileges."

"If I stumble over you or any of your things even once, you're out."

"Agreed." She held out a hand, sensing he was a man who would stand by a handshake. She was even more certain of it when she saw him hesitate. Jackie brought out what she hoped would be the coup de grâce. "You really would hate yourself if you threw me out, you know."

Nathan scowled at her but found his palm resting against hers. A small hand, and a soft one, he thought, but the grip was firm. If he lived to regret this temporary arrangement, he'd have one more score to settle with Fred. "I'm going to take a spa."

"Good idea. Loosen up all those tense muscles. By the way, what would you like for lunch?"

He didn't look back. "Surprise me."

Jackie picked up his plate and did a quick dance around the kitchen.

* * *

Temporary insanity. Nathan debated the wisdom of pleading that cause to his associates, his family or the higher courts. He had a boarder. A nonpaying one at that. Nathan Powell, a conservative, upstanding member of society, a member of the Fortune 500, the thirty-two-year-old wunderkind of architecture, had a strange woman in his house.

He didn't necessarily mean strange as in unknown. Jackie MacNamara *was* strange. He'd come to that conclusion when he'd seen her meditating by the pool after lunch. He'd glanced out and spotted her, sitting cross-legged on the stone apron, head tilted back, eyes closed, hands resting lightly on her knees, palms up. He'd been mortally afraid she was reciting a mantra. Did people still do that sort of thing?

He must have been insane to agree to her arrangement because of blueberry pancakes and a smile. Jet lag, he decided as he poured another glass of iced tea Jackie had made to go with a truly exceptional spinach salad. Even a competent, intelligent man could fall victim to the weakness of the body after a transatlantic flight.

Two weeks, he reminded himself. Technically, he'd only agreed to two weeks. After that time had passed, he could gently but firmly ease her on her way. In the meantime, he would do what he should have done hours ago—make certain he didn't have a maniac on his hands.

There was a neat leather-bound address book by the kitchen phone, as there was by every phone in the house. Nathan flipped through it to the *L*'s. Jackie was upstairs working on her book—if indeed there was a book at all. He would make the call, glean a few pertinent facts, then decide how to move from there.

"Lindstrom residence."

"Adele Lindstrom, please, Nathan Powell calling."

"One moment, Mr. Powell."

Nathan sipped tea as he waited. A man could become addicted to having it made fresh instead of digging crystallized chemicals out of a jar. Absently he drew a cigarette out of his pocket and tapped the filter on the counter.

"Nathan, dear, how are you?"

"Adele. I'm very well, and you?"

"Couldn't be better, though March insists on going out like a lion here. What can I do for you, dear? Are you in Chicago?"

"No, actually I've just arrived home. Your nephew Fred was, ah…house-sitting for me."

"Of course, I remember." There was a long, and to Nathan pregnant, pause. "Fred hasn't done something naughty, has he?"

Naughty? Nathan passed a hand over his face. After a moment, he decided not to blast Adele with the sad facts of the situation, but to tone it down. "We do have a bit of a mix-up. Your niece is here."

"Niece? Well, I have several of those. Jacqueline? Of course it's Jacqueline. I remember now that Honoria—that's Fred's mother—told me that little Jack was going south. Poor Nathan, you've a houseful of MacNamaras."

"Actually, Fred's in San Diego."

"San Diego? What are you all doing in San Diego?"

Nathan tried to remember if Adele Lindstrom had been quite this scattered in Chicago. "Fred's in San Diego—at least I think he is. I'm in Florida, with your niece."

"Oh… Oh!" The second *oh* had enough delight in it to put Nathan on guard. "Well, isn't that lovely? I've always said that all our Jacqueline needed was a nice, stable man.

She's a bit of a butterfly, of course, but very bright and wonderfully good-hearted."

"I'm sure she is." Nathan found it necessary to put the record straight, and to put it straight quickly. "She's only here because of a misunderstanding. It seems Fred…didn't understand that I was coming back, and he…offered the house to Jackie."

"I see." And she did, perfectly. Fortunately for Nathan, he couldn't see her eyes light with amusement. "How awkward for you. I hope you and Jacqueline have worked things out."

"More or less. You're her mother's sister?"

"That's right. Jackie favors Patricia physically. Such a piquant look. I was always jealous as a child. Otherwise, none of us have ever been quite sure who little Jackie takes after."

Nathan blew out a stream of smoke. "That doesn't surprise me."

"What is it now…painting? No, it's writing. Jackie's a novelist these days."

"So she says."

"I'm sure she'll tell a delightful story. She's always been full of them."

"I'll just bet."

"Well, dear, I know the two of you will get along fine. Our little Jack manages to get along with just about anyone. A talent of hers. Not to say that Patricia and I hadn't hoped she'd be settled down and married by now—put some of that energy into raising a nice family. She's a sweet girl—a bit flighty, but sweet. You're still single, aren't you, Nathan?"

With his eyes cast up to the ceiling, he shook his head. "Yes, I am. It's been nice talking to you, Adele. I'll suggest to your niece that she get in touch when she relocates."

"That would be nice. It's always a pleasure to hear from

Jack. And you, too, Nathan. Be sure to let me know if you get to Chicago again."

"I will. Take care of yourself, Adele."

He hung up, still frowning at the phone. There was little doubt that his unwanted tenant was exactly who she said she was. But that didn't really accomplish anything. He could talk to her again, but when he'd tried to do that over lunch, he'd gotten a small, and very nagging, headache. It might be the coward's way, but for the rest of the day he was going to pretend that Jacqueline MacNamara, with her long legs and her brilliant smile, didn't exist.

Upstairs, in front of her typewriter, Jackie wasn't giving Nathan a thought. Or if she was she'd twined him so completely with the hard-bitten and heroic Jake that she wasn't able to see the difference.

It was working. Sometimes, when her fingers slowed just a bit and her mind whipped back to the present, she was struck by the wonderful and delightful thought that she was really writing. Not playing at it, as she had played at so many other things.

She knew her family tut-tutted about her. All those brains and all that breeding, and Jackie could never seem to make up her mind what to do with them. She was happy to announce that this time she had found something, and that it had found her.

Sitting back, her tongue caught between her teeth, she read the last scene over. It was good, she was sure of that. She knew that back in Newport there were those who would shake their heads and smile indulgently. So what if the scene was good, or even if several chapters were good? Dear little Jack never finished anything.

In her stint at remodeling, she'd bought a huge rattrap of a house and scraped, planed, painted and papered. She'd learned about plumbing and rewiring, haunted lumberyards and hardware stores. The first floor—she'd always believed in starting from the bottom up—had been fabulous. She was creative and competent. The problem had been, as it always had been, that once the first rush of excitement was over something else had caught her interest. The house had lost its charm for her. True, she'd sold it at a nice profit, but she'd never touched the two upper stories.

This was different.

Jackie cradled her chin in her hand. How many times had she said that before? The photography studio, the dance classes, the potter's wheel. But this *was* different. She'd been fascinated by each field she'd tampered in, and in each had shown a nice ability to apply what she'd learned, but she was beginning to see, or hope, that all those experiments, all those false starts, had been leading up to this.

She had to be right about the story. This time she had to carry it through from start to finish. Nothing else she'd tried had been so important or seemed so right. It didn't matter that her family and friends saw her as eccentric and fickle. She *was* eccentric and fickle. But there had to be something, something strong and meaningful, in her life. She couldn't go on playing at being an adult forever.

The great American novel. That made her smile. No, it wouldn't be that. In fact, Jackie couldn't think of many things more tedious than attempting to write the great American novel. But it could be a good book, a book people might care about and enjoy, one they might curl up with on a quiet evening. That would be enough. She hadn't realized that before, but once she'd really begun to care about it herself she'd known that would be more than enough.

It was coming so fast, almost faster than she could handle. The room was stacked with reference books and manuals, writers' how-tos and guides. She'd pored over them all. Researching her subject was the one discipline Jackie had always followed strictly. She'd been grateful for the road maps, the explanations of pitfalls and the suggestions. Oddly, now that she was hip deep in the story, none of that seemed to matter. She was writing on instinct and by the seat of her pants. As far as she could remember—and her memory was keen—she'd never had more fun in her life.

She closed her eyes to think about Jake. Instantly her mind took a leap to Nathan. Wasn't it strange how much he looked like her own conception of the hero of her story? It really did make it all seem fated. Jackie had a healthy respect for fate, particularly after her study of astrology.

Not that Nathan was a reckless gunslinger. No, he was rather sweetly conservative. A man, she was sure, who thought of himself as organized and practical. She doubted seriously that he considered himself an artist, though he was undoubtedly a talented one. He'd also be a list-maker and a plan-follower. She respected that, though she'd never been able to stick with a list in her life. What she admired even more was that he was a man who knew what he wanted and had accomplished it.

He was also a pleasure to look at—particularly when he smiled. The smile was usually reluctant, which made it all the sweeter. Already she'd decided it was her duty to nudge that smile from him as often as possible.

It shouldn't be difficult. Obviously he had a good heart; otherwise he would have given her the heave-ho the first night. That he hadn't, though he'd certainly wanted to, made Jackie think rather kindly of him. Because she did, she was determined to make their cohabitation as painless for him as possible.

She didn't doubt that they could deal very nicely with

each other for a few months. In truth, she preferred company, even his reluctant sort, to solitude.

She liked his subtlety, and his well-bred sarcasm. Even someone much less sensitive than she would have recognized the fact that nothing would have made him happier than to dispose of her. It was a pity she couldn't oblige him, but she really was determined to finish her book, and to finish it where she had started it.

While she was at it, she'd stay out of his way as much as was humanly possible, and fix him some of the best meals of his life.

That thought made her glance at her watch. She swore a little, but turned off her machine. It really was a pain to have to think about dinner when Jake was tethered by a leather thong to the wrist of an Apache brave. The knife fight was just heating up; but a bargain was a bargain.

Humming to herself, she started down to the kitchen.

Once again it was the scents that lured him. Nathan had been perfectly happy catching up on his back issues of *Architectural Digest*. He burrowed in his office, content simply to be there with the warm paneled walls and the faded Persian carpet. Terrace doors opened onto the patio and out to the garden. It was his refuge, with the faint scent of leather from books and the sharp light of sun through etched glass. If a man couldn't be alone in his office, he couldn't be alone anywhere.

Late in the afternoon he'd nearly been able to erase Jackie MacNamara and her conniving cousin from his mind. He'd heard her humming, and had ignored it. That had pleased him. A servant. He would think of her as a servant and nothing more.

Then the aromas had started teasing him. Hot, spicy aromas. She was playing the radio again. Loud. He really was going to have to speak to her about that. Nathan shifted in his office chair and tried to concentrate.

Was that chicken? he wondered, and lost his place in an article on earth homes. He thought about closing the door, flipped a page and found the Top 40 number Jackie was playing at top volume juggling around in his head. Telling himself she needed a lecture on music appreciation, he set the magazine aside—after marking his place—then headed toward the kitchen.

He had to speak to her twice before she heard him. Jackie kept a hand on the handle of the frying pan, shaking it gently as she pitched her voice to a shout.

"It'll be ready in a few minutes. Would you like some wine?"

"No. What I'd like is for you to turn that thing off."

"To what?"

"To turn that thing—" Almost growling in disgust, Nathan walked over to the kitchen speaker and hit the switch. "Haven't you ever heard about inner-ear damage?"

Jackie gave the pan another shake before turning off the flame. "I always play the music loud when I'm cooking. It inspires me."

"Invest in headphones," he suggested.

With a shrug, Jackie took the lid off the rice and gave it a quick swipe with a fork. "Sorry. I figured since you had speakers in every room you liked music. How was your day? Did you get plenty of rest?"

Something in her tone made him feel like a cranky grandfather. "I'm fine," he said between his teeth.

"Good. I hope you like Chinese. I have a friend who owns a really wonderful little Oriental restaurant in San Francisco. I persuaded his chef to share some recipes." Jackie poured Nathan a glass of wine. She was using his

Waterford this time. In the smooth and economical way she had in the kitchen, she scooped the sweet-and-sour chicken onto a bed of rice. "I didn't have time for fortune cookies, but there's an upside-down cake in the oven." She licked sauce from her thumb before she began to serve herself. "You don't want to let that get cold."

Wary of her, he sat. A man had to eat, after all. As he forked a cube of chicken, he watched her. Nothing seemed to break her rhythm, or her breezy sense of self-confidence. He'd see about that, Nathan thought, and waited until she'd joined him at the bar.

"I spoke with your aunt today."

"Really? Aunt Adele?" Jackie hooked one bare foot around the leg of the stool. "Did she give me a good reference?"

"More or less."

"You brought it on yourself," she said, then began to eat with the steady enthusiasm of one who liked food for food's sake.

"I beg your pardon?"

Jackie sampled a bamboo shoot. "Word's going to spread like wildfire, through the Lindstrom branch and over to the MacNamaras. I imagine it'll detour through the O'Brians too. That's my father's sister's married name." She took a forkful of saffron rice. "I can't take the responsibility."

Now it was he who'd lost his rhythm. Again. "I don't know what you're talking about."

"The wedding."

"What wedding?"

"Ours." She picked up her glass and sipped, smiling at him over the rim. "What do you think of the wine?"

"Back up. What do you mean, our wedding?"

"Well, I don't mean it, and you don't mean it. But Aunt Adele will mean it. Twenty minutes after you spoke with her she'd have been chirping happily about our romance to anyone who'd listen. People do listen to Aunt Adele. I've never understood why. You're letting that chicken get cold, Nathan."

He set his fork down, keeping his voice even and his eyes steady. "I never gave her any reason to think we were involved."

"Of course you didn't." Obviously on his side, Jackie squeezed his arm. "All you did was tell Aunt Adele I was living here." The timer buzzed, so Jackie scooted up to pull the cake out of the oven. Wanting a moment to think, Nathan waited until she'd set it out to cool and joined him again.

"I explained there'd been a misunderstanding."

"She has a very selective memory." Jackie took another generous bite. "Don't worry, I won't hold you to it. Do you think there's enough ginger in this?"

"There's nothing to hold me to."

"Not between us." She sent him a sympathetic glance. "Don't let it ruin your appetite. I can handle the family. Can I ask you a personal question?"

Nathan picked up his fork again. Somehow he'd opened the door to his own house and fallen down the rabbit hole. "Why not?"

"Are you involved with anyone? It doesn't have to be particularly serious."

She liked the way his eyes narrowed. There was something about gray eyes, really gray eyes, that could cut right through you.

He debated half a dozen answers before settling on the truth. "No."

"That's too bad." Her forehead wrinkled briefly before smoothing out again. "It would have helped if you were, but

I'll just make something up. Would you mind very much if
I threw you over, maybe for a marine biologist?"

He was laughing. He didn't know why, but when he
reached for his wine, his lips were still curved. "Not at all."

She hadn't counted on that—that his laugh would be so
appealing. The little flutter came. Jackie acknowledged it,
savored it briefly, then banked it down. It wouldn't do. No,
it wouldn't do at all. "You're a good sport, Nathan. Not everyone would think so, but they don't know you like I do.
Let me get you some more chicken."

"No, I'll get it."

It was a small mistake, the kind people make every day
when they step into a doorway at the same time or bump
elbows in a crowded elevator. The kind of small mistake
that is rarely recognized and soon forgotten.

They rose simultaneously, both reaching for his plate.
Their hands closed over it, and each other's. Their bodies
bumped. He took her arm to steady her. The usual quick
smile and the automatic apology didn't come from either
of them.

Jackie felt her breath snag and her heart stumble. The
feeling didn't surprise her. She was too much in tune with
her emotions, too comfortable with them, to be surprised.
It was the depth of them that caught at her. The contact was
casual, more funny than romantic, but she felt as though
she'd been waiting all her life for it.

She'd remember the feel of his hand, and the china, and
the heat of his body as it barely brushed hers. She'd remember the look of surprised suspicion in his eyes, and the scent
of spices and wine. She'd remember the quiet, the absolute
and sudden quiet. As if the world had held its breath for a
moment. For just a moment.

What the hell was this? That was his first and only coherent thought. He was gripping her harder than he should have, as if he were holding on—but that was absurd. However absurd it was, he couldn't quite make himself let go. Her eyes were so big, so soft. Was it foolish to believe he saw absolute honesty in them? That scent, her scent, was there, the one he'd first come across in his own bedroom. The one, Nathan thought now, that still lingered, ridiculously, after she'd moved into a guest room. He heard her breath suck in, then shudder out. Or maybe it was his own.

And he wanted her, as clearly and as logically as he'd ever wanted anything. It lasted only a moment, but the desire was strong.

They moved away together, with the quick, almost jerky motion one uses when one steps back from an unexpected flame. Jackie cleared her throat. Nathan let out a long, quiet breath.

"It's no trouble," she said.

"Thanks."

She moved to the stove before she thought she could breathe easily. As she scooped up chicken and vegetables, she wondered if this was one adventure she should have passed on.

Chapter 3

When he looked at her something happened, something frantic, something she'd never experienced before. Her heart beat just a little too fast, and dampness sprang out on the palms of her hands. A look was all that was necessary. His eyes were so dark, so penetrating. When he looked at her it was as if he could see everything she was, or could be, or wanted to be.

It was absurd. He was a man who lived by the gun, who took what he wanted without regret or compassion. All of her life she'd been taught that the line between right and wrong was clear and wide, and couldn't be crossed.

To kill was the greatest sin, the most unforgivable. Yet he had killed, and would surely kill again. Knowing it, she couldn't care for him. But care she did. And want she did. And need.

Sitting back, Jackie reviewed Sarah's confused and contrasting feelings for Jake. How would a sheltered young woman, barely eighteen, respond to a man who had lived all his life by rules she couldn't possibly understand or approve of? And how would a man who had seen and done all that Jake Redman had seen and done react to an innocent, convent-bred woman?

There was no way their dealings with each other could run smoothly. Their coming together and its resolution couldn't be impossible, it just had to be difficult. Two different worlds, she thought. Two sets of values, two opposing ambitions. Those would be difficult conflicts to overcome. Then you added gunfights, betrayal, kidnapping and revenge. Just to keep things interesting. Still, for all the action and adventure, Jackie had come to think that the love story was really the heart of her book. How these two people were going to change and complement each other, how they would compromise, adjust and stand firm.

She didn't think Sarah or Jake would understand about emotional commitment or mutually supportive relationships. Those were twentieth-century terms. Her psychology course on modern marriage had given Jackie a basketful of catchphrases. The words might change, but love was love. As far as she was concerned, Sarah and Jake had a good chance. That was more than a great many people could say.

It occurred to her that that was all she wanted for herself. A good chance. Someone to love who would love her back, someone to make adjustments for, to make long-range plans with. Wasn't it strange that in making a relationship on paper she had begun to fantasize about making one for herself?

She wouldn't ask for perfection, not only because it would be boring but because she would never be able to achieve perfection herself. It wouldn't be necessary, or even appealing, to settle down with a man who agreed with you on every point.

Would she like dashing? Probably. It might be fun to have someone flash in and out of your life, dropping off dew-kissed roses and magnums of champagne. It would be a nice interlude, but she was dead certain she couldn't live with dashing. Dashing would never take out the trash or unclog a drain.

Sensitive. Jackie rolled the word around in her mind, coming up with a picture of a sweet, caring man who wrote bad poetry. Horn-rimmed glasses and a voice like cream. Sensitive would always understand a woman's needs and a woman's moods. She could be very fond of sensitive. Until sensitive began to drive her crazy.

Passionate would be nice, as well. Someone who would toss her over his shoulder and make mad love in sun-drenched fields. But it might get a bit tough to do that sort of thing once they hit eighty.

Funny, intelligent, reckless and dependable.

That was the trouble, she supposed. She could think of a dozen different qualities she would enjoy in a man, but not of a combination that would pull her in for the long haul. With a sigh, she cupped her chin in her hand and stared over the typewriter through the window. Maybe she just wasn't ready to think about wedding rings and picket fences. Maybe she'd never be ready.

It wasn't easy to accept, but if it was true she could see herself living in some quaint little house near the water and writing about other people's love affairs. She could spend her days dreaming up characters and places, puttering around in a garden and playing aunt to all the little MacNamaras. It wouldn't be so bad.

She wouldn't be a hermit, of course. And it wasn't as

though she didn't appreciate men. Any man she'd ever been close to had possessed at least one of the qualities she admired. She'd cared for and about them, even loved them a little. But then, love was easy for her, falling in and falling out of it without bruises or scars. That wasn't real romance, she thought as she looked at the words she'd written. Real romance scraped off a little skin. It had to if love was going to bloom out of it and heal.

Lord, she was getting philosophical since she'd started putting words on paper. Maybe that explained her reaction to Nathan.

The problem was, though she was clever with words and always had been, she couldn't quite come up with the right ones to describe that one brief moment of contact.

Intense, confusing, illuminating, scary. It had been all of those, yet she wasn't sure what the sum of the parts equaled.

Attraction, certainly. But then, she'd found him attractive even when she'd thought she was hallucinating. Most women found dark, brooding types with aloof qualities attractive. God knew why. Yet that one moment, that quick link, had been more than simple attraction. The fact was, it hadn't been simple anything. She'd wanted him in the strong, vital way that usually came only with understanding and time.

I know you, something had seemed to say inside her. *And I've been waiting.*

He'd felt something too. She was certain of that. Maybe it had been that same kind of instant knowledge and instant desire. Whatever he'd felt hadn't pleased him, because he'd been very careful to avoid her for the better part of two days. Not an easy trick, since they were living in the same house, but he'd managed.

She still thought it had been rather rude of him to go out on his boat for an entire day and not ask her along.

Maybe he had to think things through. Jackie gauged him as the type of man who would have to compute and analyze and reason out every area of his life, including the emotional. That was too bad, but she'd have been the first to say that everyone was entitled to their own quirks.

He didn't have to worry about her, she decided as she dipped into a bowl of cheese curls. She wasn't interested in flirting with a relationship, and certainly not one with a man as buttoned-down as Nathan Powell. If she were, then he'd have reason to worry. Jackie chuckled to herself as she nibbled. She could be very tenacious and very persuasive when her mind was set. Fortunately for him, and perhaps for both of them, she was much too involved with writing to give him more than a passing thought.

Still, she checked her watch and noticed that it was nearly dinnertime and he wasn't back. His problem, she thought as she took another handful of cheese curls. She'd agreed to cook, but not to cater. When he came home he could make himself a sandwich. It certainly didn't matter to her.

She peered out her window at the sound of a boat, then settled back with the smallest of sighs when it passed by.

She wasn't really thinking of him, she told herself. She was just…passing the time. She didn't really wish he'd asked her to join him today so that they could have spent some time alone together, getting to know each other better. She wasn't really wondering what kind of man he was— except in the most intellectual terms.

What did it matter that she liked the way he laughed when he briefly let his guard down? It certainly wasn't important that his eyes were dark and dangerous one minute and quietly sensitive another. He was just a man, bound up in his work and his self-image in the same way she was bound up in her work and her future. It wasn't any of her business that he seemed more tense than he should be, and more solitary. It wasn't her goal in life to draw him out and urge him to relax and enjoy.

Her goal in life, Jackie reminded herself, was to finish the story, sell it and reap the benefits of being a published novelist. Whatever they might be. Straightening in her seat, she pushed Nathan Powell aside and went back to work.

This was what he'd come home for, Nathan told himself as he cruised down one of the narrow, deserted channels. Peace and quiet. There were no deadlines, no contract dates to worry about, no supply shortages to work around or inspectors to answer to. Sun and water. He didn't want to think beyond them.

He was beginning to feel almost like himself again. It was odd that he hadn't thought of this before—taking the boat out and disappearing for the day. He might have agreed to have a boarder for a couple of weeks, but that didn't mean he had to chain himself to the house. Or to her.

He couldn't say that it was entirely unpleasant having her there. She was keeping her end of the bargain. Most days passed without him seeing her at all except in the kitchen. Somehow he'd even gotten used to hearing her pounding away at the keys of her typewriter for hours on end. She might have been writing nursery rhymes for all he knew, but he couldn't say she wasn't keeping at it.

Actually, there were a lot of things he couldn't say about her. The problem started with the things he could say.

She talked too fast. It might have seemed an odd complaint, but not for a man who preferred quiet and structured conversations. If they talked about the weather she'd mention her brief career as a meteorologist and end by saying she liked rain because it smelled nice. Who could keep up with that sort of thought pattern?

She anticipated him. He might just begin to think he could use a cold drink and he'd find her in the kitchen making iced tea or pouring him a beer. Though she hadn't yet indicated that she'd trained as a psychic, he found it disconcerting.

She always looked at ease. It was a difficult thing to fault her for, but he found himself growing tenser the more casual she became. Invariably she was dressed in shorts and some breezy top with no makeup and her hair curling as it chose. She stopped just short of being sloppy, and he shouldn't have found it alluring. He preferred well-groomed, polished women—women with a little gloss and style. So why couldn't he keep his mind off one coltish, unpainted throwback who didn't do anything more to attract him than scrub her face and grin?

Because she was different? Nathan could easily reject that notion. He was a man who preferred the comfortable, and the comfortable usually meant the familiar. There was certainly nothing remotely familiar about Jackie. Some might accuse him of being in a rut, but he thought himself entitled. When your career took you to different cities and different countries and involved different people and problems on a regular basis, you deserved a nice comfortable rut in your personal life.

Solitude, quiet, a good book, an occasional congenial companion over drinks or dinner. It didn't seem like too much to ask. Jacqueline MacNamara had thrown a wrench in the works.

He didn't like to admit it, but he was getting used to her.

After only a few days, he was used to her company. That in itself, for a loner, was a shattering discovery.

Nathan opened the throttle to let his boat race. He might have been more comfortable if she'd been dull or drab. For social purposes he preferred refined and composed, but for a housemate—boarder, he reminded himself firmly—for a boarder he'd have been happy with dull.

The trouble was, no matter how quiet or unobtrusive she was for most of the day, she was impossible to ignore with her rapid-fire conversations, her dazzling smiles and her bright clothes. Especially since she never seemed to dress in anything that covered more than ten percent of her.

Maybe he could admit it now, alone, with the wind breezing through his hair and over his face, that as annoying and inconvenient as it was to have his sanctuary invaded, she was, well…fun.

He hadn't allowed himself a great deal of fun in the past few years. Work had been and still was his first priority. Building, the creative process and the actual nuts and bolts, absorbed his time. He'd never resented the responsibility. If anyone had asked him if he enjoyed his work, he would have given them a peculiar look and answered, "Of course." Why else would he do it?

He would have accepted the term *dedicated* but would have knit his brows at the word *obsessed*, though obsessed was exactly what he was. He could picture a building in his mind, complete, down to the smallest detail, but he didn't consider himself an artist when he drew up the blueprints. He was a professional, educated and trained, nothing more or less.

He loved his work and considered himself lucky to have found a profession for which he had both skill and affection. There were moments of sweaty, gritty work, head-throbbing

concentration and absolute pride. Nothing, absolutely nothing, had ever given him the same thrill of accomplishment
as seeing one of his buildings completed.

If he absorbed himself in his work, it wasn't that his life
was lacking in other areas. It was simply that no other area
had the same appeal or excitement for him. He enjoyed the
company of women, but had never met one who could keep
him awake at night the way an engineering problem with
a building could.

Unless, of course, he counted Jackie. He didn't care to.

He squinted into the sun, then steered away from it until
it spread its warmth across his back. Still his frown remained.

Her conversations were like puzzles he had to sort out.
No one had made him think that intricately in years. Her
constant cheerfulness was contagious. It would be foolish
to deny he hadn't eaten better since his childhood—and
probably not even then.

She did have an affecting smile, he thought as he wound
his way down an alley of the waterway. And her eyes were
so big and dark. Dark, yes, but they had this trick, this illusion of lighting up when she smiled. And her mouth was
so wide and so generous, always ready to curve.

Nathan pulled himself up short. Her physical attributes
weren't of any consequence. Shouldn't be.

That one moment of connection had been a fluke. And
he was undoubtedly exaggerating the depth of it. There
might have been a passing attraction. That was natural
enough. But there certainly hadn't been the affinity he'd
imagined. He didn't believe in such things. Love at first
sight was a convenience used by novelists—usually bad
ones. And instant desire was only lust given a prettier name.

Whatever he had felt, if he'd felt anything at all, had

been a vague and temporary tug, purely physical and easily subdued.

Nathan could almost hear her laughing at him, though he was alone on the water and the banks of the waterway were almost deserted. Grimly he headed home.

It was dusk when she heard his boat. Jackie was certain it was Nathan. For the past two hours her ears had been fine-tuned for his return. The wave of relief came first. He hadn't met with any of the hideous boating accidents her mind had conjured up for him. Nor had he been kidnapped and held for ransom. He was back, safe and sound. She wanted to punch him right in the mouth.

Twelve hours, she thought as she dived cleanly into the pool. He'd been gone for nearly twelve hours. The man obviously had no sense of consideration.

Naturally, she hadn't been worried. She'd been much too busy with her own projects to give him more than a passing thought—every five minutes for the last two hours.

Jackie began to do laps in a steady freestyle to release her pent-up energy. She wasn't angry. Why, she wasn't even mildly annoyed. His life was most certainly his own, to do with exactly as he chose. She wouldn't say a word about it. Not a word.

She did twenty laps, then tossed her wet hair back before resting her elbows on the edge of the pool.

"Training for the Olympics?" Nathan asked her. He stood only a few feet away, a glass of clear, fizzing liquid in his hand. Jackie blinked water out of her eyes and frowned at him.

He was wearing shorts, pleated and pressed, and a short-sleeved polo shirt that was so neat and tidy it might have come straight from the box. Nathan Powell's casual wear, she thought nastily.

"I didn't realize you were back." She glanced at his feet as she lied. Despite all her accomplishments, Jackie had never been able to manage an eyeball-to-eyeball lie.

"I haven't been for long." She was annoyed, Nathan realized. He found it enormously satisfying. Abandoning his rule against small talk, he smiled down at her. "So, how was your day?"

"Busy." Jackie pushed away from the side and began lazily treading water. In the east, the sky was nearly dark, but the last light from the sun touched the pool and garden. She didn't trust the way he was smiling right now, but she found she liked it. There was probably nothing more tedious than a man a woman could trust unconditionally. "And yours?"

"Relaxing." He had an urge, odd and unexpected, to slide into the pool with her. The water would be cool and soft; so would her skin. Maybe he was punchy, Nathan thought, after a hot day on the water.

As she continued to float, Jackie studied him. He did look relaxed—for him. She'd already discovered he was one of those people who carried around tension like a responsibility. She smiled, forgiving him as abruptly as she'd become angry.

"Want an omelet?"

"What?" Distracted, he pulled himself back. She was wearing two thin strips as an excuse for a bathing suit. The water, and perhaps a trick of the light, made them glimmer against her skin. A great deal of skin.

"Are you hungry? I could fix you an omelet."

"No. No, thanks." He took a sip of his drink to ease a suddenly dry throat, then sat the glass down to stuff his hands in his pockets. "It's cooling off." If that was the best he could do, he thought with a scowl, he'd best put the lid on small talk again.

"You're telling me." After sleeking her hair back, Jackie pulled herself out of the pool. She was skinny, Nathan told himself. There was no reason such a skinny, even lanky woman should move so athletically. In the fading sunlight, drops of water scattered over her skin like some primitive decoration.

"I forgot a towel." She shrugged, then shook herself. Nathan swallowed and looked elsewhere. It wasn't wise to look when he'd begun to imagine how easy it would be to slip those two tiny swatches of material off her and slide back into the water with her.

"I should go in," he managed after a moment. "I've got reading to catch up on."

"Me too. I'm reading tons of Westerns. Ever try Zane Grey or Louis L'Amour?" She was walking toward him as she spoke, and he found himself fascinated by the way the water clung to and darkened her hair and lashes. "Great stuff. I'll take this in for you."

"That's all right."

For the second time they reached at the same instant. For the second time their fingers touched and tangled. Nathan felt hers tense on the glass. So she felt it, too. That jolt… that connection, as he'd come to think of it. It wasn't his imagination. Wanting to avoid it, Nathan loosened his grip and stepped back. For the same reason, Jackie mirrored his move. The glass tipped, teetering on the edge of the table. They made the grab simultaneously, caught it, then stood holding the glass between them.

It should have been funny, she thought, but she managed only a quick, nervous laugh. In his eyes she saw exactly what she felt. Desire, hot and dangerous and edgy.

"Looks like we need a choreographer."

"I've got it." His voice was stiff as they waged a brief tug-of-war.

After relinquishing the glass to him, Jackie let out a slow, careful breath. She made the decision quickly, as she believed all the best decisions were made. "It might be better if we just got it over with."

"Got what over with?"

"The kiss. It's simple, really. I wonder what it would be like, you wonder what it would be like." Though her voice was casual, she moistened her lips. "Don't you think we'd be more comfortable if we stopped wondering?"

He set the glass down again as he studied her. It wasn't a romantic proposal, it was a logical one. That appealed to him. "That's a very pragmatic way of looking at it."

"I can be, occasionally." She shivered a little in the cooling air. "Look, odds are it won't be nearly as important after. Imagination magnifies things. At least mine does." The smile came again, quick and stunning, with the flash of a dimple at the corner of her mouth. "You're not my type. No offense. And I doubt I'm yours."

"No, you're not," he answered, stung a bit.

She took this statement with an agreeable nod. "So, we get the kiss out of the way and get back to normal. Deal?"

He didn't know if she'd done it on purpose—in fact, he was all but certain she hadn't—but she'd managed a direct hit to his male pride. She was so casual, so damn friendly about it. So sure that kissing him would leave her unaffected. Kissing him would be like brushing a pesky fly aside. Get it over with and get back to normal. He'd see about that.

She should have been warned by the look in his eyes— what she still thought of as his Jake look. Perhaps she had been, but it was knowledge gained too late.

With one hand he cupped her neck so that his fingers tangled in her dripping hair. The touch itself was a surprise—quietly intimate. There was a quick and sudden instinct to back away, but she ignored it. Jackie was used to approaching things head-on. So she stepped forward, tilting her head up. She expected something pleasant, warm, even ordinary. It wasn't the first time in her life she'd gotten more than she'd bargained for.

Rockets. They were her first image as his lips closed over hers. Rockets, with that flash of color and that fast, deadly boom. It had always been the boom she'd liked the best. Her little murmur wasn't of protest but of surprise and of pleasure. Accepting the pleasure, she leaned into him and absorbed it.

She could smell the water on him, not the clear, chlorinated water of the pool, but the darker, more exciting water that ran out to sea. The air was cooling rapidly as night fell, but the chill was gone. Her skin warmed as she moved against him and felt the soft brush of his shirt, and then of his hands.

And she *had* been waiting. The knowledge clicked quietly into place. She had been waiting years and years for this. Just this.

Unlike Jackie, Nathan had stopped thinking almost instantly—or thought he had. She tasted…exotic. There had been no warning of that in her pretty, piquant looks and wiry body, no indication of milk and honey heated with spice. She tasted of the desert, of something a dying man might drink greedily in the oasis of his mind.

He hadn't meant to hold her, not closely. He hadn't meant to let his hands roam over her, not freely. Somehow he'd lost control over them. With each touch and stroke over her damp skin, he lost a bit more.

Her back was long and lean and slick. He trailed his fingers over it and felt her tremble. The need jolted again until his mouth was hard on hers, more demanding than he'd ever intended. He pillaged. She accepted. When her sigh whispered against his tongue, his heartbeat doubled.

She pressed against him, her mouth open and willing, her body soft but not submissive. Her generosity was all-consuming. As was his temptation.

She'd never forget this, Jackie thought, not one detail. The heavy, heated scent of flowers, the soft hum of insects, the lapping of water close by. She'd never forget this first kiss, begun at dusk and carried into the night.

Her hands were in his hair, a smile just forming on her lips, as they drew apart. Unashamed of her reaction to him, she let out a long, contented sigh.

"I love surprises," she murmured.

He didn't. Nathan reminded himself of that and pulled back before he could stroke a hand through her hair. It amazed him and infuriated him to see that it wasn't steady. He wanted, unbearably, what he had no intention of taking.

"Now that we've satisfied our curiosity, we shouldn't have any more problems."

He expected anger. Indeed, that came first, a flash in her eyes. They were exceptionally expressive, he thought, and felt a pang when he read hurt in them. Then that, like the anger, disappeared, to be replaced by amusement.

"Don't bet the farm on it, Nathan." She patted his cheek—though she would have preferred to use her fist—and strolled into the house.

She was going to give him problems, all right, she thought as the screen door shut behind her. And it would be her pleasure.

Chapter 4

She would poison his poached eggs. Jackie could see the justice in that. He would come down for breakfast, cool-eyed and smug. She could even imagine what he'd be wearing—beige cotton slacks and a navy-blue shirt. Without a wrinkle in either.

She, giving him no reason to suspect, would serve him a lovely plate of Canadian bacon, lightly grilled, and poached eggs on toast. With a touch of cyanide.

He would sip his coffee. Nathan always went for the coffee first. Then he'd slice the meat. Jackie would fix herself a plate so everything would seem perfectly normal. They'd discuss the weather. A bit humid today, isn't it? Perhaps we're in for some rain.

As he took the first forkful of eggs, the sweat would break out cold on her brow as she waited…and waited.

In moments he would be writhing on the floor, gasping for air, clutching his throat. His eyes would be wide and shocked, then all too aware, as she stood over him, triumphant and smiling. With his last breath, he would beg for forgiveness.

But that wasn't subtle enough.

She was a great believer in revenge. People who forgave and forgot with a pious smile deserved to be stepped on. Not that she couldn't forgive small slights or unconscious hurts, but the big ones, the deliberate ones, required—no, demanded—payback.

She was going to give Nathan Powell the payback he deserved.

She told herself he was a cold fish, an unfeeling slug, a cardboard cutout. But she didn't believe it. Unfortunately for her, she'd seen the kindness and sense of fair play in him. Perhaps he was rigid, but he wasn't cold.

Maybe, just maybe, she had read too much into the kiss. Perhaps her emotions were closer to the surface than most people's, and there was a possibility that he hadn't heard the boom. But he'd felt something. A man didn't hold a woman as if he were falling off a cliff if he'd only slipped off a curb.

He'd felt something, all right, and she was going to see to it that he felt that and more. And suffered miserably.

She could take rejection, Jackie told herself as she ground fresh beans for coffee. Smashing something into dust gave her enormous satisfaction. Rejection was that part of life that toughened you enough to make you try harder. True, she hadn't had to deal with it very often, but she thought of herself as gracious enough to accept it when it was warranted.

Frowning, she watched the kettle begin to steam. It wasn't as though she expected men to fall at her feet—though she had enough ego to want one to trip a little now and again. She certainly didn't expect pledges of undying love and fidelity after one embrace, no matter how torrid.

But damn it, there had been something special between them, something rare and close to wonderful. He'd had no business turning it off with a shrug.

And he'd pay, she thought viciously as she poured boiling water over the ground coffee. He'd pay for the shrug, for the pretending disinterest, and more, he'd pay for the night she'd spent tossing in bed remembering every second she'd been in his arms.

It was a pity she wasn't stunning, Jackie mused as she heated a skillet. Really stunning, with razor-edged cheekbones and a statuesque build—or petite and fragile-looking, with melting blue eyes and porcelain skin. Frowning a bit, she tried to get a good look at her reflection in the stainless-steel range hood. What she saw was distorted and vague. Experimenting, she sucked in her cheeks, then let them out again with a puff of air.

Since her appearance was something she couldn't change, she would make the very best of what she had. Nathan Powell, man of stone and steel, would be eating out of her hand in no time.

She heard him come in but took her time before turning. The skimpy halter made the most of her tanned back. For the first time in days she'd raided her supply of makeup. Nothing jarring, she'd told herself. Just a bit of blush and gloss, with most of the accent on the eyes.

Jackie tossed one of her best smiles over her shoulders and had to stifle a shout of laughter. He looked dreadful. Wasn't that a shame?

He felt worse. While Jackie had been fuming and tossing in her bed, Nathan had been cursing and turning in his own. Her cheerful smile made him want to bare his teeth and snarl.

One kiss and they'd get back to normal? He'd have liked to strangle her. Things hadn't been normal since she'd forced herself into his life. As far as he could recall, his body hadn't ached like this since he'd been a teenager, when, fortunately, his imagination had outdistanced his experience. Now he knew exactly what it could be like and had spent most of the night thinking about it.

"Morning, Nate. Coffee?"

Nate? *Nate?* Because he was sure it would hurt too much to argue, he merely nodded.

"Hot and fresh, just the way you like it." If her voice had been any sweeter, she'd have grown wings. "We have Canadian bacon and eggs on the menu this morning. Ready in five minutes."

He downed the first cup. He set it back on the counter, and she filled it again. She'd used a freer hand with her scent. Her fragrance still wasn't rich or overpowering, but this morning it seemed just a bit more pungent than usual. Remember? it seemed to say. Cautious, he glanced up at her.

Did she look prettier, or was it just his imagination? How did she manage to make her skin always look so glowing, so soft? It wasn't right, it wasn't even fair, that her hair could be constantly disheveled and appealing whether she was tossing a salad or napping on his couch.

He'd have sworn he'd never seen anyone look so alive, so vivid, in the morning. It was infuriating that she should be so fresh when he felt as though he'd spent the night being pummeled by rubber-tipped sledgehammers.

Despite his best intentions, his gaze was drawn to her mouth. She'd put something on it, something that left it looking as moist and as warm as he remembered it tasted. Dirty pool, he thought, and scowled at her.

"Mrs. Grange is coming in today."

"Oh?" Jackie smiled at him again as she turned the sizzling bacon. "Isn't that nice? Things really are getting back to normal, aren't they?" Jackie broke an egg, one-handed, and dropped it in the poacher. "Do you plan to be here for lunch?"

The yolk didn't break, and the shell was neatly dispatched. A nice trick, Nathan thought. He was sure she had a million of them. "I'll be in all day. I've got a lot of calls to make."

"Good. I'll be sure to fix something special." She turned to him again to give him a long, interested study. "You know, Nathan, you look a little haggard this morning. Trouble sleeping?"

No matter how much it cost him, he wouldn't snarl. "I had some paperwork I wanted to clear up."

Jackie clucked her tongue sympathetically as she arranged his breakfast on a plate. "You work too hard. It makes you tense. You should try yoga. There's nothing like a little meditation and proper exercise to relax the body and mind."

"Work relaxes me."

"A common misconception." Jackie set the plate neatly in front of him, then scooted around the counter. "The fact is that work occupies your mind and can take your mind off other problems, but it doesn't cleanse. Take a good massage."

Jackie began to knead his neck and shoulders while she spoke, pleased that at the first touch he jerked like a spring. "A really good massage," she continued as her fingers pressed and stroked, "relieves both mind and body of tension. A little oil, some soothing music, and you'll sleep like a baby. Oh, you've got yourself a real knot here at the base of your neck."

"I'm fine," he managed. In another minute the fork he

was holding was going to snap in two. She had magic in her hands. Black magic. "I'm never tense."

Jackie frowned a moment, losing track of the purpose of the exercise. Did he believe that? she wondered. Probably. When a man was always tense, he obviously thought of it as normal. When her heart started to warm toward him, she lectured herself.

"Let's just say there's relaxed and there's relaxed." She concentrated on the teres minor. "After a really good rub, my muscles are like butter. I slide right off the table. I've got some wonderful oil. Hans swears by it."

"Hans?" Why was he asking? Nathan thought as, despite himself, he stretched under her hands.

"My masseur. He's from Norway and has the hands of an artist. He taught me his technique."

"I'll just bet," Nathan muttered, and had Jackie grinning behind his back.

God, who would have suspected he had muscles like this? The man drew up blueprints and argued with engineers. Jackie hadn't suspected that his conservative shirts hid all those wonderful ridges. Last night, when he'd held her, she'd been too dazed to notice how well he was built. She ran her hands over his shoulders.

"You've got a terrific build," she told him. "I've got lousy deltoids myself. When I was into bodybuilding, I never managed to do much more than sweat."

Enough was enough, Nathan thought. One more squeeze of those long, limber fingers and he'd do something embarrassing. Like whimpering. Instead, he spun around on the stool and caught her hands in his.

"What the hell are you trying to do?"

She didn't mind her heart skipping a beat. In fact, it was

a delightful feeling. Still, she remembered that revenge was her first order of business.

"Just trying to loosen you up, Nate. Tension's bad for the digestion."

"I'm not tense. And don't call me Nate."

"Sorry. It suits you when you get that look in your eyes. That look," she explained, and she would have gestured if her hands hadn't been clamped in his. "The one that says shoot first and ask questions later."

He would be patient. Nathan told himself to count to ten, but only made it to four. "Careful, Jack. You're here on probation. You'd be wise to back off from whatever game you're playing."

"Game?" She smiled, but her eyes held the first hint of frost he'd ever seen in them. For some reason, even that attracted him. "I don't know what you're talking about."

"What about that stuff you put on your mouth?"

"This?" Deliberately she ran her tongue over her upper, then her lower lip. "A woman's entitled to a little lipstick now and then. Don't you like it?"

He wouldn't dignify the question with an answer. "You put stuff on your eyes, too."

"Are cosmetics against the law in this state? Really, Nate—sorry, Nathan—you're being silly. Surely you don't think I'm trying to…seduce you?" She smiled again, daring him to comment. "I'd think a big strong man like you could take care of himself." She liked the way his eyes could darken from slate to smoke. "But if it stirs you up, I'll be certain to keep my mouth absolutely naked from now on. Will that be better?"

His voice was so soft, so very controlled, that she was fooled into thinking she was still at the wheel. "People who fight dirty end up in the mud themselves."

"So I've heard." She tossed back her head and looked at him from beneath her lashes. "But you see, I can take care of myself, too."

She saw then that she had misjudged him. Perhaps by no more than a few degrees, but such miscalculations could often be fatal. The look that came into his eyes was so utterly reckless, so coolly dangerous, that her heart thudded to a halt.

Jake was back, and his guns were smoking.

It would be more than a kiss now, whether she wanted it or not. It would be exactly as he chose, when he chose and how he chose. No amount of glib chatter or charming smiles was going to help.

When the doorbell rang, neither of them moved. With a hard, painful thump, Jackie's heart started again. Saved by the bell. She would have giggled if she hadn't been ready to collapse.

"That must be Mrs. Grange," she said brightly, just a shade too brightly. "If you'd let go of my hands now, Nathan, I'd be glad to answer the door while you finish your breakfast."

He did release her, but only after making her suffer through the longest five seconds of her life, during which she believed he would ignore the door and finish what his eyes had told her he intended to do. Saying nothing, Nathan let her go, then swiveled back around to the counter. The pity of it was that he no longer wanted coffee, but a nice stiff drink.

Jackie slipped out of the kitchen. She hoped his eggs were stone-cold.

She loved Mrs. Grange. When Jackie opened the door, she wasn't sure what to make of the large woman in the flowered housedress and high-top sneakers. Mrs. Grange gave Jackie a long, narrowed look with watery blue eyes, pursed her lips and said, "Well, well."

Understanding the implications of that, Jackie smiled and offered a hand. "Good morning. You must be Mrs. Grange. I'm Jack MacNamara, and Nathan's stuck with me for a few weeks because he can't bring himself to toss me out. Have you had breakfast?"

"An hour ago." After she stepped inside, Mrs. Grange set a huge canvas bag on the floor. "MacNamara. You must be related to that no-account."

Jackie didn't need a name. "Guilty. We're cousins. He's gone."

"And good riddance." With a sniff, Mrs. Grange cast a look around the living area. Though she approved of the fresh flowers, she was determined to withhold final judgment. "I'll tell you like I told him. I don't clean up after pigs."

"And who could blame you?" Jackie's grin was fast and brilliant. If dear cousin Fred had tried to charm Mrs. Grange, he'd fallen flat on his baby face. "I'm using the guest room, the blue-and-white one? I'm working in there, too, so if you'll just let me know where that room fits into your schedule I'll make sure I'm out of your way. I'm planning on fixing lunch about twelve-thirty," she continued, mentally adjusting her menu with the idea of carving a few pounds from Mrs. Grange's prodigious bulk.

Mrs. Grange's lips pursed again. It was a rare thing for an employer to offer her a meal. For the most part she was treated with polite, and bland, disregard. "I brought some sandwiches."

"Of course, if you'd rather, but I was hoping you'd join us. I'll be upstairs if you need anything. Nathan's in the kitchen and the coffee's fresh." She smiled again, then left Mrs. Grange to begin while she went upstairs.

Throughout the morning, Jackie heard the sounds of vac-
uuming and the heavy thud of Mrs. Grange's sneakers moving up and down the hallway. It pleased her that the noise
and activity didn't intrude on her concentration. A real
writer, in her opinion, should have imagination enough to
overcome any outside interference. By noon, she was well
on her way to sending Jake and Sarah on another adventure.

Jackie decided on a cracked-wheat-and-parsley salad for
the lunch break. With the radio on, she set about dicing and
cubing and humming to herself while she tried to imagine
what it would be like to outrun desperadoes. When Nathan came in, she turned the music down, then set a huge
bowl on the counter.

"Iced coffee all right?"

"Fine." His answer was casual, but he was watching her.
One wrong move, he thought, and he was going to pounce.
He wasn't certain what would constitute a wrong move, or
what he'd do once he'd pounced, but he was ready for her.

"I'd like to use the phone later, if you don't mind. Anything long-distance I'll charge to my credit card."

"All right."

"Thanks. I think it's about time to start planting the
seeds of Fred's downfall."

With his fork halfway to his mouth, Nathan stopped.
"What kind of seeds?"

"You're better off not knowing. Oh, hello, Mrs. Grange."

Annoyed with the interruption, Nathan turned to look
at his housekeeper. "Mrs. Grange?"

"Sit down right here," Jackie said before Nathan could
continue. "I hope you like this. It's called *tabouleh*. Very
popular in Syria."

Mrs. Grange settled her bulk on a stool and eyed the

bowl doubtfully. "It doesn't have any of that funny stuff in it, does it?"

"Absolutely not." Jackie set a glass of iced coffee next to the bowl. "If you like it, I'll give you the recipe for your family. Do you have a family, Mrs. Grange?"

"Boys are grown." Cautiously Mrs. Grange took the first forkful. Her hands, Jackie noticed, were work-reddened and ringless.

"You have sons?"

With a nod, Mrs. Grange dipped into the salad again. "Had four of them. Two of them are married now. Got three grandkids."

"Three grandchildren. That's marvelous, isn't it, Nathan? Do you have pictures?"

Mrs. Grange took another forkful. She'd never tasted anything quite like this. It wasn't cold meat loaf on rye, but it was nice. Real nice. "Got some in my bag."

"I'd love to see them." Jackie took a seat that set Mrs. Grange squarely between her and Nathan. He was eating in silence, like a man who found himself placed next to strangers at a diner. "Four sons. You must be very proud."

"They're good boys." Her wide, stern face relaxed a bit. "The youngest is in college. Going to be a teacher. He's smart, that one, never gave me a minute's trouble. The others…" She paused, then shook her head. "Well, that's what having kids is all about. This is a real nice salad, Miss Mac-Namara. Real pretty."

"Jack. And I'm glad you like it. Would you like some more coffee?"

"No, I'd best get back to work. You want me to take those shirts to the cleaners, Mr. Powell?"

"I'd appreciate it."

"If you don't need to use it now, I'll do your office."

Loving Jack

"That's fine."

She turned to Jackie, and her eyes were friendly. "Don't worry about keeping out of the way upstairs. I can work around you."

"Thanks. Don't bother, I'll get these." She started to gather up bowls as Mrs. Grange plodded out. Nathan frowned at her over the rim of his iced coffee.

"What was all that about?"

"Hmm?" Jackie glanced at him as she transferred the leftover salad into a smaller dish.

"That business with Mrs. Grange. What were you doing?"

"Eating lunch. Would you mind if I gave her the rest of this to take home?"

"No, go ahead." He drew out a cigarette. "Do you usually have lunch with the help?"

She looked at him again, one brow lifting. "Why not?"

Every answer he thought of seemed stilted and snobbish, so he merely shrugged and lit his cigarette. Because she could see he was embarrassed, Jackie let it pass.

"Is Mrs. Grange divorced or widowed?"

"What?" Nathan blew out a stream of smoke and shook his head. "How would I know? How do you know she's either?"

"Because she talked about her sons and her grandchildren, but she didn't mention her husband. Therefore it's elementary, my dear Nathan, that she hasn't got one." As an afterthought, she popped one last crouton into her mouth. "I opt for divorce because widows usually continue to wear a wedding ring. Hasn't it ever come up?"

"No." He brooded, staring into his coffee. For some reason he didn't want to confess that Mrs. Grange had worked for him for five—no, it was nearly six years now—and he hadn't known she had four sons and three grandchildren until five minutes ago. "It wasn't part of her job description, and I didn't want to pry."

"That's nonsense. Everyone likes to talk about their families. I wonder how long she's been single." She moved around the kitchen rinsing bowls, tidying counters. The rings on her fingers flashed with wealth, while her hands spoke of confidence. "I can't think of anything tougher than raising kids on your own. Do you ever think about that?"

"Think about what?"

"About having a family." She poured herself another glass with the idea of taking the coffee upstairs. "Thinking about kids always makes me feel very traditional. White picket fence, two-car garage, wood-paneled station wagon and all of that. I'm surprised you're not married, Nathan. Being a traditional man."

Her tone had him scowling. "I know when I've been insulted."

"Of course you do." She touched his cheek lightly with her fingertips. "Being traditional's nothing to be ashamed of. I admire you, Nathan, really I do. There's something endearing about a man who always knows where his socks are. When the right woman comes along, she's going to get a real prize."

His hand clamped over her wrist before she could draw away. "Have you ever had your nose broken?"

Absolutely delighted, she grinned at him. "Not so far. Want to fight?"

"Let's try this."

Jackie found herself sprawled over him as he sat on the stool. He'd caught her off balance, and she had to grab his shoulders to keep from falling on her face. She hadn't expected him to move that quickly, or precisely in that way.

Before she could decide how to counter it—or whether she should counter it—his mouth was on hers. And it was searing.

He didn't know why he'd done it. What he'd really wanted to do, ached to do, was slug her. Of course, a man didn't slug a woman, so he'd really been left with no choice.

Why he'd thought a kiss would be revenge was beyond him now that it was begun. She didn't struggle, though he knew from the way her breath caught and her fingers tightened that he had at least surprised her.

But she couldn't have been more surprised than he.

Damn it, he wasn't the kind of man who yanked women around. Yet it seemed right when it was Jackie. It seemed… fated. He could rationalize for hours, he could reason and deliberate until everything was crystal-clear. Then he could touch her and blow logic to smithereens.

He didn't want her. He was eaten up with wanting her. He didn't even like her. He was fascinated by her. He thought she was crazy. And he was beginning to be sure he was. Always he'd known there was a pattern to everything, a structure. Until Jackie.

He nipped his teeth into her bottom lip and heard her low, quiet moan. Apparently life wasn't always geometrical.

She'd asked for it, Jackie thought to herself. And, thank God, she'd gotten it. Thoughts of revenge, of making him suffer and sweat, flew out of her mind as she dived into the kiss. It was wonderful, sweet, sharp, hot, trembling, the way she'd imagined and hoped a kiss might be.

Her heart went into it, completely, trustingly. This was a man who could love her, accept her. She wasn't a fool, and she wasn't naive. She felt it from him as clearly as if he'd spoken the words. This was special, unique, the kind of loving poems were written about and wars were fought for. Some people waited a lifetime for only this. And not everyone found it. She knew it, and she wrapped her arms around him, ready to give him everything she was. No questions, no doubts.

Something was happening. Over the desire, over the passion, he could sense it. There was a change inside him, an opening, a recklessness. When her mouth was on his, her body melting in his arms, he couldn't think beyond the moment. That was crazy. He never thought of today without taking tomorrow into account. But now, just now, he could think only of holding her like this. Of tasting more of her, bit by slow bit. Of exploring her, discovering her. He couldn't think of anything but her.

It was insanity. He knew it, feared it, even as he pressed her closer. Sinking. He was sinking into her. It was an odd and erotic sensation to feel himself lose his grip. He had to stop this, and stop it cold, before whatever was growing inside him grew too big to be controlled.

He drew her away, struggling to be firm, planning to be cruel. If she smiled at him instead of striking back, he knew, he'd be on his knees. He knew he should tell her all bets were off, to pack her things and leave. But he couldn't. No matter how much he told himself he wanted her out of his life, he couldn't ask her to go.

"Nathan." Aroused, pliant, already in love, she cupped her hand over his cheek. "Let's give Mrs. Grange the rest of the day off. I want to be with you."

Words caught in his throat, trapped in a fresh surge of desire. He'd never known a woman who was more open with her feelings, more honest with her needs. She scared him to death. He gave himself an extra moment. He couldn't afford to have his voice sound unsteady or to have her see how flexible his resolve was.

"You're getting ahead of yourself." As if the kiss had been only a kiss, he set her back on the floor. He hadn't realized how much warmth she'd brought to him until he'd no longer been touching her. "I don't think having an affair is in your best interests, or mine, considering our current arrangement. But thanks."

She went pale, and he knew that he'd gone too far in his rush for self-protection.

"Jackie, I didn't mean that the way it sounded."

"Didn't you? Well, whatever." She was amazed, absolutely amazed, at how much it hurt. She'd always dreamed of falling in love, deeply, blindly, beautifully in love. So this was how it felt, she thought as she pressed a hand to her stomach. The poets could keep it.

"Jack, listen—"

"No, I'd really rather not." When she smiled at him now, he realized just how special her genuine smile was. "No explanations required, Nathan. It was only a suggestion. I should apologize for coming on too strong."

"Damn it, I don't want an apology."

"No? Well, that's good, because I think I'd choke on it. I really should get back to work, but before I go there's just one thing." Deadly calm, Jackie picked up her glass of iced coffee and emptied it in his lap. "See you at dinner."

She worked like a maniac, barely noticing when Mrs. Grange came in to change the bed linen and dust the furniture. She was both amazed and infuriated at how close, how dangerously close, she'd been to tears. It wasn't that she minded shedding tears. There were times when she enjoyed nothing more than a wailing crying jag. But she knew that if she gave in to this one she wouldn't enjoy it a bit.

How could he have been so insensitive, so unfeeling, as

to think she'd been offering him nothing more than sex, a quick afternoon romp? And how could she have been so stupid as to think she'd fallen in love?

Love took two people. She knew that. Wasn't she even now pouring her heart out in a story that involved two people's feelings and needs? And those feelings hadn't sprung out of a kiss but out of time and struggle.

Same old Jack, she accused herself. Still believing that everything in life came as easily as slipping off a log. She'd deserved a swift kick and gotten one. But deserving or not, it didn't make it any less humiliating that Nathan had been the one to plant it.

Mrs. Grange cleared her throat for the third time as she fluffed Jackie's pillows. The minute the typewriter stilled, she stepped in.

"You sure do type fast," she began. "You do secretarial work?"

There was no reason to take out her foul mood on the housekeeper, Jackie reminded herself as she forced a smile. "No, actually I'm writing a book."

"Is that so?" Interested, Mrs. Grange walked to the foot of the bed to tug on the spread. "I like a good story myself."

Mrs. Grange was the first person Jackie had told about her writing who hadn't raised a brow or rolled her eyes. Encouraged, she swiveled around in her chair. The devil with Nathan, she thought. Jacqueline R. MacNamara had come to write a book, and that was just what she was going to do.

"Do you get much of a chance to read?"

"Nothing I like better after a day on my feet than to sit down with a nice story for an hour or two." Mrs. Grange edged a little closer, passing a dustrag over the lamp. "What kind of book are you writing?"

"A romance, a historical romance."

"No fooling? I'm partial to love stories. You been writing long?"

"Actually, this is my first try. I spent about a month doing research and compiling information and dates and things, then I just dived in."

Mrs. Grange shifted her gaze to the typewriter, then looked back at the lamp. "I guess it's like painting. You don't want anybody looking till it's all done."

"Are you kidding?" Laughing, Jackie tucked her feet under her. "I've been dying for somebody to want to read some of it." But not her family, Jackie thought, nibbling on her lower lip. They had already seen too much of what she'd begun, then left undone. "Want to see the first page?" Jackie was already whipping it from the pile and offering it.

"Well, now." Mrs. Grange took the typed sheet and held it out at arm's length until she focused on it. She read with her lips pursed and her eyes narrowed. After a moment she let out three wheezes that Jackie recognized as a laugh. Nothing, absolutely nothing, could have pleased her more.

"You sure did start out with a bang, didn't you?" There was both admiration and approval in Mrs. Grange's eyes as she looked over the end of the sheet. "Nothing like a gunfight to pique the interest."

"That's what I was hoping. Of course, it's just a first draft, but it's going fast." She accepted the page back and studied it. "I'm hoping to have enough to send off in a couple of weeks."

"I'll be mighty pleased to read the whole thing when you've finished."

"Me too." Jackie laughed again as she placed the first page on top of the pile. "Every day when I see how many pages I've done I can't believe it." A bit hesitantly, she laid her hand on top of the manuscript pages. "I haven't figured out what I'm going to do when it's all finished."

"Well, I guess you'll just have to write another one, won't you?" Bending, Mrs. Grange hefted her box of cleaning tools and clumped out.

Why, she was right, Jackie thought. Win or lose, life didn't begin or end on the first try. There couldn't be anyone who knew that better than herself. If something worked, you kept at it. And if something didn't work, and you wanted it, you kept right at that, too.

Turning around, she smiled at the half-typed page in her machine. She could apply that philosophy nicely to her writing. And while she was at it she might just apply it to Nathan.

Chapter 5

He was furious with himself. Still, it was easier, and a lot more comfortable, to turn his fury on her. He hadn't wanted to kiss her. She'd goaded him into it. He certainly hadn't wanted to hurt her. She'd forced him to do so. In a matter of days she'd turned him into a short-tempered villain with an overactive libido.

He was really a very nice man. Nathan was certain of it. Sure, he could be tough-minded, and he was often an impatient perfectionist on the job. He could hire and fire with impersonal speed. But that was business. In his personal life he'd never given anyone reason to dislike him.

When he saw a woman socially, he was always careful to see that the rules were posted up front. If the relationship deepened, both would be fully aware of its possibilities and its limitations. No one would ever have called him a womanizer.

Not that he didn't have a certain number of female...

friends. It would be impossible for a grown man, a healthy man, to go through life without some companionship and affection. But, damn it, he made the moves, the overtures— and there was a certain flow to how these things worked. When a man and a woman decided to go beyond being friends, they did so responsibly, with as much caution as affection. By the time they did, if they did, they'd developed a certain rapport and understanding.

Groping in the kitchen after a parsley salad wasn't his idea of a sensible adult relationship.

If that was old-fashioned, then he was old-fashioned.

The problem was, that kiss over the kitchen counter had meant more, had shaken him more, than any of the carefully programmed, considerate and mature relationships he'd ever experienced. And it wasn't the way he wanted his life to run.

He hadn't learned much from his father, other than how to knot a tie correctly, but he had learned that a woman was to be treated with respect, admiration and care. He was— always had been—a gentleman. Roses for the proper occasion, a light touch and a certain amount of courtship.

He knew how to treat a woman, how to steer a relationship along the right course and how to end one without scenes and recriminations. If he was overly careful not to allow anyone to get too close, he had good reason. Another thing he'd learned from his father, in reverse, was never to make promises he wouldn't keep or establish bonds he would certainly break. It had always been a matter of pride to him that whenever it had become necessary to end a relationship he and the woman involved had parted as friends.

How could he and Jackie part as friends when they hadn't yet become friends? In any case, Nathan considered himself sharp enough to know that if a relationship was begun, then ended, with a woman like Jackie, it wouldn't end without scenes or recriminations. The end, he was sure, would be just as explosive and illogical as the beginning.

He didn't like mercurial personalities or flash-fire tempers. They interfered with his concentration.

What he needed to do was to get back in gear—start the preliminaries on his next project, resume his social life. He'd spent too much time on the troubles and triumphs with the complex in Germany. Now that he'd gotten home, he hadn't had a peaceful moment.

His own fault. Nathan was willing to accept responsibility. His uninvited guest had another week—after all, she had his word on that. Then she was out. Out and forgotten. Well, out, in any case.

He started upstairs with the intention of changing and drowning himself in the pool. Then he heard her laugh. It was just his bad luck, he supposed, that she had such an appealing laugh. He heard her speak in that quicksilver way she had, and he stopped. Her bedroom door was open, and her voice raced out. It wasn't eavesdropping, he told himself. It was, after all, his house.

"Aunt Honoria, what in the world gave you that idea?" Kicked back in a chair, Jackie held the phone between her shoulder and chin as she painted her toenails. "Of course I'm not annoyed with Fred. Why should I be? He did me a wonderful favor." Jackie dipped her brush in the bottle of Sizzling Cerise polish and played her cards close to her chest. "The house is absolutely perfect, exactly what I'd been looking for, and Nathan—Nathan's the owner, darling—yes, he's just adorable."

She held her foot out to admire her handiwork. Between writing and cooking, she hadn't had time for a pedicure in weeks. No matter how busy, her mother would have said, a woman should always look her best from head to toe.

"No, dear, we've worked things out beautifully. He's a bit of a hermit, so we keep to ourselves. I'm fixing his meals for him. The darling's developing a bit of a paunch."

Outside the door, Nathan automatically reached a hand to his stomach.

"No, he couldn't be sweeter. We're rubbing along just fine. He might be one of my uncles. As a matter of fact, his hairline's receding just like Uncle Bob's."

This time both of Nathan's hands went to his hair.

"I'm just glad I could put your mind at ease. No, be sure to let Fred know everything couldn't be better. I'd have gotten in touch with him myself, but I wasn't sure just where he'd popped off to."

There was a pause. For some reason, Nathan felt it was a particularly cold one.

"Of course, dear, I know exactly how our Fred is."

In the hallway, Nathan heard little murmurs of agreement and a few light laughs. He was just about to continue when Jackie spoke again.

"Oh, Aunt Honoria, I nearly forgot. What was the name of that wonderful Realtor you used on the Hawkins property?"

Jackie switched feet and moved in for the kill.

"Well, dear, it's rather confidential still, but I know I can trust you. It seems there's this block of land, about twenty-five acres. South of here, a place called Shutter's Creek. Yes, it is rather precious, isn't it? In any case...you will keep this to yourself, won't you?"

Jackie smiled and continued to paint as she received her aunt's assurances. Aunt Honoria's promises were as easily smeared as wet nail polish. "Yes, I knew you would.

Anyway, it's being sold at rock bottom, and naturally I wouldn't have been interested. Who would? It's hardly more than a swamp at this point. But the beauty is, dear, that Allegheny Enterprises—you know, the contractors who put up all those marvelous resorts? Yes, that's the one. They're scouting out the location. They're thinking about pumping it and filling it in and putting up one of those chichi places like they did in Arizona. Yes, it was marvelous what they did with a few acres of desert, wasn't it?"

She listened a few more moments, knowing how to play a line until the bait was well taken.

"Just a little tip from a friend of mine. I want to snap it up quickly, then resell it to Allegheny. Word from my friend is that they'll pay triple the asking price. Yes, I know, sounds too good to be true. Do keep this under your hat, Auntie. I want to see if I can have the Realtor rush this through settlement before the lid's off."

Jackie listened for a moment as she debated putting on a third coat.

"Yes, it could be exciting, and very hush-hush. That's why I don't want to tip my hand to the Realtor here in Florida. No, I haven't said a thing to Mother and Daddy yet. You know how I love surprises. Oh, darling, there's the door. Must run. Do give my best to everyone. I'll be in touch. *Ciao*."

Delighted with herself, Jackie stretched in the chair and sent it spinning in a circle.

"Well, hello, Nathan."

"I don't know where you get your information," he began, "but unless you want to lose even more money, I'd look for someplace other than Shutter's Creek. It's twenty-five acres of sludge and mosquitoes."

"Yes, I know." With the ease of the limber, Jackie brought

her leg around so that she could blow on her painted toe-nails. Nathan wouldn't have been surprised if she'd tucked her heel behind her ear and grinned at him. "And unless I miss my guess, dear old Fred will own all those lovely mosquitoes within forty-eight hours." Smiling at Nathan, she pillowed her head on her folded arms. "I always figure when you pay back you should pay back where it'll hurt the most. For Fred, that's his wallet."

Impressed, Nathan stepped farther into the room. "You planted the seeds of his downfall?"

"Exactly, and like Jack's beanstalk, it should sprout over-night."

Nathan mulled it over. It was a nasty trick, a very nasty trick. He only wished he'd thought of it. "How do you know he'll go for it?"

Jackie merely continued to smile. "Want to make a wager on it?"

"No," he said after a moment. "No, I don't think I do. How much are they asking an acre?"

"Oh, only two thousand. Fred should be able to beg, borrow or steal fifty without too much trouble." Deciding against a third coat, she capped the bottle. "I always pay my debts, Nathan. Without exception."

He was aware he'd been warned and decided he deserved it. "If it's any consolation, I doubt I'll be able to drink iced coffee again."

She crossed her legs lazily. "I suppose that's something."

"And I'm not losing my hair."

She flicked her gaze over it. It was thick and full and dark. She could remember with absolute clarity how it had felt between her fingers. "Probably not."

"Nor do I have a paunch."

With her tongue caught between her teeth, she let her

glance slide down to his taut and very flat stomach. "Well, not yet."

"And I am not adorable."

"Well…" Her eyes were laughing when they came back to his. "Cute, then—in a staid and very masculine sort of way."

He opened his mouth to argue, then decided it was safer to give up. "I'm sorry," he said instead before he knew he'd meant to tell her.

Jackie's eyes softened along with her smile. Revenge always took a back seat to an apology. "Yes, I think you are. Do you like fresh starts, Nathan?"

So it was that easy. He should have known it would be that easy with her. "Yes, actually, I do."

"All right, then." She unwound herself from the chair. If he found himself looking at her legs again, he was only human. When she stood, she offered a hand. "Friends?"

He knew he could have given her a list of reasons they couldn't be, certainly a lengthy one of reasons why they shouldn't be. But he put his hand in hers. "Friends. Do you want to take a swim?"

"Yeah." She could have kissed him. God, she wanted to. Lecturing herself, Jackie smiled instead. "Give me five minutes to change."

She took less than that. When she arrived, Nathan was just surfacing. Before he had the chance to shake the water out of his eyes and spot her, she dived in beside him. She came up cleanly, head tilted back so that her hair was slick against her head.

"Hi."

"You move fast."

"Mostly." She moved into a smooth sidestroke and did a length and a half. "I love your pool. That helped sell me on the place, you know. I grew up with a pool, so I'd have hated to spend three months without one."

"Glad I could oblige," he told her, but it didn't come out nearly as sarcastic as he'd expected. She smiled and switched to a breaststroke that barely rippled the water. "I take it you do a lot of swimming."

"Not as much as I used to." With what looked like no effort at all, she rolled onto her back to float. "I was on a swim team for a couple of years in my teens. Gave some serious thought to the Olympics."

"I'm not surprised."

"Then I fell in love with my swim coach. His name was Hank." She sighed and closed her eyes on the memory. "I couldn't seem to concentrate on my form after that. I was fifteen and Hank was twenty-five. I imagined us married and raising a relay team. He was only interested in my backstroke. I've always been able to go backward well."

"You don't say."

"No, really. I was all-state with my backstroke. Anyway, Hank was about five-eight, with shoulders like I beams. I've always been a sucker for shoulders." She opened her eyes briefly to study him. Without a shirt, his body seemed tougher and more disciplined than she had expected. "Yours are very nice."

"Thanks." He discovered it was both relaxing and invigorating to float beside her.

"Also, Hank had the greatest blue eyes. Like lanterns. I wove some wonderful fantasies around those eyes."

Irrationally he began to detest Hank. "But he was only interested in your backstroke."

"Exactly. To get him to notice me, I pretended I was drowning. I imagined him pulling me out and doing mouth-to-mouth until he realized he was madly in love and couldn't live without me. How was I supposed to know that my father had picked that day to come in and watch practice?"

"No one could have."

"I knew you'd understand. So there's my father jumping into the pool in his three-piece wool suit and Swiss watch. Neither were ever quite the same again, by the way. By the time he dragged me to the side he was hysterical. Some of my teammates thought it was a reaction from shock, but my father knew me too well. Before I could blink, I was off the swim team and on the tennis courts. With a female pro."

"Your father sounds like a very wise man."

"Oh, he's as sharp as they come, J. D. MacNamara. No one's ever been able to put anything over on him for long. God knows I've tried." She sighed and let the water lap around her. "He'll get a tremendous charge out of it when I tell him about the sting I pulled on Fred."

"You're close to your family?"

Jackie thought, but couldn't be sure, that his voice sounded wistful. "Very. Sometimes almost too much, which may be why I'm always pulling myself off somewhere to try something new. If Daddy had his way, I'd be safely housed in Newport with the man of his choice, raising his grandchildren and keeping out of trouble. Do you have any family here in Florida?"

"No."

She didn't have any doubts about it this time. The subject was definitely on posted ground. Not wanting to irritate him again so soon, Jackie let it pass. "Want to race?"

"Where?" He nearly yawned as he said it. He couldn't remember the last time he'd been so completely relaxed.

"To one end and back to the other. I'll give you a three-stroke lead."

He opened his eyes at that. Jackie was treading water now, her face only inches from his. As he looked at her, Nathan realized he could yank her to him and have his mouth on hers in a heartbeat. Racing, he decided, was a much better idea.

"Fine." He took three easy strokes, then saw the bullet pass him. Amused, and challenged, he kicked in.

It might have been a few years since she'd been on a swim team, but after five yards Nathan saw that she'd retained her competitive spirit. With some women, with most women, he'd have been inclined to lose, knowing that the woman involved would know he'd done so purposely.

He didn't feel inclined to lose to Jackie.

When they touched the wall and rolled into a turn, they were head-to-head. He couldn't, as he'd expected, sprint ahead of her. Her long legs propelled her forward, and her slim arms cut through the water in quick, smooth strokes. Gradually he inched ahead, one stroke, then two, with the advantage of his longer reach. When they came to the side he touched only half a body length ahead.

"I must be slipping." A little breathless, Jackie leaned her forearms on the edge, pillowed her cheek on them and studied him. His skin was shiny with water now, drops running off of and clinging to muscular forearms and shoulders. The kind of arms and shoulders, Jackie thought, that a woman could depend on. "You're in good shape, Nathan."

"You too." He was out of breath himself.

"No handicap next time."

He grinned. "I'll still beat you."

"Maybe." Jackie dragged a hand through her hair so that it curled, wet and charming, around her face. "How's your tennis?"

"Not bad."

"Well, that's a possibility." She pulled herself up and out, then sat on the edge, legs dangling. "How about Latin?"

"What about Latin?"

"We could have a Latin tournament."

With a shake of his head, he pulled himself up to sit beside her. "I don't know any Latin."

"Everyone knows some Latin. Corpus delicti or magna cum laude." She leaned back on her elbows. "I can never understand why they call it a dead language when it's used every day."

"That's certainly something to think about."

She laughed. She couldn't help it. He had such a droll way of telling her he thought she was crazy. When his eyes were light and friendly and the smile was beginning to play around his mouth, he seemed like someone she'd known all her life. Or wished she had.

"I like you, Nathan. I really do."

"I like you, too. I think." It wasn't possible not to smile back at her, just as it wasn't possible not to look at her if she was anywhere nearby. She drew you in. Being with her was like plunging into a cold lake on a sultry day. It was a shock to the system, but a welcome one.

Before he realized what he was doing, Nathan reached over to tuck a dripping curl behind her ear. It wasn't like him; he didn't touch casually. The moment his fingers brushed her cheek he knew it was just one more mistake. How could you want more when you weren't even certain what it was you were taking?

As he started to draw away, she leaned up just a little and took his hand in hers. She brought his fingers to her lips in a gesture that stunned him with the naturalness of it.

"Nathan, is there some woman I should be concerned about?"

He didn't pull away, though he knew he should. Somehow his fingers had curled with hers and were holding on. "What do you mean?"

"I mean, you said you weren't involved, but I wondered if there was someone. I don't mind competing, I just like to know."

There was no one. Even if there had been, her memory would have vanished like a puff of smoke. That was what worried him. "Jack, you're taking two steps to my one."

"Am I?" She shifted. It only took a small movement to have her lips whisper against his. She didn't press, content for now with only a taste. "How long do you think it'll take you to catch up?"

He didn't remember moving, but somehow his hands were framing her face. He could feel the water turning to steam on his skin. It should have been easy, uncomplicated. She was willing, he was desirous. They were adults who understood the rules and the risks. There were no promises between them, and no demands for any.

But even as her lips parted beneath his, even as he took what she offered and ached for more, he knew there would be nothing simple about it.

"I don't think I'm ready for you," he murmured, but lowered her onto the concrete apron of the pool.

"Then don't think." Her arms went around him. She'd been waiting. There was no way she could explain to him that she'd been waiting for him, just for him, all her life. It was so easy, so natural, to want him and to give in to that wanting.

Somehow, even as a girl, she'd known there would only be one man for her. She hadn't known how or when she'd find him, or even if she would. Without him, she would have been content to live on her own, satisfying herself with the love of family and friends. Jackie had never believed in settling for second best.

But now he was here, his mouth on her mouth, his body warming hers. She didn't have to think about tomorrow or the day after that when she was holding a lifelong dream in her arms.

What she wanted was here and now. Turning into him, Jackie murmured his name and cherished the sensation of being wanted in turn.

She wasn't like other women. But why? He'd wanted before, been charmed and baffled and achy before. But not like this. He couldn't think when he was close to her. He could only feel. Tenderness, passion, frustration, desire. It was as if when he held her intellect clicked off and emotion, pure emotion, took over.

Was it that she was every man's fantasy? A generous, willing woman with needs and demands to match a man's—a woman without inhibitions or pretenses. He wished he could believe it was that. He wanted to believe it was only that. But he knew it was more. Somehow it was much more.

And he was losing himself, degree by degree, layer by layer. All his life he'd known where he was going and why. It wasn't possible, it wasn't right, to allow this—to allow her—to change it.

He had to stop it now, while he still had a choice, or at least while he could still pretend he had one.

Slowly, and with much more difficulty than he'd imagined, he pulled away from her. The sun was hanging in the west, still bright, vivid enough to bring out the highlights in her hair. It wasn't just brown as he'd thought, it had dozens and dozens of variations of the shade. Soft, warm, rich. Like her eyes. Like her skin.

He forced himself not to lift a hand to her cheek to touch just once more.

"We'd better go in."

She'd melted inside. Completely. He could have asked anything of her in that moment and she'd have given it without a second thought. Such was the power of loving. She blinked, struggling against coming back to earth. If the choice had been hers, and hers alone, she would have stayed where she was, in his arms, forever.

But she wasn't a fool. He wasn't talking about going in to continue what they'd begun, but to end it. She closed her eyes, accepting the hurt.

"Go ahead. I think I'll get a little more sun."

"Jack."

She opened her eyes. He was surprised to see such patience in them. He shifted away, knowing that if he remained too close he'd touch her again and start the merry-go-round spinning. "I don't like to start anything until I know how it's going to finish."

She let out a long sigh because she understood. "That's too bad. You miss an awful lot that way, Nathan."

"And make less mistakes. I don't like to make mistakes."

"Is that what I am?" There was just enough amusement in her voice for him to be relieved.

"Yes. You've been a mistake right from the beginning." He turned to her again, noting that she was looking at him the way he sometimes saw her look when she was putting together a complicated dish. "You know it would be better if you didn't stay here."

She lifted a brow. It was the only change in the quietly intense look. "Are you kicking me out?"

"No." He said it too quickly and cursed himself for it. "I should, but I don't seem to be able to."

She laid a hand on his shoulder lightly. He was tense again. "You want me, Nathan. Is that so terrible?"

"I don't take everything I want."

She frowned a moment, thinking. "No, you wouldn't. You're too sensible. It's one of the things I like best about you. But you will take me eventually, Nathan. Because there's something right about us. And we both know it."

"I don't sleep with every woman who attracts me."

"I'm glad to hear it." Jackie sat up completely, tucked up her knees and wrapped her arms around them. "Indulging like that is dangerous in more ways than one." Turning her head, she studied him. "Do you think I sleep with every man who raises my blood pressure?"

Restless and not entirely comfortable, he moved his shoulders. "I don't know you or your lifestyle."

"Well, that's fair." She preferred things to be fair. "Let's get the sex out of the way, then. It dims the romance a bit, but it's sensible. I'm twenty-five, and I've fallen in and out of love countless times. I like falling in better, but I've never been able to stick. Nathan, this might be difficult for you to accept, but I'm not a virgin."

When he shook his head and dropped his chin on his chest, she patted his shoulder.

"I know, shocking, isn't it? I confess, I've been with a man. Actually, I've been with two. The first time was on my twenty-first birthday."

"Jack—"

"I know," she interrupted with a wave of her hand. "That's a little late in this day and age, but I hate to follow trends. I was crazy about him. He could quote Yeats."

"That explains it," Nathan muttered.

"I knew you'd understand. Then a couple of years ago I was into photography. Moody black-and-whites. Very esoteric. I met this man. Black leather jacket. Very sullen good looks." There was more amusement in her eyes now than sentiment.

"He moved in with me and sat around being attractive and despondent. It only took me a couple of weeks to discover I wasn't meant to be depressed. But I got some wonderful pictures. Since then, there hasn't been anyone who's made my toes curl. Until you."

He sat still, wondering why he should be glad there had only been two important men in her life. And why he was now jealous of both of them. After a moment he looked at her again. The light had changed subtly. It warmed her skin now.

"I can't decide whether you have no guile whatsoever or if you have more than anyone I've ever met."

"Isn't it nice to have something to wonder about? I guess that's why I want to write. You can 'I wonder' yourself from beginning to end." She was silent only a moment. Jackie's debates with herself never lasted long. "Nathan, there's another thing you might want to wonder about. I'm in love with you."

She rose after she told him, feeling it would be best for both of them.

"I don't want you to worry about it," she said as he sat in stunned silence. "It's just that I hate it when people try to pretend things away. Good things, I mean. I think I'll go in after all and change before I start dinner."

She left him alone. He wondered if anyone else could drop a bombshell so casually, then wander off without checking the damage. Jackie could.

He frowned, watching the way the sun danced in diamonds on the water. There was a boat running north. He could just hear the purr of the motor. The air smelled richly of spring, flowers sun-warmed and burgeoning, grass freshly cut. The days were lengthening, and the heat remained well into evening.

That was life. It went on. It had a pattern.

She was in love with him.

That was absurd...so why wasn't he surprised? It all had to do with who she was, he decided. While he wasn't one to use words like *love* casually, she would be much freer with words, and with feelings.

He didn't even know what love meant to her. An attraction, an affection, a spark. That would be more than enough for many people. She was impetuous. Hadn't she just told him she'd fallen in and out of love countless times? This was just one more adventure for her.

Wasn't that what he wanted to believe? If it was, why did the thought leave him cold and angry?

Because he didn't want to be another adventure. Not for her. He didn't want her to be in love with him...but if she was, he wanted it to be real.

Rising, Nathan walked over to where his land gave way to the wall and the wall to the water. Once his life had moved that smoothly—like a calm channel flowing effortlessly out to sea. That was what he wanted, and that was what he had. He didn't have time to deal with impulsive women who talked about love and romance.

Sometime in the future there would be time for such things—with the proper woman. Someone sensible and polished, Nathan thought. Then he wondered why that suddenly sounded like a nice piece of furniture instead of a wife.

She was doing this to him, he realized, and he resented it. She had no business telling him she was in love with him, making him think that maybe, just maybe, what he was feeling was—

No. He brought himself up short as he turned to scowl back at his house. It was beyond ridiculous to imagine, even for an instant, that he could be in love with her. He barely knew the woman, and for the most part she was an annoyance. If he was attracted it was simply because she was attractive. And he'd kept himself so tied up with work in Germany that he hadn't had time for the softer things a man needed.

And, damn it, that was a lie. Disgusted, he turned back to the water again. He did feel something for her. He wasn't sure what or why, but he felt it. He wanted more than to tumble into bed with her and satisfy an itch. He wanted to be with her, hold her, let that low, fascinating voice drain away his tensions.

But that wasn't love, he assured himself. It might have been a little like caring. That was almost acceptable. A man could come to care for a woman without sinking in over his head.

But not a woman like Jackie.

Dragging a hand through his hair, he started back to the house. They weren't going to talk about this, not now, and not later. Whatever it took, he was going to get back to normal.

He told himself it was expedient, not cowardly, to go in through the side door and avoid her.

Chapter 6

Jackie wasn't ashamed of having told Nathan what she felt. Nor did she wish the words back. One of her firmest beliefs was that it was useless to second-guess a decision once it had been made.

In any case, taking the words back or regretting them wouldn't change the fact that they were true. She hadn't meant to fall in love with him, which made it all the sweeter and more important. At other times in her life she had seen a man, thought that he might be the one and set about falling in love.

With Nathan, love had come unexpectedly, without plan or consideration. It had simply happened, as she had always secretly hoped it would. In her heart she'd known that love couldn't be planned, so she'd begun to believe that it would never be there for her.

He was not the perfect match for her, at least not in the way she'd once imagined. Even now she couldn't be sure he had all the qualities she had sometimes listed as desirable in a man.

None of that mattered, because she loved him.

She was willing to give him time—a few days, even a week—to respond in whatever way suited him. As far as she was concerned, there were no doubts as to how things would resolve themselves. She loved him. Fate had taken a hand, in the person of cousin Fred, and tossed them together. Perhaps Nathan didn't know it yet. As she whipped eggs for a soufflé, Jackie smiled. In fact, she was sure Nathan didn't know it yet, but she was exactly what he needed.

When a man was logical, conservative and—well, yes, even just a tad stuffy—he needed the love and understanding of a woman who wasn't any of those things. And that same woman—herself, in this case—would love the man, Nathan, because he was all the things he was. She would find his traits endearing and at the same time not allow him to become so starched he cracked down the middle.

She could see exactly the way it would be for them over the years. They would grow closer with an understanding so keen that each would be able to know what the other was thinking. Agreement wouldn't always be possible, but understanding would. He would work at his drawing board and attend his meetings, while she wrote and took occasional trips to New York to lunch with her publisher.

When his work took him away, she'd go with him, supporting his career just as he would support hers. While he supervised the construction of one of his buildings, she would fill reams of notebooks with research.

Until the children came. Then, for a few years, they would both stay closer to home while they raised their family. Jackie didn't want to imagine boys or girls or hair color, because something that precious should be a surprise. But she was sure that Nathan would be a marshmallow when it came to his children.

And she would be there for him, always, to knead the tension from his shoulders, to laugh him out of his sullen moods, to watch his genius grow and expand. With her, he would smile more. With him, she would become more stable. She would be proud of him, and he of her. When she won the Pulitzer they would drink a magnum of champagne and make love through the night.

It was really very simple. Now all she had to do was wait for him to realize how simple.

Then the phone rang.

With her mixing bowl held in the crook of her elbow, Jackie picked up the receiver from the wall unit. "Hello."

After a brief hesitation came a beautifully modulated voice. "Yes, is this the Powell residence?"

"Yes, it is. May I help you?"

"I'd like to speak to Nathan, please. This is Justine Chesterfield calling."

The name rang a bell. In fact, it rang several. Justine Chesterfield, the recently divorced darling of the society pages. The name opened doors in Bridgeport, Monte Carlo and St. Moritz. All in the proper season, naturally. Jackie believed in premonitions, and she didn't care for the one she was having at the moment.

She was tempted to hang up, but she didn't think that would solve anything.

"Of course." Her mother would have been delighted with the richly rounded tones. "I'll see if he's available, Mrs. Chesterfield."

It was ridiculous to be jealous of a voice over the phone. Besides, she didn't have a jealous bone in her body. Regardless, Jackie gained enormous satisfaction from sticking her tongue out at the receiver before she went to find Nathan.

Since he was just coming down the stairs, she didn't have to look far. "You have a phone call. Justine Chesterfield."

"Oh." He had a flash of guilt that baffled him. Why should receiving a call from an old friend make him feel guilty? "Thanks. I'll take it in my office."

She didn't linger in the hall. Not on purpose, anyway. Could she help it if she had a sudden and unavoidable itch on the back of her knee? So she stood, scratching, while Nathan stepped into his office and picked up the phone.

"Justine, hello. A few days ago. A new housekeeper? No, that was…" How did he, or anyone, explain Jackie? "Actually, I've been meaning to call you. Yes, about Fred MacNamara."

When she decided that if she scratched much longer she'd draw blood, Jackie wandered back into the kitchen. Once there, she stared at the phone. It would be easy to pick up the receiver, very slowly, very quietly—just to see if he was still on the line, of course. She began to, and very nearly did. Then, with a muttered oath, she set it back on the hook. Audibly.

She wasn't interested in anything he had to say to *that woman*. Already Justine had taken on an italicized quality in her mind. Let him explain to *her* why he had a woman living with him. Because the idea amused her, Jackie turned up the radio a little louder and began to sing along with it.

With the care of a woman who loved to cook, she continued to mix the soufflé. She wouldn't slam pots and pans around the kitchen. Jackie knew how to control herself. She didn't make a habit of it, but she knew how. It was only a phone call, after all. As far as Jackie knew, *that woman* had phoned Nathan to make a plug for her favorite charity. Or maybe she wanted to remodel her den. There were a dozen very innocent and perfectly logical reasons for Justine Chesterfield to call Nathan.

Because she wants to get her hooks into him, Jackie thought, and made herself pour the soufflé mixture into the pan without spilling a drop.

"Jackie?"

She turned, as careful with her smile as she'd been with the batter. "All done? Did you have a nice chat with Justine?"

"I wanted to let you know I'll be going out so you wouldn't worry about dinner."

"Mmm-hmm." Without missing a beat, Jackie set a cucumber on the chopping block and began to slice it. "I wonder, did Justine's second—or is it third—divorce ever come through?"

"As far as I know." He paused a moment, leaning against the doorjamb as he watched Jackie bring the knife down with deadly accuracy. Jealousy, he thought, recognizing it when it slammed into his face. He had a jealous woman on his hands, through no fault of his own. Nathan opened his mouth, then shut it again. He'd be damned if he'd explain himself. Perhaps it was absurd, but if she thought he and Justine were romantically involved it might be the best thing for everyone. "I'll see you later."

"Have a good time," she said, and brought the knife down with a satisfying *thwack*.

Jackie didn't turn, nor did she stop her steady slicing until she heard the front door shut. Blowing the hair out of her eyes, she poured the soufflé mixture down the drain. She'd eat a hot dog.

It helped to get back to work, to hear the comforting hum of her typewriter. What helped even more was the development of a new character. Justine—make that Carlotta—was the frowsy, scheming, overendowed madam of the local brothel. Her heart was brass, like her hair. She was a woman who used men like poker chips.

Jake, being only a man, was taken in by her. But Sarah, with the clear eyes of a woman, saw Justine—Carlotta—for exactly what she was.

Afraid of his growing feelings for Sarah, Jake turned to Carlotta. The cad. Eventually Carlotta would betray him, and her betrayal would nearly cost Sarah her life, but for now Sarah had to deal with the fact that the man she'd come to love would turn to another woman to release his passion.

Jackie would have preferred to make Carlotta frumpy and faded. She'd even toyed with a wart. Just a small one. But a hard-faced woman wouldn't do justice to Jake or her book. Dutifully tearing up the first page, Jackie got down to business.

Carlotta was stunning. In a cold, calculated sort of way. Jackie had seen Justine's picture often enough to describe her. Pale and willowy, with eyes the clear blue of a mountain lake and a thin, almost childish mouth. A slender neck and wheat-blond hair. There were ice-edged cheekbones and balletic limbs. Taking literary license, Jackie allowed herself to toughen the looks, add a few dissipated lines and a drinking problem.

As she wrote, she began to see the character more clearly, even began to understand Carlotta's drive to use and discard men, to make a living off their baser drives and weaknesses. She discovered that Carlotta had had a miserable childhood and an abusive first marriage. Unfortunately, this softened her mood toward Justine even as she had Carlotta plotting dreadful problems for Jake and Sarah.

When Jackie ran out of steam, it was still shy of midnight. Telling herself it had nothing to do with waiting up for Nathan, she dawdled, applying a facial she remembered once or twice a month at best, filing her nails and leafing through magazines.

At one she deliberately turned the bedside light off, then lay staring at the ceiling.

Maybe everyone was right after all. Maybe she *was* crazy. A woman who fell in love with a man who had virtually no interest in her had to be asking for trouble. And heartache. This was her first experience with real heartache, and she couldn't say she cared for it.

But she did love him, with all the energy and devotion she was capable of. It wasn't anything like the way it had been with the Yeats buff or the leather jacket. They had brought on a sense of excitement—the way a runner might feel, she thought, when she was about to race the fifty-yard dash full-out. It was different, very different, from preparing for a marathon. The excitement was still there, but with it was a steady determination that came from the knowledge of being ready to start and finish, of being prepared for the long haul.

Like her writing, Jackie thought, and sat up in bed. The parallel was so clear. With all her other projects there had been that quick, almost frantic flash of energy and power. It had been as if she'd known going in that there would be a short, perhaps memorable thrill, then disenchantment.

With the writing, there had been the certainty that this was it for her. It hadn't been her last chance so much as her only one. What she was beginning now was the one thing she'd been looking for through all the years of experimenting.

Falling for Nathan was precisely the same. Other men she'd cared for had been like stepping-stones or springboards that had boosted her up for that one and only man she would want for the rest of her life.

If someone had gotten in the way of her and her writing, would she have tolerated it? Not for a minute. Mentally pushing up her sleeves, she settled back. No one was going to step in the way of her and her man, either. Justine Chesterfield was going to have a fight on her hands.

He'd been home for nearly an hour, but Nathan sat in his parked car and let the smoke from his cigarette trail out the window. It was an odd thing for a man to be wary about going into his own house, but there it was. She was in there. In the bedroom. Her bedroom now. It would never be just a guest room again.

He'd seen her light burning, and he'd seen her light shut off. She might be sleeping. He wasn't sure he'd ever get a decent night's sleep again.

My God, he wanted to go in, walk up the stairs into her room and lose himself in the promise of her. Or the threat.

There was nothing in his feelings for her that made sense, nothing he could put his finger on and analyze. Over and over again his mind played back the way she'd looked at him as they'd sat by the pool, the way her skin had felt with water drying on it, the way her voice had sounded.

I'm in love with you.

Could it be, could it possibly be that easy for her? Yes, he thought it was. Now that he was beginning to know and understand her, he was sure that falling in love and declaring that love would be as natural for Jackie as breathing. But this time she was in love with him.

He could take advantage of it. She wouldn't even blame him for it. He could, without conscience or guilt, do exactly what he was dreaming of doing—walk into her room and finish what had been started that evening.

But he couldn't. He'd never be able to forget the way her eyes had looked. Trusting, honest and incredibly vulnerable. She thought she was tough, resilient. And he believed that she was, to a point. If she really loved him and he hurt her by casually taking what love urged her to give, she wouldn't bounce back.

So how did he handle her?

He'd thought he'd known earlier that evening. Going to see Justine had been a calculated move to distance himself from Jackie and to show both her and himself how ridiculously implausible any relationship between them would be.

Then he'd found himself in Justine's elegant condo with its gold-and-white rooms and its tasteful French antiques and he'd been unable to think of anything but Jackie. There'd been an excellent poached salmon, prepared to a turn by Justine's housekeeper. Nathan had found himself with a yen for the spicy chicken Jackie had prepared that first night.

He'd smiled as Justine, dressed in sleek white lounging pajamas, her wheat-colored hair twisted back in a sleek knot, had served him brandy. And he'd thought of the way Jackie looked in shorts.

With Justine he'd discussed mutual friends and compared viewpoints on Frankfurt and Paris. Her voice was low and soothing, her observations were concise and mildly amusing. He'd remembered the fits and starts and wild paths Jackie's conversations could take.

Justine was an old friend, a valued one. She was a woman he had always been completely at ease with. He knew her family, and she knew his. Their opinions might not always agree precisely, but they were invariably compatible. Over the ten years they'd known each other, they'd never become lovers. Justine's marriages and Nathan's travels had prevented that, though there had always been a light and companionable attraction between them.

That could change now, and they were both aware of it. She was single, and he was home. There would very likely never be a woman he knew better, a woman better suited to his tastes, than Justine Chesterfield.

He'd wanted, as he'd sat comfortably, to be back in his kitchen watching Jackie concoct a meal, even if the damn radio was playing.

He thought it entirely possible that he was losing his mind.

The evening had ended with a chaste, almost brotherly kiss. He hadn't wanted to make love with Justine, though God knew he was stirred up enough to need a woman. It infuriated him to realize that if he'd slept with Justine he would have thought of Jackie and felt like an adulterer.

There was no doubt about it. He was going crazy.

Giving up on trying to reason, even with himself, Nathan got out of the car. As he let himself in to the house he thought a long soak in the whirlpool might tire him out enough to let him sleep.

Jackie heard the movement downstairs and sat up in bed again. Nathan? She hadn't heard a car drive up and stop. She'd been listening for his return for over a half hour, and even in a half doze she would have heard. Crawling down to the foot of the bed, she strained to hear.

Silence.

If it was Nathan, why wasn't he coming upstairs? Annoyed because her heart was beginning to race, she crept to the door and peeked out.

If it was Nathan, why was he walking around in the dark?

Because it wasn't Nathan, she decided. It was a burglar who'd probably been watching the house for weeks, learning the routine and waiting for his chance. He'd know that she was alone in the house and asleep, so he'd broken in to rob Nathan blind.

With a hand to her heart, she glanced back toward her bed. She could call the police, then crawl under the covers. It sounded like a wonderful idea. Even as she took the first tiptoeing step back, she stopped.

But what if she hadn't really heard anything other than the house settling? If Nathan wasn't already fed up, he certainly would be if he got home from *that woman*'s and found the house full of police because she'd jumped the gun.

Taking a deep breath, Jackie decided to creep down and make sure there was a good reason to panic.

She descended the stairs slowly, keeping her back to the wall. Still no sound. The house was absolutely dark and absolutely silent. A burglar had to make some noise when he stole the family silver.

Probably just your imagination, she told herself as she reached the lower landing. In the dark she strained her ears but still heard nothing. As her heartbeat slowed to normal she decided to take one quick check around the house, knowing her imagination would play havoc if she went back to bed without satisfying her curiosity.

She began to whistle, just under her breath, as she moved from room to room. There was no one there, of course, but if there was, Jackie preferred to have them know she was on her way. Jackie's imagination, according to her mother, had always been bizarre.

By the time she'd wound through the living room, passed

by Nathan's office and the powder room and gone into the dining area, she'd imagined not just your everyday intruder but a gang of psychotic thugs who'd recently escaped from a maximum-security prison in Kentucky. Determined to beat her own wayward fantasies, she stepped into the kitchen. Every light in the house blazed behind her. Now, as she reached for the switch in the kitchen, she heard a shuffle of footsteps.

Her fingers froze, but her mind didn't. They were in the sunroom—at least six of them by now. One of them had a scar running from his temple to his jawline and had been serving time for bludgeoning senior citizens in their sleep. She took a step back, thinking of the phone in her room behind a locked door when the footsteps came closer.

Too late, her mind flashed. Going with impulse and desperation, she grabbed the closest weapon—the soufflé pan. Swinging it above her head, she prepared to defend herself.

When Nathan stepped into the room, dressed only in his briefs, it was a toss-up as to who was the more surprised. He jerked back, finding himself ridiculously embarrassed as Jackie let out a scream and dropped the pan. It landed with a resounding clatter just before she doubled over with hysterical giggles.

"What the hell are you doing, sneaking around the house?" If it wouldn't have made him feel that much more foolish, Nathan would have grabbed a dishcloth for cover.

Jackie slammed both hands over her mouth as she gasped and choked. "I thought you were six men with homicidal intentions. One of you had a scar, and the little one had a face like a weasel."

"So naturally you came down to beat us all off with a soufflé pan."

"Not exactly." Still giggling, she propped herself against the counter. "I'm sorry, I always laugh when I'm terrified."

"Who doesn't?"

"It was just that I thought there was a burglar, then I convinced myself there wasn't, and then…" She began to hiccup. "Then I thought you were this gang from Kentucky led by a man named Bubba. I need some water." Grabbing a glass, Jackie filled it to the rim while Nathan tried to follow.

"You've obviously picked the right field at last, Jack. With an imagination like that, you'll make a million."

"Thanks." Picking up the glass, she drank while running her finger in circles over the bottom.

"What the hell are you doing now?"

"Getting rid of the hiccups. Surefire." She set the glass down and waited. "See? All clear. Now it's your turn. What were you doing sneaking around the house in the dark in your underwear?"

"It's my house."

"Right you are. And it's very nice underwear, too. Sorry I scared you."

"You didn't scare me." Finding his temper once more on a short fuse, he bent down and scooped up the pan. "I was about to take a spa and decided I wanted a drink."

"Oh. Well, that explains that." Jackie pressed her lips together. It wouldn't do to start giggling again. "Did you have a nice time?"

"What? Yes, fine." This was a hell of a time, Nathan decided, to notice that she was wearing nothing but an oversize T-shirt with a faded picture of Mozart on the front. With care and effort, he kept his eyes on her face, but it didn't help very much. "I don't want to keep you up."

"Oh, that's okay. I'll fix you a drink."

"I can do it." He had his hand on her wrist before she could open the cupboard.

"No need to be cranky. I said I was sorry."

"I'm not cranky. Go to bed, Jack."

"I'm bothering you, aren't I?" she murmured as she turned to face him. With her free hand, she reached up to touch his cheek. "That's nice."

"Yes, you're bothering me, and it's not particularly nice." Her face was scrubbed free of cosmetics, but her scent still lingered. "Now go to bed."

"Want to come with me?"

His eyes narrowed at the smile in hers. "You're going to push too far."

"It was only a suggestion." She felt a wave of tenderness as she thought of how he would view his position and what was happening between them. An honorable man who thought his intentions were dishonorable. "Nathan, is it so hard for you to understand that I love you and want to make love with you?"

He didn't want it to make sense, couldn't allow it to make sense. "What's hard for me to understand and impossible for me to believe is that anyone could consider themselves in love after a matter of days. Things don't work that easily, Jack."

"Sometimes they do. Look at Romeo and Juliet. No, that's a bad example when you think of how things worked out." Fascinated by his mouth, warmed by the memory of how it felt on hers, she traced it with her fingertip. "Sorry, I guess I can't think of a good example right now because I'm thinking about you."

His stomach wound itself into a tight knot. "If you're trying to make this difficult, you're succeeding."

"Impossible was the idea, but I'll settle for difficult."

She shifted closer. Their thighs brushed. Her eyelids lowered. "Kiss me, Nathan. Even my imagination falls short of what it's like when you do."

He swore at her, or tried to, but his mouth was already against hers. Each time it was a little sweeter, a little sharper, a little more difficult to forget. He was losing, and he knew it. Once he gave in to his own needs, he wasn't sure he'd be able to pull back. Nor did he know precisely what he would find himself trapped in.

She was a drug to a man who had always been obsessively clear-minded, a slide down a cliff to one who had always been firmly surefooted.

And she was naked beneath that loose shirt. Soft and naked and already warm for him. He found himself reaching, testing, taking, even as warning bells rang inside his head. DANGER. PROCEED AT YOUR OWN RISK.

His own risk. He'd always carefully calculated the risk, the odds, the degrees and angles, before he took the first step. Her body seemed to have been molded for his hands, for his pleasure, for his needs. There was no way to calculate this, or her, or what happened every time they touched each other.

It was so easy, so mindlessly easy, to take the next step. Blindly, recklessly. She was murmuring his name as her hands glided up his back, then down to his hips. He could feel every curve and angle of her body as his hands moved over and under the thin cotton. How could it be so familiar yet so fresh, so comforting yet so unnerving?

He wanted to scoop her up, to wallow in her, to lose himself. It would have been so easy. Her body was poised against his, ready, waiting, eager. And the heat, the heat he'd begun to recognize and expect, was weighing down on his brain. There was nothing and no one he'd ever wanted more.

Somewhere in the back of his mind he heard a door slam and a key turn in a lock. In a last attempt at self-defense, he pulled her away.

"Hold it."

Sighing, half dreaming, she opened her eyes. "Hmm?"

If she kept looking at him like that he was going to fall apart. Or rip that excuse for nightgear off her back. "Look, I don't know why this is happening, but it has to stop. I'm not hypocrite enough to say I don't want you, but I'm not crazy enough to start something that's going to make us both miserable."

"Why should making love make either of us miserable?"

"Because it could never go beyond that." Because she swayed toward him, he put his hands on her shoulders. Damn it, she was trembling. Or he was. "I don't have room for you, for anyone, in my life, Jack. I don't want to make room. I don't think you understand that."

"No, I don't." She leaned forward to brush her lips over his chin. "If I believed it, I'd think it was very sad."

"Believe it." But he was no longer certain he did. "My work comes first. It takes all my time, my energy and my concentration. That's the way I want it. A blistering affair with you has its appeal, but...for some reason I care about you, and I don't think that's all you want or need."

"It doesn't have to be all."

"But it does, and that's something for you to think about." He had to stay calm now, calm enough to make her listen. "In six weeks I go to Denver. When I've finished there, it's Sydney. After that I don't know where I'll be or for how long. I travel light, and that doesn't include a lover, or the worry about someone waiting for me back home."

She shook her head as she took a small step back. "I wonder what happened to make you so unwilling to share yourself, so determined to keep to some straight-and-narrow path. No curves, no detours, Nathan?" She tilted her head to study him. There was no anger in her eyes, just a sympathy he didn't want. "It's more than sad, it's sinful, really, to turn away someone who loves you because you don't want to spoil your routine."

He opened his mouth so that the words nearly tumbled out. Reasons, explanations, an anger he barely remembered or thought he'd forgotten. Years of control snapped into place.

"Maybe it is, but that's the way I live. The way I've chosen to live." He'd hurt her again, badly this time. The shiver of pain sliced back at him, and he knew he was hurting himself, as well. "I can tell you that if you were another woman it would be a lot easier to turn away. I don't want to feel what I'm feeling for you. Do you understand?"

"Yes. I wish I didn't." She looked down at the floor. When her eyes lifted again, the hurt was still there, but it had been joined by a flash of something stronger. "What you don't understand is that I don't give up. Blame it on the Irish. A stubborn breed. I want you, Nathan, and no matter how far you run or how fast, I'll catch up. When I do, all your neat little plans are going to tumble like a stack of dominoes." Taking his face in her hands, she kissed him hard. "And you'll thank me for it, because no one's ever going to love you the way I do."

She kissed him again, more gently this time, then turned away. "I made some fresh lemonade, if you still want a drink. Night."

He watched her go with the sinking feeling that he could already hear the clatter of dominoes.

Chapter 7

She should have hated him. Sarah wanted to, wished the strong, destructive emotions would come, filling all the cracks in her feelings, blocking out everything else. With hate, a coolheaded, sharply honed hate, she would have felt in control again. She needed badly to feel in control again. But she didn't hate him. Couldn't.

Even knowing Jake had spent the night with another woman, kissing another woman's lips, touching another woman's skin, she couldn't hate him. But she could grieve for the loss, for the death of a beauty that had never had the chance to bloom fully.

She had come to understand what they might have had together. She had nearly come to accept that they belonged together, whatever their differences, whatever the risks. He would always live by his gun and by his own set of rules, but with her, briefly, perhaps reluctantly, he had shown such kindness, such tenderness.

There was a place for her in his heart. Sarah knew it. Beneath the rough-hewn exterior was a man who believed in justice, who was capable of small, endearing kindnesses. He'd allowed her to see that part of him, a part she knew he'd shared with few others.

Then why, the moment she had begun to soften toward him, to accept him for what and who he was, had he turned to another woman, a woman of easy virtue?

A woman of easy virtue? Jackie said to herself, and rolled her eyes. If that was the best she could come up with, she'd better hang it up right now.

It hadn't been one of her better days. Nathan had been up and gone before she'd started breakfast. He'd left her a note—she couldn't even say a scribbled note, because his handwriting was as disciplined as the rest of him—telling her he'd be out most of the day.

She'd munched on a candy bar and the last of the ginger ale as she'd mulled over the current situation. As far as she could see, it stank.

She was in love with a man who was determined to hold her, and his own feelings, at arm's length. A man who insisted on rationalizing those feelings away—not because he was committed to another woman, not because he was suffering from a fatal disease, not because he was hiding a criminal past, but because they were inconvenient.

He was too honorable to take advantage of the situation, and too stubborn to admit that he and she belonged together.

No room in his life for her? Jackie thought as she pushed away from the typewriter and began to pace. Did he really believe she would take a ridiculous statement like that and back off? Of course she wouldn't, but what bothered her more was that he would make a statement like that in the first place.

What made him so determined not to accept love when it was given, so determined not to acknowledge his own emotions? Her own family could sometimes be annoyingly proper, but there had always been a wealth of love generously given. She'd grown up unafraid of feelings. If you didn't feel, you weren't alive, so what was the purpose? She knew Nathan felt, and felt deeply, but whenever his emotions took control he stepped back and put up those walls.

He did love her, Jackie thought as she flopped down on the bed. She couldn't be mistaken about that. But he was going to fight her every inch of the way. So she'd handle it. It wasn't that she objected to a good fight, it was just that this one hurt. Every time he drew back, every time he denied what they had together, it hurt a little more.

She'd been honest with him, and that hadn't worked. She'd been deliberately provocative, and that hadn't done so well, either. She'd been annoying, and she'd been cooperative. She wasn't sure what step to take next.

Rolling onto her stomach, she debated the idea of taking a nap. It was midafternoon, she'd worked nonstop since breakfast, and she couldn't drum up any enthusiasm for the pool. Perhaps if she went to sleep with Nathan on her mind she would wake up with a solution. Deciding to trust the Fates—after all, they'd gotten her this far—she closed her eyes. She'd nearly dozed off when the doorbell rang.

Someone selling encyclopedias, she thought groggily, with the idea of ignoring them. Or it was three men in white suits passing out pamphlets for a tent revival—which actually might be fairly interesting. With a yawn, she snuggled into the pillow. She'd nearly shut off her mind when a last

thought intruded. It was a telegram from home, and someone had been in a horrible accident.

Springing up, she sprinted downstairs.

"Yes, I'm coming!" As she pushed the hair out of her
eyes, she yanked the door open.

It wasn't a telegram or a door-to-door salesman. It was
Justine Chesterfield. Jackie decided it really wasn't one
of her better days. She leaned on the door and offered a
chilly smile.

"Hello."

"Hello. I wonder if Nathan might be around."

"Sorry, he's out." Her fingers on the knob itched to close
the door quietly and completely. That would be rude. Jackie
could almost hear her mother upbraiding her. She took a
long breath before moderating her tone. "He didn't say
where he was going or when he'd be back, but you're welcome to wait if you'd like."

"Thanks." They exchanged appraising glances before
Justine stepped over the threshold.

The woman's dressed as if she's just stepped off a yacht,
Jackie thought nastily. In Hyannis Port. At the beginning
of the season. Justine's tall, softly curved body was set off
nicely by white slacks and a boat-necked silk T-shirt in
crimson. She'd added a quietly elegant necklace of twisted
gold links and discreetly stylish matching earrings. Her
hair had been left down to wave gently on her shoulders,
scooped back at the temples by two mother-of-pearl combs.

She was perfect. Perfectly lovely, perfectly groomed,
perfectly mannerly. Jackie was glad she could hate her.

"I hope I'm not disturbing you…" Justine began.

"Not at all." Jackie gestured toward the living room.
"Make yourself at home."

"Thanks." Justine wandered in, then set her envelope

bag on a small table. The bag matched her open-toed white snakeskin pumps. "You must be Jacqueline, Fred's cousin."

"I must be."

"I'm Justine Chesterfield. An old friend of Nathan's."

"I recognized your voice." Ingrained manners had Jackie offering a hand. As their fingers touched briefly, a smile hovered around Justine's mouth. Unfortunately for Jackie, the smile was friendly and entirely too appealing.

"And I yours. According to Nathan, Fred's as devious as he is charming."

"More so, believe me." So this was the kind of woman Nathan preferred. Quietly polished, quietly stylish, quietly stunning. Trying not to sigh, Jackie played hostess. "Can I get you something? A cold drink, some coffee?"

"I'd love something cold, if you wouldn't mind."

"All right, have a seat. I'll just be a minute."

Jackie muttered to herself the entire time she fixed lemonade and arranged shortbread cookies on Nathan's Depression glass platter. It rarely occurred to her to think how she looked when she planned on staying in. But she would have picked today to wear her most comfortable and most ragged pair of cutoffs, with a baggy athletic-style T-shirt in garish green-and-yellow stripes. There was a small fortune in gold and gems on her fingers, and her feet were bare. The Sizzling Cerise on her toes had begun to chip.

The hell with that, she thought, and made one vague and futile attempt to finger-comb her hair. She'd let Ms. Sleek-and-Stylish have her say.

She was sure that Sarah would have been just as gracious to Carlotta, but she had a feeling that Sarah was a much nicer person than Jacqueline R. MacNamara. Determined to give Nathan nothing to snarl about, she lifted the tray and started back to her guest. Nathan's guest.

The sunlight and the strong masculine colors of the room were certainly flattering to Justine. It didn't help to admit it, but Jackie was nothing if not honest.

"This is awfully nice of you," Justine began as she took a seat. "Actually, I was hoping we'd have a chance to talk. Are you very busy? Nathan told me you were working on a book."

"He did?" It was surprise more than a desire to chat that had Jackie sitting. She hadn't thought Nathan even remembered she was writing, much less that he would tell someone else about it. And Justine was the second person, after Mrs. Grange, who hadn't smirked when she'd spoken of her writing.

"Yes, he said you were writing a novel and that you were very dedicated and disciplined about your work. Nathan's a big believer in discipline."

"So I've noticed." Jackie discovered she didn't mind sipping a glass of lemonade after all. Justine had just handed her the perfect route to make her excuses and disappear back upstairs. After a second sip, Jackie decided to detour around it. "As it turns out, I was just taking a break when you rang the bell."

"That's lucky." Justine chose a cookie and nibbled. Her scent was very sophisticated, not opulent but rich and feminine. Jackie noticed that her nails were long, rounded and painted a pale rose. She wore only one ring, a stunning opal surrounded by diamonds. "I suppose I should apologize first."

Jackie left off her study long enough to lift a brow. "Apologize?"

"For the mix-up here between you and Nathan." Justine noticed with a little stab of envy that Jackie's skin was free of cosmetics and as clear as springwater. "It was I who talked Nathan into letting Fred move in while he was away in Europe. It seemed like such a perfect solution at the time, as Nathan was concerned about leaving his house empty for that length of time and Fred seemed to be at loose ends."

"Fred's always at loose ends," Jackie said over the rim of her glass. She looked at Justine with a trace of sympathy. Fred's charm might not have swayed Mrs. Grange, but the housekeeper was the exception to the rule. "He also has a way of making you believe he can spin straw into gold. As long as you're paying for the straw."

"So I understand." Appreciation for the analogy showed in Justine's eyes. "I feel, well…a little guilty that Fred absconded with your money under false pretenses."

"No need." Jackie took a healthy bite out of a cookie. "I've known Fred all my life. If anyone should have seen through him, I should have. In any case," she added with what she thought was a wonderfully cool smile, "Nathan and I have come to a satisfactory arrangement."

"So he said." Justine took another sip of lemonade, watching Jackie over the rim. "Apparently you're a first-class cook."

"Yes." She didn't believe in denying the truth, but she wondered what else Nathan had felt obligated to tell Justine. If they were going to fight, she thought restlessly, why didn't they just get on with it?

"I've never been able to put two ingredients together and have either one come out recognizable. Did you really study in Paris?"

"Which time?" Despite herself, Jackie smiled. She hadn't wanted to like Justine. True, the woman was very cool and very polished, but there was something kind in her eyes. Kindness, no matter what the package, always drew her in.

Justine smiled in return, and the restraint between them

lowered by another few degrees. "Miss MacNamara—Jacqueline—may I be frank?"

"Things usually get done faster that way."

"You're not at all what I expected."

Jackie sat back, tucking up her legs beneath her. "What did you expect?"

"I always thought when Nathan became besotted about someone she'd be very sleek and self-contained. Possibly boring."

The lemonade that was halfway down Jackie's throat had to be swallowed in a hard gulp. "Back up. Did you say Nathan was besotted?"

"A wreck. Didn't you know?"

"He hides it well," Jackie murmured.

"Well, it was perfectly obvious to me last night." The heat in Jackie's eyes came instantly and automatically. "We've never been anything but friends, by the way." Justine gave a small shrug. "If I were in your position, I'd appreciate someone making that clear to me."

The heat simmered a moment longer, then snuffed itself out. She didn't often feel like a fool, but she was willing to accept it when she did. "I do appreciate it—your telling me, and the fact that you've never been anything but friends. Would you mind if I asked you why?"

"I've wondered myself." With the ease of a woman who never gained an ounce, Justine took another cookie. "The timing's never been quite right. I'm not independent." This was said with another shrug. "I enjoy being married, being part of a couple, so I end up doing it quite a bit. I was married when I met Nathan. Then, after my first divorce, we were in different parts of the country. It's continued to work out about the same way for close to a decade. In any case, it's enough to say that I was always involved with someone else and Nathan was always involved with his work. For his own reasons, he prefers things that way."

Jackie wanted to ask why, suspected that Justine might have some of the answers. But she couldn't go that far. If what she had with Nathan was going to work, the explanations would have to come from him. "I appreciate you telling me. I suppose I should tell you that you're not what I expected, either."

"And what did you expect?"

"A calculating adventuress with icicles on her heart and designs on my man. I spent most of last night detesting you." When Justine's lips curved at the description, Jackie was very glad she'd refrained from giving Carlotta that wart.

"Then I wasn't wrong in thinking you care about Nathan?"

"I'm in love with him."

Justine smiled again. There was a trace of wistfulness in it that told Jackie more than words could have. "He needs someone. He doesn't think so, but he does."

"I know. And it's going to be me."

"Then I'll wish you luck. I didn't intend to when I came."

"What changed your mind?"

"You invited me in and offered me a drink when you wished me to hell."

Jackie grinned. "And I thought I was so discreet."

"No, you weren't. Jack...that's what Nathan calls you, isn't it?"

"Most of the time."

"Jack, my track record with relationships isn't what you would call impressive—in fact, let's continue to be frank and admit it's lousy—but I'd like to offer you a little advice."

"I'll take anything I can get."

"Some men need more of a push than others. Use both hands with Nathan."

"I intend to." With her head tilted to one side, Jackie considered. "You know, Justine, I have this cousin. Second cousin on my father's side. Not Fred," she said quickly. "This one's a college professor at the University of Michigan. Do you like the intellectual type?"

With a laugh, Justine set down her glass. "Ask me again in six months. I'm on sabbatical."

When Nathan arrived home a few hours later, he knew nothing of Justine's visit or of the conclusions that had been reached in his living room. Perhaps that was for the best.

It was bad enough that he was glad to be home. It was a different sort of glad from the feeling he'd had when he'd arrived from Germany. Then he'd been looking forward to the familiar, to solitude, to the routine he had set for himself over the years. He didn't—wouldn't have—considered it stuffy, just convenient.

Now a part of him, a part he still wasn't ready to acknowledge, was glad to come home to Jackie. There was an anticipation, a surge of excitement at knowing she was there to talk with, to relax with, even to spar with. The unfamiliar, and the companionship, added a new dimension to an evening at home. The challenge of outmaneuvering her had become a habit he hadn't been aware of forming. Somewhere along the line he'd stopped resenting the fact that she'd invaded his privacy.

He heard the music the moment he opened the door. It wasn't the rock he'd grown accustomed to hearing from the kitchen but one of Strauss's lovely and sensual waltzes. Though he wasn't sure if her change in radio stations was something to worry about, he was cautious as he slipped into his office to put away his briefcase and the reinforced tubes that held the blueprints from his project in Denver.

Loosening his tie, he started into the kitchen. As usual, something smelled wonderful.

She wasn't wearing her habitual shorts. Instead, she wore a jumpsuit in some soft, silky material the color of melted butter. It didn't cling to her body so much as shift around it, offering hints. Her feet were bare, and she wore one long wooden earring. She was busy slicing a round loaf of crusty bread. He had a sudden feeling, strong and lucid, that he should turn and run, as fast and as far as he could. Because it annoyed him, Nathan stepped through the archway.

"Hello, Jack."

She'd known he was there, but she managed to look mildly and credibly surprised when she turned. "Hi." He looked so attractive in a suit, with the knot of his tie pulled loose. Because her heart turned to mush, she walked over and kissed his cheek. "How was your day?"

He didn't know what to make of her. So what else was new? But he did know that her casual greeting kiss was exactly what he'd needed, and it worried him. "Busy," he told her.

"Well, you'll have to tell me all about it, but you should have some wine first." She was already pouring two glasses. The sun hit the liquid as it rushed into the crystal and shot it through with gold. "I hope you're hungry. It'll be ready in just a couple minutes."

He accepted the wine and didn't ask why her timing always seemed so perfect. It made him wonder if she'd managed to slip a homing device on him. "Did you get much done today?"

"Quite a bit." Jackie began to arrange the bread she'd sliced in a basket. "I had a little lull this afternoon, but things really picked up afterward." Her lips curved as she lifted her wine, and once again he had the feeling that there was something he should know, but he didn't want to ask. "I've decided to concentrate on the first hundred pages for the next week or so, until it's ready to send off to an agent I know in New York."

"That's good," he managed, wondering why the idea sent him into a panic. He wanted her to progress, didn't he? The more she did, the less guilty he'd feel about telling her that her time was up. No amount of logic could erase the niggling fear that she would tell him she no longer needed the house to work in and was moving on. "It must be going well."

"Better than I expected, and I always expect quite a lot." The timer buzzed, and she turned to the oven. Fortunately, the move hid her smile. "I thought we'd eat on the patio. It's such a nice evening."

The warning bells sounded again, but they were dimmer and less urgent. "It's going to rain."

"Not for a couple of hours yet." With her hands buried in oven mitts, she drew out a casserole. "I hope you like this. It's called *schinkenfleckerln*." Jackie whipped out the foreign name like a native.

There was something very homey and nonthreatening about the pot of browned noodles and ham in bubbling sauce. "It looks terrific."

"A very simple Austrian recipe," she told him. That explained the Viennese waltz, he thought. "Grab the bread, will you? I've already set up outside."

Again, she timed it perfectly. The sun was dropping in the sky. The clouds that were gathering to bring rain during the night were tipped with pink and orange. The air was cool, with a catchy breeze from the east that brought just a hint of the sea.

The round patio table was set for two. Informally. Nathan

would have to have stretched a point to call it deliberately romantic. Colorful mats she must have bought herself were under his white everyday dishes. She'd added flowers, but they were only a few sprigs of daisies in a colored bottle. The bottle wasn't his, either, so he could only suppose that she'd been foraging in some of the local shops.

He settled back as Jackie began the business of serving. "I haven't thanked you for all the meals."

She only smiled as she sat across from him. "That was the deal."

"I know, but you've gone to more trouble than you had to. I appreciate it."

"That's nice. I really like to cook when there's someone to share it with. Nothing more depressing than cooking for one."

He hadn't thought so. Once. "Jack..." She looked up at him, her eyes big and round and soft, and he lost track of what he'd planned to say. Groping, he picked up his wine. "I, ah... I feel like we got off on the wrong foot. Since we're both victims, so to speak, I'd like to call a truce."

"I thought we had."

"An official one."

"All right." She lifted her glass and tapped it against his. "Live long and prosper."

"I beg your pardon?"

Jackie chuckled into her wine. "I should have known you wouldn't be a fan of *Star Trek*. That's the Vulcan greeting, Nathan, but to keep it simple, I'll just wish you the best."

"Thanks." Unconsciously he loosened his tie a little more. "Why don't you tell me about your book?"

It was a first, Nathan decided, to see Jackie speechless. Her lips parted, not to smile or to toss a quip, but in utter surprise. "Really?" she managed after a moment.

"Yes, I'd like to hear what it's about." He picked up a hunk of bread and began to butter it. "Don't you want to talk about it?"

"Well, yes, it's just that I didn't think you were interested. You never asked, or even commented, and I know that I usually beat people over the head with whatever I'm doing at the time because I get too involved and lose perspective. So I thought it would be better if I just kept the book to myself since I was already driving you crazy. I figured under the circumstances, counting Fred and six months in Frankfurt, you'd probably hate it anyway."

Nathan scooped up some of the casserole, chewed and considered. "I understand that," he said. "I can't tell you how much that terrifies me, but I understand. Now, why don't you tell me about your book?"

"Okay." She moistened her lips. "I've set it in what is now Arizona, in the 1870s—a decade or so after the Mexican War, when it was ceded to the U.S. as part of New Mexico. I'd toyed around with doing a generational thing and starting in the eighteenth century, when it was still a European settlement, but I found that I wanted to get into the meat right away."

"No meat in the eighteenth century?"

"Oh, pounds of it." She took a piece of bread herself and shredded it before she realized she was nervous. "But Jake and Sarah weren't alive then. My protagonists," Jackie explained. "It's really their story, and I was too impatient to start the book a hundred years before they came along. He's a gunfighter and she's convent-bred. I liked the idea of putting them in Arizona because it really epitomizes America's Old West. The Earps, the Claytons, Tombstone, Tucson, Apaches." Nerves disappeared as she began to imagine. "It gives it that nice bloody frontier tradition."

"Shoot-outs, bounty hunters and Indian raids?"

"That's the idea. The setup has Sarah coming West after her father dies. He, Sarah's father, had led her to believe that he's a prosperous miner. She's grown up in the East, learning all the things that well-bred young ladies of good families are supposed to learn. Then, after his sudden death, she comes out to the Arizona Territory and discovers that for all the years she was living in moderate luxury back East, her father had barely been scraping by on this dilapidated gold mine, spending every penny he could spare on her education."

"Now she's penniless, orphaned and out of her element."

"Exactly." Pleased with him, Jackie poured more wine. "I figure that makes her instantly vulnerable and sympathetic, as well as plunging her into immediate jeopardy. Anyway, it doesn't take her long to discover that her father didn't die in an accidental cave-in, but was murdered. By this time, she's already had a few run-ins with Jake Redman, the hard-bitten gun-for-hire renegade who stands for everything she's been taught to detest. He saved her life during an Apache raid."

"So he's not all bad."

"A diamond in the rough," Jackie explained over a bite of bread. "See, there were a lot of miners and adventurers in the territory during this period, but the War between the States and troop withdrawal were delaying settlement, so the Apaches were still dominant. That made it a very wild and dangerous place for a gently bred young woman to be."

"But she stays."

"If she'd turned to run, she'd have been pitiful rather than sympathetic. Big difference. She's compelled to discover who killed her father and why. Then there's the fact that she's desperately, though unwillingly, attracted to Jake Redman."

"And he to her?"

"You've got it." She smiled at him as she toyed with her wine. "You see, Jake, like a lot of men—and women, for that matter—doesn't believe he needs anyone, certainly not someone who would interfere with his lifestyle and convince him to settle down. He's a loner, has always been a loner, and intends to keep it that way."

His brow lifted as he sipped. "Very clever," he said mildly.

Pleased that he saw the correlation, she smiled. "Yes, I thought so. But Sarah's quite determined. Once she discovers that she loves him, that her life would never be complete without him, she wears him down. Of course, Carlotta does her best to botch things up."

"Carlotta?"

"The town's leading woman of ill repute. It's not so much that she wants Jake, though of course she does. They all do. But she hates Sarah and everything Sarah stands for. Then there's the fact that she knows Sarah's father had been murdered because, after five years, he'd finally hit the mother lode. The mine Sarah now holds the claim for is worth a fortune. That's as far as I've gotten."

"But how does it end?"

"I don't know."

"What do you mean, you don't know? You're writing it, you have to know."

"No, I don't. In fact, I'm almost certain if I knew, exactly, it wouldn't be half as much fun to sit down every day." She offered him more of the casserole, but he shook his head. "It's a story for me, too, and I am getting closer, but it's not like a blueprint, Nathan."

Because she could see he didn't understand, she leaned closer, elbows propped on the table. "I'll tell you why I think I'd never have made a good architect, though I found the whole process fascinating and the idea of taking an empty lot and bringing it alive with a building incredible."

He glanced over again at that. What she'd said, and how she'd phrased it, encompassed his own feelings so perfectly that he could almost believe she'd stepped into his mind.

"You have to know every detail, beginning to end. You have to be certain before you take out the first shovel of dirt how it's going to end up. When you build, you're not just responsible for creating an attractive, functional piece of work. You're also responsible for the lives of the people who will work or live in or pass through the building, climb the stairs, ride the elevators. Nothing can be left to chance, and imagination has to conform to safety and practicality."

"I think you're wrong," he said after a moment. "I think you'd have made an excellent architect."

She smiled at him. "No, just because I understand doesn't mean I can do. Believe me, I've been there." She touched his hand easily, friend to friend. "You're an excellent architect because not only do you understand, but you're able to combine art with practicality, creativity with reality."

He studied her, both moved and pleased by her insight. "Is that what you're doing with your writing?"

"I hope so." She sat back to watch the clouds roll in. It would rain soon after nightfall. "All my life I've been scrambling around, looking for one creative outlet after another. Music, painting, dancing. I composed my first sonata when I was ten." Her lips tilted in a self-deprecating grin. "I was precocious."

"No, really?"

She chuckled as she slipped her hand under the bowl of her glass. "It wasn't a particularly good sonata, but I always knew there was something I had to do. My parents have been very patient, even indulgent, and I didn't always deserve it. This time… I guess this sounds silly at my age, but this time I want them to be proud of me."

"It doesn't sound silly," he murmured. "We never grow out of wanting our parents' approval."

"Do you have yours, Nathan?"

"Yes." The word was clipped. Because he heard it himself, he added a smile. "They're both very pleased with the route my career's taken."

She decided to press just a little farther. "Your father isn't an architect, is he?"

"No. Finance."

"Ah. That's funny, when you think of it. I imagine our parents have had cocktails together more than once. J.D.'s biggest interests are in finance."

"You call your father J.D.?"

"Only when I'm thinking of him as a businessman. He'd always get such a kick out of it when I'd march into his office, plop on his desk and say, 'All right, J.D., is it buy or sell?'"

"You're very fond of him."

"I'm crazy about him. Mother, too, even when she nags. She's always wanting me to fly to Paris and be redone." With only the faintest of frowns, she touched the tips of her hair. "She's certain the French could find a way to make me elegant and demure."

"I like you the way you are."

Again he saw that quick look of astonishment on her face. "That's the nicest thing you've ever said to me."

He thought, as he stared into her eyes, that he heard the first rumble of thunder. "We'd better get this stuff inside. Rain's coming."

"All right." She rose easily enough and helped clear the table. It was foolish to be moved by such a simple statement. He hadn't told her she was beautiful or brilliant. He hadn't said he loved her madly. He'd simply told her that he liked her the way she was. Nothing he could have said would have meant more to a woman like Jackie.

Inside the kitchen, they worked together for a few moments in companionable silence.

"I suppose," she began, "since you're dressed like that, you didn't spend the day at the beach."

"No, I had meetings. My clients from Denver."

Jackie looked at what was left in the wine bottle, decided it wasn't enough to cork and poured the remainder into their glasses. "You never mentioned what you were going to build."

"S and S Industries is putting a branch in Denver. They need an office building."

"You designed another one of them in Dallas a few years ago."

Surprised, he glanced over. "Yes, I did."

"Is this one going to be along the same lines?"

"No. I went for slick and futuristic in Dallas. Lots of glass and steel, with an uncluttered look. I want something more classic for this. Softer, more distinguished lines."

"Can I see the drawings?"

"I suppose, if you'd like."

"I really would." She dried her hands on a cloth, then handed him his half-filled glass. "Can I see them now?"

"All right." He didn't question the fact that he wanted her to see them, that her opinion mattered to him. Both were new concepts for him, and something to think about later. They walked through the house as the light grew dim from the gathering clouds.

His desk was clear. Nathan would never have gone to a meeting without dealing with any leftover paperwork or correspondence. Drawing the blueprints from the tube, he spread them out. Genuinely interested, Jackie leaned over his shoulder with her lips pursed.

"The exterior is brown brick," he began, trying to ignore the brush of her hair against his cheek as she leaned closer. "I'm using curves rather than straight lines."

"It has a deco look."

"Exactly." Why hadn't he noticed her scent earlier? Was he just growing accustomed to it, or was it because she was standing so close, close enough to touch or to taste with the slightest effort? "I've arched the windows, and…"

When he let his words trail off, she glanced up and smiled. Understanding and patience shouldn't make a man uncomfortable, but he looked back deliberately at the papers on his desk.

"And every individual office will have at least one. I've always felt that it's more conducive to productivity if you don't feel caged in."

"Yes." She was still smiling, and neither of them were looking at the blueprints. "It's a beautiful building, very strong without being oppressive. Classic without being staid. The trim and accents are in rose, I imagine."

"To blend with the bricks." Her mouth was rose, a very soft, very subtle rose. He found himself turning his head just enough to taste it.

This time he knew he heard thunder, and it was much closer.

He drew away, shaken. Without speaking, he began to roll up the blueprints.

"I'd like to see the sketches of the interior."

"Jack—"

"It's not really fair to leave things half done."

Nodding, Nathan unrolled the next set. She was right. He supposed he'd known that all along. A thing begun required a finish.

Chapter 8

Jackie drew a long, steadying breath. She felt like a diver who'd just taken the last bounce on the board. There could be no turning back now.

She hadn't known when she'd started the evening that he would allow her to get this close. The defenses he had were lowering, and the distance he insisted on was narrowing. It was difficult, very difficult, to accept that the reason for that might only be his own desire. But if that was all he could feel for her now, that was all she would ask for. Desire, at least, was honest.

She couldn't love him any more than she already did. That was what she had thought, but now she knew it wasn't true. With every step closer, with every hour spent with him, her heart expanded.

Patient, even sympathetic to his dilemma, she listened while he explained the floor plans.

It was an excellent piece of work. Her eye and her knowl-

edge were sharp enough to recognize that. But so was he.
An excellent piece of work. His hands were wide palmed
and long fingered, tanned from the hours he spent outdoors
watching over his projects, artistic in their own competent,
no-nonsense way. His voice was strong, masculine without
being gruff, cultured without being affected. There was a
trace of lime scent on his skin from his soap.

She murmured in agreement and put a hand on his arm
as he pointed out a facet of the building. There were muscles beneath the creaseless material of his tailored, conservative suit. She heard his voice hesitate at her touch. And
she, too, heard the thunder.

"There'll be an atrium here, in the executive offices.
We're going to use tile rather than carpet for a cooler,
cleaner look. And here…" His mouth was drying up on
the words, his muscles tightening at her casual touch. He
found it necessary to sit.

"The boardroom?" Jackie prompted, and sat on the arm
of his chair.

"What? Yes." His tie was strangling him. Nathan tugged
at it and struggled to concentrate. "We'll continue with the
arches, but on a larger scale. The paneling will—" He wondered why in the hell the paneling had ever mattered. Her
hand was on his shoulder now, kneading away the tension
he hadn't even been aware had lodged there.

"What about the paneling?"

What about it? he thought as she leaned forward to trail
one of her slender, ringed fingers over the prints. "We're
going with mahogany. Honduras."

"It'll be beautiful. Now, and a hundred years from now.
Indirect lighting?"

"Yes." He looked at her again. She was smiling, her head
tilted just inches above his, her body curved just slightly

toward him. The ink on the blueprint of his life seemed to fade. "Jack, this can't go on."

"I agree completely." In one lithe move, she was in his lap.

"What are you doing?" It shouldn't have amused him. His stomach had just contracted into a fist, one with claws, but he found himself smiling at her.

"You're right, this can't go on. I'm sure you're going as crazy as I am, and we can't have that, can we?" A trio of rings glittered on her hand as she tucked her hair back.

"I suppose not."

"No. So I'm going to put a stop to it."

"To what?" He put a hand on her wrist as she slipped off his tie.

"To the uncertainty, to the what-ifs." Ignoring his hand, she began to unbutton his shirt. "This is very nice material," she commented. "I'm taking full responsibility, Nathan. You really have no say in the matter."

"What are you talking about, Jack?" He took her by the shoulders when she started to peel off his jacket. "What the hell do you think you're doing?"

"I'm having my way with you, Nathan." She pressed her mouth to his, and the laugh he'd thought he was ready to form became a moan. "It's no use trying to fight it, you know," she murmured against his lips as she pulled off his jacket. "I'm a very determined woman."

"So I see." He felt her tug at his shirt from the waistband of his slacks and tried again. "Jack—damn it, Jackie, we'd better talk about this."

"No more talk." She nipped lightly at his collarbone, then slid her tongue to his ear. "I'm going to have you, Nathan, willing or not." She closed her teeth over his earlobe. "Don't make me hurt you."

This time he did laugh, though not steadily. "Jack, I out-weigh you by seventy pounds."

"The bigger they are..." she told him, and unhooked his slacks. In an automatic defensive gesture, his hands covered hers.

"You're serious."

She drew back far enough to look at him just as the first slice of lightning lit the sky. The flash leaped into her eyes as if it had always been there, waiting. "Deadly." With her eyes on his, she caught the zipper of her jumpsuit between her thumb and fingers and drew it down. "You're not get-ting out of this room until I'm finished with you, Nathan. Cooperate, and I'll be gentle. Otherwise..." She shrugged, and the jumpsuit slithered tantalizingly down her shoulders.

It was too late, much too late, to pretend he didn't want to be with her, didn't have to be with her. The game she was playing was taking the responsibility and the reper-cussions away from him and onto her. Though it touched him, he couldn't allow it.

"I want you." He brushed her cheeks with his hands and combed his fingers through her hair as he said it. "Come upstairs."

She turned her face so that her lips pressed into his palm. It was a gesture of great tenderness, a gesture that bordered on submission. But when she looked back at him, she shook her head. "Right here. Right now." Jackie pressed her open mouth to his, leaving him no choice.

She tantalized, tormented, teased. Her body curled it-self around his, and her lips were quick and urgent. They lingered on his, drawing in, drawing out, then sped away to trace the planes and angles of his face. His blood was hammering. He could feel it, in his head, in his loins, in

his fingertips. Her hands were unmerciful…wonderful…
as they roamed over him.

No hesitation. She didn't know the meaning of the word.
Like the storm that whipped at the windows, she was all
flash and fire. A man could get burned by her, he thought,
and always bear the scars. Yet his arms banded around her,
holding her hard and close as he fought to maintain some
control. She was driving him beyond the limits he'd always
set for himself, away from reason, away from the civilized.

That was his own breath he heard, fast and uneven. That
was his skin springing moist and hot from a need that had
grown titanic in mere moments. He was pulling the material from her shoulders with a gnawing demand to feel
her flesh against his. And it was with an insatiable greed
that he took it.

"Jack." His mouth was against her throat as he tasted,
devoured. More…he could only think of having more. He'd
have absorbed her into him if he'd known how. "Jack," he
repeated. "Give me a minute, will you?"

But her mouth was just as greedy when it came to his.
She only laughed.

He swore, but even the oath caught in his throat. He
was tearing the jumpsuit from her as they slid to the floor.

She couldn't make her fingers work fast enough. Jackie
pulled and yanked to strip the last barriers of his clothing
away. She wanted to feel him, all of him. As they rolled
over on the carpet, her skin was on fire from the friction
of flesh against flesh.

She'd thought she would guide him, coerce, cajole, se-
duce. She'd been wrong. Like a pebble in a slingshot, she'd
been flung high and fast, no longer in control. But with
some trace of reason, she knew he was as lost as she.

Desire held control, steered by a love only one of them

could admit. But in the lamplight, with the storm reaching its peak, desire was enough.

Wrapped together, they rolled mindlessly, each searching and finding more. The capacity for intense concentration was inherent in them both, but neither had used it so fully in the act of love until tonight. The clothes they'd discarded tangled with their naked legs and were kicked heedlessly away. Rain, tossed by a restless wind, hit the windows like bullets but was ignored. Something teetered on a table as it was jolted, then thudded to the carpet. Neither of them heard.

There were no murmured promises, no whispered endearments. Only sighs and shudders. Neither were there tender caresses or gentle kisses. Only demands and hunger.

Breath heaving, Nathan moved above her. Lightning still flashed sporadically, highlighting her face and hair. Her head was thrown back, her eyes clear and open, when he took her.

Perfect. Naked, damp and dazed, Jackie curled into him while that one word ran around in her head. Nothing had ever been so perfect. His heart was still pounding against hers, his breath still warming her cheek. The rain had slowed, and the thunder was only a murmur in the distance. Storms passed. Some storms.

She hadn't needed the physical act of love to confirm her feelings for Nathan. Lovemaking was only an extension of being in love. But even with her vivid and often far-reaching imagination, she'd never known anything could be like this.

He'd emptied her, and he'd filled her.

No matter how many times they came together, no matter how many years they shared, there would never be another first time. Her eyes closed, her arms wrapped around him, she savored it.

He didn't know what to say to her, or if he was capable of speech at all. He'd thought he knew himself, the man he was and the man he'd chosen to be. The Nathan Powell he'd lived with most of his life wasn't the same man who had plunged so recklessly into passion, giving and taking with greedy disregard.

He'd lost all sense of time, of place, even of self, as he'd driven himself restlessly, even abandonedly, into her. The way he had never done before. The way, he already understood, he would never do again. Unless it was with Jackie.

He should have taken her with more care, and certainly with more consideration. But once begun he had lost whatever foothold he'd still had on reason and had cartwheeled off the cliff with her.

It had been what she'd wanted—what he'd wanted—but did that make it right? There had been no words, no questions. He hadn't even given a thought to his responsibility or her protection. That had made him wince a bit even as he stroked a hand through her hair.

They'd have to talk about that, and soon, because he was going to have to admit that what had happened between them was going to happen again. That didn't make it permanent, he assured himself as his hand fitted possessively over the curve of her shoulder.

"Jack?"

When she tilted her head to look up at him, he was struck by such an unexpected wave of tenderness that he couldn't speak at all. Lips curved, she leaned closer and pressed them to his. It took no more than that to have the embers of desire glowing again. The fingers that had been strok-

ing her hair tightened and dragged her closer. Limber and
sleek, she shifted onto him.

"I love you, Nathan. No, don't say anything." Her lips
nibbled and rubbed against his as she sought to soothe
more than to arouse. "You don't have to say anything. I
just need to tell you. And I want to make love with you
again and again."

Her hands had already told him as much, and now her
mouth was moving lower, nipping and gliding along his
neck. His response was so immediate it stunned him.

"Jack, wait a minute."

"No more complaints," she murmured. "I ravished you
once, and I can do it again."

"Thank God for that, but wait." Firmly now, thinking
only of her, he drew her away by the shoulders. "We have
to talk a minute."

"We can talk when we're old—though I did want to mention that I'm crazy about your carpet."

"I've grown fond of it myself. Now, hold on," he said
again when she tried to squirm away from his restraining
hands. "Jack, I'm serious."

She let out a huge and exaggerated sigh. "Do you have
to be?"

"Yes."

"All right, then." She composed her features and settled
herself comfortably. "Shoot."

"I'm already doing it backward," he began, furious
with himself. "But I don't intend to make the same mistake again. Things happened so quickly before that I never
asked, never even thought to ask, if it was all right."

"Of course it was all right," she began with a laugh.
"Oh." Her brows rose as realization struck. "You really
are a very good man, aren't you?" Despite his grip on her

shoulders, she managed to kiss him. "Yes, it's all right. I realize I look like a scatterbrain, but I'm not. Well, at least I'm a responsible one."

The tenderness crept back unexpectedly, and he cupped her face in his hands. "You don't look like a scatterbrain. You may act like one, but you look beautiful."

"Now I know I'm getting to you." She tried to say it lightly, but her eyes glistened. "I'd like you to think I'm beautiful. I always wanted to be."

Her hair fell over her brow, tempting him to brush at it, to tangle his fingers in it. "The first time I saw you, when I was tired and annoyed and you were sitting in my whirl-pool, I thought you were beautiful."

"And I thought you were Jake."

"What?"

"I'd been sitting there, thinking about my story, and about Jake—the way he looked, you know." Her fingers roamed over his face as she remembered. "Build, color-ing, features. I opened my eyes and saw you and thought… there he is." She rested her cheek on his chest. "My hero."

Troubled, he curled an arm around her. "I'm no hero, Jack."

"You are to me." She shimmied up his body a bit, then rested her forehead against his. "Nathan, I forgot the stru-del."

"Did you? What strudel?"

"The apple strudel I made for dessert. Why don't I dish some out and we can eat it in bed?"

Later, he thought, later he'd think about Jackie's idea of love and heroes. "Sounds very sensible."

"Okay." She kissed the tip of his nose, then smiled. "Your bed or mine?"

"Mine," he murmured, as though the word had been waiting to be said. "I want you in mine."

Laziness was its own reward. Jackie embraced the idea as she stretched in bed. Nothing seemed more glorious at the moment than to sleep in after so many days of rising early and going straight to the typewriter.

She snuggled, half dozing, pretending she was twelve and it was Saturday. There had been nothing she'd liked better at twelve than Saturdays. But as she shifted her leg brushed against Nathan's. It took no more than that for her to be very, very glad she was no longer twelve.

"Are you awake?" she asked without opening her eyes.

"No." His arm came around her possessively and remained.

Still drowsy, a smile just forming on her lips, she nibbled on him. "Would you like to be?"

"Depends." He shifted closer to her, enjoying the quiet, cozy feel of warm body against warm body. "Did we get all the strudel out of the bed?"

"Can't say for sure. Shall I look?" With that, Jackie tossed the sheets over their heads and attacked him.

She had more energy than she was entitled to, Nathan thought later as she lay sprawled over him. The sheets were now balled and twisted somewhere below their feet. Still trying to catch his breath, he kept his eyes half-shut as he looked at her.

She was long and lean and curved very subtly. Her skin was gold in the late-morning light, except for a remarkably thin line over her hips where it remained white, unexposed to the sun. Tousled from the pillow and from his hands, her hair sprang in a distracted halo.

He'd always thought he preferred long hair on a woman,

but with Jackie's short, free-swinging style he could stroke the curve at the back of her neck. He did so now, and she began to purr like a satisfied cat.

What was he going to do with her?

The idea of nudging her gently along was no longer even a remote possibility. He wanted her with him. Needed her. *Need.* That was a word he'd always been careful to avoid. Now that it had slammed into him, he hadn't any idea how to handle it.

He tried to think of what he would do tomorrow, a week, even a month from now, without her. His mind remained stubbornly blank. This wasn't like him. He hadn't been like himself since she'd spun her way into his life.

What did she want from him? Nathan detested himself because he knew he wouldn't ask her. He already knew what she wanted, as if it had been discussed and debated and deliberated. She loved him, at least for today. And he…he cared for her. *Love* was one four-letter word he wouldn't allow himself. Love meant promises. He never made promises unless he was sure he could keep them. A promise given casually and broken was worse than a lie.

With the morning sun shining through the windows and the birds singing the praises of spring, he wished it could be as simple as Jackie would like it. Love, marriage, family. He knew all too well that love didn't guarantee the success of a marriage and that marriage didn't equal family.

His parents had a marriage in which love no longer was an issue. No one would ever have accused the three of them of being a family.

He wasn't his father, Nathan thought as he held Jackie and studied the ceiling. He'd made certain that he would never be his father. But he understood the pride in success and the drive for accomplishment that had been his father's. That were still his father's. And were his.

He shook his head. He hadn't thought of his father or his lack of family life as much in a decade as he had since he'd met Jackie. She did that to him, as well. She made him consider possibilities that he'd rejected long ago with perfect logic and sense. She made him wish and regret what he'd never had reason to wish or regret before.

He couldn't let himself love her, because then he would make promises. And when the promises were broken he'd hate himself. She deserved better than what he could give her or, more accurately, what he couldn't give her.

"Nathan?"

"Hmm."

"What are you thinking about?"

"You."

When she lifted her head, her eyes were unexpectedly solemn. "I hope not."

Puzzled, he combed his fingers through the tangle of her hair. "Why?"

"Because you're tensing up again." Something came and went in her face—the first shadow of sorrow he'd ever seen in it. "Don't regret. I don't think I could bear it."

"No." He drew her up to cradle her in his arms. "No, I don't. How could I?"

She turned her face into his throat. He didn't know she was forcing back tears, and she couldn't have explained them to him. "I love you, Nathan, and I don't want you to regret that, either, or worry about it. I want you to just let things happen as they're meant to happen."

He tilted her head back with a finger under her chin. Her eyes were dry now. His were intense. "And that's enough for you?"

"Enough for today." The smile was back. Even he couldn't detect the effort it cost her. "I never know what's going to be enough for tomorrow. How do you feel about brunch? You haven't had my crepes yet. I make really wonderful crepes, but I don't remember if there's any whipping cream. There's always omelets, of course—if the mushrooms haven't dried up. Or we could make do with leftover strudel. Maybe we should have a swim first, and then—"

"Jack?"

"Uh-huh?"

"Shut up."

"Right now?" she asked as his hand slid down to her hip.

"Yes."

"Okay."

She started to laugh, but his lips met hers with such quiet, such fragile tenderness that the laughter became a helpless moan. Her eyes, once alight with amusement, shuttered closed at the sound. She was a strong woman, often valiant in her way, but she had no defense against tenderness.

It had been just as unexpected for him. There had been no flash of fire, no rumble of thunder. Just warmth, a drugging, languorous warmth that crept under his skin, into his brain, into his heart. With one kiss, one easy merging of lips, she filled him.

He hadn't thought of her as delicate. But she was delicate now, as her bones seemed to dissolve under his hands, leaving her smaller somehow, softer. Woman at her most vulnerable. As the kiss spun out, he lifted a hand to her cheek, as if to hold her there, captive.

Patience. She'd known there was a steady, rock-solid patience in him. But until now he'd never shown it to her. Compassion. That, too, she'd sensed in him. But to feel it now, to have him give her the gift of it, was more precious than diamonds. She was lost in him again, not in the frantic race she'd become used to, but in a slow, lengthy search she already knew would lead her where she had always wanted to go.

He caressed where he'd once taken greedily. Her skin was like satin and shivered under his touch. There was a fluidity to her now rather than a frenzy, a quiescence that had taken the place of energy.

His fingertips skimmed over her, and he delighted in making discoveries in territory already conquered. The same woman, yet a different one; her generosity was still there, but merged now with a vulnerability that humbled him. He found her flavor somehow sweeter. When he pressed his lips to her breast, he felt her heartbeat. It hammered fast, not with the heady, energetic rhythm of their past loving, but quick and light.

Experimentally he ran a finger over the inside of her wrist, feeling her pulse beating there, as well. For him. Curling his fingers through hers, he brought them to his lips to kiss and caress them one by one.

The bottom seemed to drop out of her world. With each touch she had fallen deeper, still deeper, into his. Into him. Now, as he did nothing more than brush his mouth over her fingertips, she tumbled headfirst into the dark, trusting him implicitly to catch her.

He could have asked her anything, demanded anything. In that moment her love was so overwhelming that she would have granted any wish without a thought to self or survival. It wasn't possible for her to gather him close and take their loving to another plane. He had a prisoner. Though he might not know it, she would stay enslaved as long as he'd have her.

He only knew that something had changed yet again. He was protector now as well as lover, giver as well as taker. The excitement that knowledge brought was tinged with a trace of fear he struggled to ignore. He couldn't think about tomorrow and tomorrow's consequences when he wanted her, possibly more, impossibly more, than he had only moments ago. She wouldn't object if he took her quickly, if he dragged them both to the top without preamble or delicacy. Perhaps it was because of that, because he understood that she would accept him on any terms, that he found himself needing to give her everything he could.

Slow loving. Almost tortuous. Tender stroking. Lazy tastes. There were quiet sighs that rippled the air until even the sunlight seemed to dim. If it had been possible, he would have had flowers for her, a bouquet of them. Soft petals, shimmering fragrances; he would have poured them over her skin. But he only had himself.

It was enough. He was more than enough for her. She showed him that in the way her lips parted, in the way her arms encircled him. No dream she'd ever indulged in, no wish she'd ever given herself, could compare with the reality of him cherishing her.

His hands were so cool, so calm, on her skin. With each touch she felt herself glow. The heat came from within her now, so that it was possible to bank it, to prevent it from becoming overpowering. Just flickers of flame, burning softly.

As gentle as he, she reached for him, offering the pleasure and temptation of unconditional love. When she trembled, he murmured. In reassurance. And she, who had never believed she would need a man to watch over her, understood that she would wither to dust without him.

Generosity, given without restrictions. That she offered,

openhanded, was no longer a surprise to him. But to discover that he could give equally, to find that he was compelled to match her, was something new.

He slipped into her, and the tenderness remained.

Slow, harmonious movements. A breath caught, then sighed away like the wind. With his mouth on hers, they continued. Like a Viennese waltz, their dance was light and elegant. When the tempo increased, they surged with the music, spinning, whirling, their eyes open and locked together.

The dance ended as gently as it had begun.

The sun was higher now. Contentedly, her body curved into his, Jackie watched the curtains move with the faint breeze. If she concentrated hard enough she could catch the light fragrance of flowers from the garden below. Nothing identifiable, but a mixture of scents that spoke of spring and new life.

Every moment of the hours they'd had together was lodged firmly in her mind. She knew she would take them out often and enjoy them over and over.

"You know what I'd like?" she asked him.

"Hmm?" If he hadn't been so dazed, it would have amazed him that he could be dozing in bed this close to noon.

"To stay here, right here in this bed, all day."

"We've got a pretty good start."

Her grin wicked, she turned to face him. Nose to nose, she leered. "Why don't we—" She swore when the phone rang. "It's the wrong number," she told him, climbing over his shoulder as he reached for it. "It's just a woman with a squeaky voice who's going to tell you your name's been selected in a sweepstakes and you've won ten free magazine subscriptions as long as you pay $7.75 a month for handling."

He hesitated a moment because when she said it it was too easy to believe. "What if it isn't?"

"Ah, but what if it is? Do you have enough willpower to resist ten free magazines a month? Be sure, Nathan. Be very sure."

He put a hand over her face and shoved her back against the pillows. "Hello."

"You were warned," Jackie said in a voice that spoke of doom. This time he put the pillow over her face.

"Carla?"

"Carla?" Her voice was muffled by the pillows. Jackie tossed it aside and sank her teeth into his shoulder.

"Ouch! Damn it! No, Carla, I— What is it?" To protect himself, Nathan rolled and trapped Jackie under him. "Yes, I was expecting that." Ignoring the flailing arms and muttered curses beneath him, Nathan listened. "All right, we'll push up the schedule if necessary. No, I've already taken care of that from here. Set this up for tomorrow. Nine. Ten, then," he said. "Contact Cody. I'll want him there. Fine, Carla." Jackie wriggled beneath him and made loud gasping noises. He ignored that, as well. "Yes, I've enjoyed having a few days of relaxation. See you tomorrow."

When he leaned over to hang up the receiver, Jackie managed to squirm out from under him. Face flushed, pulling in exaggerated gulps of air, she thudded a pillow over his head.

"So," she began. "You decided to smother me so that you could run off with the Italian countess and make mad, illicit passion in the Holiday Inn. Don't try to deny it," she warned. "The signs are all too clear."

"Okay. Which Italian countess was that?"

"Carla." She slammed the pillow at him again, aiming lower, then had to bite back a laugh when he grabbed her around the waist. "No, don't try to make up, Nathan. It's too late. I've already decided to murder both you and the countess. I'll electrocute you while you're sharing your bubble bath. No jury would convict me."

"Not if they did a psychiatric profile first."

She made another grab, this time for a very vulnerable area. He avoided her by throwing her onto her back and once again using his body to shield and protect himself. Arms locked, they rolled. Nathan was just beginning to enjoy it when her momentum sent them tumbling to the floor.

Out of breath and rubbing his shoulder, he narrowed his eyes. "You are crazy."

Jackie straddled him and planted her arms on either side of his head. "Okay, Powell, if you value your life, come clean. Who's Carla?"

He considered her. Her eyes were bright, her cheeks flushed with amusement. Her wide, incredible mouth was curved. Casually he cupped her hips in his hands. "You want the truth?"

"And nothing but."

"The Countess Carla Mandolini and I have been having a blazing adulterous affair for years. She fools her husband, the elderly and impotent count, by doubling as my secretary. The fool actually believes that the twins are his."

He really was adorable, Jackie decided as she leaned closer. "A likely story," she told him just before her mouth covered his.

Chapter 9

"All right, Nathan, consider yourself kidnapped. You might as well go peacefully."

As he wrapped a towel around his waist, Nathan glanced up. Without bothering to knock, Jackie pushed open the door to the bathroom and strode in. He should be used to it by now, he thought as he secured the towel. She could pop up anytime and anywhere.

"Mind if I put my shoes on?"

"You've got ten minutes."

Before she could turn to go, he had her by the arm. "Where have you been?"

He was becoming too attached to her, Nathan told himself even as the words came out. When he'd woken up alone that morning it had taken all of his control not to dash around the house looking for her. They'd been lovers three days, and already he felt bereft if she wasn't beside him when he opened his eyes in the morning.

"Some of us have work to do, even on Saturdays." She let her gaze roam down, then up. He was damp, tanned and mostly naked. She thought it a pity she'd made plans. "Downstairs in ten minutes, or I'll make you suffer."

"What's going on, Jack?"

"You're not in a position to ask questions." With a last smile, she left him. He heard her run lightly downstairs.

What did she have in store for him now? Nathan wondered as he reached for his razor. With Jackie there were never any guarantees, and there was rarely any rhyme or reason. It should have annoyed him, he thought as he lathered his face. It was supposed to annoy him. He'd already planned his day.

A few hours in his office dealing with the preliminaries on the Sydney project and snipping any loose ends from Denver would take care of the morning. After that he'd thought it might be nice to treat Jackie, and himself, to lunch and tennis at the country club. Being kidnapped hadn't been in his plans.

But he wasn't annoyed. Nathan brought the razor over lather and beard in short, smooth strokes. Because he'd left the window open, the mirror was only lightly steamed at the edges. He could see himself clearly. What had changed?

He was still Nathan Powell, a man with certain responsibilities and priorities. It wasn't a stranger looking back at him in the mirror, but a man he knew very well. The eyes were the same, as was the shape of the face, the hairline. If he looked the same, why didn't he feel the same? More, why couldn't he, a man who knew himself so well, put his finger on exactly what his feelings were?

Shaking the thought aside, he rinsed off the traces of lather. It was absurd. He was exactly who he had always been. The only change in his life was Jackie.

And what the hell was he going to do about her?

It wasn't a question he could avoid much longer. The more involved he became with her, the more certain he was that he was going to hurt her. That was something he would regret the rest of his life. In a matter of weeks he would have to leave her to go to Denver. He couldn't leave her with promises and vows, nor could he expect her to stay when he couldn't tell her what she needed to hear.

He wanted to believe she was nothing more than a few colorful pages in the very straightforward book of his life. But he knew, he already knew, that as his life went on he would keep turning back to look over those few pages again and again.

They should talk. He slapped on aftershave that left his skin cool and stinging. It was up to him to see that they did, quietly, seriously and as soon as possible. The world, as much as he might now wish it could be, was not composed of two people. And neither of them had begun to live the moment they'd met.

"You're running out of time, Nathan."

Jackie's voice came rushing up the stairs and caught him daydreaming. Daydreams were also something new in his life. Swearing at himself, Nathan whipped off the towel and began to dress.

He found her in the kitchen, securing the lid on a cooler, while on the radio some group from the fifties harmonized about love and devotion.

"You're lucky I decided to be generous and give you another five minutes." She turned to study him. He wore black shorts with a white shirt, and his hair was still slightly damp. "I guess it was worth it."

He was almost but not quite used to her frank and unabashed appraisals. "What's going on, Jack?"

"I told you. You're kidnapped." She stepped forward to slip her arms around his waist. "If you try to escape, it'll go hard on you." Pressing her face in his throat, she began to sniff. "I love your aftershave."

"What's in the cooler?"

"Surprises. Sit down, you can have some cereal."

"Cereal?"

"Man doesn't live by hotcakes alone, Nathan." She kissed him quick. "And some bananas." She moved away to get one, changed her mind and took two. As she peeled her own, she began to explain. "You might as well consider yourself my hostage for the day and make this simple."

"Make what simple?"

"We've both been working hard the last few days— well, except for one very memorable day." She smiled as she took the first bite. "And that was exhausting in its own way. So…" She slapped a palm on the cooler. "I'm taking you for a ride."

"I see." Nathan sliced the banana over a bowl of corn-flakes. "Anywhere in particular?"

"No. Anywhere at all. You eat, I'll put this in the boat."

"Boat?" He paused, the banana peel in his hand. "My boat?"

"Of course." Hefting the cooler, she turned back with an easy smile. "As much as I love you, Nathan, I know even you can't walk on water. Coffee's hot, by the way, but make it quick, will you?"

He did, because he was more interested in what she had up her sleeve than in a bowl of cold cereal. She'd left the radio on, he supposed for his benefit. After he'd rinsed his bowl, Nathan switched it off. As a matter of course he went to check the front door. Jackie had left it open. He shut it, locked it, then went to join her.

Outside, he found her competently storing supplies in the hatch. She wore a visor in a blazing orange that matched her shorts and the frames of a pair of mirrored wraparound sunglasses.

"All set?" she asked him. "Cast off, will you?"

"You're driving?"

"Sure. I was practically born on a boat." She slipped behind the wheel and tossed a look over her shoulder as Nathan hesitated, his hands on the line. "Trust me. I looked at a map."

"Well, then." Wondering if he was taking his life in his hands, he cast off and came aboard.

"Sun block," she said, handing him a tube. With that she pulled smoothly away from the dock. "How do you feel about St. Thomas?"

"Jack..."

"Only kidding. I've thought what a kick it would be to travel the whole Intracoastal. Take a whole summer and just cruise."

He'd thought of it, too, as something he might find time for—someday. After retirement, perhaps. When Jackie said it, it seemed possible it could happen tomorrow. And it made him wish it would happen tomorrow. He only murmured as he watched her handle the boat.

He should have known she'd be fine. Maybe she couldn't remember to close doors behind her, but it seemed to him that whatever she did she did with careless skill. Her hand was light on the wheel as she negotiated the channel. Even when she picked up speed, he relaxed.

"You picked a good day for a kidnapping."

"I thought so." She threw him a grin, then settled more comfortably in her seat.

The boat handled like a dream. Of course, she'd known

that Nathan would keep it in tip-top shape. That was one of the things she admired about him. He didn't take his possessions for granted. If it belonged to him, it deserved his attention. Too many people she knew, herself included, could develop a casual disregard for what was theirs. She'd learned something from him about pride of possession and the responsibility that went along with it.

She belonged to him now. Jackie hoped he'd begin to care for her with the same kind of devotion.

You're moving too fast, as usual, she cautioned herself. Caution was something else she'd learned from Nathan. It had to be enough, for now, that he no longer looked alarmed whenever she told him she loved him. The fact that he was beginning to accept that she did was a giant step. And soon—eventually, she thought, correcting herself—eventually he would accept the fact that he loved her back.

She knew he did. It wasn't a matter of wish fulfillment or hopeful dreams. She saw it when he looked at her, felt it when he touched her. Because she did, it made it that much more difficult to wait.

She'd always looked for instant gratification. Even as a child she'd been able to learn quickly and apply what she'd learned so that the rewards came quickly. Writing had shown her more than a love for storytelling. It had also shown her that some rewards were best waited for. Having Nathan, really having him, would be worth waiting a lifetime.

She turned down an alley of water where the bush was thick and green. It was hardly wide enough for two boats to pass. Near the verges, limbs of deadwood poked through the surface like twisted arms. Behind them the wake churned white, while ahead the water was darker, more mysterious. Above, the sun was a white flash, hinting, perhaps threatening, of the sultry summer still weeks away. Spray flew, glinting in the light. The motor purred, sending a flurry of birds rocketing above the trees.

"Ever been on the Amazon?"

"No." Nathan turned to her. "Have you?"

"Not yet," she told him, as if it were only a small oversight. "It might be something like this. Brown water, thick vegetation hiding all sorts of dangerous jungle life. Is it crocodiles or alligators down there?"

"I couldn't say."

"I'll have to look it up." A dragonfly dashed blue and gleaming across the bow, catching her attention. It skimmed over the water without making a ripple, then flashed into the bush. "It's wonderful here." Abruptly she cut the engine.

"What are you doing?"

"Listening."

Within moments the birds began to call, rustling through the leaves and growing bold in the silence. Insects sent up a soprano chorus. There was a watery plop, then two, as a frog swallowed an insect for an early lunch. Even the water itself had sound, a low, murmurous voice that invited laziness. From far off, too far off to be important, came the hum of another boat.

"I used to love to go camping," Jackie remembered. "I'd drag one of my brothers, and—"

"I didn't know you had any brothers."

"Two. Fortunately for me, they've both taken an avid interest in my father's many empires, leaving me free to do as I please." He couldn't see her eyes as she spoke, but from the tone of her voice he knew they were smiling.

"Never any interest in being a corporate climber?"

"Oh, God, no. Well, actually, I did think of being chairman of the board when I was six. Then I decided I'd rather be a brain surgeon. So I was more than happy when Ryan and Brandon took me off the hook." Lazily she slipped out of her deck shoes to stretch her toes. "I've always thought it would be difficult to be a son of a demanding father and not want to follow in his footsteps."

She'd said it casually, but Nathan was so completely silent that she realized she'd hit part of the mark. She opened her mouth to question, then shut it again. In his own time, she reminded herself. "Anyway, even though it often took blackmail to get one of my brothers to go with me, I really loved sitting by the fire and listening. You could be anywhere you wanted to be."

"Where did you go?"

"Oh, here and there. Arizona was the best. There's something indescribable about the desert when you're sitting beside a tent." She grinned again. "Of course, there's also something special about the presidential suite and room service. Depends on the mood. You want to drive?"

"No, you're doing fine."

With a laugh, Jackie kicked the motor on. "I hate to say it, but you ain't seen nothin' yet."

She spun the boat through the waterway, taking any out-of-the-way canal or inlet that caught her fancy. She was delighted to chug along behind the *Jungle Queen*, Lauderdale's triple-decker party boat, and wave to the tourists. For a time she was content to follow its wake and direction as it toured the Intracoastal's estates.

The houses pleased her, with their sweeping grounds and sturdy pillars. She enjoyed the flood of the spring flowers and the wink and shimmer of the pools. When another boat passed, she'd make up stories about the occupants that had Nathan laughing or just rolling his eyes.

It pleased her just as much to turn off the more traveled

routes and pretend she was lost in the quiet, serpentine waters where the brush grew heavy and close at the edges. Shutting down again under the shade of bending palms and cypress, she took out Jackie's idea of a picnic.

There was Pouilly-Fuissé in paper cups, and cracked crab to be dug out with plastic forks, and tiny Swiss meringues, white and glossy. After she'd badgered Nathan into taking off his shirt, she rubbed sunblock over him, rambling all the while about the idea of setting a book in the Everglades.

But what she noticed most as she stroked the cream over his skin was that he was relaxed. There was no band of tension over his shoulders, no knot of nerves at the base of his neck. When he reciprocated by applying the cream to wherever her skinny blue tank top exposed her skin, there was none in her, either.

When the cooler was packed away again, she jumped back behind the wheel. The morning laziness was over, she told him. Turning the boat around, she headed out.

She burst into Port Everglades to join the pleasure and cruise ships, the freighters and sailboats. Here the water was wide and open, the spray cool and the air full of sound.

"Do you ever come here?" she shouted.

"No." Nathan clamped a hand on the orange visor she'd transferred from her head to his. "Not often."

"I love it! Think of all the places these ships have been before they come here. And where they're going when they leave. Hundreds of people, thousands, come here on their way to—I don't know… Mexico, Cuba."

"The Amazon?"

"Yes." Laughing, she turned the boat in a circle that had spray spurting up the sides. "There are so many places to go and see. You don't live long enough, you just can't live long enough to do everything you should." Her hair danced madly away from her face as she rode into the wind. "That's why I'm coming back."

"To Florida?"

"No. To life."

He watched her laugh again and raise her arm to another boat. If anyone could, Nathan thought, it would be Jackie.

He let her have her head. Indeed, he didn't know if he could have stopped her if he'd been inclined to. Besides, he'd long since acknowledged that he enjoyed the race.

At midafternoon, she pulled up to a dock and advised Nathan to secure the lines. While he obliged, she dug her purse out of the hatch.

"Where are we going now?"

"Shopping."

He held out a hand to help her onto the pier. "For what?"

"For anything. Maybe nothing." With her hand in his, she began to walk. "You know, spring break's nearly here. In a couple of weeks the college crowd will flock to this, the mecca of the East."

"Don't remind me."

"Oh, don't be a stick-in-the-mud, Nathan. Kids have to blow off steam, too. But I was thinking the shops would be a madhouse then, and as much as I might appreciate that, you wouldn't, so we should do this now."

"Do what now?"

"Shop," she explained patiently. "Play tourist, buy tacky souvenirs and T-shirts with vulgar sayings, haggle over a shell ashtray."

"I can't tell you how much I appreciate you thinking of me."

"My pleasure, darling." She planted a quick kiss on his

cheek. "Listen, unless I miss my guess, this is something you never do."

He was surprised when she paused, waiting for his answer. "No, it's not."

"It's time you did." She adjusted the visor to a cockier angle. "You very sensibly moved south and chose Fort Lauderdale because of its growth, but you don't take too many walks on the beach."

"I thought we were going shopping."

"It's the same thing." She slipped her arm around his waist. "You know, Nathan, as far as I can see, you don't have one T-shirt with a beer slogan, a rock concert or an obscene saying."

"I've been deprived."

"I know. That's why I'd like to help you out."

"Jack." He stopped, turning around to gently take her shoulders. "Please don't."

"You'll thank me later."

"We'll compromise. I'll buy a tie."

"Only if it has a naked mermaid on it."

Jackie found exactly what she wanted bordering Las Olas Boulevard. There was a labyrinth of small cross streets bulging with shops selling everything from snorkels to sapphires. Telling him it was for his own good, Jackie dragged him into a small, crowded store with a doorway flanked by two garish red flamingos.

"They're becoming entirely too trendy," she said to Nathan with a flick of her hand toward the slim-legged birds. "It's a shame I'm so fond of them. Oh, look, just what I've always wanted. A music box with shells stuck all over it. What do you suppose it plays?"

Jackie wound up what Nathan considered one of the most

hideous-looking things he'd ever seen. It played "Moon River."

"No." Jackie shook her head over the melody. "I can do without that."

"Thank God."

Chuckling, she replaced it and began to poke through rows of equally moronic whatnots. "I understand, Nathan, that you have an eye for the aesthetic and harmonious, but there really is something to be said for the ugly and useless."

"Yes, but I can't say it here. There are children present."

"Now take this."

"No," he said as she held up a pelican made entirely of clamshells. "Please, I can't thank you enough for the thought, but I couldn't."

"Only for demonstration purposes. This has a certain charm." She laughed as his brow rose. "No, really. Think of this. Say a couple comes here on their honeymoon and they want something silly and very personal to remember the day by. They need something they can look at in ten years and bring back that very heady, very intimate time before insurance payments and wet diapers." She flourished the bird. *"Voilà."*

"Voilà? One doesn't *voilà* a pelican, especially a shell one."

"More imagination," she said with a sigh. "All you need is a little more imagination." With what seemed like genuine regret, she set the pelican down. Just when he thought it was safe, Jackie dragged him over to a maze of T-shirts. She seemed very taken with one in teal with an alligator lounging in a hammock drinking a wine cooler. Passing it by, she dragged out one of a grinning shark in dark glasses.

"This," she told him grandly, "is you."

"It is?"

"Absolutely. Not to say you're a predator, but sharks are

notorious for being loners, and the sunglasses are a symbol of a need for privacy."

He studied it, frowning and intrigued. "You know, I've never known anyone to be philosophical about T-shirts."

"Clothes make the man, Nathan." Draping it over her arm, she continued to browse. When she loitered by a rack of ties screen-printed with fish, he put his foot down.

"No, Jack, not even for you."

Sighing at his lack of vision, she settled for the shirt.

She hauled him through a dozen shops until pictures of neon palms, plastic mugs and garish straw hats blurred in his head. She bought with a blatant disregard for style or use. Then, suddenly inspired, she shipped off a huge papier-mâché parrot to her father.

"My mother will make him take it off to one of his offices, but he'll love it. Daddy has a wonderful sense of the ridiculous."

"Is that where you get it?"

"I suppose." Hands on her hips, she turned in a circle to be certain she hadn't missed anything. "Well, since I've done that, I'd better run by that little jewelry store and see if there's anything appropriate for my mother." She pocketed the receipt, then relieved Nathan of two packages. "How are you holding up?"

"I'm game if you are."

"You're sweet." She leaned over, between packages, to kiss him. "Why don't I buy you an ice-cream cone?"

"Why don't you?"

She grinned at that, thinking he was certainly coming along. "Right after I find something tasteful for my mother," she promised, and she proved as good as her word.

Some fifteen minutes later, she chose an ebony pin

crusted with pearls. It was a very mature, very elegant piece in faultless taste.

The purchase showed Nathan two things. First that she glanced only casually at the price, so casually that he was certain she would have bought it no matter what the amount. An impulse buyer she certainly was, but he sensed that once she'd decided an item was right, the dollar amount was unimportant. And second that the pin was both conventional and elegant, making it a far cry from the parrot she'd chosen for her father.

It made him wonder, as she loitered over some of the more colorful pieces in the shop, if her parents were as different as her vision of them.

He'd always believed, perhaps too strongly, that children inherited traits, good and bad. Yet here was Jackie, nothing like a woman who would wear a classically tasteful pin, and also nothing like a man who had spent his adult life wheeling and dealing in the business world.

Moments later, he had other things to worry about. They were out on the street again, and Jackie was making arrangements to rent a bicycle built for two.

"Jack, I don't think this is—"

"Why don't you put those packages in the basket, Nathan?" She patted his hand before paying for the rental.

"Listen, I haven't been on a bike since I was a teenager."

"It'll come back to you." The transaction complete, she turned to him and smiled. "I'll take the front if you're worried."

Perhaps she hadn't meant to bait him, but he didn't believe it. Nathan swung his leg over and settled on the front seat. "Get on," he told her. "And remember, you asked for it."

"I love a masterful man," she cooed. Nathan found his lips twitching at the phony southern accent as he set off.

She'd been right. It did come back to him. They pedaled smoothly, even sedately, across the street to ride along the seawall.

Jackie was glad he'd taken the lead. It gave her the opportunity to daydream and sightsee. Which, she thought with a smile, she would have done even if she'd been steering. This way, she didn't have to worry about running into a parked car or barreling down on pedestrians. Nathan could be trusted to steer true. It was only one more reason she loved him.

Matching her rhythm to his, she watched his shoulders. Strong and dependable. She found those both such lovely words. Strange…she'd never known she would find dependability so fiercely attractive until she'd found it. Found him.

Now he was relaxed, enjoying the sun and the day in it. She could give that to him. Not every day of the week, Jackie mused. He wouldn't always fall in with whatever last-minute plans she cooked up. But often enough, she thought, and wished there wasn't so much space between them so that she could wrap her arms around him and just hug.

He'd never pictured himself biking along the oceanfront—much less enjoying it. The fact was, Nathan rarely even came to this section of town. It was for tourists and teenagers. Being with Jackie made him feel like both. She was showing him new things not only about the city where he'd lived for nearly a decade but about the life he'd had more than thirty years to experience.

Everything about her was unexpected. How could he have known that the unexpected could also be the fresh? For a few hours he hadn't given a thought to Denver or penalty clauses or the responsibilities of tomorrow. He hadn't thought of tomorrow at all.

This was today, and the sun was bright, and the water

was a rich blue against the golden sand. There were children squealing as they played in the surf, and there was the smell of oils and lotions. Someone was walking a dog along the beach, and a vendor was hawking nachos.

Across the street, beach towels waved colorfully over rails, making a tawdry little hotel seem exotic. He could smell hot dogs, he realized, and some kind of colored ice was being sold to children so that it would drip sticky down their arms as they slurped it. Oddly enough, he had a sudden yen for it himself.

When he looked up, he spotted the black-and-yellow colors of a kite shaped like a wasp. It had caught the wind and was climbing. A light plane flew over, trailing a flowing message about the special at a local restaurant.

He took it all in, wondering why he'd thought the beach held no magic for him. Perhaps it hadn't when he'd been alone.

On impulse, he signaled Jackie, then stopped.

"You owe me some ice cream."

"So I do." She slipped lithely off the bike, kissed him, then backtracked a few steps to a vendor. She considered, debated and studied her choices, taking a longer and more serious deliberation over ice cream on a stick than she had over a five-hundred-dollar brooch. After weighing the pros and cons, she settled on chocolate and nuts wrapped around a slab of vanilla.

Stuffing her change in her pocket, she turned and saw Nathan. He was holding a big orange balloon. "Goes with your outfit," he told her, then gently looped the string around her wrist.

She was going to cry. Jackie felt the tears well up. It was only a ball of colorful rubber held by a string, she knew. But as symbols went, it was the best. She knew that when the air had finally escaped she would press the remains between the pages of a book as sentimentally as she would a rose.

"Thanks," she managed, then dutifully handed him the ice cream before she threw her arms around him.

He held her close, trying not to show the awkwardness he was suddenly feeling. How did a man deal with a woman who cried over a balloon? He'd expected her to laugh. Kissing her temple, he reminded himself that she rarely did the expected.

"You're welcome."

"I love you, Nathan."

"I think maybe you do," he murmured. The idea left him both exhilarated and shaken. What was he going to do about her? he wondered as his arms tightened around her. What the hell was he going to do about her, and them?

Looking up, Jackie saw the concern and the doubt in his eyes. She bit back a sigh, touching his face instead. There was time, she told herself. There was still plenty of time.

"Ice cream's melting." She was smiling as she brushed his lips with hers. "Why don't we sit on the wall while we eat it? Then you can change into your new shirt."

He cupped her chin in his hand, lingering over another kiss. He didn't know Justine had used the word *besotted* in describing his feelings for Jackie, but that was precisely what he was.

"I'm not changing shirts on the street."

She smiled again and took his hand.

When their hour was up, they pedaled back. Nathan was wearing his shark.

Chapter 10

From the doorway, Jackie watched Nathan drive off. She lifted her hand as his car headed down the street. For a moment there was only the sound of his fading engine breaking the morning quiet. Then, standing there, she heard the neighborhood noises of children being loaded into cars for school, doors slamming, goodbyes and last-minute instructions being given.

Nice sounds, Jackie thought as she leaned against the doorjamb. Regular everyday sounds that would be repeated morning after morning. There was a solidity to them, and a comfort.

She wondered if wives felt this way, seeing off their husbands after sharing that last cup of coffee and before the workday really began. It was an odd mixture of emotions, the pleasure of watching her man tidily on his way and the regret of knowing it would be hours before he came back.

But she wasn't a wife, Jackie reminded herself as she

wandered away from the door without remembering to shut it. It didn't do any good to imagine herself as one. It did less good to regret knowing that Nathan was still far from ready for commitments and wedding rings.

It shouldn't be so important.

Chewing on her bottom lip, she started back upstairs. Mrs. Grange was already scrubbing and mopping the kitchen, and she herself had enough work to do to keep her occupied throughout the day. When Nathan came home, he would be glad to see her, and they'd share the casual talk of couples.

It couldn't be so important.

She was happy, after all, happier with Nathan than she'd ever been before or than she could imagine herself being without him. Since there had never been any major trage-dies in her life, that was saying quite a lot. He cared for her, and if there were still restrictions on how much he would allow himself to care, what they had now was more than many people ever had.

He laughed more. It was very gratifying to know she'd given him that. Now, when she put her arms around him, it was a rare thing for her to find him tense. She wondered if he knew he reached for her in his sleep and held her close. She didn't think so. His subconscious had already accepted that they belonged together. That they were together. It would take a bit longer for him to accept that consciously.

So she'd be patient. Until Nathan, Jackie hadn't realized she had such an enormous capacity for patience. It pleased her to be able to find a virtue in herself that, because it had so seldom been tapped, seemed to run free.

He'd changed her. Jackie took her seat in front of her typewriter, thinking Nathan probably didn't realize that, either. She hadn't fully realized it herself until it had al-

ready happened. She thought of the future more, without the
need for rose-colored glasses. She'd come to appreciate the
ability to make plans—not that she wouldn't always enjoy
an interesting detour, but she'd come to understand that
happiness and good times didn't always hinge on impulse.

She'd begun to look at life a little differently. It had come
home to her that a sense of responsibility wasn't necessarily a burden. It could also bring a sense of satisfaction and
accomplishment. Seeing something through, even when
the pace began to drag and the enthusiasm began to wane,
was part of living. Nathan had shown her that.

She wasn't certain she could explain it to him so that
he would understand or even believe her. After all, she'd
never given anyone reason to believe she could be sensible, dependable and tenacious. Things were different now.

Surprised at her own nerves, she looked down at the pad-
ded envelope sitting beside the neatly typed pile of manuscript pages. For the first time in her life, she was ready
to put herself on the line. To prove herself, Jackie thought,
taking a deep breath. To prove herself to herself first, then
to Nathan, then to her family.

There was no guarantee that the agent would accept the
proposal, nor, though he'd been gracious and marginally
encouraging, that he would find anything appealing in her
work. Risks didn't frighten her, Jackie told herself. But still
she hesitated, not quite able to take the next step and slip
the pages into the envelope.

This risk frightened her. It hurt to admit it, but she was
scared to death. It was no longer just a matter of telling an
entertaining story from start to finish. It was her future
on the line now, the future she had once blithely believed
could take care of itself. If she failed now, she had no one
to blame but herself.

She couldn't, as she had with so many of her other projects, claim that she'd discovered something that interested her more. Writing was it, win or lose, and somehow, though she knew it was foolish, the success or failure of her work was inevitably tied up with her success or failure with Nathan.

She crossed her fingers tight, eyes closed, and recited the first prayer that came into her head, though "Now I lay me down to sleep" wasn't quite appropriate. This done, Jackie shoved the proposal into the bag. Clutching it to her chest, she ran downstairs.

"Mrs. Grange, I've got to go out for a few minutes. I won't be long."

The housekeeper barely glanced up from her polishing. "Take your time."

It was done within fifteen minutes. Jackie stood in front of the post office, certain she'd just made the biggest mistake of her life. She should have gone over the first chapter again. A dozen glaring errors leaped into her mind, errors that seemed so obvious now that the manuscript was sealed and stamped and handed over to some post office clerk she didn't even know.

It occurred to her that there had been a wonderful angle she hadn't bothered to explore and that her characterization of the sheriff was much too weak. He should have chewed tobacco. That was the answer, the perfect answer. All she had to do was go in and stick a wad of tobacco in his mouth and the book would be a best-seller.

She took a step toward the door, stopped and took a step back. She was being ridiculous. Worse, if she didn't get hold of herself, she was going to be sick. Weak-kneed, she sat on the curb and dropped her head into her hands. Sink or swim, the proposal was going to New York, and it was going today. It amazed her to remember that she'd once thought of celebrating with champagne when she had enough to ship off. She didn't feel like celebrating. She felt like crawling home and burying herself under the covers.

What if she was wrong? Why hadn't she ever considered the fact that she could be totally and completely wrong— about the book, about Nathan, about herself? Only a fool, only a stupid fool, left herself without any route to survival.

She'd poured her heart into that story, then sent it off to a relative stranger who would then have the authority to give a thumbs-up or a thumbs-down without any regard for her as a person. It was business.

She'd given her heart to Nathan. She'd held it out to him in both hands and all but forced him to take it. If he tried to give it back to her, no matter how gently he handled it, it would be cracked and bruised.

There were tears on her cheeks. Feeling them, Jackie let out a little huff of disgust and dragged the heels of her hands over them. What a pitiful sight. A grown woman sitting on a curb crying because things might not work out the way she wanted them to. She sniffled, then rose to her feet. Maybe they wouldn't work out and she'd have to deal with it. But in the meantime she was going to do her damnedest to win.

By noon, Jackie was sitting at the counter, elbows up, looking at Mrs. Grange's latest pictures of her grandchildren while they shared a pasta salad.

"These are great. This one here… Lawrence, right?"

"That's Lawrence. He's three. A pistol."

Jackie studied the little towhead with the smear of what might have been peanut butter on his chin. "Looks like a heartbreaker to me. Do you get to spend much time with them?"

"Oh, now and again. Don't seem enough, though, with grandkids. They grow up faster than your own. This one, Anne Marie, she favors me." A big knuckled finger tapped a snapshot of a little girl in a frilly blue dress. "Hard to believe now—" Mrs. Grange patted an ample hip "—but I was a good-looking woman a few years and a few pounds back."

"You're still a good-looking woman, Mrs. Grange." Jackie poured out more of the fruit drink she'd concocted. "And you have a beautiful family."

Because the compliment had been given easily, Mrs. Grange accepted it. "Families, they make up for a lot. I was eighteen when I ran off to marry Clint. Oh, he was something to look at, let me tell you. Lean as a snake and twice as mean." She chuckled, the way a woman could over an old and almost faded mistake. "I was what you might call swept away."

She took a bite of pasta as she looked back. It didn't occur to her that she was talking about private things to someone she hardly knew. Jackie made it easy to talk. "Girls got no sense at that age, and I wasn't any different. Marry in haste, they say, but who listens?"

"People who say that probably haven't been lucky enough to have been swept away."

Admiring Jackie's logic, Mrs. Grange smiled. "That's true enough, and I can't say I regret it, even though at twenty-four I found myself in a crowded little apartment without a husband, without a penny, and with four little boys wanting their supper. Clinton had walked out on the lot of us, smooth as you please."

"I'm sorry. It must have been awful for you."

"I've had better moments." She turned then, seeing

Jackie looking at her not with polite interest but with eyes filled with sympathy and understanding. "Sometimes we get what we ask for, Miss Jack, and I'd asked for Clint Grange, worthless snake that he was."

"What did you do after he'd left?"

"I cried. Spent the night and the better part of a day at it. It felt mighty good, that self-pity, but my boys needed a mother, not some wet-eyed female pining after her man. So I took a look around, figured I'd made enough of a mess of things for a while and decided to fix what I could. That's when I started cleaning houses. Twenty-eight years later, I'm still cleaning them." She looked around the tidy kitchen with a sense of simple satisfaction. "My kids are grown up, and two of them have families of their own. I guess you might say Clint did me a favor, but I don't think I'd thank him if we happened to run into each other in the checkout line at the supermarket."

Jackie understood the last of the sentiment, but not the beginning. If a man had left her high and dry with four children, hanging was too good for him. "How do you figure he did you a favor?"

"If he'd stayed with me, I'd never have been the same kind of mother, the same kind of person. I guess you could say that some people change your life by coming into it, and others change it by going out." Mrs. Grange smiled as she finished off her salad. "Course, I don't suppose I'd shed any tears if I heard old Clinton was lying in a gutter somewheres begging for loose change."

Jackie laughed and toasted her. "I like you, Mrs. Grange."

"I like you, too, Miss Jack. And I hope you find what you're looking for with Mr. Powell." She rose then, but hesitated. She'd always been a good mother, but she'd never been lavish with praise. "You're one of those people who change lives by coming in. You've done something nice for Mr. Powell."

"I hope so. I love him a lot." With a sigh, she stacked Mrs. Grange's snapshots. "That's not always enough, is it?"

"It's better than a stick in the eye." In her gruff way, she patted Jackie's shoulder, then went about her business.

Jackie thought that over, nodded, then walked upstairs, where she went to work with a vengeance.

Long after Mrs. Grange had gone home and afternoon had turned to evening, Nathan found her there. She was hunched over the machine, posture forgotten, her hair falling into her face and her bare feet hooked around the legs of the chair.

He watched her, more than a little intrigued. He'd never really seen her work before. Whenever he'd come up, she'd somehow sensed his approach and swung around in her chair the moment he'd entered.

Now her fingers would drum on the keys, then stop, drum again, then pause while she stared out of the window as if she'd gone into a trance. She'd begin to type again, frowning at the paper in front of her, then smiling, then muttering to herself.

He glanced over at the pile of pages to her right, unaware that the bulk of them were copies of what she'd mailed that morning. He had an uncomfortable feeling that she was more done than undone by this time. Then he cursed himself for being so selfish. What she was doing was important. He'd understood that since the night she'd spun part of the tale for him. It was wrong of him to wish it wouldn't move so quickly or so well, but he'd come to equate the end of her book with the end of their relationship. Yet he knew, even as he stood in the doorway and watched her, that it was he who would end it, and soon.

It had been a month. Only a month, he thought, dragging a hand through his hair. How had she managed to turn his life upside down in a matter of weeks? Despite all his resolutions, all his plans to the contrary, he'd fallen in love with her. That only made it worse. Loving, he wanted to give her all those pretty, unrealistic promises. Marriage, family, a lifetime. Years of shared days and nights. But all he could give her was disappointment.

It was best, really for the best, that Denver was only two weeks away. Even now the wheels were turning that would keep him at the office and in meetings more and at home less. In twelve days he would get on a plane and head west, away from her. Nathan had come to understand that if he didn't love her, if it were only need now, he might be tempted to make those promises to keep her there.

She deserved better. Despite both of them, he was going to make sure she didn't settle for less.

But there were twelve days left.

Quietly he moved toward her. When her fingers stilled again, he laid his hands on her shoulders. Jackie came off the chair with a yelp.

"I'm sorry," he said, but he had to laugh. "I didn't mean to startle you."

"You didn't. You scared me out of my skin." She sank back into the chair with a hand to her heart. "What are you doing home so early?"

"I'm not. It's after six."

"Oh. No wonder my back feels like it belongs to an eighty-year-old weight lifter."

He began to massage her shoulders. That, too, was something he'd learned from her. "How long have you been at it?"

"I don't know. Lost track. Right there… Mmm." Sighing her approval, she shifted under his hands. "I was going to set an alarm or something after Mrs. Grange left, but Burt Donley rode into town, and I forgot."

"Burt Donley?"

"The cold-blooded hired hand of Samuel Carlson."

"Oh, of course, Burt."

Chuckling, she looked over her shoulder. "Burt murdered Sarah's father, at Carlson's bidding. He and Jake have unfinished business from Laramie. That's when Burt gunned down Jake's best friend—in the back, of course."

"Of course."

"And how was your day?"

"Not as exciting. No major shootouts or encounters with loose women."

"Lucky for you I happen to be feeling very loose." She rose, sliding her body up his until her arms were linked around his neck. "Why don't I go see what I can mix together for dinner? Then we'll talk about it."

"Jack, you don't have to cook for me every night."

"We made a deal."

He stilled her mouth with a kiss, a longer and more intense one than he'd realized he needed. When he drew away, her eyes had that soft, unfocused look he'd come to love. "I'd say all those bets were off. Wouldn't you?"

"I don't mind cooking for you, Nathan."

"I know." She could have no idea how such a simple statement humbled him. "But I'd guess of the two of us you've had the tougher day." He drew her closer, wanting to smell her hair, brush his lips over her temple. He was hardly aware that his hands had slipped under her shirt just to stroke the long line of her back. "I'd offer to go down and throw something together, but I doubt you'd be able to eat it. Over the past few weeks I've learned my cooking's not just bad, it's embarrassing."

"We could send out for pizza."

"An excellent idea." He drew her toward the bed. "In an hour."

"An even better idea," she murmured, and melted into him.

Later, much later, after the sun had set and the cicadas had started their serenade, they sat on the patio, an empty carton between them and wine growing warm in glasses. The silence between them had stretched out, long and comfortable. Lovemaking and food had left them content. There was an ease between that usually came only from years of friendship or from complete understanding.

The moon was round and white and generous with its light. With her legs stretched out and her eyes half closed, Jackie decided she could happily stay where she was for hours. It could be like this, just like this, she thought, for the rest of her life.

"You know, Nathan, I've been thinking."

"Hmm?" He stirred himself enough to look at her. Moonlight did something special to her skin, to her eyes. Though he knew he would remember her best in the sunlight, with energy vibrating through her, there would be times when he would need a memory like this—of Jackie, almost bonelessly relaxed, in the light of a full moon.

"Are you listening?"

"No, I'm looking. There are times you are incredibly lovely."

She smiled, almost shyly, then reached out to take his hands. "Keep that up and I won't be able to think at all."

"Is that all it takes?"

"Do you want to hear my idea or not?"

"I'm never sure if I want to hear your ideas."

"This is a good one. I think we should have a party."

"A party?"

"Yes, you know what a party is, Nathan. A social gathering, often including music, food, drink and a group of people brought together for entertainment purposes."

"I've heard of them."

"Then we've passed the first hurdle." She kissed his hand, but he could tell that her mind was already leaping forward. "You've been back from Europe for weeks now and you haven't seen any of your friends. You do have friends, don't you?"

"One or two."

"There we go, over the second hurdle." Lazily she stretched out her legs, rubbing the arch of her foot over his calf. "As a businessman and a pillar of the community— I'm sure you're a pillar of the community—it's practically your obligation to entertain."

He lifted a brow. "I've never been much of a pillar, Jack."

"That's where you're wrong. Anyone who wears a suit the way you do is an absolute pillar." She grinned at him, knowing she'd ruffled his feathers. "A man of distinction, that's you, darling. A tower of strength and conservatism. A dyed-in-the-wool Republican."

"How do you know I'm a Republican?"

Her smile became sympathetic. "Please, Nathan, let's not debate the obvious. Have you ever owned a foreign car?"

"I don't see what that has to do with it."

"Never mind, your politics are entirely your affair." She patted his hand. "Myself, I'm a political agnostic. I'm not entirely convinced they exist. But we're getting off the subject."

"What else is new?"

"Let's talk party, Nathan." As she spoke, she leaned closer, enthusiasm already bubbling. "You've got those fat little address books at every phone in the house. I'm sure out of them you could find enough convivial bodies to make up a party."

"Convivial bodies?"

"A party's nothing without them. It doesn't have to be elaborate—just a couple dozen people, some nice little canapés and an air of good cheer. It could be a combination welcome-home and bon-voyage party for you."

He glanced over sharply at that. Her eyes were steady and a great deal more serious than her words. So, she was thinking about Denver, too. It was like her not to have mentioned it directly or to have asked questions. His fingers tightened on hers. "When did you have in mind?"

She could smile again. Now that his leaving had been brought up and acknowledged, she could push it firmly to the back of her mind. "How about next week?"

"All right. I have an agency we can call."

"No, a party's personal."

"And a lot of work."

She shook her head. She wasn't able to explain that she needed something to keep her mind occupied. "Don't worry, Nathan. If there's one thing I know how to do, it's throw a party. You take care of contacting your friends. I'll do the rest."

"If that's what you want."

"Very much. Now that that's settled, how about a swim?"

He glanced over at the pool. It was inviting and tempting, but so was sitting doing nothing. "Go ahead. The idea of changing into a suit seems too complicated."

"Who needs a suit?" To prove a point, she rose and shimmied out of her shorts.

"Jack…"

"Nathan," she said, mimicking his tone, "one of the ten great pleasures of life is skinny-dipping in the moonlight." The thin bikinis she wore joined her shorts. Her baggy T-shirt skimmed her thighs. "You have a very private pool here," she continued. "Your neighbors would need a step-ladder and binoculars to sneak a peak." Carelessly she pulled the T-shirt over her head and stood, slim and naked. "If they want to that badly, we may as well oblige them."

His mouth went dry. He should have been beyond that by now. Over the past few weeks he'd seen, touched, tasted every inch of her. Yet watching Jackie poised at the edge of the pool, her body gold and gleaming in the moonlight, made his heart thud like a teenager's on a first date.

She rose on her toes, arched and dived cleanly into the water. And surfaced, laughing. "God, I've missed this." Her body glimmered beneath the surface, darker and some-how more lush with the illusion of moonlight and water. "I used to sneak out at one in the morning to swim like this. My mother would have been horrified, even though there was a six-foot wall around the estate and the pool was hid-den by trees. There was something wonderfully decadent about swimming nude at one in the morning. Aren't you coming in?"

He was already having trouble breathing, and he only shook his head. If he went in, he wouldn't do much swim-ming.

"And you said you weren't a pillar of the community." She laughed at him and trailed her fingers through the water. "All right, then, I guess I've got to get tough. It's for your own good." With a sigh, she lifted a hand out of the water. Like a child playing cowboy, she pointed it at him, finger out, thumb up. "Okay, Nathan, get up slow. Don't make any sudden moves."

"Give me a break, Jack."

"This is a hair trigger," she warned him. "Get up, and keep your hands where I can see them."

He couldn't have said why he did it. Maybe it was the full moon. He rose to a more interesting view.

"Okay, strip." She touched her tongue to her top lip. "Slow."

"You really are out of your mind."

"Don't beg, Nathan, it's pitiful." She cocked her thumb back over an invisible hammer. "Do you have any idea what a .38 slug can do to the human body? Take my word for it, it's not a pretty sight."

With a shrug, he pulled off his shirt. It wouldn't hurt to go in wearing his shorts. "You haven't got the guts to use that thing."

"Don't bet on it." But her lips twitched as she struggled with a grin. "Come a step closer with your pants on and I'll blow off a kneecap. Something like that gives a whole new meaning to the word *pain*."

She was crazy, he had no doubt about that. But apparently some of it had rubbed off. Nathan unsnapped his shorts and stepped out of them. She was going to get a surprise when he joined her in the water.

"That's good, very good." Deliberately she took her time evaluating him. "Now the rest."

With his eyes on hers, he stripped off his briefs. "You have no shame."

"Not a bit. Aren't you lucky?" Laughing, she gestured with her imaginary gun. "Into the pool, Nathan. Face the music."

He dived in, no more than an arm's length from her.

When he surfaced, Jackie was treading water and smiling. "You dropped your gun."

She glanced down, as if surprised, at her open hand. "So I did."

"Let's see how tough you are unarmed."

He lunged for her, but she was quick. Anticipating him, Jackie dived deep, kicked out and glided under him. When she surfaced, she was six feet away with a smug smile. "Missed," she said lightly, and waited for his next move.

Slowly they circled, eyes locked. Jackie bit her lip, knowing that if she gave in to the laughter she would be sunk in more ways than one. Nathan was as strong a swimmer as she, but she was counting on speed and agility to see her through. Until she was ready to lose.

He advanced, she evaded. He feinted, she adjusted. He maneuvered, she outmaneuvered. For the next few minutes there were only the sounds of insects and lapping water, giving them both a sense of solitude. Suddenly inspired, he brought a hand out of the water, cupping his fingers in his palm, pointing the index and cocking the thumb.

"Look what I found."

That was all it took to have her laughter breaking through. In two long strokes, he had her.

"Cheat. You cheated. Nathan, there's hope for you yet." Giggling, she reached to hug him. Then his hand was hard and fast around her hair. The roughness was so uncharacteristic that her eyes flew to his. What she saw had her breath catching. This time it was her mouth that went dry. "Nathan," she managed before her lips were imprisoned by his.

The need was fiercer, edgier, more frenzied than it had ever been before. He felt as though his body were full of springs that had all been wound too tightly. Against his own, her heart was beating desperately as he dived into her mouth, taking, tasting, devouring all. His teeth scraped her lips, his tongue invaded, tantalized by her breathless moan. Her body, at first taut as wire, went limp against him. They slipped beneath the surface without a thought for air.

The water enveloped them, making their movements slow and sluggish but no less urgent. The sensuous kiss of the cool, night-darkened water flowed around them, then ran off in torrents as they rose above it, still wrapped close.

Her first submission had passed. Now she was as desperate and anxious as he. She clung to him, head thrown back as he brought her up so that he could suckle her damp, water-cooled breasts. With each greedy pull, her stomach contracted and her pulse thudded out the new rhythm. The fingers on his shoulders dug in, leaving thin crescents. Then her mouth was on his again, thirsty.

She took her hands under, then over him, while her mind spun faster than her movements. Their bodies were captured in a slow-motion dream world, but their thoughts, their needs, raced.

Reaching down, he found her, cool and inviting. At his touch, his name burst from her. The sound of it across the quiet moonlight had his madness growing. She clung to him, her hands slipping over his slick body, then grasping for purchase. Her lips were wet and open when he took them again.

Jackie found her back braced against the side of the pool. Trembling with anticipation, she opened for him, then groaned when he filled her. Her hands fell lifelessly in the water, and he was there, holding her, moving in her.

The moonlight was on her face, making it both exotic and beautiful, but he could only press his own into her shoulder and ride the wave.

Chapter 11

Some people were born knowing how to entertain, and Jackie was one of them. The fact that she was using a party as a way of blocking out the knowledge that she had only a few more days until Nathan left didn't mean she was any less determined to make it a success.

She wrote for eight, sometimes ten, hours a day, losing herself in another romance, in another catastrophe. When she wasn't chained to her machine, she was shopping, planning menus, checking off lists and supplies.

She insisted on doing all the cooking herself but had decided to enlist Mrs. Grange to help serve and her son, the future teacher, to tend bar.

She was delighted when Nathan joined her in the kitchen the afternoon of the party, his sleeves rolled up and his mind set on helping her make hors d'oeuvres. Determined he was, and clumsy. Jackie found both traits endearing. Tactfully she buried his attempts on the bottom tray.

Jackie, optimistic about the weather, had planned to set up tables outside so that the guests could wander out among the colored lights she'd hung. Her faith was rewarded when the day remained clear and promised a star-filled, breezy night.

She rarely worried about the success or failure of a party, but this was different. She wanted it to be perfect, to prove to herself and to Nathan that she belonged in his world as much as she belonged in his arms.

She had only a matter of days left before he would fly thousands of miles away from her. It was difficult not to dwell on that, and on the fact that he had never told her what he wanted of her. What he wanted for them. She refused to believe that he still considered permanence impossible.

He'd never told her he loved her. That was a thought that hit her painfully at the oddest times. But he'd shown her in so many ways. Often he'd call her in the middle of the day just to hear her voice. He'd bring her flowers, from his garden or from a roadside stand, just when the ones she'd put in a vase had begun to fade. He'd draw her close, just to hold her after lovemaking, after passion had ebbed and contentment remained.

A woman didn't need words when she had everything else.

The hell she didn't.

Pushing back her gnawing doubts, Jackie told herself that for once she would have to be content with what she had instead of what she wanted.

An hour before the party she began to pamper herself. This was one of her mother's traditions that Jackie approved of. She was using her old room after telling Nathan he'd only be in her way. There was some truth in that, but more, Jackie had discovered she wanted to add a touch of mystery to the evening. She wanted him to see not the step-by-step preparation but the completed woman.

A long, leisurely bubble bath was first on her list. She soaked, the radio playing quietly while she looked out through the skylight over the tub. The only clouds in the sky were as harmless as white spun sugar.

She took time and care with her makeup, shooting for the exotic. When she studied her face from every angle in the mirror, she was satisfied with the results. She indulged in the feminine pleasure of slathering on perfumed cream before she took the dress she'd bought only the day before out of the closet.

Nathan was already downstairs when she started out. She could hear him talking to Mrs. Grange, and she could hear the woman's gruff replies. Always one to enjoy a bit of drama, Jackie put her hand on the rail and started slowly down.

She wasn't disappointed. Nathan glanced up, saw her and stopped in midsentence. Intent on him, she didn't notice the tall sandy-haired man beside Mrs. Grange. Nor did she see his mouth fall open.

Her eyes dominated her face, smudged on the lids with blending tones of bronze. Her hair, a combination of nature and womanly art, was windswept and cunningly tousled. Oversize silver stars glinted at her ears.

When Nathan could drag his gaze away from her face to take in the rest of her, it was another shock to the system.

The dress she'd chosen was stunning, eye-burning white that fell in a narrow column from her breasts to her ankles, leaving her shoulders bare and her arms unadorned but for the dozen silver bracelets that encircled her arm from her wrist almost to her elbow. Smiling, she reached the bottom, then turned in a circle, revealing the slit in the back of the dress that reached to midthigh.

"What do you think?"

"You're stunning."

Finishing the circle, she studied him in turn. No one wore a black suit with quite as much style as Nathan, Jackie thought. It must have been that broad-shouldered, muscled body that gave conservatism a dangerous look. She took a step closer to kiss him. Then, with her hand in his, she turned to Mrs. Grange.

"I really appreciate you helping us out tonight. And this is your son? You must be Charlie."

"Yes, ma'am." He swallowed audibly, then accepted the hand she offered. His palm was sweaty. His mother hadn't told him that Miss Jack was a goddess.

"It's nice to meet you, Charlie. Your mom's told us a lot about you. Shall I show you where we've set up the bar?"

Mrs. Grange gave him an elbow in the ribs. The boy looked as if he had rocks in his head when he stared that way. "I'll show him what he needs to know. Come on, Charlie, get the lead out."

Charlie went with his mother—because she had a death grip on his arm—but sent one last moonstruck look over his shoulder.

"The kid's jaw dropped on his shoes when he saw you."

With a laugh, Jackie tucked her arm through Nathan's. "That's kind of sweet."

"Mine hit the floor."

She looked at him, nearly level with him in her heeled sandals. "That's even sweeter."

"You always manage to surprise me, Jack."

"I hope so."

With his free hand he touched her shoulder, then ran his

fingertips down her arm. "This is the first time I remember wishing a party was over before it began." It wasn't her usual scent tonight, but something stunningly sexy and taunting. "What did you do to yourself up there?"

"Tricks of the trade." She had to shift only slightly for her lips to meet his. "It's still me, Nathan."

"I know." His arm curled around her waist to keep her there. "That's why I wish the party was over."

"Tell you what." She slid her hands over his shoulders. "When it is, we'll have one all our own."

"I'm counting on it." He lowered his lips to hers as the doorbell rang.

"Round one," she said. Keeping his hand in hers, she went to answer the door.

Within an hour, the house was milling with people. Most of them were every bit as interested in finding out about the woman in Nathan's life as they were in an evening of socializing. She didn't mind. She was just as curious about them.

She discovered Nathan knew a wide variety of people, from the staunch and stuffy to the easygoing. It took only a smile and a greeting for her to click with Cody Johnson, an architect who had joined Nathan's firm two years before. He favored scuffed boots and faded jeans but had made a concession to formality by tossing on a suit jacket. Since her brother favored the same style and brand, Jackie recognized it as murderously expensive. He clamped a hand over hers, looked her up and down with eyes as brown as her own, then winked.

"I've been wanting to get a look at you."

"Check out the boss's outside interests?"

"Something like that." He still held her hand, but there was nothing flirtatious in the gesture. Jackie had the feeling that Cody got his impressions as much by touch as by sight. "One thing you can never fault Nathan for is his taste. I always figured whenever he looked more than twice at a woman she'd have to be special."

"That seemed like both a compliment and approval."

"You could say that." He didn't often give both so easily. "I'm glad, because Nathan's a good friend. The best. You planning on sticking around?"

Her brow lifted. Though she preferred direct questions, Jackie didn't feel obligated to respond with a direct answer. "You cut right through, don't you?"

"Hate to waste time."

Yes, she decided, she liked Cody Johnson just fine. With her hand still in his, she looked over and spotted Nathan. "I plan on sticking around."

His lips curved. He had one of those quick, arrogant grins that women found devastating. Because, Jackie thought, a woman could never be sure what he was thinking. "Then why don't I buy you a drink?"

Tucking her arm through his, she headed for the bar. "Have you met Justine Chesterfield?"

His laugh was full and rich. Jackie liked that as much as she did the sun-bronzed hair that fell over his forehead. "Anyone ever tell you you're clear as glass?"

"Hate to waste time."

"I appreciate that." He stopped at the bar and was amused by the way the college boy gaped at his hostess. "She's a nice lady, but a little rich for my blood."

"Is there anyone special?"

"Depends. You got a sister?"

With a laugh, Jackie turned and ordered champagne. Neither of them noticed Nathan watching them with a small, preoccupied frown.

He wasn't a jealous man. Nathan had always considered

that one of the most foolish and unproductive emotions. Not only was jealousy the green-eyed monster, it invariably made the affected party look, and act, like an idiot.

He was neither an idiot nor jealous, but watching Jackie with Cody made him feel suspiciously like both. It was not, Nathan discovered, a sensation that could be enjoyed or ignored.

Cody was certainly more her type. Nathan managed to smile at the squeaky-voiced engineer who thought he had his attention. Cody could easily have passed for a gunfighter. Jackie's diamond-in-the-rough Jake Redman. That was Cody, with his loose limbed, rangy build and his sunbleached hair that always looked as though it were one week past time for the barber. And there was the drawl. Nathan had always considered Cody's slight drawl soothing, but it began to occur to him that a woman might find it exciting. Some women.

Added to that was a deceptively laid-back attitude, a total lack of interest in convention and a restless, unerring eye for quality. Fast cars, late nights and bright lights. That was Cody.

When Nathan saw Jackie glance up and laugh into Cody's wide grin, he considered the potential satisfaction of strangling them both.

Ridiculous. Nathan sipped his drink, then reached for a cigarette. He wasn't fully aware that he rarely wanted— needed—a cigarette these days. Cody was a friend, probably the best friend Nathan had now, or had ever had. And Jackie… What was Jackie?

Lover, friend, companion. A delight and, oddly enough, a rock. It was strange to think of someone who looked and acted like a butterfly as something so solid and secure. She could be loyal when loyalty was deserved and strong when strength was needed. But rock or not, he'd given her no reason to pledge her fidelity. For her own good. He didn't want to cage her in or narrow her horizons.

The hell he didn't.

Cutting off the engineer in midsentence, Nathan made a vague excuse and moved toward Jackie.

She was laughing again, her face glowing with it, her eyes brilliant as they slanted upward over the rim of her champagne flute. "Nathan, you didn't tell me your associate was the kind of man mothers warn their daughters about." But as she spoke, her hand linked casually with Nathan's. It was the kind of ease that spoke of certain intimacy.

"I'm happy to take that as a compliment." Cody was drinking vodka straight up, and he toasted her with the squat glass. "Nice party, boss. I've already complimented you on your taste."

"Thanks. You know there are tables loaded with food outside. Knowing your appetite, I'm surprised you haven't found them."

"I'm on my way." He sent Jackie a final wink, then sauntered off.

"Well, that was certainly a subtle heave-ho," she commented.

"It seemed he was taking up a great deal of your time."

Her head swiveled around, her brows lifted, and then her face glowed again with a fresh smile. "That's nice. That's very, very nice." She brushed her lips lightly over his. "Some women don't care for possessive men. Myself, I like them a lot. To a point."

"I simply meant—"

"Don't spoil it." She kissed him again before she tucked her arm through his. "Well, shall we stroll around looking convivial, or shall we dive into that food before I starve to death?"

He raised her hand to his lips. The quick bout of jealousy, if that was what it was, hadn't caused him to look or act like an idiot. That was one more thing he'd have to rearrange his thinking about.

"We'll dive," he decided. "It's hard to be convivial on an empty stomach."

The evening was a complete success. Cards and calls came in over the next few days complimenting and commenting. Invitations were extended. It should have been a delightful time for Jackie. She had met Nathan's friends and associates and had won them over. But it wasn't Nathan's friends and associates who mattered. The bottom line was Nathan himself, and he was going to Denver.

It was no longer something she could think about later, not when his plane ticket was tucked in his briefcase. She'd been to Denver herself once, to sit on the fifty-yard line at Mile High Stadium and cheer. She'd enjoyed it well enough. Now she hated it, as a city and as a symbol.

He was leaving in a matter of hours, and they'd settled nothing. Once or twice he'd tried to talk to her, but she'd put him off. It was cowardly, but if he was going to brush her out of his life, she wanted every moment she could grab before it happened.

Now she was out of time, but she'd made herself a firm promise. He would at least tell her why. If he didn't want her any longer—wouldn't let himself want her—she would have the reasons.

She braced herself outside the bedroom door, squared her shoulders, then walked in. "I brought you some coffee."

Nathan glanced up from his packing. "Thanks." He'd

thought he'd been miserable a few times before in his life. He'd been wrong.

"Need any help with this?" She lifted her own cup and sipped. Somehow it was easier to have serious, life-altering discussions when you were doing something as casual as drinking coffee.

"No. I'm almost finished."

Nodding, she sat on the edge of the bed. If she paced, as she wanted to, it would be easy to slam the cup against the wall and watch it shatter. As she wanted to. "You haven't said how long you'll be out of town."

"That's because I can't be sure." He'd never hated packing before. It had always been just one more small, slightly annoying chore. He hated it now. "It could be three weeks, more likely four, on this first trip. If we don't run into any major complications, I should be able to spot-check it as we go."

She sipped again, but the coffee was bitter. "Should I be here when you get back?"

It was like her to put it that way, not a demand or even a request, but a question. He wanted to say yes, please, yes, but "It's up to you" was what he told her.

"No, it's not. We both know how I feel, what I want. I haven't made a secret out of it." She paused a moment, wondering if she should feel a loss of pride. But none came. "Now it comes down to what you feel and what you want."

Her eyes were so solemn. There was no hint of a smile on her lips. He missed that, already missed that bright, vivid look she wore the way other women wore jewelry. "You mean a lot to me, Jackie." The word *love* was there, in his mind, in his heart, but he couldn't say it. "More than anyone else."

It amazed her that she was almost desperate enough, almost hungry enough, to accept those crumbs and be content. But she lifted a brow and continued watching him. "And?"

He packed another freshly laundered shirt. He wanted to choose the right words, say the right thing. Over and over during the last twenty-four hours he'd imagined what he would say to her, what he would do. In one wildly satisfying fantasy he'd dragged her to the airport with him and they'd flown away together. On a shell pelican.

But this was real. If he couldn't give her anything else, he could give her fairness.

"I can't ask you to stay, to wait, then live your life day by day. That's not what I want for you, Jack."

The hurting came from his honesty. He wouldn't lie or give her what she thought might be the comfort of pretense. "I'd like you to take a step back and tell me what you want for yourself. Is it what you had before, Nathan? Peace and quiet and no complications?"

Wasn't it? But somehow, when she said it, that life no longer sounded settled and comfortable, it sounded stagnant and boring. Yet it was the only one he was sure of. "I can't give you what you want," he said, struggling for calm. "I can't give you marriage and family and a lifetime commitment, because I don't believe in those things, Jack. I'd rather hurt you now than hurt you consistently over the rest of our lives."

She said nothing for a moment, afraid she would say too much. Her heart had gone out to him. There had been more misery in those last few words than she'd known he felt, or could feel. Though she hurt with him, she wasn't sorry she'd dredged it up.

"Was it that bad?" she said quietly. "Were you that unhappy growing up?"

He could have sworn at her for putting her slim, sensitive finger on the core of it. "That's not relevant."

"Oh, it is, and we both know it." She rose. She had to move, just a little, or the tension inside of her was going to explode and shatter her into a million pieces. "Nathan, I won't say you owe me an explanation. People are always saying, 'He owes me,' or 'I owe him.' I've always felt that when you do something for someone, or give something away, that you should do it freely or not at all. So there's no debt." She sat again, calmer, then looked at him again. "But I have to say that I think it's right for you to tell me why."

He fished out a cigarette and lit it as he sat on the opposite end of the bed. "Yes, you're right. You're entitled to reasons." He was silent for a long time, trying to sort out the words, but it wasn't possible to plan them. So he simply began.

"My mother came from a wealthy and established family. She was expected to make a good marriage. A proper marriage. She'd been raised and educated with that in mind."

Jackie frowned a little, but tried to be fair. "That wasn't so unusual a generation ago."

"No, and it was the rule of thumb in her family. My father had more ambition than security, but had earned a reputation as an up-and-comer. He was, I've been told, dynamic and charismatic. When my mother fell in love with him, her family wasn't overjoyed, but they didn't object. Marriage to her gave my father exactly what he wanted. Family name, family backing, a well-bred wife who could entertain properly and give him an heir."

Jackie looked down at her empty cup. "I see," she murmured, and she was beginning to.

"He didn't love her. The marriage was a business decision."

He paused again, studying the column of smoke rising toward the ceiling. Was that the core of it? he wondered. Was that what had damaged his parents, and him, the most? Restless, he moved his shoulders. It was history, ancient history.

"I don't doubt that he had a certain amount of affection for her. He wasn't able, he'd never been able, to give too much of himself. His business took him away from home quite a bit. He was obsessed with making a fortune, with personal and professional success. When I was born, he gave my mother an emerald necklace as a reward for producing a son."

She started to speak, struck by the bitterness in his tone, then closed her mouth. Sometimes it was best only to listen.

"My mother adored him, was almost fanatic about it. As a child I had a nurse, a nanny and a bodyguard. She was terrified of what he might do if anything happened to me. It wasn't so much that she worried about me as a son, but as *his* son. His symbol."

"Oh, Nathan…" she began, but he shook his head.

"She told me in almost those words when I was five, six years old. She told me that and a great deal more once her feelings for him had changed. I rarely saw either of them when I was growing up. She was so determined to be the perfect society wife, and he was always flying off somewhere or another to close a deal. His idea of being a father consisted of periodic checks on my progress in school, lectures on responsibility and family honor. The trouble was, he had no honor himself."

With slow, deliberate motions he crushed out his cigarette. "There were other women. My mother knew and ignored it. He told me once there was nothing serious in those relationships. A man away from home so often required certain comforts."

"He told you?" Jackie demanded, stupidly shocked.

"When I was sixteen. I believe he considered it a heart-to-heart. My mother's feelings for him were dead by that time, and we were living like three polite strangers in the same house."

"Couldn't you have gone to your grandparents?"

"My grandmother was dead. She might have understood. I can't be sure. My grandfather considered the marriage a success. My mother certainly never complained, and my father had lived up to his potential. He would have been horrified if I'd arrived on his doorstep saying I couldn't live in the same house with my own parents. Besides, I had the place to myself a great deal of the time."

Privacy, she thought. She certainly understood his need for privacy. But what would it have done to a young boy to have his privacy in such an unhealthy place? "It must have been terrible for you."

She thought of her own family, wealthy, prestigious, respected. But their house had never been quiet, not the way she imagined Nathan's childhood home. It had never been cold. Hers had been filled with screams of laughter and accusations. With fists raised, the emotion in the threat heatedly real at the moment, then laughed about later.

"Nathan," she began slowly, "did you ever tell them how they made you feel?"

"Once. They were simply appalled with me for my lack of gratitude. And my lack of…graciousness in bringing up the subject. You learn not to beat your head against a wall that isn't going to move and find other ways."

"What other ways?"

"Study, personal ambitions. I can't say they ceased to exist for me as parents, but I shifted priorities. My father was away when I graduated from high school. I went to Europe that summer, so I didn't see him again until I was in college. He'd discovered I was studying architecture and came, he thought, to pull the rug out from under my feet.

"He wanted, as you put it once, for me to follow in his footsteps. He expected it. He demanded it. I'd lived under his thumb for eighteen years, totally cowed by my, and my mother's, perception of him. But something had happened. When I'd decided I wanted to build, the idea, the dream of that, became bigger than he."

"You'd grown up," she murmured.

"Enough, apparently, to stand up to him. He threatened to stop my tuition. I had a responsibility to him and the family business. That's all the family was, you see. A business. My mother was in full agreement. The fact was, once she'd stopped loving him, she couldn't have cared less. For her, I was my father's son."

"Surely that's too harsh, Nathan. Your mother—"

"Told me she hadn't wanted me." He reached for another cigarette, then broke it in half. "She said she believed if I hadn't been born her marriage could have been saved. Without the responsibility of a child she could have traveled with my father."

Her face had gone very white. She didn't want to believe him. She didn't want to think that anyone could be so cruel to her own child. "They didn't deserve you." Swallowing a lump of tears, she rose to go to him.

"That's not the point." He put his hands out, knowing if she put her arms around him now he would fall apart. He had never spoken of this with anyone before, hadn't wanted to think it through stage by stage. "I made a decision that day I faced my father. I had no family, had never had one and didn't need one. My grandmother had left me enough to get me through college. So I used that, and took nothing from him. What I did from that point, I did on my own, for myself. That hasn't changed."

She let her arms rest at her sides. He wouldn't allow her to comfort him, and as much as her heart ached to, her mind told her that perhaps it wasn't comfort he needed.

"You're still letting them run your life." Her voice wasn't soft now, but angry, angry with him, angry for him. "Their marriage was ugly, so marriage itself is ugly? That's stupid."

"Not marriage itself, marriage for me." Fury hit him suddenly. He'd opened up an old and tender wound for her, yet she still wanted more. "Do you think people only inherit brown eyes or a cleft chin from their parents? Don't you be stupid, Jack. They give us a great deal more than that. My father was a selfish man. I'm a selfish man, but at least I have the common sense to know I can't put myself, you or the children we'd have through that kind of misery."

"Common sense?" The MacNamara temper, famed for generations, leaped out. "You can stand there spouting off that kind of drivel and call it common sense? You haven't got enough sense to fill a teaspoon. For God's sake, Nathan, if your father had been an ax murderer, does that mean you'd be lunging around looking for people to chop up? My father loves raw oysters, and I can't stand to look at them. Does that mean I'm adopted?"

"You're being absurd."

"I'm being absurd? *I'm* being absurd?" With a sound of disgust, she reached for the closest thing at hand—a nineteenth-century Venetian bowl—and smashed it to the floor. "You obviously wouldn't recognize absurd if it shot you between the eyes. I'll tell you what's absurd. Absurd is loving someone and having them love you right back, then refusing to do anything solid about it because maybe, just maybe, it wouldn't work out perfectly."

"I'm not talking about perfect. Damn it, Jack, not that vase."

But it was already a pile of French porcelain shards on the floor. "Of course you're talking about perfect. Perfect's your middle name. Nathan Perfect Powell, projecting his life years into the future, making certain there aren't any loose ends or uneven edges."

"Fine." He swung her around before she could grab something else. "That should be enough right there to show you I'm right about this, about us. I like things done a certain way, I do plan ahead and insist on completing things as carefully as they're begun. You, by your own admission, never finish anything."

Her chin came up. Her eyes were dry. The tears would come later, she knew, torrents of them. "I wondered how long it would take you to throw that in my face. You're right about one thing, Nathan. The world's made up of two kinds of people, the careful and the careless. I'm a careless person and content to be so. But I don't think less of you for being a careful one."

He let out a quiet breath. He wasn't used to fighting, not unless it was over the quality of materials or working conditions for his men. "I didn't mean that as an insult."

"No? Well, maybe not, but the point's taken. We're not alike, and though I think we're both capable of a certain amount of growth and compromise, we'll never be alike. That doesn't change the fact that I love you and want to spend my life with you." This time she grabbed him, by the shirtfront. "You're not your father, Nathan, and I'm sure as hell not your mother. Don't let them do this to you, to us."

He covered her hands with his. "Maybe if you weren't so

important it would be easier to risk it. I could say all right, we want each other, so let's take the chance. But I care for you too much to go into this with two strikes against me."

"You care too much." The tears were going to come, and soon, so she backed away. "Damn you for that, Nathan. For not having the guts to say you love me, even now."

She whirled around and ran out. He heard the front door slam.

Chapter 12

"The masons lost two days with the rain. I'm putting on double shifts."

Nathan stood at the building site, squinting into the sun, which had finally made an appearance. It was cold in Denver. Spring hadn't floated in gently. The few hopeful wildflowers that had poked up had been carelessly trampled over. By next spring, the grounds would be green and trimmed. Looking at the scarred earth and the skeleton of the building, he already saw it.

"Considering the filthy weather you've been having, there's been a lot of progress in just under three weeks." Cody, a Stetson shading his eyes, his booted feet planted wide apart, looked at the beams and girders. Unlike Nathan, he didn't see the finished product. He preferred this stage, when there were still possibilities. "It looks good," he decided. "You, on the other hand, look like hell."

"It's always nice to have you around, Cody." Studying

his clipboard, Nathan began a steady and detailed analysis of work completed and work projected. Schedules had to be adjusted, and deadlines met.

"You seem to have everything under control, as usual."

"Yeah." Nathan pulled out a cigarette, cupping his hands over his lighter.

As the flame leaped on, Cody noticed the shadows under Nathan's eyes, the lines of strain that had dug in around his mouth. To Cody's mind, there was only one thing that could make a strong man look battered. That was a woman.

Nathan dropped his lighter back in his pocket. "The building inspector should make his pass through today."

"Bless his heart." Cody helped himself to a cigarette from Nathan's pack. "I thought you were quitting these?"

"Eventually." One of the laborers had a portable radio turned up full. Nathan thought of Jackie blaring music through the kitchen speakers. "Any problems back home?"

"Businesswise? No. But I was about to ask you the same thing."

"I haven't been there, remember? Got an update on the Sydney project?"

"Ready to break ground in about six weeks." He took another drag, then broke the filter off the cigarette. Cody figured if you were going to kill yourself you might as well do it straight out. "You and Jack have a disagreement?"

"Why?"

"Because from the looks of you you haven't had a decent night's sleep since you got out here." He found a bent pack of matches in his pocket, remembered the club that was printed on the front with some fondness, then struck a match. "Want to talk about it?"

"There's nothing to talk about."

Cody merely lifted a brow and drew in more smoke. "Whatever you say, boss."

Nathan swore and pinched at the tension between his eyes. "Sorry."

"Okay." He stood quiet for a time, smoking and watching the men at work. "I could do with some coffee and a plateful of eggs." He pitched the stub of the cigarette into the construction rubble. "Since I'm on an expense account, I'll buy."

"You're a sport, Cody." But Nathan walked back to the pickup truck.

Within ten minutes they were sitting in a greasy little diner where the menu was written on a chalkboard and the waitresses wore holsters and short shocking-pink uniforms. There was a bald man dozing over his coffee at the counter and booths with ashtrays in the shape of saddles. The smell of onions hung stubbornly in the air.

"You always could pick a class joint," Nathan muttered as they slid into a booth, but all he could think of was how Jackie would have enjoyed it.

"It ain't the package, son." Cody settled back and grinned as one of the waitresses shrieked out an order to a stocky, grim-faced man at the grill.

A pot of coffee was plopped down without being asked for. Cody poured it himself and watched the steam rise. "You can keep your fancy French restaurants. Nobody makes coffee like a diner."

Jackie did, Nathan thought, and found he'd lost his taste for it.

Cody grinned up at the frowsy blonde who stopped, pad in hand, by their booth. "That blue plate special. I want two of them."

"Two blue plates," she muttered, writing.

"On one plate, darling," he added.

She looked over her pad and let her gaze roam over him. "I guess you do have a lot to fill up."

"That's the idea. Bring my friend the same."

She turned to study Nathan and decided it was her lucky day. Two hunks at her station, though the dark one looked as if he'd put in a rough night. Or a week of rough nights. She smiled at Nathan, showing crooked incisors. "How do you want your eggs, sweetie?"

"Over light," Cody told her, drawing her attention back to him. "And don't wring all the grease out of the home fries."

She chuckled and started off, her voice pitched high. "Double up on a couple of blue plates. Flip the eggs but make it easy."

For the first time in weeks, Nathan had the urge to smile. "What is the blue plate?"

"Two eggs, a rasher of bacon, home fries, biscuits and coffee by the barrel." As he took out one of his own cigarettes, Cody stretched his legs to rest his feet on the seat beside Nathan. "So, have you called her?"

It wasn't any use pretending he didn't want to talk about it. If that had been the case, he could have made some excuse and remained on the building site. He'd come because Cody could be counted on to be honest, whether the truth was pretty or not.

"No, I haven't called her."

"So you did have a fight?"

"I don't think you could call it a fight." Frowning, he remembered the china shattering on the floor. "No, you could call it that."

"People in love fight all the time."

Nathan smiled again. "That sounds like something she'd say."

"Sensible woman." He poured a second cup of coffee and

noted that Nathan had left his untouched. "From the looks of you, I'd say whatever you two fought about, she won."

"No. Neither of us did."

Cody was silent for a moment, tapping his spoon on the table with the tinny country song playing on the jukebox. "My old man was big on sending flowers whenever he and my mother went at each other. Worked every time."

"This isn't as simple as that."

Cody waited until two heaping plates were set in front of them. He sent the waitress a cheeky wink, then dug in. "Nathan, I know you're the kind of man who likes to keep things to himself. I respect that. Working with you the last couple of years has been an education for me, in organization and control, in professionalism. But I figure by this time we're more than associates. A man has trouble with a woman, it usually helps if he dumps it out on another man. Not that another man understands women any better. They can just be confused about it together."

A semi pulled up in front of the diner's dusty window, gears groaning. "Jack wanted a commitment. I couldn't give her one."

"Couldn't?" Cody took his time pouring honey on a biscuit. "Isn't the word *wouldn't*?"

"Not in this case. For reasons I don't want to get into, I couldn't give her the marriage and family she wanted. Needed. Jack needed promises. I don't make promises."

"Well, that's for you to decide." Cody scooped up more eggs. "But it seems to me you're not too happy about it. If you don't love her—"

"I didn't say I didn't love her."

"Didn't you? Guess I misunderstood."

"Look, Cody, marriage is impossible enough when people think alike, when they have the same attitudes and habits. When they're as different as Jack and I, it's worse than impossible. She wants a home, kids and all the confusion that goes with it. I'm on the road for weeks at a time, and when I come home I want..." He let his words trail off because he no longer knew. He used to know.

"Yeah, that's a problem, all right," Cody continued as if Nathan weren't staring out of the window. "I guess dragging a woman along, having her to share those nameless hotel rooms and solitary meals, would be inconvenient. And having one who loved you waiting for you when you got home would be a pain."

Nathan turned back from the window and gave Cody a level look. "It would be unfair to her."

"Probably right. It's better to move on and be unhappy without her than risk being happy with her. Your eggs are getting cold, boss."

"Marriages break up as often as they work out."

"Yeah, the statistics are lousy. Makes you wonder why people keep jumping in."

"You haven't."

"Nope. Haven't found a woman mean enough." He grinned as he shoveled in the last of his eggs. "Maybe I'll look Jack up next week." The sudden deadly fury on Nathan's face had Cody stretching an arm over the back of the booth. "Figure this, Nathan, when a woman puts light into a man's life and he pulls the shade, he's asking for somebody else to enjoy it. Is that what you want?"

"Don't push it, Cody."

"No, I think you've already pushed yourself." He leaned forward again, his face quietly serious. "Let me tell you something, Nathan. You're a good man and a hell of an architect. You don't lie or look for the easy way. You fight for your men and for your principles, but you're not so hardheaded you won't compromise when it's time. You'll still be all of those things without her, but you could be a hell of a lot more with her. She did something for you."

"I know that." He shoved his all-but-untouched meal aside. "I'm worried about what I might do to her. If it were up to me…"

"If it were up to you, what?"

"It comes down to the fact that I'm not better off without her." That was a tough one to bring out in the open, to say plainly and live with. "But she may be better off without me."

"I guess she's the only one who can answer that." He drew out his wallet and riffled through bills. "I figure I know as much about this project here as you."

"What? Yes, so?"

"So I got an airline ticket in my room. Booked to leave day after tomorrow. I'll trade you for your hotel room."

Nathan started to make excuses, to give all the reasons why he was responsible for the project. Excuses, he realized, were all they would be. "Keep it," he said abruptly. "I'm leaving today."

"Smart move." Cody added a generous tip to the bill.

Nathan arrived home at 2:00 a.m. after a frenzied stop-and-go day of traveling. He'd had to route through St. Louis, bump into Chicago, then pace restlessly through O'Hare for two and a half hours waiting for his connection to Baltimore. From there he took his only option, a puddle jumper that touched down hourly.

He was sure she'd be there. He'd kept himself going with that alone. True, she hadn't answered when he'd called, but she could have been out shopping, in the pool, taking a walk. He didn't believe she'd left.

Somewhere in his heart he'd been sure all along that no

matter what he'd said or how they'd left things she would be there when he returned. She was too stubborn and too self-confident to give up on him because he'd been an idiot.

She loved him, and when a woman like Jackie loved, she continued to love, for better or for worse. He'd given her worse. Now, if she'd let him, he was going to try for better.

But she wasn't there. He knew it almost from the minute he opened his front door. The house had that same quiet, almost respectful feel it had had before she'd come into it. A lonely feel. Swearing, he took the steps two at a time, calling her.

The bed was empty, made up with Mrs. Grange's no-nonsense tucks. There were no colorful shirts or grubby shoes tossed anywhere. The room was neat as a pin. He detested it on sight. Still unable to accept it, he pulled open the closet. Only his own ordered clothes were there.

Furious with her, as well as himself, he strode into the guest room. And had to accept. She wasn't there, curled under tangled sheets. The clutter of books and papers was gone. So was her typewriter.

He stared for a long time, wondering how he could ever had thought it preferable to come home to order and peace. Tired, he sat on the edge of the bed. Her scent was still there, but it was fading. That was the worst of it, to have a trace of her without the rest.

He lay back on the bed, unwilling to sleep in the one he'd shared with her night after night. She wasn't going to get away with it, he thought, and instantly fell asleep.

"It's worse than pitiful for a grown man to cheat at Scrabble."

"I don't have to cheat." J. D. MacNamara narrowed his eyes and focused them on his daughter. "*Zuckly* is an adjective, meaning graceful. As in 'the ballerina executed a zuckly pirouette.'"

"That's a load of you-know-what," Jackie said, and scowled at him. "I let you get away with *quoho*, Daddy, but this is too much."

"Just because you're a writer now doesn't mean you know every word in the dictionary. Go ahead, look it up, but you lose fifty points if you find it."

Jackie's fingers hovered over the dictionary. She knew her father could lie beautifully, but she also knew he had an uncanny way of coming out on top. With a sigh of disgust, she dropped her hand. "I'll concede. I know how to be a zuckly player."

"That's my girl." Pleased with himself, he began to add points to his score. Jackie lifted her glass of wine and considered him.

J. D. MacNamara was quite a man. But then, she'd always known that. She supposed it was Nathan's description of his own father, his family life, that had made her stand back and appreciate fully what she'd been given. She knew her father had a tough-as-nails reputation in the business world. He derived great pleasure from wheeling and dealing and outwitting competitors. Yet she'd seen the same self-satisfied look on his face after pulling off a multimillion-dollar business coup as she saw on it now as he outscored his daughter in a game of Scrabble.

He just loved life, with all its twists and turns. Perhaps Nathan was right about children inheriting more than eye color, and if she'd inherited that joie de vivre from her father, she was grateful.

"I love you, Daddy, even if you are a rotten cheat."

"I love you, too, Jackie." He beamed at the totals. "But

I'm not going to let that interfere with destroying you. Your turn, you know."

Folding up her legs, she propped her elbows and stared owlishly at her letters. The room was gracefully lit, the drapes yet to be drawn as sunset exploded in the eastern sky. The second parlor, as her mother insisted on calling it, was for family or informal gatherings, but it was a study in elegance and taste.

The rose-and-gray pattern of the Aubusson was picked up prettily in soft floor-length drapes and the upholstery of a curvy sofa. Her mother's prize collection of crystal had been moved out some years before when Jackie and Brandon had broken a candy dish while wrestling over some forgotten disagreement. Patricia had stubbornly left a few dainty pieces of porcelain.

There was a wide window seat in the east wall, where Jackie had hidden playing hide-and-seek as a child and dreamed of her latest crush as a teenager. She'd spent thousands of hours in that room, happy ones, furious ones, tearful ones. It was home. She hadn't fully understood or appreciated that until now.

"What's the matter with you, girl? Writers are supposed to have a way with words."

Her lips twitched a bit. J.D. had already fallen into the habit of calling her a writer several times a day. "Off my case, J.D."

"Hell of a way to talk to your father. Why, I ought to take a strap to you."

She grinned. "You and who else?"

He grinned back. He had a full, generous face with that oh-so-Irish ruddy skin. His eyes were a bright blue even through the glasses he had perched on his nose. He wore a suit because dressing for dinner was expected, but the vest was unbuttoned and the tie pulled crooked. A cigar was clamped between his big teeth, a cigar that Patricia tolerated in dignified silence.

Jackie pushed her letters around. "You know, Daddy, I've just began to think about it, but you and Mother, you're so different."

"Hmm?" He glanced up, distracted from the creative demands of inventing a new word.

"I mean, Mother is so elegant, so well-groomed."

"What am I, a slob?"

"Not exactly." When he frowned, she spread out her letters on the board. "There, *hyfoxal*."

"What the hell is this?" J.D. waved a blunt finger at the word. "No such thing."

"It's from the Latin for sly or cleverly adept. As in 'My father is well-known for his hyfoxal business dealings.'"

In answer, J.D. used a brief four-letter word that would have had his wife clucking her tongue. "Look it up," Jackie invited. "If you want to lose fifty points. Daddy," she said to distract him again, "how do you and Mother stay so happy?"

"I let her do what she does best, she lets me do what I do best. Besides, I'm crazy about the old prude."

"I know." Jackie felt her eyes fill with the tears that never seemed far away these days. "I've been thinking a lot lately about what you've both done for me and the boys. And loving each other might be the most important part of all."

"Jack, why don't you tell me what's on your mind?"

She shook her head but leaned over to stroke his cheek. "I just grew up this spring. Thought you'd like to know."

"And does growing up have anything to do with the man you're in love with?"

"Just about everything. Oh, you'd like him, Daddy. He's strong, sometimes too strong. He's kind and funny in the oddest sorts of ways. He likes me the way I am." The tears threatened again, and she put a hand to her eyes, pressing hard for a moment. "He makes lists for everything and always makes sure that *B* follows *A*. He, uh…" Letting out a long breath, she dropped her hands. "He's the kind of man who opens the door for you, not because he thinks it's the gentlemanly or proper thing to do, but because he is a gentleman. A very gentle man." She smiled again, her tears under control. "Mother would like him, too."

"Then what's the problem, Jackie?"

"He's just not ready for me or for the way we feel about each other. And I'm not sure how long I can wait for him to get ready."

J.D. frowned a moment. "Want me to give him a kick in the pants?"

That made her laugh. She was up and in his lap, her arms tight around him. "I'll let you know."

Patricia glided into the room, slim and pretty in a silk sheath the same pale blue as her eyes. "John, if the chef continues to throw these disgraceful temper tantrums, you're going to have to speak to him yourself. I'm at my wit's end." She went to the bar, poured a small glass of dry sherry, then settled in a chair. She crossed her legs, which her husband still considered the best on the East Coast, and sipped. "Jackie, I came across a new hairdresser last week. I'm convinced he could do wonders for you."

Jackie grinned and blew her hair out of her eyes. "I love you, Mother."

Instantly, and in the way Jackie had always adored, Patricia's eyes softened. "I love you too, darling. I meant to tell you that your tan is wonderfully flattering, particularly with your coloring, but after all I've been reading lately I'm worried about the long-term effects." Then she smiled in a way that made her look remarkably like her daughter. "It's good to have you home for a little while. The house is always too quiet without you and the boys."

"Won't be seeing too much of her now." J.D. gave her a fatherly pinch on the rump. "Now that she's a big-time author."

"It's only one book," she reminded him, then grinned. "So far."

"It did give me a great deal of satisfaction to mention, very casually, of course, to Honoria that you'd sold your manuscript to Harlequin Historicals." Patricia took a delicate sip as she settled back on the cushions.

"Casual?" J.D. gave a shout of laughter. "She couldn't wait to pick up the phone and brag. Hey, there, what do you think you're doing?"

Jackie turned back from her study of his letters. "Nothing." She gave him a loud kiss on the cheek. "You're doomed, you know. You're never going to be able to use that ridiculous collection."

"We'll see about that." J.D. dumped her off of his lap, then rubbed his palms together. "Sit down and shut up."

"John, really," Patricia said, in a tone that had Jackie running over to hug her. When the doorbell rang, Jackie straightened, but her mother waved her back. "Philip will get the door, Jacqueline. Do fix your hair."

Dutifully Jackie dragged her fingers through it as their graying butler came to the parlor entrance. "I beg your pardon, Mrs. MacNamara, but there's a Nathan Powell here to see Miss Jacqueline."

With a quick squeal, Jackie leaped forward. Her mother's firm command stopped her. "Jacqueline, sit down and pretend you're a lady. Philip will show the man in."

"But—"

"Sit down," J.D. told her. "And shut up."

"Quite," Patricia murmured, then nodded to Philip.

She sat with a thud.

"And I'd take that sulky look off your pointy face," her

father suggested. "Unless you want him to turn right around and leave again."

Jackie gritted her teeth, glared arrows at him, then settled down. Maybe they were right, she thought. Just this once, she'd look before she leaped. But when she saw him she would have been out of her chair in an instant if her father's foot hadn't stamped down on hers.

"Jack." There was something strained and husky about his voice, as though he hadn't spoken for days.

"Hello, Nathan." Pulling herself in, she rose easily and offered a hand. "I didn't expect you."

"No, I…" He felt suddenly and completely foolish standing there in a travel-stained suit with a brightly ribboned box under his arm. "I should have called."

"Of course not." As if there had never been any strain between them, or any passion, she tucked her arm through his. "I'd like you to meet my parents. J. D. and Patricia Mac-Namara, Nathan Powell."

J.D. shoved himself to his feet. He'd already made his assessment, and if he'd ever seen a more lovesick, frustrated man before, he couldn't bring it to mind. It was with both sympathy and interest that he offered a hand.

"Pleased to meet you. Admire your work." He shook his hand with a hefty pumping stroke. "Jack's told us all about you. I'll get you a drink."

Nathan managed to nod through these rapid-fire statements before turning to greet Jackie's mother. This was what she would look like in twenty or twenty-five years, Nathan realized with a jolt. Still lovely, with her skin clear as a bell and the grace that only years could add.

"Mrs. MacNamara, I apologize for dropping in on you like this."

"No need for that." But it pleased her that he had the manners to do so. She took stock in much the same way her husband had and saw a breeding and a kindness that she approved of. "Won't you sit down, Mr. Powell?"

"Well, I—"

"Here you are, nothing like a nice shot of whiskey to put hair on your chest." J.D. slapped him on the back as he offered the glass. "So you design buildings? Do any remodeling?"

"Yes, when there's—"

"Good, good. I'd like to talk to you about this building I'd had my eye on. Place is a mess, but it has potential. Now if I—"

"Excuse me." Forgetting his manners, Nathan shoved the glass back in J.D.'s hand and grabbed Jackie's arm. Without another word, he dragged her through the terrace doors he'd spotted.

"Well." Patricia raised both brows as if scandalized and hid her smile in her drink. J.D. merely hooted and downed the whiskey himself.

"Up to planning a wedding, Patty, old girl?"

The air was balmy and full of flowers. The stars were close enough to touch, vying with the moon for brilliance. Nathan noticed none of it as he stopped, dropped his package on a gleaming white table and hauled Jackie into his arms.

She fit perfectly.

"I'm sorry," he managed after a moment. "I was rude to your parents."

"That's all right. We often are." She lifted both hands to his face and studied him. "You look tired."

"No, I'm fine." He was anything but. Searching for lost control, he stepped back. "I wasn't sure you'd be here, either."

"Either?"

"You were gone when I got home, and then I tracked down your apartment, but you weren't there, either, so I came looking here."

Hoping she could take it slowly, she leaned back against the table. "You've been looking for me?"

"For a couple of days."

"I'm sorry. I didn't expect you back from Denver until next week. Your office certainly didn't."

"I came back sooner than— You called my office?"

"Yes. You came back sooner than what, Nathan?"

"Sooner than expected," he said with a snap. "I left Cody in charge, dumped the project in his lap and flew home. You'd gone. You'd left me."

She nearly flew at him, laughing, but decided to play it out. "Did you expect me to stay on?"

"Yes. No. Yes, damn it." He dragged both hands through his hair. "I know I hadn't any right to expect it, but I did. Then, when I got home, the house was empty. I hated it there without you. I can't think without you. That's your fault. You've done something to my brain." He'd begun to pace, which made her lift a brow. The Nathan she'd come to know rarely made unnecessary moves. "Every time I see something I wonder what you'd think about it, what you'd say. I couldn't even eat a blue plate special without thinking about you."

"That's really dreadful." She drew a breath. It needed to be asked. "Do you want me back, Nathan?"

There was fury in his eyes when he turned, a kind of vivid, blazing fury that made her want to launch herself into his arms again. "Do you want me to crawl?"

"Let me think about it." She touched the bow on the package, wondering what was inside. Wondering was almost as good as knowing. "You deserve to crawl a bit, but I don't have the heart for it." She smiled at him, her hands folded neatly. "I hadn't gone anywhere, Nathan."

"You'd cleared out. The place was tidy as a tomb."

"Didn't you look in the closet?"

Impatience shimmered, then stilled. "What do you mean?"

"I mean, I hadn't left. My clothes are still in the guest room. I couldn't sleep in your bed without you, so I moved, but I didn't leave." She touched his face again, gently. "I had no intention of letting you ruin your life."

He grabbed her hand as if it were a lifeline. "Then why are you here and not there?"

"I wanted to see my parents. Partly because of the things you'd told me. It made me realize I needed to see them, to thank them somehow for being as wonderful as they are. And partly because I wanted to tell them I'd finally done something from beginning to end." Her fingers curved nervously over his. "I sold my book."

"Sold it? I didn't know you'd sent it in."

"I didn't want to tell you. I didn't want you to be disappointed in me if it didn't work."

"I wouldn't have been." He drew her close. Her scent, so needed, was all around him. It was only then that he understood that you could come home even without the familiar walls. "I'm happy for you. I'm proud of you. I wish... I wish I'd been here."

"This is something I had to do, this first time, by myself." She shifted back, not out of his arms, but circled by them. "I'd like you to be around the next time."

His fingers tensed on the back of her waist, and his eyes went dark. Jake's look, she thought yet again, giddy with love for him. "It's that easy? All I had to do was walk in and ask?"

"That's all you've ever had to do."

"I don't deserve you."

She smiled. "I know."

With a laugh, he swung her in a circle, then brought her down to crush his lips to hers in a long, breathless kiss. "I came prepared to make all kinds of offers and promises. You aren't going to ask for any."

"That's not to say I wouldn't like to hear them." She laid her head on his shoulder. "Why don't you tell me what you've got in mind?"

"I want you, but I want it to be right. No long separations, no broken promises. I'm doing something I should have done a year ago and making Cody a partner."

When she drew her head back, he noticed that her eyes could be as shrewd as her father's. "That's an excellent decision."

"A personal one, as well as a business one. I'm learning, Jack."

"I can see that."

"Between the two of us, the pressure will lighten enough to make it possible to start a family, a real family. I don't know what kind of husband I'll make, or father, but—"

She touched her fingers to his lips. "We'll find out together."

"Yes." Reaching up, he took her hands again. "I'll still have to travel some, but I hope you'll agree to come with me whenever you can."

"Just try to stop me."

"And you'll be there to make certain I don't forget that marriage and family come first."

She turned her face into his throat. "You can count on it."

"I'm doing this backward. I do that a lot since I met you." He ran his hands down her arms, then drew her away. "I wanted to tell you that since I found you everything changed for me. Losing you would be worse than losing my eyes or my arms, because without you I can't see or touch anything. I need you in my life, I want you to share it all with me. We can learn from each other, make mistakes together, and I love you more than I know how to say."

"I think you said it very nicely." She sniffled, then shook her head. "I don't want to cry. I look really awful when I cry, and I want to be beautiful tonight. Let me have my present, will you, before I start babbling?"

"I like it when you babble." He pressed a kiss to her brow, to her temple, to the dimple at the corner of her mouth. "Oh, God, I do owe cousin Fred."

Jackie gave a watery laugh. "He's trying to find a buyer for twenty-five acres of swampland."

"Sold." He caught her face in his hands again, just to look, just to touch what was more real to him than his own heart. "I do love you, Jack."

"I know, but you can repeat yourself all you want."

"I intend to, but first I think you should have this." He picked up the package and offered it to her. "I wanted you to have something that would show you, if I couldn't make myself clear, how I felt about you. How you'd given me hope for a future I never believed in."

She dragged the heels of her hands under her eyes. "Well, let's see. Diamonds are forever, but I've always had a fondness for colored stones." She ripped at the paper ruthlessly, then pulled out her gift.

For a moment she was speechless, standing in the moonlight, her cheeks still gleaming with tears. In her hands was a shell-covered pelican. When she looked at him again, her eyes were drenched. "Nobody understands me the way you do."

"Don't change," he murmured, holding her close again with the tacky bird between them. "Let's go home, Jack."

* * * * *

BEST LAID PLANS

For Bruce,
who knows how to build and make it last.

Chapter 1

She was definitely worth a second look.

There were more reasons—more basic reasons—than the fact that she was one of the few women on the building site. It was human nature for a man's eyes to be lured by the female form, especially when it was found in what was still predominantly a man's domain. True, a good many women donned hard hats to work construction, and as long as they could hammer a nail or lay a brick it didn't matter to Cody how they buttoned their shirts. But there was something about this particular woman that pulled his gaze back.

Style. Though she wore work clothes and stood on a mound of debris, she had it. Confidence, he mused as he rocked back on the worn heels of his boots. He supposed confidence was its own brand of style. It appealed to him as much—well, nearly as much—as black lace or white silk.

He didn't have the time to sit and speculate, though. He'd been almost a week late making the trip from Florida to Arizona to take over this project, and there was a lot of catching up to do. The morning was a busy one, with plenty of distractions: the noise of men and machines; orders being shouted and followed; cranes lifting heavy metal beams to form the skeleton of a building where there had been only rock and dirt; the vivid color of that rock and dirt under the white sun; even his own growing thirst. But he didn't mind distractions.

Cody had spent enough time on building sites to be able to look beyond the rubble, through what to the uninitiated might seem like confusion or even destruction. He saw instead the sweat, the strain, the thought and the possibilities.

But just now he found himself watching the woman. There were possibilities there, as well.

She was tall, he noted, five-nine or five-ten in her work boots, and lean rather than slender. Her shoulders looked strong under a dandelion-yellow T-shirt that was dark with sweat down the back. As an architect, he appreciated clean, economical lines. As a man, he appreciated the way her worn jeans fit snugly over her hips. Beneath a hard hat as bright as her shirt was a thick short braid the color of polished mahogany—one of his favorite woods to work with because of its beauty and richness.

He pushed his sunglasses farther up on his nose as the eyes behind them scanned her from hard hat to boot tip. Definitely worth a second look, he thought again, admiring the way she moved, with no wasted gestures as she leaned over to look through a surveyor's transit. There was a faint white outline worn into her back pocket, where he imagined she tucked her wallet. A practical woman, he decided. A purse would get in the way on the site.

She didn't have a redhead's pale, fragile complexion, but a warm, golden tan that probably came from the blistering

Arizona sun. Wherever it came from, he approved, just as he approved of the long, somewhat sharp angles of her face. Her tough-looking chin was offset by elegant cheekbones, and both were balanced by a soft, unpainted mouth that was even now turning down.

He couldn't see her eyes because of the distance and the shade from the brim of her hat, but her voice as she called out an order was clear enough. It sounded more appropriate for quiet, misty nights than for sweaty afternoons.

Tucking his thumbs in the pockets of his jeans, he grinned. Yes, indeed, there were endless possibilities.

Unaware of his study, Abra continued to frown as she swiped an arm over her damp brow. The sun was merciless today. At 8:00 a.m., it was already blistering. Sweat rolled down her back, evaporated, then rolled again in a cycle she had learned to live with.

You could only move so fast in this heat, she thought. You could only haul so much metal and chip so much rock when the temperature hovered in the nineties. Even with water barrels filled and salt tablets dispensed, every day was a struggle to stay ahead of the clock. So far they were pulling it off, but... There couldn't be any buts, she reminded herself. The construction of this resort was the biggest thing she'd been involved with in her career, and she wasn't going to mess it up. It was her springboard.

Though she could have murdered Tim Thornway for tying Thornway Construction, and her, to such a tightly scheduled project. The penalty clauses were outrageous, and in the way Tim had of delegating he'd put the responsibility for avoiding them squarely on her shoulders.

Abra straightened as if she could actually feel the weight. It would take a miracle to bring the project in on time and under budget. Since she didn't believe in miracles, she accepted the long hours and hard days ahead. The resort would be built, and built on time, if she had to pick up hammer and saw herself. But this was the last time, she promised herself as she watched a steel girder rise majestically into place. After this project she was cutting her ties with Thornway and striking out on her own.

She owed them for giving her a shot, for having enough faith in her to let her fight her way up from assistant to structural engineer. It wasn't something she'd forget—not now, not ever. But her loyalty had been to Thomas Thornway. Now that he was gone, she was doing her best to see that Tim didn't run the business into the ground. But she'd be damned if she was going to baby-sit him for the rest of her career.

She took a moment to wish for one of the cold drinks stashed in the cooler, then picked her way around and over the rubble of construction to supervise the placing of the beams.

Charlie Gray, the ever-eager assistant Cody had found himself stuck with, all but tugged at his shirt. "Want me to tell Ms. Wilson you're here?" Cody tried to remember that he, too, had once been twenty-two and annoying.

"Got her hands full at the moment." Cody pulled out his cigarettes, then searched through two pockets before he found some matches. They were from some little hotel in Natchez and were damp with his own sweat.

"Mr. Thornway wanted you to get together."

Cody's lips curved a little. He'd just been thinking that it wouldn't be such a hardship to get together with Abra Wilson. "We'll get around to it." He struck a match, automatically curling his fingers around the flame, though there wasn't a breath of wind.

"You missed yesterday's meeting, so—"

"Yeah." The fact that he'd missed the meeting wouldn't cause him to lose any sleep. The design for the resort was Cody's, but when family problems had cropped up his partner had handled most of the preliminary work. Looking back at Abra, Cody began to think that was a shame.

There was a trailer parked a few yards away. Cody headed for it, with Charlie scrambling to keep up with him. He pulled a beer from a cooler, then pried the top off as he walked inside, where portable fans battled the heat. The temperature dropped a few precious degrees.

"I want to take a look at the plans for the main building again."

"Yes, sir, I have them right here." Like a good soldier, Charlie produced the tube of blueprints, then practically stood at attention. "At the meeting—" he cleared his throat "—Ms. Wilson pointed out a few changes she wanted made. From an engineering standpoint."

"Did she now?" Unconcerned, Cody propped himself on the thin, narrow cushions of the convertible couch. The sun had mercifully faded the vivid orange-and-green upholstery to a nearly inoffensive blur. He glanced around for an ashtray and settled on an empty cup, then unrolled the blueprints.

He liked the look of it, the feel of it. The building would be dome-shaped, topped by stained glass at the apex. Floors of offices would circle a center atrium, giving a sense of open, unstructured space. Breathing room, he thought. What was the use of coming west if you didn't have room to take a breath? Each office would have thick tinted glass to hold out the brilliance of the sun while affording an unhampered view of the resort and the mountains.

On the ground level the lobby would curve in a half circle, making it easily accessible from the entrance, from the double-level bar and the glassed-in coffee shop.

Patrons could take the glass elevators or the winding staircase up a floor to dine in one of three restaurants, or they could venture a bit higher and explore one of the lounges.

Cody took a long swallow of his beer as he looked it over. He saw in it a sense of fantasy, even of humor, and more basically a marriage of the modern with the ancient. No, he couldn't see anything in his basic design that needed changing, or that he'd allow to be changed.

Abra Wilson, he thought, was going to have to grin and bear it.

When he heard the door of the trailer open, he glanced over. She was even better close up, Cody decided as Abra stepped inside. A little sweaty, a little dusty and, from the looks of her, a lot mad.

He was right about the mad. Abra had enough to do without having to chase down errant laborers taking un-scheduled breaks. "What the hell are you doing in here?" she demanded as Cody lifted the can to his lips again. "We need everyone out there." She snatched the beer away be-fore Cody could swallow. "Thornway isn't paying you to sit on your butt, and nobody on this project drinks on the job." She set the beer on the counter before she could be tempted to soothe her own dry throat with it.

"Ms. Wilson—"

"What?" Her patience in tatters, she turned on Charlie. "Oh, it's Mr. Gray, right? Hold on a minute." First things first, she thought as she rubbed her damp cheek against the sticky sleeve of her shirt. "Listen, pal," she said to Cody, "unless you want your walking papers, get yourself up and report to your foreman."

He grinned insolently at her. Abra felt reckless, unprofessional words bubble to her lips and battled them back with what control she had left. Just as she battled back the urge to jam her fist into his cocky chin.

A good-looking sonofa— She caught herself there, as well. Men with those kind of rough-and-ready looks always thought they could smile their way out of trouble—and they usually could. Not with her, though, Abra reminded herself. Still, it wouldn't do any good to threaten a union employee.

"You're not allowed in here." Frustrated, she bit the words off and snatched up the blueprints. Maybe if the morning had gone more smoothly she wouldn't have been ready to bite someone's—anyone's—head off. But he was in the wrong place at the wrong time. "And you certainly have no business poking around in these." She wondered what color his eyes were behind his dark glasses. If for no other reason than his continued grin, she would have been delighted to blacken them.

"Ms. Wilson…" Charlie said again, desperately.

"What, damn it?" She shook off his hand even as she reminded herself to be polite. The devil with polite, she thought. She was hot, tired, frustrated and delighted to have a target. "Have you got that illustrious architect of yours out of his hot tub yet, Gray? Thornway's interested in seeing this project move on schedule."

"Yes, you see—"

"Just a minute." Cutting him off again, she turned to Cody again. "Look, I told you to move. You speak English, don't you?"

"Yes, ma'am."

"Then move."

He did, but not as she'd expected. Lazily, like a cat stretching before it jumps off a windowsill, he unfolded his body. It appeared that most of him was leg. He didn't look like a man afraid of losing his job as he sidled between the table and the sofa, plucking his beer from the counter. He took a long, easy sip, leaned against the compact refrigerator and grinned at her again.

"You're a tall one, aren't you, Red?"

Barely, just barely, she caught herself before her mouth fell open. Building might still be primarily a man's trade, but no one Abra worked with had the nerve to be condescending. At least not to her face. He was out, she told herself. Schedule or no schedule, union or no union, she was going to issue him his walking papers personally.

"Find your lunch bucket, get in your pickup and make tracks, jerk." She snatched his beer again, and this time she poured the contents on his head. Fortunately for Cody, there was only a swallow left. "File that with your union representative."

"Ms. Wilson…" Charlie's face had gone bone white, and his voice was shaking. "You don't understand."

"Take a walk, Charlie." Cody's voice was mild as he lifted a hand to tunnel his fingers through his damp hair.

"But…but…"

"Out."

"Yes, sir." More than willing to desert a sinking ship, Charlie fled. Because he did, and because he'd called the lanky, pretty-faced cowboy "sir," Abra began to suspect that she'd taken a wrong turn down a blind alley. Automatically her eyes narrowed and her shoulders tensed.

"I don't guess we've been introduced." Cody drew his shaded glasses off. She saw that his eyes were brown, a soft, golden brown. They weren't lit with anger or embarrassment. Rather, they assessed her with a flat neutrality. "I'm Cody Johnson. Your architect."

She could have babbled. She could have apologized. She could have laughed off the incident and offered him another beer. All three options occurred to her but, because of his calm, unblinking stare, were rejected. "Nice of you to stop by," she said instead.

A tough one, he decided, despite the hazel eyes and the sultry mouth. Well, he'd cracked tough ones before. "If I'd known what a warm reception I'd get, I'd have been here sooner."

"Sorry, we had to let the brass band go." Because she wanted to salvage her pride, she started to move past him, and discovered quickly that if she wanted to get to the door, the sofa or anywhere else she'd have to move through him. She didn't question why the prospect appealed to her. He was an obstacle, and obstacles were meant to be knocked down. An angling of her chin, very slight, was all she needed to keep her eyes level with his.

"Questions?" she asked him.

"Oh, a few." Like who do I have to kill to have you? Does your chin really take a punch as well as you think? And since when is a hard hat sexy? "Do you always pour beer on your men?"

"Depends on the man." Leaving it at that, she started by him again—and found herself lodged between him and the refrigerator. He'd only had to turn to accomplish it. He took a moment, keeping his eyes on hers. He didn't see fear or discomfort in them, only a spitting fury that made him want to grin again. So he did.

"Close quarters in here… *Ms.* Wilson."

She might be an engineer, she might be a professional who had come up the hard way and knew the ropes, but she was still a woman, and very much aware of the press of his body against hers, the hard line of hip, the solid length of thigh. Whatever her reaction might have been, the glint of amusement in his eyes erased it.

"Are those teeth yours?" she asked calmly.

He lifted a brow. "Last time I checked."

"If you want to keep it that way, back off."

He would have liked to kiss her then, as much in appreciation for her guts as in desire for her taste. Though he was often impulsive, he also knew when to change tactics and take the long route. "Yes, ma'am."

When he moved aside, she slipped past him. She would have preferred to walk through the door and keep going, but she sat on the sofa and spread the prints out again. "I assume that Gray filled you in on the meeting you missed?"

"Yeah." He slid behind the table and sat down. As he'd said, the quarters were close. For the second time, their thighs brushed, denim against denim, muscle against muscle. "You wanted some changes."

She shouldn't be defensive. It did no good to be defensive. She couldn't help it. "I've had a problem with the basic design from the beginning, Mr. Johnson. I made no secret of it."

"I've seen the correspondence." Stretching out his legs was a bit of a trick in such cramped quarters, but he managed it. "You wanted standard desert architecture."

Her eyes narrowed fractionally, and he caught the glint. "I don't recall the word *standard* coming up, but there are good reasons for the style of architecture in this region."

"There are also good reasons for trying something new, don't you think?" He said it easily as he lit another cigarette. "Barlow and Barlow want the ultimate resort," he continued before she could comment. "Totally self-contained, and exclusive enough to draw in big bucks from the clientele. They wanted a different look, a different mood, from what can be found in the resorts sprinkled around Phoenix. That's what I'm giving them."

"With a few modifications—"

"No changes, *Ms.* Wilson."

She nearly ground her teeth. Not only was he being pig-headed—a typical architect—but it infuriated her the way he drew out "Ms." in that sarcastic drawl. "For some reason," she began calmly, "we've been unfortunate enough to have been chosen to work together on this."

"Must have been fate," he murmured.

She let that pass. "I'm going to tell you up front, Mr. Johnson, that from an engineering standpoint your design stinks."

He dragged on his cigarette, letting the smoke escape in a slow stream. She had amber flecks in her eyes, he noted. Eyes that couldn't make up their mind whether they wanted to be gray or green. Moody eyes. He smiled into them. "That's your problem. If you're not good enough, Thornway can assign someone else."

Her fingers curled into her palms. The idea of stuffing the plans down his throat had a certain appeal, but she reminded herself that she was committed to this project. "I'm good enough, Mr. Johnson."

"Then we shouldn't have any problems." He crossed his booted ankles. The noise from the site was steady. A productive sound, Cody had always thought. He didn't find it intrusive as he studied the woman across from him. It helped remind him that there was a time for business and a time for... pleasure.

"Why don't you fill me in on the progress?"

It wasn't her job. She almost snapped that at him. But she was tied to a contract, one that didn't leave much margin for error. By God, she'd pay her debt to Thornway, even if it meant working hand in glove with some overconfident, high-flying East Coast architect. She pushed the hard hat back on her head but didn't relax.

"As you've probably seen, the blasting went on schedule. Fortunately, we were able to keep it to a minimum and preserve the integrity of the landscape."

"That was the idea."

"Was it?" She glanced at the prints, then back at him. "In any case, we'll have the frame of the main building completed by the end of the week. If no changes are made—"

"None will be."

"If no changes are made," she repeated between clenched teeth, "we'll meet the first contract deadline. Work on the individual cabanas won't begin until the main building and the health center are under roof. The golf course and tennis courts aren't my province, so you'll have to discuss them with Kendall. That also goes for the landscaping."

"Fine. Do you know if the tiles for the lobby have been ordered?"

"I'm an engineer, not a purchaser. Marie Lopez handles supplies."

"I'll keep that in mind. Question."

Rather than give him a go-ahead nod, she rose and opened the refrigerator. It was stockpiled with sodas, juices and bottled water. Taking her time with her selection, she opted for the water. She was thirsty, she told herself. The move didn't have anything to do with wanting to put some distance between them. That was just a side benefit. Though she knew it was nasty, she screwed the top off the bottle and drank without offering him any.

"What?"

"Is it because I'm a man, an architect or an Easterner?"

Abra took another long sip. It only took a day in the sun

to make you realize that paradise could be found in a bottle of water. "You'll have to clarify that."

"Is it because I'm a man, an architect or an Easterner that makes you want to spit in my eye?"

She wouldn't have been annoyed by the question itself, not in the least. But he grinned while he asked. After less than an hour's acquaintance, she'd already damned him a half-dozen times for that smile. Still, she leaned back against the counter, crossed her own ankles and considered him.

"I don't give a damn about your sex."

He continued to grin, but something quick and dangerous came into his eyes. "You like waving red flags at bulls, Wilson?"

"Yes." It was her turn to smile. Though the curving of her lips softened her mouth, it did nothing to dim the flash of challenge in her eyes. "But to finish my answer— architects are often pompous, temperamental artists who put their egos on paper and expect engineers and builders to preserve it for posterity. I can live with that. I can even respect it—when the architect takes a good, hard look at the environment and creates with it rather than for himself. As for you being an Easterner, that might be the biggest problem. You don't understand the desert, the mountains, the heritage of this land. I don't like the idea of you sitting under an orange tree two thousand miles away and deciding what people here are going to live with."

Because he was more interested in her than in defending himself, he didn't mention that he had made three trips to the site months before. Most of the design work had been done almost where he was sitting now, rather than back at his home base. He had a vision, but he was a man who drew and built his visions more than a man who spoke of them.

"If you don't want to build, why do you?"

"I didn't say I didn't want to build," she said. "I've never thought it necessary to destroy in order to do so."

"Every time you put a shovel in the ground you take away some land. That's life."

"Every time you take away some land you should think hard about what you're going to give back. That's morality."

"An engineer *and* a philosopher." He was baiting her, and he knew it. Even as he watched, angry color rose to her cheeks. "Before you pour that over my head, let's say I agree with you—to a point. But we're not putting up neon and plastic here. Whether you agree with my design or not, it is my design. It's your job to put it together."

"I know what my job is."

"Well, then." As if dismissing the disagreement, Cody began to roll up the plans. "How about dinner?"

"I beg your pardon?"

"Dinner," he repeated. When the prints were rolled up, he slid them into their cylinder and rose. "I'd like to have dinner with you."

Abra wasn't sure it was the most ridiculous statement she'd ever heard, but it certainly ranked in the top ten. "No thanks."

"You're not married?" That would have mattered.

"No."

"Involved?" That wouldn't have.

Patience wasn't her strong suit. Abra didn't bother to dig for it. "None of your business."

"You've got a quick trigger, Red." He picked up his hard hat but didn't put it on. "I like that."

"You've got nerve, Johnson. I don't like that." She moved to the door, pausing just a moment with her hand on the

knob. "If you have any questions that deal with the construction, I'll be around."

He didn't have to move much to put a hand on her shoulder. Under his palm he felt her coil up like a cat ready to spring. "So will I," he reminded her. "We'll have dinner some other time. I figure you owe me a beer."

After one self-satisfied glance at the top of his head, Abra stepped out into the sun.

He certainly wasn't what she'd been expecting. He was attractive, but she could handle that. When a woman took root in male territory, she was bound to come into contact with an attractive man from time to time. Still, he looked more like one of her crew than a partner in one of the country's top architectural firms. His dark blond hair, with its sun-bleached tips, was worn too long for the nine-to-five set, and his rangy build held ripples of muscle under the taut, tanned skin. His broad, callused hands were those of a workingman. She moved her shoulders as if shrugging off the memory of his touch. She'd felt the strength, the roughness and the appeal of those hands. Then there was that voice, that slow take-your-time drawl.

She settled the hard hat more securely as she approached the steel skeleton of the building. Some women would have found that voice appealing. She didn't have time to be charmed by a southern drawl or a cocky grin. She didn't, when it came right down to it, have much time to think of herself as a woman.

He'd made her feel like one.

Scowling against the sun, she watched beams being riveted into place. She didn't care for Cody Johnson's ability to make her feel feminine. "Feminine" too often meant "defenseless" and "dependent." Abra had no intention of being either of those. She'd worked too hard and too long

at self-sufficiency. A couple of...flutters, she decided, just flutters...weren't going to affect her.

She wished the can of beer had been full.

With a grim smile she watched the next beam swing into place. There was something beautiful about watching a building grow. Piece by piece, level by level. It had always fascinated her to watch something strong and useful take shape—just as it had always disturbed her to see the land marred by progress. She'd never been able to resolve that mixture of feelings, and it was because of that that she'd chosen a field that allowed her to have a part in seeing that progress was made with integrity.

But this one... She shook her head as the sound of riveting guns split the air. This one struck her as an outsider's fantasy, the domed shape, the curves and spirals. She'd spent countless nights at her drawing board with slide rule and calculator, struggling to come up with a satisfactory support system. Architects didn't worry about mundane matters like that, she thought. It was all aesthetics with them. All ego. She'd build the damn thing, she thought, kicking some debris out of her way. She'd build it and build it well. But she didn't have to like it.

With the sun baking her back, she bent over the transit. They'd had the mountain to deal with, and an uneven bed of rock and sand, but the measurements and placement were right on. She felt a tug of pride as she checked angles and degrees. Inappropriate or not, the structure was going to be perfectly engineered.

That was important—being perfect. Most of her life she'd had to deal with second best. Her education, her training and her skill had lifted her beyond that. She had no intention of ever settling for second best again, not for herself, and not in her work.

She caught his scent and felt the light tickle of aware-
ness at the back of her neck. Soap and sweat, she thought,
and had to fight not to shift uncomfortably. Everybody on
the site smelled of soap and sweat, so why was she certain
Cody was behind her? She only knew she was certain, and
she determinedly remained bent over the eyepiece.

"Problem?" she said, pleased with the disdain she was
able to put into the single word.

"I don't know until I look. Do you mind?"

She took her time before stepping back. "Be my guest."

When he moved forward, she hooked her thumbs in her
back pockets and waited. He'd find no discrepancies—even
if he knew enough to recognize one. Hearing a shout, she
glanced over to see two members of the crew arguing. The
heat, she knew, had a nasty way of bringing tempers to a
boil. Leaving Cody to his survey, she strode across the
broken ground.

"It's a little early for a break," she said calmly as one
crewman grabbed the other by the shirtfront.

"This sonofabitch nearly took my fingers off with that
beam."

"If this idiot doesn't know when to get out of the way,
he deserves to lose a few fingers."

Neither man had much on her in height, but they were
burly, sweaty and on the edge. Without thinking twice,
she stepped between them as fists were raised. "Cool off,"
she ordered.

"I don't have to take that sh—"

"You may not have to take his," Abra said levelly, "but
you have to take mine. Now cool off or take a walk." She
looked from one angry face to the other. "If you two want
to beat each other senseless when you're off the clock, be
my guest, but either of you takes a swing on my time, you're

unemployed. You." She pointed to the man she judged the more volatile of the two. "What's your name?"

The dark-haired man hesitated briefly, then spit out, "Rodriguez."

"Well, Rodriguez, go take a break and pour some water over your head." She turned away as if she had no doubts about his immediate obedience. "And you?"

The second man was ruddy and full-faced and was smirking. "Swaggart."

"Okay, Swaggart, get back to work. And I'd have a little more respect for my partner's hands if I were you, unless you want to count your own fingers and come up short."

Rodriguez snorted at that but did as he was told and moved away toward the water barrels. Satisfied, Abra signaled to the foreman and advised him to keep the men apart for a few days.

She'd nearly forgotten about Cody by the time she turned and saw him. He was still standing by the transit, but he wasn't looking through it. Legs spread, hands resting lightly on his hips, he was watching her. When she didn't make a move toward him, he made one toward her.

"You always step into the middle of a brawl?"

"When it's necessary."

He tipped his shaded glasses down to study her, then scooted them up again. "Ever get that chip knocked off your shoulder?"

She couldn't have said why she had to fight back a grin, but she managed to. "Not yet."

"Good. Maybe I'll be the first."

"You can try, but you'd be better off concentrating on this project. More productive."

He smiled slowly, and the angles of his face shifted with

the movement. "I can concentrate on more than one thing at a time. How about you?"

Instead of answering, she took out a bandanna and wiped the back of her neck. "You know, Johnson, your partner seemed like a sensible man."

"Nathan *is* sensible." Before she could stop him, he took the bandanna from her and dabbed at her temples. "He saw you as a perfectionist."

"And what are you?" She had to resist the urge to grab the cloth back. There was something soothing, a little too soothing, in his touch.

"You'll have to judge that for yourself." He glanced back at the building. The foundation was strong, the angles were clear, but it was just the beginning. "We're going to be working together for some time yet."

She, too, glanced toward the building. "I can take it if you can." Now she did take the bandanna back, stuffing it casually in her back pocket.

"Abra." He said her name as if he were experimenting with a taste. "I'm looking forward to it." She jolted involuntarily when he brushed a thumb down her cheek. Pleased with the reaction, he grinned. "See you around."

Jerk, she thought again as she stomped across the rubble and tried to ignore the tingling along her skin.

Chapter 2

If there was one thing she didn't need, Abra thought a few days later, it was to be pulled off the job and into a meeting. She had mechanics working on the main building, riveters working on the health club, and a running feud between Rodriguez and Swaggart to deal with. It wasn't as though those things couldn't be handled without her—it was simply that they could be handled better with her. And here she was cooling her heels in Tim's office waiting for him to show up.

She didn't have to be told how tight the schedule was. Damn it, she knew what she had to do to see that the contract was brought in on time. She knew all about time.

Her every waking moment was devoted to this job. Each day was spent sweating out on the site with the crews and the supervisors, dealing with details as small as the delivery of rivets. At night she either tumbled into bed at sundown or worked until three, fueled by coffee and ambition, over her drawing board. The project was hers, hers more than it could ever be Tim Thornway's. It had become personal, in a way she could never have explained. For her, it was a tribute to the man who had had enough faith in her to push her to try for more than second best. In a way, it was her last job for Thomas Thornway, and she wanted it to be perfect.

It didn't help to have an architect who demanded materials that made cost overruns and shipping delays inevitable. Despite him and his marble sinks and his oversize ceramic tiles, she was going to pull it off. If she wasn't constantly being dragged into the office for endless meetings.

Impatient, she paced to the window and back again. Time was wasting, and there were few things that annoyed her more than waste of any kind. If she hadn't had a specific point to bring up to Tim, she would have found a way to avoid the meeting altogether. The one good thing about Tim, she thought with a humorless smile, was that he wasn't really bright enough to recognize double-talk. In this case, she wanted to make the pitch herself, so she'd come. But— she glanced at her watch—she wasn't going to twiddle her thumbs much longer.

This had been Thornway's office. She'd always liked the cool, authoritative colors and the lack of frills. Since Tim had taken over, he'd made some changes. Plants, she thought, scowling at a ficus. It wasn't that she disliked plants and thick, splashy pillows, but it annoyed her to find them here.

Then there were the paintings. Thornway had preferred Indian paintings and landscapes. Tim had replaced them with abstracts that tended to jar Abra's nerves. The new carpet seemed three inches thick and was salmon-colored. The elder Thornway had used a short-napped buff so that the dust and dirt wouldn't show. But then, Tim didn't often visit the sites or ask his foremen to join him for an after-hours drink.

Stop it, Abra ordered herself. Tim ran things differently, and that was his privilege. It was his business in every way. The fact that she had loved and admired the father so much didn't mean she had to find fault with the son.

But she did find fault with him, she thought as she studied the tidy, polished surface of his desk. He lacked both the drive and the compassion that had been so much a part of his father. Thornway had wanted to build first for the love of building. With Tim, the profit margin was the bottom line.

If Thomas Thornway had still been alive, she wouldn't have been preparing to make a break. There was a certain freedom in that, in knowing that this current project would be her last for the company. There would be no regrets in leaving, as there might once have been. Instead, there was excitement, anticipation. Whatever happened next, she would be doing it for herself.

Terrifying, she thought, closing her eyes. The idea was as terrifying as it was compelling. All unknowns were. Like Cody Johnson.

Catching herself, she walked back to the window. That was ridiculous. He was neither terrifying nor compelling. Nor was he an unknown. He was just a man—a bit of a pest, with the way he kept popping up on the site. He was the kind of man who knew he was a pleasure to look at and exploited it. The kind who always had a line, an angle and an escape route.

She'd seen men like Cody operate before. Looking back, Abra considered herself lucky that she'd only fallen for a pretty face and a smooth line once. Some women never learned and kept walking blindly into the trap again and again. Her mother was one, Abra thought with a shake of her head. Jessie Wilson would have taken one look at a man like Cody and taken the plunge. Thank God, in this way it was not "like mother like daughter."

As for herself, Abra wasn't interested in Cody Johnson personally and could barely tolerate him professionally.

When he walked in seconds later, she wondered why her thoughts and her feelings didn't seem to jibe.

"Abra, sorry to keep you waiting." Tim, trim in a three-piece suit, offered her a hearty smile. "Lunch ran a bit over."

She only lifted a brow. This meeting in the middle of the day had caused her to miss her lunch altogether. "I'm more interested in why you called me in from the field."

"Thought we needed a little one-on-one." He settled comfortably behind his desk and gestured for both her and Cody to sit.

"You've seen the reports."

"Absolutely." He tapped a finger on a file. He had a nice, engaging grin that suited his round face. More than once Abra had thought he'd have done well in politics. If anyone knew how to answer a question without committing himself, it was Tim Thornway. "Efficient, as always. I'm having a dinner meeting with Barlow senior this evening. I'd like to give him something more than facts and figures."

"You can give him my objections to the interior layout of the main building." She crossed her ankles and spared Cody the briefest glance. Tim began to fiddle with one of his monogrammed pens.

"I thought we'd settled all that."

Abra merely shrugged. "You asked. You can tell him that the wiring should be completed on the main structure by the end of the week. It's a tricky process, given the size and shape of the building. And it's going to cost his company a fortune to cool."

"He has a fortune," Cody commented. "I believe they're more interested in style than saving on the electric bill."

"Indeed." Tim cleared his throat. The way things stood, the Barlow project was going to bring him a tidy profit. He wanted to keep it that way. "Of course, I've looked over the specs and can assure our client that he's receiving only the best in materials and in brainpower."

"I'd suggest you tell him to come see for himself," Abra said.

"Well, I don't think—"

Cody cut in. "I agree with Ms. Wilson. Better he should buck now about something that doesn't suit him than buck later, after it's in concrete."

Tim frowned and backpedaled. "The plans have been approved."

"Things look different on paper," Cody said, looking at Abra. "Sometimes people are surprised by the finished product."

"Naturally, I'll suggest it." Tim tapped his pen on his spotless blotter. "Abra, you have a suggestion in your report about extending the lunch break to an hour."

"Yes, I wanted to talk with you about that. After a few weeks on the site I've seen that until and unless we get some relief in the weather the men are going to need a longer break at midday."

Tim set down the pen and folded his hands. "You have to understand what a thirty-minute extension means in terms of overall time and money."

"You have to understand that men can't work in that sun without a reasonable reprieve. Chugging salt tablets isn't enough. It may be March, and it may be cool inside when you're having your second martini, but out there it's a killer."

"These men get paid to sweat," Tim reminded her. "And I think you can only agree that they'll be better off to have the buildings under roof by summer."

"They can't build if they drop from heat exhaustion or sunstroke."

"I don't believe I've had any reports of that happening."

"Not yet." It would be a miracle if she held on to her temper. He'd always been pompous, she thought. When he'd been a junior executive she'd been able to skirt him and go straight to the top. Now he *was* the top. Abra gritted her teeth and tried again. "Tim, they need the extra time off. Working out in that sun drains you. You get weak, you get sloppy, then you make mistakes—dangerous mistakes."

"I pay a foreman to see that no one makes mistakes."

Abra was on her feet and ready to explode when Cody's calm voice cut in. "You know, Tim, men tend to stretch out breaks in the heat in any case. You give them an extra thirty minutes, makes them feel good—obliged, even. Most of them won't be as liable to take more. You end up getting the same amount of work and good PR."

Tim ran his pen through his fingers. "Makes sense. I'll keep it in mind."

"You do that." With an easy smile, he rose. "I'm going to hitch a ride back to the site with Ms. Wilson. Then we can discuss that idea about our working more closely together. Thanks for lunch, Tim."

"Any time, any time."

Before Abra could speak, Cody had her by the elbow and was leading her out. They were in front of the elevators before she managed to jerk away. "I don't need to be shown the way," she said through clenched teeth.

"Well, *Ms.* Wilson, looks like we disagree again." He strolled into the elevator with her, then punched the button for the parking garage. "In my opinion, you could definitely use some guidance—in how to handle birdbrains."

"I don't need you to…" She let her words trail off, glancing over at his face. The hint of amusement in his eyes matched the reluctant smile in hers. "I assume you're referring to Tim."

"Did I say that?"

"I have to assume you were—unless you were talking about yourself."

"Take your choice."

"That leaves me with a tough decision." The elevator shuddered slightly when it reached the parking level. Abra put her hand out to keep the door from sliding shut again as she studied him. There was a sharp intelligence in his eyes, and an easy confidence around his mouth. Abra nearly sighed as she moved through the doors and into the garage.

"Made up your mind?" he asked as he fell into step beside her.

"Let's just say I've already made up my mind how to handle you."

The slap of their boots echoed as they walked between the lines of cars. "How's that?"

"You've heard of ten-foot poles?"

His mouth quirked at the corners. She was wearing a braid again. It gave him the urge to loosen it, strand by strand. "That's downright unfriendly."

"Yeah." She stopped in front of a compact station wagon. Its white paint was scarred and dusty, and its windows were tinted violet to combat the merciless sun. Thoughtfully she dug out her keys. "Are you sure you want to go to the site? I could drop you by your hotel."

"I do have a mild interest in this project."

She moved her shoulders in a quick, restless gesture. "Suit yourself."

"Usually do."

Once in he cocked his seat back and nearly managed to stretch out his legs. When she turned the key, the engine coughed, objected, then caught. The radio and air conditioner sprang to life. Music jangled out, but she didn't bother to turn it down. Scattered across the dashboard were a family of decorative magnets—a banana, an ostrich, a map of Arizona, a grinning cat and a lady's hand with pink fingernails. Scribbled notes were held in place by them. As far as Cody could make out, she had to pick up milk and bread and check on fifty tons of concrete. And call Mongo? He narrowed his eyes and tried again. Her mother. She was supposed to call her mother.

"Nice car," he commented when it shuddered and bucked to a stop at a light.

"Needs a tune-up." She shifted into neutral to let the engine idle. "I haven't gotten around to it."

He studied her hand as she jammed the car into first and accelerated. It was long and lean and suited her build. She wore her nails short and, unlike the plastic depiction of a lady's hand, unpainted. No jewelry. He could imagine those hands serving delicate cups of tea—just as he could imagine them changing spark plugs.

"So how would you handle Tim?"

"What?" He'd been lost in a quiet little fantasy about how those narrow, competent hands would feel stroking along his skin.

"Tim," she repeated. She gave the car more gas as they headed south out of Phoenix. "How would you handle him?"

At the moment he was more interested in how he was

going to handle her. "I take it you two don't always see things the same way."

"You're the observant type, Johnson."

"Sarcasm, Red." He didn't ask permission to smoke, just rolled the window down an inch and began to search through his pockets for matches. "Personally, I don't mind it a bit, but when you're dealing with Thornway you'll find oil does better than vinegar."

It was true, absolutely true. It annoyed her that she'd put herself in a position where she'd had to be reminded of that. "He doesn't recognize sarcasm if you pour it over his head." She punched in the car lighter for him.

"Not nine times out of ten, maybe." He touched the tip of the lighter against his cigarette. "It's that tenth time that could get you in trouble. Before you say it, I already know you don't mind a little trouble."

Despite herself, she smiled, and she didn't object when he turned the radio down. "You know those horses, the parade horses that wear blinders so they'll follow the route and not look around and get spooked by crowds?"

"Yeah, and I've already seen that Thornway wears blinders so that he can follow the route to profit without being distracted. You want better working conditions for the men, a higher grade of material, whatever, you've got to learn how to be subtle."

She made that quick, restless movement with her shoulders again. "I can't."

"Sure you can. You're smarter than Thornway, Red, so you sure as hell ought to be able to outwit him."

"He makes me mad. When I think about—" She shrugged again, but this time there was sorrow in the movement. "He just makes me mad. When I get mad, whatever I think comes out."

That was something he'd already figured out for himself. "All you have to do is use the common denominator. With Thornway, that's profit. You want the men to have an hour lunch break in the heat of the day, you don't tell him it's for their benefit, you tell him he'll get higher efficiency and therefore higher profits."

She scowled for a minute, then let out a long breath. "I suppose I'll have to thank you for talking him into it."

"Okay. How about dinner?"

She cast him a short, level look. "No."

"Why not?"

"Because you've got a pretty face." When he grinned, she granted him the briefest of smiles. "I don't trust men with pretty faces."

"You've got a pretty face. I don't hold it against you."

Her smile widened for a moment, but she kept staring at the long road ahead. "There's the difference between you and me, Johnson."

"If we had dinner, we could find others."

It was tempting. And it shouldn't have been. "Why should we want to find others?"

"Passes the time. Why don't we—" He broke off when the car swerved. Abra swore and wrestled the car to the shoulder of the road.

"A flat," she said in disgust. "A lousy flat, and I'm already late getting back." With that, she slammed out of the car and stomped around to the back, swearing with admirable expertise. By the time Cody joined her, she'd already rolled out her spare.

"That one doesn't seem to be in much better shape," he commented, eyeing the tread.

"I need new ones all around, but this one should hold awhile." She hauled out the jack and, still muttering curses, hooked it under the bumper. It was on the tip of Cody's tongue to offer to change it himself. Then he remembered how much he enjoyed watching her work. He hooked his thumbs in his belt loops and stayed out of her way.

"Where I come from, engineers do pretty well for themselves. Ever think about a new car?"

"This one does the job." She spun the lug nuts off. With easy efficiency she pulled off the flat and rolled the spare into place. The breeze from a passing car fluttered through her hair.

"This is bald," Cody said when he took a look at the flat.

"Probably."

"Probably, hell. I've got more tread on my sneakers. Haven't you got more sense than to drive around on bald tires?" Even as he asked he started around the car to examine the tread on the remaining three. "These aren't much better."

"I said I needed new ones." She brushed the hair out of her eyes. "I haven't had the time to take it in and deal with it."

"Make time."

He was standing behind her now. From her crouched position, she aimed a look over her shoulder. "Back off."

"When I work with someone who's this careless personally, I have to wonder how careless they might be professionally."

"I don't make mistakes on the job." She went back to tightening the lug nuts. He was right. Because it embarrassed her, she refused to admit it out loud. "Check the records."

She stood, and was more annoyed than surprised when he turned her around to face him. It didn't bother her to be close. It bothered her to *feel* close. "How many do you make off the job?"

"Not many." She should move away. The warning flashed in and out of her mind as her throat went dry. They were standing toe-to-toe. She could see the light sheen of dampness on his face and throat, just as she could see, whether she wanted to or not, the flicker of desire in his eyes.

"I don't like to argue with a woman who's holding a tire iron." He took it from her and leaned it against the bumper. Her hands curled into fists at her sides, but it was nerves, pure nerves, and had nothing to do with anger.

"I've got an inspector coming this afternoon."

"At two-thirty." He took her hand, turning the wrist up to glance at her watch. "You've got some time."

"Not my own," she said evenly. "I'm on Thornway's clock."

"Conscientious." He looked down at the bald tire. "Mostly."

It was uncomfortable and unnerving to feel her heart thud against her ribs. As if she'd been running, Abra thought. She didn't want to admit that she'd been running since she'd first laid eyes on him.

"If you've got something you want to say, say it. I've got work to do."

"Can't think of a thing at the moment." But he still held her hand. His thumb lightly grazed the underside of her wrist, where her pulse beat hard and steady. "Can you?"

"No." She started to move past him and found herself brought up firmly against his chest. She'd always been lousy at chess, she thought, flustered. Never looking past the immediate move to the future consequences. It took more effort than it should have to keep her voice steady. "What's your problem, Cody?"

"I don't know." He was every bit as intrigued as she. "There's one way to find out." His free hand was on her face now, not resting there but holding her still. "Do you mind?" Even as he spoke, his lips lowered toward hers.

She wasn't sure what made her pull back at the last moment—or what made her able to pull back. She lifted a hand to his chest and pressed firmly, even as she tasted the warmth of his breath on her lips. "Yes," she said, and was amazed to realize that it was a lie. She wouldn't have minded. In fact, she'd wanted the feel and taste of his mouth on hers.

There was only an inch separating them, perhaps less. He felt, unexpectedly, a churning, a tug, a heat that drew together and centered in his gut. It was more than curiosity, he realized, and he found himself not entirely comfortable with the knowledge. When he stepped back, it was as much for his own sake as anything.

"I shouldn't have asked," he said easily. "Next time I won't."

She'd start trembling in a moment. It stunned her to realize that any second her system was going to betray her and shudder and quake. Again, not from anger. She held it off through sheer will and bent to the ruined tire. "Go find someone else to play with, Cody."

"I don't think so." He took the tire from her and stored it in the rear of the car. Before she could see to it herself, he had lowered the jack and stored that, as well.

Taking slow, steadying breaths, she walked around to her door. A tractor-trailer rattled by, and the force of the air it displaced hit her like a wall. She braced herself against it, as she had braced herself against him. Her palms were sweaty. Carefully she rubbed them against the thighs of her jeans before settling inside and turning the key.

"You don't strike me as the kind of man who keeps knocking at a door when no one answers."

"You're right." He leaned back again as she pulled onto the road. "After a while I just open it myself." With a friendly grin, he turned the radio up again.

The inspector had come early. Abra swore about it but couldn't do much else, since the wiring passed. She walked through the building, which was already taking shape, and climbed to the second and third floors to supervise the insulating and the first delivery of drywall. It was moving like clockwork, and she should have been more than satisfied.

All she could think of was how she had felt standing on the shoulder of the road with Cody's lips an inch from hers.

She was an engineer, not a romantic, she reminded herself as she stood on a platform twenty feet up and unrolled a drawing. The cooling system, she thought as she went over the specs again. That was going to take enough of her time and energy over the next few days. She didn't have the time or the inclination to stand around and wonder what it would have been like to kiss Cody Johnson.

Hot. Hot and exciting. No woman could look at that mouth and not see the kind of damage it could do to the nervous system. It had already jangled hers, and without even making contact. He probably knew it. Men like him always knew what kind of effect they had on a woman. They could hardly be blamed for it, but they could—and should—be avoided.

With another oath, she rolled up the drawings. She wouldn't think about him or what would have happened if she'd said yes instead of no. Or if she'd said nothing at all and had moved on instinct rather than brainpower.

There were the elevators to consider. It wouldn't be long before they'd be going in. She'd worked hard and long with another engineer on the design. What was now on paper would be reality soon enough, running up and down the walls, glass glittering as they rose and fell without a sound.

Some men could do that—make your heart rise and fall, make your pulse hammer though it couldn't be heard by anyone but you. No matter how you tried, how you pretended it wasn't happening, inside you'd be shooting up and shooting down so fast that a crash was inevitable. No matter how clever you were with a calculator, you could never quite fix the kinks in the system.

Damn him. Damn him for that—for taking that one step beyond and making her vulnerable. She couldn't forget the way her hand had felt in his, the way his eyes had looked when his face had been that close. So now she would wonder. The blame for that was his. She'd do well to remember that.

Glancing down, she saw him on the first floor, talking with Charlie Gray. Cody was gesturing toward the rear wall, where the side of the mountain sloped in to become part of the building—or the building to become part of the mountain. There would be long panes of glass there to form the ceiling, curved glass that would blend the line from the rock to the dome. She'd already decided it would be ostentatious and impractical, but as she'd been told, it was her job to make it work, not to approve.

Cody shook his head at something Gray told him, and his voice rose a little, enough to carry but not enough to make the words clear. Annoyance was there. It pleased her.

Let him be annoyed, she thought. Let him go back east and be annoyed where he would be out of her way.

She started down, using the temporary stairs. She had the progress on the health club to check out, and the excavation work on the first set of cabanas. As long as they could keep one job overlapping the next, they'd be all right. Tim should have been there, overseeing the scheduling. Abra moved a shoulder to work out a kink. It was better that he wasn't, that he had left the responsibility to her. He had a way of irritating the men when he showed up on the site in his expensive suits.

Just as she checked her watch, she heard a shout from above. She had enough time to see the metal stud falling toward her before she was grabbed by the waist and dragged aside.

The stud landed inches from her feet, spewing up dust and clattering. Hard hat or no, she'd have been taking a trip to the hospital now if she'd been under it.

"You all right? Hey." Arms were still around her waist, but now she was turned and pressed against a hard male body. She didn't have to see to know who was holding her.

"Yes." But her voice wasn't steady. Neither were her hands. "I'm okay. Let me—"

"Who the hell's responsible for this?" Cody shouted up, still holding Abra against him. He knew now what it meant to be sick with fear. He'd moved instinctively, but the moment the stud had hit harmlessly his stomach had heaved. Looking at it, he could envision her lying there, bleeding. Two men were already scurrying down the ladder, their faces as white as his.

"It got away from us. God, Ms. Wilson, are you okay? There was an electric box on the floor. It tripped me up, and the stud just went."

"It didn't hit me." She tried to move away from Cody but didn't have the strength.

"Get up there and make sure those floors and platforms are clear. If there's any more carelessness, people are going to be out of a job."

"Yes, sir."

The hammering, which had stopped dead, resumed hesitantly, then with more vigor.

"Look, I'm all right." She had to be. Even if her hands were clammy, she had to be all right. "I can handle the men."

"Just shut up." He fought back the urge to pick her up, and pulled her along instead. "You're white as a sheet." He shoved her down on a crate. "Sit."

Because her legs felt like rubber, she didn't argue. A few deep breaths, she told herself, and she'd be fine.

"Here." Cody pushed a cup of water into her hand.

"Thanks." She drank, forcing herself to take it slow. "You don't have to bother."

"No, I could just leave you in a puddle on the ground." It hadn't come out the way he'd intended, but he was angry, as sick with anger as he'd been with fear. It had been too close, way too close. If he hadn't glanced over at her... "I could've stood there and watched you get smashed, but it seemed a shame to get blood all over the fresh concrete."

"That's not what I meant." She swallowed the last of the water and balled up the paper cup in her hand. He'd saved her from a major injury. She'd wanted to thank him, nicely. And she would have, too, Abra thought, if he hadn't been scowling at her. "I would have gotten out of the way myself, in any case."

"Fine. Next time I'll just go about my business."

"Do that." Biting off the words, she tossed the paper cup aside. She rose and fought back a wave of giddiness. Hammers were still pounding, but more than one man was watching out of the corner of an eye. "There's no need to cause a scene."

"You've no idea the kind of scene I can cause, Wilson." He was tempted to show her, to release some of the fury that had boiled together with the fear and let her have a good long look at what he could throw. But her face was chalk white, and whether she knew it or not her hands were shaking. "If I were you, I'd have your foreman drill some safety rules into these men."

"I'll take that under advisement. Now, if you'll excuse me, I have to get back to work."

When his fingers curled around her arm, she felt the temper in them. She was grateful for it. It made her stronger. Very slowly she turned her head so that she could look at him again. Fury, she thought with a kind of edgy curiosity. The man was absolutely furious—more than a few cross words warranted. His problem, Abra told herself.

"I'm not going to keep telling you to back off, Johnson."

He waited a moment until he was sure he could speak calmly. In his mind he could still hear the sickening crack of metal hitting concrete. "That's something we can agree on, Red. You won't keep telling me to back off."

He let her go. After the briefest hesitation, she strode away.

She wouldn't keep telling him, Cody thought as he watched her disappear outside. And even if she did, it wasn't going to do her any good.

Chapter 3

He had other things to think about. Cody let the hot spray of the shower beat over his head and reminded himself that Abra Wilson wasn't his problem. A problem she undoubtedly was, but not his.

Women that skittish were best avoided, particularly when they had those pretty feminine looks that contrasted with a mean temper. The Barlow project was giving him enough headaches. He didn't need to add her to the list.

But then, she was mighty easy to look at. Cody smiled to himself as he turned off the shower. Easy to look at didn't mean easy to handle. Usually he appreciated challenges, but just now he had enough on his plate. Now that his partner was married and expecting his first baby, Cody was doing what he could to shoulder the excess. With business booming, the excess meant twelve-hour days. In addition to overseeing the construction of the resort, there were in-

numerable phone calls to make and take, telegrams to send
and receive, decisions, approvals and rejections.

He didn't mind the responsibility or the long hours. He
was grateful for them. It didn't take much prodding for him
to remember the boy who had grown up on a muddy farm
on the Georgia-Florida border. The boy had wanted more,
and the man had worked to get it.

Come a long way, Cody thought as he knotted the towel
at his waist. His body was lean, the torso tanned. He still
worked outdoors, though that was from choice now, rather
than necessity. It wasn't only drawing boards and dreams
with Cody. There was a house on a lake in Florida that was
half-built. He was determined to finish it himself. A matter of pride now, rather than lack of funds.

The money was there, and he'd never deny he enjoyed
its benefits. Still, he'd grown up working with his hands,
and he couldn't seem to break the habit. He corrected himself. He didn't want to break the habit. There were times
when he enjoyed nothing more than the feel of a hammer
or a piece of wood in his hand.

He dragged his fingers through his wet hair. They were
callused, as they'd been since childhood. He could run a
tractor even now, but he preferred a slide rule or a power
saw.

He strode into the bedroom of his hotel suite. The suite
was nearly as big as the home he'd grown up in. He'd gotten
used to the space, to the small luxuries, but he didn't take
them for granted. Because he'd grown up skirting poverty
he'd learned to appreciate good material, good food, good
wine. Perhaps he appreciated them with a more discern-
ing eye than someone who had been born to the good life.
But he didn't think about that.

Work, talent and ambition were the keys, with a bit of

luck thrown in. Cody remembered that luck could change, so he never avoided work.

He had come a long way from digging in the mud to make a living. Now he could dream, imagine and create—as long as he didn't forget that making dreams reality meant getting your hands dirty. He could lay a score of brick if it was required, mix mortar, pound in a stud or drive a rivet. He'd worked his way through college as a laborer. Those years had given him not only a practical bent toward building but a respect for the men who sweated to create them.

Which brought him back to Abra. She understood construction workers. He knew firsthand that many of the people who worked at drawing boards forgot the men who hammered the nails and hauled the bricks. But not Abra. Thoughtfully he slipped into a white terry-cloth robe with the vague notion of calling room service and eating in. Abra Wilson, he mused. She would have gone to the wall to get an extra thirty minutes' break for the men. She was a fiend about checking the water supply and the salt tablets.

She was also a woman who would step in between two angry construction workers to break up a fight. Or pour beer over the head of an insubordinate employee. The memory made him grin. No drinking on the job. And she'd meant what she'd said.

He appreciated that. He was a man who preferred frankness to subtleties in both his business and his personal life. She wasn't a woman who would play flirting games or give teasing hints. She would say yes or she would say no.

As she had on the side of the road, he remembered. She'd said no, Cody mused, and she'd wanted to say yes. Discovering the reasons for the contradiction would be interesting work. It was a pity he could only fit Abra into the business slot. They might have had some fun together, he thought, dragging a hand through his still-damp hair. The trouble was, she was too uptight to settle back and have a good time. Perhaps it would be fair to say that she was too honest to take intimacy on a casual level. He couldn't fault her for that, which made one more reason to keep things on a business plane.

And there was too much friction. Friction usually led to a spark, and a spark to a blaze. He didn't have the time to fight fires just now.

With a glance at the clock on the bedside table he calculated the time back east. It was far too late to make any calls to the East Coast. That meant he'd have to get up at five, pull himself together and make all the necessary calls and connections between 6:00 and 7:00 a.m.

With a shrug, he decided that what was called for was a quick room-service meal and an early night. Just as he picked up the phone, the buzzer sounded at his door.

If there was one person he hadn't been expecting, it was Abra.

She stood there, balancing a brown grocery bag on one hip. Her hair was loose—it was the first time he'd seen it unbraided or unpinned—and curled wildly to her shoulders. She still wore jeans and a T-shirt, but she'd changed from work boots to sneakers. The next surprise was that she was almost smiling.

"Hi," she managed. It was ridiculous, but she'd never been so nervous in her life.

"Hi." He leaned against the doorframe and took a long, lazy scan. "Passing by?"

"Not exactly." Her fingers dug into the stiff brown paper bag. The telltale rattle made her relax them again. "Can I come in?"

"Sure." He stepped back, and she stepped through. From

behind her, she heard the door click closed. Her heart jerked with it. "This is nice."

The living room of the suite was done in desert colors, mauves and umbers and creams. There were sketches on the walls and narrow louvered blinds at the windows. The room smelled of soap. He smelled of soap. Abra braced herself to turn.

"I wanted to apologize."

His brow lifted in an unconscious gesture as he studied her. She was doing her best, Cody realized, and hating every minute of it. Amused, he decided to draw the scene out.

"For what?"

She nearly ground her teeth. On the trip over she had prepared herself for the likelihood that he wouldn't make it easy. "For being rude and ungrateful this afternoon."

Cody slipped his hands into the pockets of his robe. "Just this afternoon?"

Venom nearly poured out, and it was hard to swallow. An apology was due, and she was damn well going to get it over with. "Yes. We're dealing with a specific instance. You helped me this afternoon, and I was ungrateful and unkind. I was wrong, and when I am I like to think I can admit it." Without asking, she moved over to the counter that separated the living space from the kitchenette. "I brought you some beer."

"To drink or to wear?" he asked when she pulled out a six pack.

"Up to you." She broke down enough to smile, really smile. The flecks in her eyes brightened. Her lips softened as if by magic. Cody felt his heart stop for two full beats. "I didn't know whether you'd eaten, so I tossed in a meatball sub and some fries."

"You brought me dinner?"

Uncomfortable, she shrugged. "It's no big deal, just a sandwich." She pulled out a twelve-inch tube wrapped in white paper.

"Some sandwich."

"Yeah." She took out the foam dish that held the french fries. If it killed her, she told herself, she was going to get the words out. And it might kill her, she thought, if he kept looking at her as though he'd rather nibble on her than the sub. "I wanted to thank you for acting so quickly this afternoon. I don't know whether I'd have gotten out of the way in time or not, but that's not the issue. The fact is, you made certain I wasn't hurt, and I never really thanked you at the time. I guess I was more shaken up than I realized."

As he had been, Cody thought. He crossed over to stand beside her. She was holding the empty bag, folding and unfolding it. The gesture showed him more than words could have how much it had cost her to come. He took the bag from her and tossed it on the counter.

"You could have written that down in a nice little note and slipped it under the door. But I don't suppose that's your style." He resisted the urge to touch her hair, knowing it would be a mistake for both of them. He would only want to touch her more, and she already looked as though she'd jump out of her shoes at the first advance. Instead, he pulled a bottle out of the pack and turned it to read the label. "Want a beer?"

She hesitated only briefly. It looked as if he was going to make it easy for her after all. "Sure."

"Half a meatball sub?"

She relaxed and smiled again. "I could probably choke it down."

A truce, undeclared but understood, had been negotiated. They shared cold beer and spicy meatballs on Cody's terrace. A small in-ground spa swirled silently at their feet. Orange and red blossoms, their scent heavy, trailed up and along the high walls that closed them in. The sun was low, and the air was cooling.

"All the comforts of home," Abra mused as she sipped her beer.

Cody thought about his house, where everything was familiar, where so many walls were still unfinished and so many yards of trim were still unpainted. "Not quite home. But it's the next best thing."

Abra stretched the toes of her sneakers toward the water. Lord, she'd like to sink into that, close her eyes and let every muscle hum. With a soft sigh of regret, she dismissed the idea. "You do much traveling?"

"Enough. You?"

"Not really. Well, around the state. Up into Utah a couple of times. I like hotels."

"Really?"

She was relaxed enough to ignore his smirk. She bit into the sub and savored the blending of meat, sauce and cheese. "I like being able to take a shower and go out and come back to find fresh towels. Ordering room service and eating in bed. Stuff like that. You must like them, too." She watched him tilt back his beer. "You don't strike me as someone who'd keep doing something he didn't care for."

"I don't mind moving around." The fries were greasy and loaded with salt. Perfect. He took two. "I like knowing I've got some place to go back to, that's all."

She understood that very well, though it surprised her that he felt the sentiment—and the need. "Have you always lived in Florida?"

"Yeah. Can't say I care much for the snow-shoveling, finger-numbing weather in the north. I like the sun."

"Me too." She dug out fries. "It only rains here a handful of times a year. Rain's an event." With a grin, she finished off her half of the sub. The best meal, she had to admit, she'd had in weeks. It was hard to believe, but his company wasn't such a trial after all. She settled back to nurse her beer and wait for nightfall. "I'd like to see the ocean, though."

"Which one?"

"Any one."

Her eyes were gray in this light, he noted. Gray and a little sleepy. "It's a short flight to the West Coast."

"I know." She moved her shoulders and continued to watch the sky darken. "I always figured I needed a bigger reason to make the trip."

"Vacation?"

"I've been pushing pretty hard the last few years. This may be the age of women's liberation, but there are still walls to break down when you're an engineer who happens to be a woman."

"Why are you an engineer?"

He reached lazily for more fries, and so did she. Their fingers brushed companionably. "I always liked to figure out how things worked—or what to do to make them work better. I was good with numbers. I like the logic of them. If you put them together and figure out the formula, you're always going to come up with the right answer."

"The right answer's not always the best answer."

Crossing her legs at the ankles, she turned her head enough to study his face in the lowering light. "That's artistic thinking, which is why an architect needs a good engineer to keep him on track."

He took a lazy swallow of beer and smiled at her. "Is that what you're doing, Red? Keeping me on track?"

"It isn't easy. Take the design of the health club."

"I figured you'd get around to it."

Mellowed by the casual meal, she ignored his sarcasm. "The waterfall on the east wall. We'll overlook the fact that it's an impractical piece of fancy."

"You've got something against waterfalls?"

"This is the desert, Johnson."

"Ever hear of an oasis?"

She sighed, determined to be patient. It was a nice night. The food had been good, and the company more pleasant than she'd expected. "I'll give you your little whimsy."

"Bless you for that."

"But if you'd put it on the west wall, as I requested—"

"It doesn't work on the west wall," he said. "You need the windows on the west wall for the evening light, the sunsets. And the view's best in the west."

"I'm talking about logistics. Think plumbing."

"I leave that up to you. You think plumbing, I'll think aesthetics, and we'll get along fine."

Typical, typical, typical, she thought with a shake of her head. "Cody, my point is that this project could have been half as difficult as it is with a few minor adjustments."

The challenging light had come back into her eyes. He nearly smiled. The evening wouldn't have been complete without at least one argument. "If you're afraid of hard work, you should have found another profession."

That had her head snapping up, and her eyes, already filled with anger, narrowing. "I'm not afraid to work, and I'm damn good at what I do. It's people like you, who come along with your six-story egos, refusing to make any adjustments, who make things impossible."

He had a temper of his own, but he managed—barely—to check it. "It's not my ego that keeps me from making adjustments. If I made them, I wouldn't be doing the job I'd been hired to do."

"You call it professional integrity, I call it ego."

"And you're wrong," he said with deceptive calm. "Again."

She could have drawn in then and tried tact and subtlety—if she had thought of it. "Are you telling me it would have compromised your integrity to move that silly waterfall from east to west?"

"Yes."

"That's the most ridiculous thing I've ever heard. But typical," she said, rising to pace the tiny walled-in terrace. "God knows it's typical. Sometimes I think architects worry more about the color of paint than stress points."

He watched her as she paced. Her stride was long and loose, the kind that ate up ground from point to point easily. A woman going places, he mused. But he wasn't about to be walked over so that she could get there.

"You've got a bad habit of generalizing, Red."

"Don't call me Red," she muttered, then tugged an orange blossom off the vine. "I'll be glad when this project's finished and I'm out on my own. Then I can pick what architect I want to work with."

"Good luck. It might just be difficult for you to find one who's willing to put up with temper tantrums and nitpicking."

She whirled back. She knew she had a temper. She wouldn't deny it or apologize for it. But as to the rest… "I don't nitpick. It's not nit-picking to make a suggestion that would save laying an extra hundred feet of pipe. And only an egocentric, hardheaded architect would see it that way."

"You've got a problem, *Ms.* Wilson." He saw and enjoyed the way she stiffened at that. "You've got a low opinion of people in my profession, but as long as you pursue yours, you're stuck with us."

She mangled the flower she was holding. "Not everyone in your field's an idiot. There are some excellent architects in Arizona."

"So it's just architects from back east you don't like."

She wasn't going to let him put words in her mouth and make her sound like a fool. "I have no idea why Tim felt he had to hire a firm from out of state to begin with. But since he did, I'm doing my best to work with you."

"Your best could use some polishing up." Setting his beer aside, he rose. His face was in shadows, but she could tell by his stance that he was as angry as she was, and primed for a fight. "If you've got any other complaints, why don't you get them out now while there's just the two of us?"

She tossed the bruised flower, like a gauntlet, between them. "All right, I will. It infuriates me that you didn't bother to come out for any of the preliminary meetings. I was against hiring an East Coast firm, but Tim wouldn't listen. The fact that you were unavailable made things more complicated. Meanwhile, I've got to deal with Gray, who bites his fingernails and is always looking up codes or shuffling papers. Then you come out and swagger around like the cock of the walk, refusing to modify even one line of your precious design."

He took a step toward her, out of the shadows. He was angry, all right, she noted. It was just her luck that his temper made him more attractive. "In the first place, I had a very good reason for missing the preliminary meetings. Good personal reasons that I don't feel obligated to discuss with you." He took another step. "The fact that your employer hired my firm over your objections is your problem, not mine."

"I prefer to think of it as his mistake, not mine."

"Fine." When he took the next step toward her, she had to fight back the urge to retreat. His eyes could be very dark, she discovered, very intense. He didn't remind her of a casual beachcomber now, or an easygoing cowboy. More like a gunslinger, she realized, but she held her ground. "As to Gray, he might be young and annoying, but he also works hard."

She felt a flush of shame and jammed her hands into her pockets. "I didn't mean…"

"Forget it." He took a final step that brought him so close that their bodies nearly brushed. Abra kept her jaw set and her eyes on his. "And I don't swagger."

She had a ridiculous urge to laugh, but something in his eyes warned her that that was the most dangerous thing she could do. Instead, she swallowed and lifted both brows. "You mean you don't do it on purpose?"

She was baiting him, plain and simple. He hadn't missed the light of amusement in her eyes. She wanted to laugh at him, and he'd be damned if she'd get away with it. "I don't do it at all. You, on the other hand, put on that hard hat and those steel-toed boots and stomp around the site trying to prove how tough you can be."

She opened her mouth in utter astonishment, then snapped it closed. "I don't stomp, and I don't have to prove anything to anyone. I'm doing the job I was trained to do."

"Then you do yours and I'll do mine."

"Fine. See you at sunup."

She started to spin toward the door, and he caught her by the arm. He didn't know what demon had prompted him to do it, to stop her when her angry exit would have been best for both of them. Now it was too late. The move was already made. Their faces were close, his hand was tight on her arm, and their bodies were turned toward each other. A half moon was rising. Outside the walls a woman's laugh ebbed and flowed as a couple strolled by beneath its light.

The friction had given birth to a spark—no, dozens of sparks, Cody thought as he felt them singe his skin. The heat from them was quick and dangerous, but still controllable. If he fanned them, they would flame. And then…

The hell with it, he thought as he closed his mouth over hers.

She was braced. She was ready. The desire and the intent had been plain to see as they'd stood there for that long, silent moment. Abra was honest enough to admit that the desire had been there all along. It had cut through her time and time again. So she was braced. She was ready.

It didn't do any good.

She should have been able to hold back her response, something she'd always been able to give or subdue as she chose. As *she* chose. It was frightening to learn in one split second that the choice wasn't always there. Response ripped out of her before a decision could be made and shattered her opinion of her own free will.

She was holding on to him without any recollection of having reached out. Her body was pressed hard against his without any memory of having moved at all. When her lips parted, it was as much in demand as in invitation. His rough answer was exactly what she wanted.

He dragged her against him, amazed that need could rise from a simmer to a boil so quickly. Another surprise. What flared between them came as much from her as from him. She hadn't protested or struggled angrily away, but had met him force for force, passion for passion. With temper adding an edge to desire, he caught her hair in his hands and took as ruthlessly as his need demanded.

He nipped at her lip. Her low, throaty moan was as arousing as the play of her tongue over his. Now he gave himself freedom, letting his hands run over her, testing, tormenting, taking. Her body shuddered against his, then pressed closer. She didn't hold back, didn't seem to believe in it.

She should think, oh, she knew she should think. But it wasn't possible when her pulse was pounding in her head and her muscles were like water. How could she think when his taste was spreading through her, filling her?

He was as breathless as she when they drew apart. She was as willing as he when they came together for one last long, lingering kiss. When they parted again they stayed close, his hands on her shoulders, hers on his arms. Anger defused, passion ignited, leaving them both weak.

"What are we going to do about this?" Cody asked her.

She could only shake her head. It was too soon to think and too late not to.

"Why don't you sit down?"

She shook her head again before he could lead her to a chair. "No. No, I don't want to sit." It was harder than she'd thought it would be to step away from him. "I've got to go."

"Not quite yet." He needed a cigarette. He fumbled in the pockets of his robe and swore when he found his hands weren't steady. It amazed and infuriated him. "We have to resolve this, Abra."

She watched the match spark and flame, then drew a steadying breath. Flames could be lit, she reminded herself, and they could be put out just as easily. "It shouldn't have happened."

"That's beside the point."

It hurt, more than a little, that he hadn't disagreed with

her. But of course he couldn't, she told herself. She was right. "No, I think that is the point." In frustration she dragged both hands through her hair, and he remembered all too clearly what it had felt like tangled around his own hands. "It shouldn't have happened, but it did, and now it's over. I think we're both too sensible and too professional to let it get in the way of our working relationship."

"Do you?" He should have known she'd handle this the same way she would a fouled-up order for concrete. "Maybe you're right. Maybe. But you're an idiot if you think it won't happen again."

She had to be careful, very careful. It wasn't easy to speak calmly when her lips were still warm and swollen from his. "If it does, we'll simply have to deal with it— separately from business."

"We agree on something." Cody blew out a long stream of smoke. "What happened just now had nothing to do with business." Through the screen of smoke his eyes met hers and held them. "But that's not going to stop me from wanting you during working hours."

She felt a warning chill race up her spine. It made her straighten her shoulders. "Look, Cody, this is—was—a momentary thing. Maybe we were attracted, but—"

"Maybe?"

"All right, all right." She tried to find the right words. "I have to think of my future. We both know there's nothing more difficult, or awkward, than becoming involved with an associate."

"Life's rough," he murmured, and pitched his cigarette high over the wall. He watched the glow fly up and arc before he turned back to her. "Let's get something straight, Red. I kissed you and you kissed me right back. And it felt damn good. I'm going to want to kiss you again, and a lot more than that. What I'm not going to do is wait until it's convenient for you."

"You make all the decisions?" she snapped. "You make all the moves?"

He considered a moment. "Okay."

Fury didn't make her speechless. Taking a step forward, she poked a finger at his chest. "It's not okay, you arrogant pinhead. I kissed you back because I wanted to, because I liked it. If I kiss you again it'll be for the same reasons, not because you set the time and place. If I go to bed with you, the same rules hold. Got that straight?"

She was wonderful. Infuriating, but wonderful. He managed not to grab her. Instead, he grinned. When a woman called a spade a spade, you couldn't argue. "Straight as an arrow," he agreed. He tucked an errant strand of hair behind her ear. "Glad you liked it."

The sound that hissed out between her teeth was anything but pleased. His grin just widened. Rather than punch him in the face, she knocked his hand aside and turned for the door.

"Abra."

She yanked the door open and stood gripping the knob. "What?"

"Thanks for dinner."

The door slammed at her back, and then he did laugh. He waited ten seconds and heard the front door of the suite slam in turn. On impulse, he stripped off his robe and, turning on the timer for the spa, eased into the hot, bubbling water. He hoped it would soothe out the aches she'd left him with and clear his mind enough to let him think.

Chapter 4

Business. From now until the last tile was caulked Abra was determined to keep it strictly business between herself and Cody. Engineer to architect. They would discuss templates and curved headers, wiring and plastic pipe, concrete and thermal mass. Abra scowled at the bare bones of the health club. With luck, she thought, they would discuss nothing at all.

What had happened on that moonlit terrace was like temporary insanity. Inherited insanity, she decided as she dug her fists into her pockets. Obviously she was more like her mother than she had ever wanted to admit. An attractive man, a little stardust and *wham*! She was ready and willing to make a fool of herself.

She took the clipboard the foreman handed her, scanned the papers, then initialed them. She'd come this far without letting any congenital weaknesses muck up her life. She intended to go a lot farther. Maybe she had inherited the flaw from her mother, but unlike the sweet, eternally optimistic Jessie she had no intention of going into a romantic spin and ending up flat on her face. That moment of weakness had passed, and now it was back to business as usual.

She spent the morning running back and forth between the health club and the main building, with an occasional foray to check on the excavation work for the cabanas. The work on each section of the project was overlapping according to plan, keeping her constantly in demand to oversee, answer questions, smooth out problems.

She had a long, technical phone conversation with the mechanical engineer Thornway had assigned. He was moving more slowly than she might have liked, but his work was first-class. She made a note to go by the offices and take a good look at the dies for both the elevator and the mechanized roof over the pool.

Those were aspects of her profession she enjoyed every bit as much as the planning and figuring, and they were aspects she took every bit as seriously. She wasn't an engineer who figured her job was over once the specs were approved and the calculations checked. She'd wanted a part in the Barlow project that didn't begin and end at the drawing board. It had been given to her, and if she still winced inwardly when a shovelful of dirt was removed from the site, she had the satisfaction of being a part of its reshaping.

No one she came in contact with would have seen beneath the competent exterior to her distracted thoughts. If she was constantly on the lookout for Cody, she told herself, it was only that she didn't care to be taken unaware. By noon she had decided he wasn't going to show. Disappointment masqueraded as relief.

She took her lunch break in the trailer with a bottle of chilled orange juice, a bag of chips and blueprints. Since her conversation with the mechanical engineer she had decided there were still a few problems to work out in the dynamics of the sliding glass roof Cody wanted over the pool. She crunched into a chip while she punched a new equation into her calculator. If it weren't for the waterfall the man insisted on having run down the wall and into the corner of the pool... Abra shook her head and tried a new angle. The man was a maniac about waterfalls, she thought. She took a long swig of juice. Basically he was just a maniac. It helped to think of him that way, as a crazy architect with delusions of grandeur, rather than as a man who could kiss the common sense right out of you.

She was going to give him his damn sliding glass arch of a roof, and his waterfalls, and his spirals and domes. Then she was going to use this foolish fancy of a design to launch her own career while he went back to his humidity and his orange groves.

Nearly satisfied, Abra sketched out a few details, then ran a new set of figures. It wasn't her job to approve, she reminded herself, it was her job to make it work. She was very good at making things work.

When the door opened, she didn't bother to glance up. "Close that quick, will you? You'll let the heat in."

"Yes, ma'am."

The lazy drawl had her head jerking up. She straightened her shoulders automatically as Cody stooped to walk through the doorway. "I didn't think we'd see you here today."

He merely smiled and stood aside to make room for Tim Thornway and the bullet-shaped form of William Walton Barlow, Sr. Awkwardly, due to the row of cabinets over her head, Abra stood.

"Abra." Though he would have preferred to have found

her knee-deep in concrete or up on the scaffolding, Tim was skilled enough to use almost any situation to his advantage. "As you can see, WW," he said, "our crew lives, sleeps and eats B and B's resort hotel. You remember Ms. Wilson, our chief structural engineer."

The little man with the thatch of white hair and the shrewd eyes held out a meaty hand. "Indeed, indeed. A Barlow never forgets a pretty face."

To her credit, Abra didn't wince, not even when Cody smirked over Barlow's head. "It's nice to see you again, Mr. Barlow."

"WW thought it was time he had a look at things," Tim explained. "Of course, we don't want to interrupt the flow or slacken the pace—"

"Don't know much about putting these places up," Barlow cut in. "Know about running them. Like what I see, though." He nodded three times. "Like the curves and arches. Classy. Barlow and Barlow stands for classy operations."

Abra ignored Cody's grin and scooted out from behind the table. "You picked a hot day to visit, Mr. Barlow. Can I get you something cold? Juice, tea?"

"Take a beer. Nothing washes away the dust like a cold beer."

Cody opened the scaled-down refrigerator himself and rooted some out. "We were about to show WW the progress on the health club."

"Oh?" Abra shook her head at the offer of a beer and was amused when Tim accepted a bottle gingerly. "Good timing. I've just been working out the final details on the pool roof. I think Lafferty and I smoothed out some of the bugs over the phone this morning."

Barlow glanced down at the blueprints and at the stacks

of paper covered with figures and calculations. "I'll leave that to you. Only numbers I'm handy with are in an account book. Looks like you know your way around, though." He gestured with his bottle before taking three healthy gulps. "Thornway always said you had a head on your shoulders. Pretty shoulders, too." He winked at her.

Rather than getting her dander up, the wink made her grin. He was nearly old enough to be her grandfather and, multimillionaire or not, he had a certain rough charm. "Thank you. He always spoke highly of you."

"I miss him," Barlow said. Then he turned to the matter at hand. "Let's get on with this tour, Tim. No use wasting time."

"Of course." Tim set aside his untouched beer. "I'm giving a little dinner party for Mr. Barlow tonight. Seven. You'll escort Mr. Johnson, Abra."

Since it wasn't a question, Abra opened her mouth with the idea of making some excuse. Cody stepped smoothly in. "I'll pick up Ms. Wilson. Why don't you start over to the health club? We'll be right with you."

"Why don't you loosen that damn tie, Tim?" Barlow asked as they stepped out of the trailer. "Man could strangle in this heat."

Cody shut the door, then leaned against it. "They *are* nice shoulders. From what I've seen of them."

From an engineering standpoint, Abra couldn't have said why the trailer seemed more crowded now than it had a moment before. Turning back to the table, she began to tidy her papers. "It isn't necessary for you to pick me up this evening."

"No." He studied her, not certain whether he was amused or annoyed by her withdrawal. He hadn't slept well, and he knew the blame lay squarely on those pretty shoulders, which were now braced for an attack. "But I will."

This was business, Abra told herself, and should be handled as such. Making up her mind, she turned to face him. "All right. You'll need an address."

He smiled again, slowly this time. "Oh, I think I can find you, Red. Same way you found me."

Since he'd brought it up, Abra told herself, it would be best to deal with it. "It's good that we have a minute here. We can clear things up."

"What things?" Cody pushed away from the door. Abra backed into the table hard. "We had a mule back home on the farm," he mused as he stepped closer. "She tended to be skittish, too."

"I'm not skittish. It's simply that I think you have the wrong impression."

"I have the right impression," he told her, reaching around to toy with the end of her braid. "Of just how your body feels when it's fitted against mine. A very right and very pleasant impression."

"That was a mistake." She would have turned away to move around him, but he tightened his grip on her hair and tugged her back.

"What was?"

"Last night." She was going to handle this calmly, Abra told herself. She was basically a calm and reasonable person. "It should never have happened."

"It?" His eyes had darkened. Abra noted that, and noted, also, that there was no anger to be seen in them. She let out a little breath of relief. Obviously he was prepared to be as reasonable as she.

"I suppose we just got caught up in the moment. The best thing to do is forget it and go on."

"Okay." She saw his smile but didn't notice how cool it was. He wasn't much of a hand at chess, but he was a killer at poker. "We'll forget last night."

Pleased at the ease with which the problem had been erased, she smiled back at him. "Well, then, why don't we—"

Her words were cut off as he dragged her against him and covered her mouth with his. Her body went rigid— from shock, she told herself. From fury. That was what she wanted to believe. Today there was none of the gentle, sensual exploration in the moonlight. This kiss was as bold and as bright as the sun that beat through the windows. And as angry, she thought as he twisted her against him and took whatever he wanted. She tried to yank free and was held fast. Those subtle muscles covered steel. Abra found herself caught up in an embrace that threatened every bit as much as it promised.

He didn't give a damn. She could stand there and talk all she wanted in that reasonable voice about mistakes. He'd made mistakes before and lived through them. She might be the biggest, she would certainly be the costliest, but he wasn't about to back off now. He remembered the way she had felt in his arms the night before, that shivering, wire-taut passion, that abrupt avalanche of emotion. Even then he'd known it was nothing he'd felt before, nothing he would feel again. Not with anyone else. He'd see them both damned before it was forgotten.

"Stop," she managed before he crushed her mouth again. She was drowning, and she knew she couldn't save herself. Drowning, she thought as she moaned against his lips. Drowning in sensations, in longings, in desires. Why was she clinging to him when she knew it was crazy? Why was she answering that hard, hungry kiss when she knew it could lead to nothing but disaster?

But her arms were around him, her lips were parted, her heart was pounding in rhythm with his. This was more than temptation, more than surrender. What she felt now wasn't a need to give but a need to take.

When they broke apart she dragged air into her lungs and braced a hand on the table for balance. She could see now that she'd been wrong. There was anger in his eyes, anger and determination and a rough-edged desire that rooted her to the spot. Still, when he spoke, his voice was mild.

"Looks as if we have another point of reference, Red." He swung to the door. "See you at seven."

There were at least a half a dozen times that evening that Abra thought of a plausible excuse and began to dial Cody at his hotel. What stopped her each time was the knowledge that if she made the call she would be acknowledging not only that there was something between them but that she was a coward. Even if she forced herself to accept the fact that she was afraid, she couldn't allow him to see it.

She was obliged to go, she reminded herself as she rummaged through her closet once again. It was really no more than a business meeting, though they would be wearing evening dress and picking at canapés on Tim's elegant patio. It was politic and necessary to show Barlow that his architect and engineer could handle a social evening together.

She had to be able to handle it. Sexual attraction aside, Cody Johnson was her associate on this project. If she couldn't handle him—and what he seemed bound and determined to make her feel—she couldn't handle the job. No slow-talking East Coast architect was going to make her admit she couldn't handle anything that came her way.

In any case, she thought with some satisfaction as she tried to decide between two dresses, once they were there there would be so many people that they would get lost in the shuffle. It was doubtful she and Cody would have to exchange more than a few words.

When the knock came, she looked at her watch and swore. She'd been talking to herself for so long that it was time to leave and she wasn't even dressed. Tightening the belt on her robe, she went out of the cramped bedroom into the tiny living area and answered the door.

Cody took one lazy look at her short cotton robe and grinned. "Nice dress."

"I'm running behind," she muttered. "You can go on without me."

"I'll wait." Without waiting for an invitation, he walked in and surveyed her apartment.

She might be a woman who dealt in precise facts and figures, but she lived in chaos. Bright pillows were tossed on a faded couch, and piles of magazines were stacked on a mismatched chair. For someone who made her living turning facts and figures into structure and form, she didn't know the first thing about decorating space—or didn't care to, Cody mused. He'd seen her work, and had admired it. If she put her mind to it, he figured, she could turn a closet into an organized and functional living area.

The room was smaller than the bedroom of his hotel suite, but no one would have called it impersonal. Dozens of pictures jockeyed for position on a long table in front of the single window. There was a comfortable layer of dust over everything except a collection of crystals that hung at the window and caught the last of the evening light.

That, more than anything else in the room, told him that she spent little time there but cared for what mattered to her.

"I won't be long," Abra told him. "If you want a drink or something, the kitchen's through there."

She escaped, clicking the door firmly behind her. God, he looked wonderful. It wasn't fair for him to look so sexy, so confident, so utterly perfect. She dragged her hands through the hair she had yet to attempt to style. It was bad enough that he looked so good in work clothes, but he looked even better in a cream-colored jacket that set off his sun-bleached hair and his tanned skin, and that didn't seem fair. Even dressed more formally for the evening he didn't lose the casual flair of the beachcomber or the masculine appeal of the cowboy. How was she supposed to fight off an attraction when every time he showed up he was that much more attractive?

The hell with it, she thought as she faced her closet again. She was going to handle him and the attraction she felt. That meant she wasn't going to wear that plain and proper blue suit after all. If she was going to play with fire, she decided, she was going to have to dress for it.

Cody found her kitchen in the same unapologetic disarray as the living room. One wouldn't have called it dirty. Something normally had to be put to use to get that way, and it was obvious that she wasn't a woman who spent a lot of time over a stove. The fact that she had a tin of cookies and a canister full of tea bags set on two of the burners made that clear.

He found a bottle of wine in the refrigerator, along with a jar of peanut butter and one lonely egg. After a search through the cupboards he located two mismatched wineglasses and a paperback copy of a horror novel by a well-known writer.

He took a sip of the wine and shook his head. He hoped he'd have a chance to teach her a little about vintages. Carrying both glasses into the living room, he listened to the sounds of movement from the bedroom. Apparently she was looking for something and pulling out every drawer she owned in the search. Sipping gingerly, he studied her photographs.

There were some of her, one a formal shot showing that she'd been very uncomfortable in pink organdy. There was another with her standing beside an attractive blonde. Since the blonde had Abra's hazel eyes, Cody wondered if she might be an older sister. There were more of the blonde, one in what might have been a wedding dress, and another of Abra in a hard hat. There were pictures of men scattered throughout, the only one he recognized being of Thornway senior. He sipped again, wondering if any were of her father, then turned. The noises in the bedroom had stopped.

"I poured some wine," he called out. "Want yours?"

"No... Yes, damn it."

"I'll go with the yes." Walking over, Cody pushed open the bedroom door.

There was something about a long, slender woman in a black dress, Cody decided. Something that made a man's mouth water. The dress dipped low in the front, and the plunge was banded with silver in a design that was repeated again at the hem, where the skirt skimmed above her knees. The glitter was designed to draw the eye before it moved down the length of slim legs clad in sheer, smoky stockings. But it was the back that was troubling Abra. She was struggling to fasten the hooks, which stopped at her waist.

"Something's stuck."

His heartbeat, Cody thought, and he waited for it to pick up speed again. If she'd attracted him in a hard hat and a sweaty T-shirt, that was nothing compared to what she was doing to him now.

"Here." He stepped over sturdy work boots and a pair of glossy black heels that were no more than a few leather straps.

"They design these things so that you have to fight your way in and out of them."

"Yeah." He handed her both glasses and tried not to think about how much more interesting it would be to help her fight her way out of this particular scrap of black silk. "You've got the hooks twisted."

She let out an impatient breath. "I know that. Can you fix it?"

He glanced up, and their eyes met in the mirror above her dresser. For the first time since he'd seen her, she had put on lipstick. Her mouth looked slick and ripe and inviting. "Probably. What are you wearing?"

She sipped because her throat was suddenly dry. "That should be obvious. A black dress with faulty hooks."

"I mean the scent." He dipped a little closer to her neck.

"I don't know." She would have moved away, but his fingers were busy at the waist of her dress. "Something my mother bought me."

"I'm going to have to meet your mother."

She sipped again. "Are you finished back there?"

"Not nearly." He skimmed his fingers up her back and had the pleasure of watching her reaction reflected in the mirror. "You're very responsive, Abra."

"We're very late," she countered, turning.

"Then a couple of minutes more shouldn't matter." He slid his hands lightly around her waist. In defense, she pressed both glasses against his chest. He took them patiently and set them on the dresser behind her. "You have lousy taste in wine."

"I know the difference between white and red." She

lifted her hands to his shoulders as he circled her waist again. His grip was loose, just the slight pressure of his fingertips against her. But she didn't shift aside.

"That's like saying I'm a man and you're a woman. There's a lot more to it than that." He bent his head to nibble at her lips. He'd been right. They were inviting. Very inviting. "A whole lot more."

"With me things are one way or another. Cody." She arched away as she felt the floor tilt under her feet. "I'm not ready for this."

A yes or no he would have dealt with swiftly. But there was a desperation in her words that made him pull back. "For what?"

"For what's happening." There were times for flat-out honesty. "For you and what I'm feeling."

His eyes skimmed over her face and came back to hers. She'd given him the leverage. They both knew it. Rather than applying weight, he gave her space. "How long do you need?"

"That's not a question I can answer." Her fingers tightened on his shoulders as his hands moved up and down her back. "You keep backing me into corners."

"So I do," he murmured. He moved aside and waited while she stepped into her shoes. "Abra." When she looked at him again, he took her hand. "This isn't the end of it. I have a feeling the end's a long way off."

She was absolutely certain he was right. That was what worried her. "I have a policy," she said carefully. "I like to know what the end looks like before I begin. I can't see a nice clean finish with you, Cody, so I'm not altogether sure I want to take you on—so to speak."

"Red." He brought her hand to his lips, leaving her flustered. "You already have."

* * *

By the time they arrived at the Thornway estate, the party was in full swing. The buffet was loaded with spicy Mexican cuisine, and wine and margaritas flowed. Beyond the spreading white-and-pink ranch house that Tim had had built for his bride was a sweep of carefully manicured lawn dotted with a few rustling palms. A pool glittered at the tip of a slight slope. Near it was a pretty gazebo shielded by trailing vines just beginning to bloom.

The scent from the side garden was as sweet as the moonlight.

There was a crowd mingling on the glassed-in terrace and the lawn. The cream of Phoenix society had turned out. Abra had already decided to find herself a nice quiet corner. She was always pleased to build for the upper crust, but she didn't have a clue how to socialize with them.

"A Chablis," Cody explained as he handed Abra a glass. "California. Nice clean color, sharp aroma and very full-bodied."

Abra lifted a shoulder as she sipped. "It's white."

"And your dress is black, but it doesn't make you look like a nun."

"Wine's wine," she said, though her palate told her differently.

"Honey—" he trailed a finger down the side of her throat "—you have a lot to learn."

"There you are." Marci Thornway, Tim's wife of two years, glided up. She wore a heavily embroidered white silk caftan, and around her neck was a jeweled collar that glittered in the moonlight. She gave Abra a pat on the hand, then lifted her sapphire-blue eyes to Cody. Her voice dripped like Spanish moss. "I suppose I can understand why you were late."

"Marci Thornway, Cody Johnson."

"The architect." Marci slipped a proprietary hand through Cody's arm. "Tim's told me all about you—except he didn't mention you were so attractive." She laughed. It was a musical sound that suited her silvery blond looks and her petite frame. "But then, husbands have to be forgiven for not telling their wives about handsome men."

"Or men about their beautiful wives."

Abra made a face behind Marci's back and began to spoon up a cheese enchilada.

"You're from Florida, aren't you?" With a little sigh, Marci began leading Cody away. "I grew up in Georgia, a little town outside of Atlanta. Sometimes I swear I could pine away from missing it."

"Little magnolia blossom," Abra muttered, and turned directly into Barlow. "Oh, excuse me, Mr. Barlow."

"That's WW to you. Ought to put more on your plate, girl. Here, try these tortillas. Don't forget the guacamole."

Abra stared down at the food he had heaped on her dish. "Thanks."

"Why don't you have a seat with me and keep an old man company in the moonlight?"

Abra wasn't sure what she'd expected of this evening, but it hadn't been to enjoy a sweet and funny hour with one of the richest men in the country. He didn't, as she had half feared, make a pass, but flirted like an old family friend across the comfortable distance of thirty-five years.

They sat on a bench by the rippling waters of the pool and talked about their mutual love of movies. It was the one vice Abra allowed herself, the only pure recreation she didn't consider a waste of time.

If her attention wandered from time to time, it wasn't because she found Barlow boring, it was because she spotted Cody off and on—more often than not in Marci Thorn-way's company.

"Selfish," Barlow decided as he finished off his drink. "Ought to let you mingle with the young people."

Feeling guilty about her lapse, she gave him a warm smile. "Oh, no, I like talking to you. To tell you the truth, WW, I'm not much on parties."

"Pretty thing like you needs a young man to fuss over her."

"I don't like to be fussed over at all." She saw Cody light Marci's cigarette.

Barlow was nothing if not shrewd. He followed the direction of Abra's gaze. "Now there's a pretty little thing," he observed. "Like spun glass—expensive and easy to look at. Young Tim must have his hands full."

"He's very devoted to her."

"Been keeping your architect close company this evening."

"*Your* architect," Abra said. Because she didn't like the way that sounded, she smiled. "They're both from the East—Southeast. I'm sure they have a lot in common."

"Mmm." Plainly amused, Barlow rose. "Like to stretch my legs. How about walking around the garden?"

"All right." She made a point of keeping her back to Cody as she took Barlow's arm and strolled off.

What the hell kind of game was she playing? Cody wondered as he watched Abra disappear with Barlow. The man was old enough—more than old enough—to be her father. She'd spent the entire evening cozying up to the man while he'd been trying to untangle himself from the wisteria vine called Marci Thornway.

Cody recognized a woman on the prowl, and the porcelain-cheeked Marci was definitely sending out signals—

ones Cody wasn't the least bit interested in receiving. Even
if he hadn't already set his sights on Abra, he wouldn't have
felt the slightest tug from a woman like Marci. Married or
not, she was trouble. Tim was welcome to her.

He wouldn't have judged Abra to be the kind of woman
to flatter an old man, to smile and flirt with one with an eye
to what it could gain her. There was no mistaking the fact
that Barlow was smitten with her, or that she had just wandered off into the roses with one of the *Fortune* 500's best.

Cody lit a cigarette, then narrowed his eyes against the
smoke. There was no mistaking the fact that she had wanted
him. He might have initiated the kiss—might even have
backed her into a corner, as she'd said—but her response
had been full-blown. No one kissed like that unless she
meant it.

Yet she'd pulled back. Each time. He'd thought it was
because she was cautious, maybe even a little afraid of
how strong the connection between them had become. And
maybe he was a fool, and she held him off because she
wanted to snag a bigger fish.

Almost as soon as the thought took root, he ripped it
out. It was unfair, he told himself. He was allowing himself to think that way because he was frustrated—because
he wanted Abra more than he had ever wanted anyone.
And, most of all, because he didn't know what the hell to
do about it.

"Excuse me." He cut Marci off in midsentence, sent her
a quick smile and strode off toward the garden.

He heard Abra's laughter, a low whispering sound that
made him think of the mist on the lake near his home. Then
he saw her, standing in the beam of one of the colored lanterns the Thornways' staff had hung all over the garden.
She was smiling, twirling a red blossom in her fingertips.

The same kind of flower, Cody noted, that she had mangled on his terrace only the night before.

"There's not much meat," Barlow was saying as he grinned at her, "but what's there is choice."

She laughed again, then slipped the stem of the flower into his lapel.

"I beg your pardon."

Both Barlow and Abra turned—guiltily, Cody thought—at the sound of his voice.

"Well, Johnson, been enjoying yourself?" Barlow gave him a quick slap on the shoulder. "Enjoy yourself more if you took a stroll in the moonlight with someone as pretty as our Abra here. Young people don't take enough time for romance these days. Going to see if I can dig up a beer."

For a broad man, he moved quickly enough and Abra found herself alone in the festively lit garden with Cody. "I should probably go mingle—" she began, but she stopped short when Cody blocked her path.

"You haven't felt the need to mingle all evening."

Her main thought was to get out of the garden and away from him, so she just gave him a vague smile. "I've been enjoying WW. He's great company."

"I noticed. It's an unusual woman who can jump from man to man so smoothly. My compliments."

The smile turned into a look of blank confusion.

Cody found a match and cupped his hand over the flame as he lit a cigarette. "He might be in his sixties, but two or three hundred million melt the years away, I imagine."

Abra stared at him for nearly a full minute. "Maybe you should go out and come in again. Then I might understand what you're talking about."

He tossed aside the match. In heels she was eye to eye with him. "I think I'm clear enough. Barlow's a very rich man, widowed for about ten years, and one who obviously appreciates a young, attractive woman."

She nearly laughed, but then she saw the disdain in his eyes. He was serious, she realized. It was incredibly insulting. "You could say he's certainly a man who knows how to treat a woman. Now, if you'll excuse me."

He grabbed her arm before she could storm past him. "I don't find any excuse for you, Red, but that doesn't stop me from wanting you." He pulled her around until they were once again face-to-face. "Can't say that I care for it, but there it is. I want you, and whatever goes on in that calculating head of yours I intend to have you."

"You can go straight to hell, Johnson." She jerked her arm away, but she wasn't through. "I don't care what you want, or what you think of me, but because I like Mr. Barlow too much to let you go on thinking he's some kind of senile fool, I'll let you in on something. We had a conversation tonight, the way some people do in social situations. We happened to hit it off. I wasn't coming on to him, nor he to me."

"What about that crack I heard when I walked up?"

"What?" She hesitated a minute, and then she did laugh. But her eyes were cold. "That was a line from a movie, you simpleton. An old Tracy-Hepburn movie. Mr. Barlow and I both happen to be fans. And I'll tell you something else." Temper lost, she shoved him, taking him back two steps. "If he *had* been coming on to me, it would've been none of your business. If I want to flirt with him, that's my business. If I want to have an affair with him—or anyone else—you don't have jack to say about it." She shoved him again, just for the satisfaction. "Maybe I prefer his kind of attention to the grab-and-go treatment I get from you."

"Now hold on."

"You hold on." Her eyes glowed green in the light from the lanterns. "I have no intention of tolerating this kind of insult from you, or anyone. So keep clear, Johnson, if you want that face of yours to stay in one piece."

She stormed off, leaving Cody singed. He let out a breath between his teeth as he dropped the cigarette onto the path and crushed it out.

"You had that one coming, Johnson," he muttered, rubbing the back of his neck. He knew what it was to dig a hole, and he knew he'd dug this one deep. He also knew that there was only one way out.

Chapter 5

He thought about flowers. Somehow Cody didn't think Abra was the type of woman to melt at the sight of a few roses. He considered a straight-out apology, the kind of no-frills shoot-from-the-hip *I'm sorry* one friend might offer another. But he didn't think Abra saw him as a friend, exactly. In any case, the ice she was dishing out would freeze the words before they got from his mouth to her ear. So he gave her the only thing he thought she would accept for the time being. Space.

They worked together over the next two weeks, often shoulder to shoulder. The distance between them was as great as that between the sun and the moon. Consultations were often necessary, but Abra always arranged it so that they weren't alone. With a skill he was forced to admire, she used Charlie Gray as a buffer. It couldn't have been easy, but she avoided Cody altogether whenever possible. Understanding the need for a cooling-off period, he did nothing to change the situation. Twice he made brief trips, once to the home office in Fort Lauderdale and once to work out a few bugs in a medical complex in San Diego.

Each time he returned he stuck a toe in the waters of Abra's temperament and found them still frigid.

With his hard hat in place and his eyes shielded by tinted glasses, Cody watched the glass of the dome being lowered into place.

"A nice touch. A class touch." Barlow looked up, grinning at the light that came through the glass in red-and-gold spears.

"WW." Cody relaxed a bit when the glass settled on the opening like a cap on a bottle. "Didn't know you were back in town."

"Doing some spot-checking." Barlow mopped his face with a handkerchief. "Hope they get that cooling system going."

"It's on today's schedule."

"Good. Good." Barlow turned around, wanting to take in the entire sweep of building. It pleased him. It had the look of a castle, noble and impregnable, yet at the same time was unabashedly modern. He strolled over to study the glass arch of roof that brought the mountain into the lobby. He approved of the dramatic touch here, where guests would check in and out. First and last impressions, he thought. Young Johnson was making certain they would be lasting ones. Landscapers would plant a few desert shrubs and cacti, then let nature take over. All along the west wall were wide arching windows that let in the vast arena of desert and butte. To the west, men were connecting pipe and laying the stone pool for the waterfall.

"I'll say this, boy—you deliver." It was the kind of blunt compliment Barlow gave only when it was deserved. "I'll admit I had some bad moments over the blueprints and the mock-ups, but my son saw something in all this. I went with his judgment, and I can say now he was right. You've made yourself something here, Cody. Not every man can look back on his life and say the same."

"I appreciate that."

"I'm going to want you to show me the rest." He slapped Cody on the back. "Meantime, is there a place a man can get a beer around here?"

"I think we can arrange it." Cody led the way outside to an ice chest and dug out two cans.

Barlow drank deeply and sighed. His thinning hair was covered by a straw hat with a paisley band. A porch hat, Cody's mother would have called it. It had the effect of making the millionaire look like a retired tobacco farmer.

"I'll be sixty-five my next birthday, and there's still nothing quite like a cold beer on a hot afternoon." Barlow glanced toward the health club and caught a glimpse of Abra. "Well, maybe one thing." With a quick bray of laughter he sat down on the ice chest and loosened his collar. "I like to think of myself as a student of human nature. Figure I made most of my money that way."

"Mmm-hmm," Cody responded absently. He, too, had spotted Abra. She was wearing baggy bib overalls that should have made her appear sexless. They didn't. Cody kept remembering how she'd looked in the little black dress.

"Seems to me you're a man with more on his mind than steel and glass." Barlow swigged his beer with simple appreciation. "Wouldn't have something to do with a long-legged engineer, would it?"

"Might." Cody sent him a mild look as he took out his cigarettes. He offered Barlow one, but the older man shook his head.

"Had to give them up. Damn doctors yammering at me. Took a liking to her," he continued, switching back easily to the subject of Abra. "'Course, most men take a liking to good looks, but she's got brains and grit. Might have scared me off in my younger days." He grinned and took off his hat to fan his face. "Seemed to me you two had a tiff at that do we had at Tim Thornway's."

"You could call it that." Cody sipped and considered. "I was jealous of you."

"Jealous?" Barlow had lifted the can to his lips. Now he had to set it on the ground for fear he'd drop it as he roared with laughter. Cutting loose, he rocked back and forth on the chest, mopping his streaming face with his handkerchief. "You just knocked twenty years off me, boy. I gotta thank you." He sucked in air, then let it out again in a wheeze. "Imagine a good-looking sonofabitch like you jealous of an old man." He caught his breath and leaned back, still grinning. "A rich old man. Well, well, I don't suppose the little lady took kindly to that."

"The little lady," Cody drawled, "came very close to knocking out my teeth."

"Told you she had grit." Barlow stuffed his handkerchief back in his pocket, then picked up his beer. Life still had some surprises, he thought. Thank God. "Fact is, I had her in mind for my son." At Cody's look, he chuckled and dropped the hat back on his head. "Don't get your dander up now, boy. A man can only take so much excitement in one day. 'Sides, decided against it when I saw the way she looked at you."

"That simplifies things."

"Between you and me, anyway," Barlow pointed out. "Otherwise, I'd say you were about waist-deep in quicksand."

"Pretty accurate estimate." Cody tossed his empty can in a trash barrel. "Any suggestions?"

"Better find yourself a rope, son, and haul your tail out."

"My father always used flowers," Cody mused.

"Couldn't hurt." Wincing at a few creaks in his joints, Barlow rose. "Neither would groveling." He noted Cody's expression and laughed again. "Too young for groveling yet," he said. "But you'll learn." He gave Cody a thump on the back. "Yes, indeed, you'll learn."

He wasn't about to grovel. Absolutely not. But he thought it might be time to give the flowers a shot. If a woman hadn't cooled off some in two weeks, she wasn't going to cool off at all—at least not without a little help.

In any case, Cody told himself, he owed her an apology. He laughed a little to himself as he shifted the tiger lilies to his other hand. It seemed as if they'd been bouncing apologies back and forth since the first minute they'd met. Why break the pattern? he mused as he stood in front of her door. If she didn't accept it now, he'd just stick around and drive her crazy until she did.

Each of them seemed to excel at driving the other crazy.

Besides, he'd missed her. It was as simple as that. He'd missed arguing with her about the project. He'd missed hearing her laugh the way she could when her guard was down. He'd missed the strong, uninhibited way her arms would come around him.

He glanced at the flowers in his hand. Tiger lilies were a pretty fragile rope, but they were better than none at all. Even if she tossed them in his face, it would be a change from the stiff politeness she'd dished out since the evening at Tim's. He knocked and wondered what he was going to say to get his foot in the door.

It wasn't Abra who answered, but the blonde from the photographs. She was a small, rosy-cheeked woman Cody guessed was about forty. She was dressed very simply, in a copper-colored jumpsuit that complemented her hair and her eyes, which were so much like Abra's. Cody smiled at her, as much for that as for the fact that, in her porcelain way, she was a knockout.

"Well, hello." She smiled back at him and offered a hand. "I'm Jessie Peters."

"Cody Johnson. I'm a—an associate of Abra's."

"I see." She gave him a slow, sweeping study that was laced with feminine approval. "Come in. I always love meeting Abra's…associates. Would you like a drink? Abra's in the shower."

"Sure." He remembered Abra's wine. "Something cold, if you have it."

"I've just made some lemonade. Fresh. Make yourself at home." She disappeared into the adjoining kitchen. "Was Abra expecting you?"

"No." He glanced around, noting that the apartment had had a swift but thorough tidying.

"A surprise, then. I love surprises." She walked back in with two tall glasses crackling with ice. "Are you an engineer?"

"I'm an architect."

Jessie paused for a moment. Then a smile wisped around her mouth. "*The* architect," she murmured, gesturing for Cody to sit. "I believe Abra's mentioned you."

"I'll bet." He set the flowers on the newly dusted table.

"She didn't mention you were so attractive." Jessie crossed her legs and settled back. "But it's like her to keep a thing like that to herself." She ran a fingertip down her glass as she summed him up. Her hand was pretty and fragile-looking, like the novelty magnet in Abra's car. There was a diamond on her finger, a small one in a rather ornate setting, but no wedding band. "You're from the East?"

"That's right. Florida."

"I never think of Florida as the East," she commented. "I always think of Disney World."

"Did I hear the door? I— Oh." Abra came out of the adjoining bedroom. She was wearing baggy white pants and an oversize sweatshirt with a pair of battered-looking sandals. Her hair was still damp and curled from the shower.

"You have company." Jessie rose and gathered up the flowers. "Bearing gifts."

"Yes, I see." Abra dug her hands into the deep pockets of her pants.

With her bright smile still in place, Jessie buried her face in the blooms. She recognized tension and romance. As far as she was concerned, one was wasted without the other. "Why don't I put these in water for you, sweetheart? You don't happen to have a vase, do you?"

"Somewhere."

"Of course."

Abra waited until Jessie went into the kitchen to search for it. Cautious, she kept her voice low. "What do you want?"

"To see you."

Abra's hands tightened into fists in her pockets when he rose. "You've done that. Now, if you'll excuse me, I'm busy this evening."

"And to apologize," Cody continued.

She hesitated, then let out a long breath. She had gone to him once with an apology, and he had accepted. If there was one thing she understood, it was how difficult it was to try to mend fences temper had broken.

"It's all right," she said, and managed what she hoped was a casual smile. "Let's forget it."

"Wouldn't you like an explanation?" He took a step forward. She took one backward.

"I don't think so. It might be best if—"

"I found one." Jessie came back in holding a milk bottle. "So to speak. Actually, I think they look charming in this, don't you?" She set the flowers in the center of the coffee table, then stepped back to admire them. "Don't forget to change the water, Abra. And it wouldn't hurt to lift the vase up when you dust."

"Mom…"

"Mom? You've got to be kidding." The genuine astonishment in Cody's voice had Jessie beaming.

"That's the nicest compliment I've had all day," she said. "If I didn't love her so much, I'd deny it." Raising up on her toes, she kissed Abra's cheek, then brushed lightly at the faint smear of lipstick she left behind. "You two have a nice evening. Don't forget to call me."

"But you just got here."

"I've a million things to do." Jessie gave her daughter's hand a squeeze, then offered her own to Cody. "It was lovely meeting you."

"I hope I see you again, Mrs. Peters."

"Jessie." She smiled again. "I insist that all handsome men call me Jessie." The sweep of her lashes was the gesture of a practiced flirt. "Good night, sweetheart. Oh, you're almost out of dish detergent."

Abra let out a huff of breath when the door closed.

"Are you sure that's your mother?"

"Most of the time." Abra tunneled her fingers through her hair. Jessie always left her feeling bewildered. "Look, Cody, I appreciate you coming by to clear the air."

"Now clear out?"

"I don't want to be rude. I think both of us have used up our share of rudeness for this year, but it would simplify things if we kept our contact limited to working hours."

"I never said I wanted things simple." He took a step closer. Her eyes stayed warily on his as he toyed with the damp ends of her hair. "But if you do, fine. I look at you and I want. It doesn't get much simpler than that."

"For you." If it was difficult not to step away, it was much more difficult not to step forward. "I don't want to get into all of the reasons, but when I told you that I wasn't ready I was being perfectly honest. Added to that is the fact that we just don't get along very well. We don't know each other. We don't understand each other."

"All right. So we'll get to know each other."

"You're simplifying."

"Isn't that what you just said you wanted?"

Feeling trapped, she turned away and sat down. "Cody, I told you, I have reasons for not wanting to get involved with you, with anyone."

"Let's just stick with me." He sat across from her. For the life of him he couldn't understand why he was so keyed up. He had very little time or energy to put into a relationship at this point in his life. He certainly wasn't looking for one. He corrected himself. Hadn't been. This one, one he couldn't seem to resist, had crashed onto his head. "Okay, Wilson, why don't we look at this logically? Engineers are logical people, right?"

"We are." She wished the flowers weren't sitting so bright and lovely between them.

"We have to work together for a few months yet. If there's tension between people, they don't work well. If we keep walking on eggshells around each other the way we have been the last couple weeks, the project's going to suffer."

"Okay, you have a point." She smiled. "But I'm not going to go to bed with you to ease the tension."

"And I thought you were dedicated." He sat back and braced his ankle on his knee. "If that's out..." He raised a questioning brow.

"Definitely."

"How about pizza and a movie?"

She started to speak, then stopped. She was logical. She was trained to take facts to the correct conclusion. "Nothing else?"

"That would depend."

"No." Shaking her head, Abra lifted her mother's untouched lemonade. "I prefer to deal in absolutes. If we agree to get to know each other, to try to develop a professional and a personal relationship, I have to know that the personal relationship will remain on a certain level. So we set ground rules."

He lifted a brow. "Should I get out my notepad?"

"If you like," she said mildly. "But I think we can keep it simple. We can see each other, as friends, as associates. No romantic situations."

Amused, Cody watched her. "Define 'romantic situation.'"

"I think you get the picture, Johnson. You're right in the sense that we are working closely together. If either one of us is in a snit, the work suffers. A personal understanding and respect can only lead to better professional communication."

"You ought to write that down for the next staff meeting." He held up a hand before she could snap at him. "Okay, we'll give it a shot your way. Pals." He leaned over and offered his hand. When she took it, he grinned. "Guess I'll have to take back the flowers."

"Oh, no. You gave them to me before we set the rules." She rose, pleased with herself. "I'll buy the pizza. You spring for the movie."

It was going to work. Over the next few days Abra congratulated herself on taking a potentially volatile situation and making it into a pleasant arrangement. There were times, inevitably, that they rubbed each other the wrong way on the job. When they saw each other after working hours, they met as casual friends to enjoy a meal or a show. If she caught herself longing for more after she dropped Cody at his hotel or he left her at her apartment, she smothered the need.

Little by little she learned more about him, about the farm he had grown up on, about his struggle to finish his education. He didn't speak of the financial hardships or the backbreaking hours he'd had to put in, but she was able, as their time together went on, to hear what he didn't say through what he did.

It changed her view of him. She'd seen him as a pampered, privileged partner in a top architectural firm. She hadn't considered the fact that he had worked his way up to where he was in much the same way she had. Abra admired ambition when it was married with drive and old-fashioned hard labor.

She was more careful than he about giving away pieces of her private life. She spoke easily about her years with Thornway and about her admiration for the man who had given her her chance. But she never mentioned her family or her childhood. Though he noted the shield, Cody made no attempt to pierce it. What was growing between them was still fragile. He had no intention of pushing harder until a firm foundation had been laid.

If Abra was pleased with herself and the arrangement, Cody was growing more and more frustrated. He wanted to touch her—a fingertip to her cheek, a hand to her hair. He knew that if he made even so gentle a move the tenuous thread that was spinning between them would snap. Time and again he told himself to back off completely, to call a halt to their platonic evenings. But he couldn't. Seeing her, spending time with her, had become a habit too strong to break.

Still, he was beginning to think that whoever had said half a loaf was better than none hadn't known anything about real hunger.

Hands on hips, Abra stood and watched the crew of engineers and mechanics work on the mechanism for the sliding roof. The envelope for the glass was completed, and the glass itself would be installed at the end of the week. The sun beat mercilessly down on the smoothed concrete while she worried over her design like a mother hen.

"Darling!"

"Mom?" Her concentration broken, Abra managed to smooth her frown into a smile. "What are you doing here?"

"You talk about this place so much, I thought it was time I came to see for myself." She tilted her hard hat at a jaunty angle. "I talked Mr. Blakerman into giving me just a smidgen longer for my lunch hour." She linked arms with her daughter as they stood in the stream of sunlight. "Abra, this place is fabulous. Absolutely fabulous. Of course, I don't know anything about these things, and all those little places over there look like a bunch of stick houses in heaps of dirt."

"Those are the cabanas."

"Whatever. But that big building I saw when I drove in.

Incredible. It looks like a castle out of the twenty-fourth century."

"That about sums it up."

"I've never seen anything like it before. It's so alluring, so majestic. Just the way I've always thought of the desert."

Abra glanced back at her mother. "Really?"

"Oh, yes. I can tell you, when I first saw it I could hardly believe my own little girl had a part in something so, well... grand." She beamed as she inspected the empty pool, which was even now being faced with mosaic tiles. She didn't miss the tanned, muscular arms of the laborers, either. "Why, it's shaped like a half-moon. How clever. Everything's curved and arched, isn't it? It makes for a relaxed tone, don't you think? Just the right effect for a resort."

"I suppose," Abra murmured, hating to admit that she was beginning to see the appeal of it herself.

"What goes up there?"

Frowning again, Abra looked up through the roof at the hard blue sky. "Glass, movable glass. It'll be tinted to filter the sunlight. When it's opened, the two panels will separate and slide into the curve of the walls."

"Wonderful. I'd love to see it when it's finished. Do you have time to show me around, or should I just wander?"

"I can't leave just now. If you can—"

"Oh, look, there's your architect." Jessie automatically smoothed her skirt. She had already zeroed in on the shorter, broader man who was walking beside Cody. "And who's that distinguished-looking man with your beau?"

"He's not my beau." Abra took a swift look around to be certain no one had heard Jessie's remark. "I don't have or want a beau."

"That's why I worry about you, sweetheart."

Patience, Abra told herself. She would be patient. "Cody Johnson is my associate."

"Whatever you say, darling. But who's that with him?"

"That's Mr. Barlow. It's his resort."

"Really?" Jessie was already aiming a smile at Cody and holding out both hands. "Hello again. I was just telling Abra how much I like your design. I'm sure this is going to be the most beautiful resort in the state."

"Thank you. William Barlow, this is Abra's mother, Jessie Peters."

"Mother?" Barlow's bushy brows rose. He'd already tried, and failed, to suck in his stomach. "I didn't know Abra was only sixteen."

Jessie gave a delighted laugh. "I hope you don't mind my popping in like this, Mr. Barlow. I've been dying to see what Abra's been working on so long and hard. Now that I have, I'm convinced it's been worth it."

"We're very pleased with Abra's work. You can be proud of her."

"I've always been proud of Abra." Her lashes swept down, then up. "But tell me, Mr. Barlow, how did you ever imagine putting a resort here, and such a beautiful one?"

"That's a long story."

"Oh." Jessie sent a rueful look at Abra. "Well, I know I'm keeping everyone from their work. I'd hoped Abra could give me a little tour, but that will have to wait."

"Perhaps you'll allow me to show you around."

"I'd love it." Jessie put a hand on Barlow's beefy arm. "But I don't want to be in the way."

"Nonsense." Barlow gave her hand a quick pat. "We'll just leave everything in capable hands and have a nice stroll."

They started off, with Jessie sending a fleeting smile over her shoulder.

"There she goes again," Abra muttered.

"Hmm?"

"Nothing." With her hands jammed into her pockets, Abra turned away to watch her men. It disturbed her, and always had, to watch her mother in action. "We should have the wiring and supports finished by the end of the day."

"Good. Now do you want to tell me what's bugging you?"

Bad-temperedly she shrugged off the hand he put on her shoulder. "I said nothing. We had some problems with the angle."

"You've worked it out."

"At considerable time and expense."

They were going to fight. Knowing it, Cody rubbed the bridge of his nose between his thumb and forefinger. "Don't you get tired of singing the same song?"

"With a slight change in degrees—"

"It would have changed the look, and the feel."

"A fly stuck on the glass wouldn't have noticed the changes I wanted."

"I would have noticed."

"You were being obstinate."

"No," Cody said slowly, struggling to pace his words well behind his temper. "I was being right."

"Stubborn. The same way you were being stubborn when you insisted we had to use solid sheets of glass rather than panes."

Without a word, Cody took her arm and dragged her away.

"What the hell are you doing?"

"Just shut up." With Abra dragging her heels, he pulled her down the steps into the empty pool. Laborers glanced over, tiles in hand, and grinned. Taking her face in his hands, he pushed her head back. "What do you see?"

"Sky, damn it. And if you don't let go you're going to see stars."

"That's right. Sky. That's what I want you to see. Whether the roof's open or whether it's closed. Not panes of glass, not a window, not a roof, but sky. It's my job to imagine, Wilson, and yours to make it work."

She shrugged out of his hold. The sides of the pool rose around them. If the water had been added, it would have been well over her head. For now the pool was like an arena.

"Let me tell you something, hotshot. Not everything that can be imagined can be engineered. Maybe that's not what people like you want to hear, but that's the way it is."

"You know the trouble with you, Red? You're too hung up to dream, too buttoned into your columns and calculations. Two and two always make four in your head, no matter how much better life might be if once in a while it came up five."

"Do you know how crazy that sounds?"

"Yeah. And I also know it sounds intriguing. Why don't you take a little time out to wonder why not instead of always assuming the negative?"

"I don't assume anything. I just believe in reality."

"This is reality," he said, grabbing her. "The wood, the glass, the steel, the sweat. That's reality. And damn it, so is this."

He clamped his mouth onto hers before either of them had a chance to think. Work around them stopped for ten humming seconds. Neither of them noticed. Neither of them cared. Abra discovered that, though the pool was indeed empty, she was still in over her head.

She'd wanted this. There was no denying it now, not when his lips were hot and demanding on hers. She curled her fingers into his work shirt, but not in protest. In possession. She held him close as the need spiraled high inside her, very fast and, yes, very real.

He hadn't meant to touch her this way, to take what he had tried to convince himself she would give him in her own time. Patience had always been an integral part of his nature—the knowing when, the knowing how. But with her none of the old rules seemed to apply.

Perhaps if her response hadn't been so complete, if he hadn't tasted desire warm and waiting on her lips, he could have pulled back. But, like Abra, he was in over his head and sinking fast. For the first time in his life he wanted to sweep a woman up and away like some knight on a white charger. He wanted just as badly to drag her to the ground and have her like a primitive warrior reaping the spoils of victory. He wanted, like a poet, to light the candles and set the music. Most of all, he wanted Abra.

When he drew her away, she was dazed and speech-less. He had kissed her before and sent the passion swimming. But there was something different, something deeper, something desperate, about this. For a moment she could only stand and stare at him, giddy with the knowledge that a woman could fall in love anywhere, anytime, even when she had barricaded her heart against it.

"That real enough for you?" Cody murmured.

She only shook her head as the buzzing in her brain cleared and separated into sounds. The whirl of drills, the slap of trowels, the murmur of men. The color rose into her cheeks quickly, and with it a combination of fury, embarrassment and self-reproach.

"How dare you do something like that here?"

He hooked his thumbs in his pockets when he realized he was still angry enough to do something rash and regrettable. "You got someplace else in mind?"

"Keep away from me, Johnson," she said under her breath. "Or you'll find yourself hauled up on sexual harassment charges."

His eyes remained very calm and very level. "We both know that what happened here has nothing to do with harassment, sexual or otherwise. It's personal, Red, and keeping my distance isn't going to make it go away."

"Fine," she said, going toe-to-toe with him. The argument interested the men around them almost as much as the kiss had. "If it's personal, let's keep it that way. Off the job, Johnson. I'm on Thornway time, and I don't intend to waste it arguing with you."

"Good."

"Good," she echoed, scrambling up the steps and out of the pool.

Cody rocked back on his heels as she stormed out of the building. They would both be off the clock soon enough.

Chapter 6

It was nearly five when Abra stopped by the trailer to splash cold water on her face. After her scene with Cody it seemed as if everything that could go wrong had. A part for the elevators had proved defective, and then there had been another tiff between Rodriguez and Swaggart. One of the carpenters had gotten a splinter in his eye, and Tim had dropped by the site to moan about the budget.

It had all started with her mother's visit, Abra thought as she wiped her dripping face with a towel. It wasn't fair to blame Jessie, but no matter when, no matter where, she was a woman who trailed complications behind her, then waited for other people to clear them up.

Maybe it wasn't right to resent the fact that her mother had hit it off so well with Barlow or to worry about the fallout. But history had a habit of repeating itself. The last thing Abra wanted added to her plate was the possibility of a romance between the owner of the project and her very susceptible mother.

Better to worry about her, Abra decided as she gathered up a load of files to take home. Jessie's varied and colorful love life was much safer to fret over than her own.

She didn't have a love life, Abra reminded herself. She didn't want a love life. Her plans, personal and professional, were all mapped out. She wasn't about to let some high-handed Florida cowboy botch them up.

What the hell had he been thinking of?

The moment the thought ran through her head, she grimaced and kicked the door open. She knew very well what he'd been thinking of, because she'd been thinking of exactly the same thing.

Rockets exploding, volcanoes erupting, tornadoes swirling. It was difficult to think of anything but power and chaos when she was in Cody's arms.

Was it that way for him, too? she wondered as she locked the trailer door. Did he lose part of himself when they came together? Did everything and everyone fade away until they seemed—no, until they *were* totally unimportant?

Of course not, she decided, and gave in enough to rest her forehead against the side of the trailer. He was just another good-looking man with a glib tongue and clever hands. The world was full of them. God knew her mother had made a science out of the search and discovery.

Not fair, Abra thought again as she straightened. Jessie's life was Jessie's life. It wasn't fair to Cody, either, she admitted, shifting the files and starting toward her car. He had initiated the kiss, but she had done nothing to stop it. That made her behavior every bit as outrageous and unprofessional as his.

She should have stopped it. A dozen times through the

rest of the day she'd asked herself why she hadn't. It hadn't been shock, it hadn't even been overpowering lust. Though she would have preferred to lay the blame on either one. It had been... Just for a moment it had been as though something strange and wonderful and completely unexpected had happened. There had been more than need, more than passion, more than desire.

There had been a bang. Those rockets again, she thought ruefully, looking at the buttes, which were shadowed in the lowering sun. But with this bang something had shaken loose. She'd almost believed she had fallen in love.

Which was nonsense, of course. She dug in her pocket for her keys. She was far too levelheaded to take that route ever again. Nonsense or not, the idea was giving her some bad moments.

So, she wouldn't think about it. There were plenty of other problems to occupy her mind, and most of them were in the files she carried. With a little effort and a lot of concentration she could dig out the calculations, work the equations and find the solutions. Finding a solution to Cody was out of her sphere, so she would leave it alone and spare herself the headache.

She turned her head at the sound of a car and had another bad moment when she recognized the sporty little toy Cody had rented. He pulled up beside her, his car spewing dust, just as she yanked her own car door open.

He'd done his own share of thinking that afternoon and he'd come to his own decisions. Before she could slide behind the wheel, he was out and taking her arm.

"Let's go."

"I was just about to."

"We'll take my car."

"You take your car." She turned back to her own.

He took her keys and the files, pocketing the first and tossing the second into the back of his convertible. "Get in."

"What do you think you're doing?" Shoving him aside, she reached in to retrieve her files. "If you think I'm going anywhere with you, you need brain surgery."

"We always do it the hard way, don't we?" he said, and scooped her up.

"You are crazy." She nearly got an elbow into his ribs before she was dumped into the passenger seat. Fuming, she grabbed for the handle. His hand closed like a vise over hers as he waited for her to toss the hair out of her eyes and glare up at him. He leaned down close, and his voice was very soft.

"You get out of this car, Wilson, and I'll make you sorry."

"Give me my keys."

"Not a chance."

She considered the possibility of wrestling the keys from him. She was mad enough, but she knew when she was outweighed. Eyes narrowed, she met him look for look. "Fine. Then I'll walk up to the road and hitch a ride."

"You already have a ride." He stepped back to walk about the hood. Abra pushed the door open. She'd no more than gotten to her feet when he shoved her back again.

"You don't scare me, Johnson."

"I should. We're off the clock, Abra, and we've got business of our own. Personal business." Reaching down, he fastened her safety belt. "I'd keep that on. It could be a rough ride."

By the time she'd fumbled the catch open, he'd slid behind the wheel. Wordlessly he jammed her belt back in its slot before he sent the car spinning up the road.

"What are you trying to prove?"

He turned off the construction road onto the highway.

"I'm not sure yet. But we're going someplace quiet until I figure it out." Dust rose in plumes behind the car. It would take some time for it to settle. "The way I look at it, our first plan didn't pan out, so we go back to the drawing board."

Someplace quiet turned out to be his hotel. Abra's reaction was to slam out of the car and head across the parking lot. Cody simply picked her up and tossed her over his shoulder. Her stream of abuse trailed behind them to his door.

Cody unlocked it and pushed it open, then took the precaution of bolting it before dropping Abra into a chair.

"Want a drink?" he asked. Abra glared at him. "Well, I do." He went to the bar and opened a bottle of wine. "A chardonnay this time. Gold highlights, a bright flavor, a bit tart. You'll like it."

She could probably have made it to the door in a dash, but she was through running. Instead, she rose very slowly, very deliberately, out of the chair. "Do you know what I would like?" she asked in a surprisingly silky voice. The tone of it alerted him even as he drew out the cork. "Do you know what I would *really* like? To see you hanging by your thumbs over a large, open fire." She advanced toward him while he poured two glasses. "A big fire, Johnson, with just enough breeze to draw the smoke away so it wouldn't dull your senses." She slapped her palms on the bar and leaned her face close to his.

"Why don't you try the wine instead?"

She snatched for the glass, but he was quicker. His fingers wrapped firmly around hers. "Red," he said in a reasonable tone, "if you pour this on me, I'm going to have to beat you up."

She jerked the glass away and downed the contents in one swallow. "Thanks for the drink." She made it to the door, dignity intact, but he was there beside her before she could unlock it.

"You'll never learn to appreciate good wine that way." Pulling her back, he shoved her into a chair. "Now sit," he told her. "We can talk this through or I can go with my more primitive instincts. Up to you."

"We have nothing to talk about."

"Fine." As quickly as he'd pushed her into the chair, he hauled her out of it. She managed one sputter of protest before she was swirled into his arms.

He kissed her as though he meant to go on kissing her forever. His mouth was hard, but skilled rather than punishing as it demanded and received response. One hand was caught in her hair, while the other roamed freely. Up and over her it stroked in one long, firm line of possession, discovering her slenderness, her softness, her weaknesses and her strengths. He'd never touched her like this before, and the result stunned both of them.

She was so alive. He could all but feel her pulse through his fingertips. An energy fueled by passion raced through her, leaving him dazed and desperate. There was no one else who had ever set off this combination of needs and sensations inside him.

No one had ever made her feel this way. No one. It terrified her. It delighted her. It was easy, almost too easy, to forget the rules she had set up for their relationship, the reason for them, and the anger he had set boiling in her only moments before. There was only now and the way her body experienced dozens of tiny explosions wherever he touched—wherever she wanted him to go on touching. With a murmur of confused pleasure, she shifted against him and offered more.

Behind them, the phone began to ring. They ignored it and listened to the pounding of their own hearts.

Cody broke away to bury his face in her hair and catch his breath. Another first, he thought. He couldn't think of another woman who had left him breathless.

He held her at arm's length to study her face. Her eyes were big and clouded and very green. He decided she looked every bit as stunned as he felt. If they moved on impulse now, their already shaky foundation would crumble.

"We'd better talk."

She nodded and sank into a chair, wondering if the strength would ever seep back into her legs. "Okay."

Turning to the bar, he poured more wine into her glass. His hand wasn't steady. Cody wondered if he'd find the energy to laugh about that later. He gave her a glass, then took his own to the chair facing hers.

She looked at him then, as she had refused to before. His hair was ruffled by the fast ride in the open car. Hours in the sun had streaked it and deepened his tan. Still, he didn't make her think of a laid-back beachcomber now. There was a sense of movement about him even when he was sitting—arrested, held in check, but ready. The energy was there, and a power she'd already experienced firsthand. If they crossed swords again while this mood was on him, she would lose.

After a long breath, she sipped. "You wanted to talk."

He had to laugh. It helped somehow to diffuse the worst of his tension. "Yeah. That was the idea."

"I don't appreciate being hauled in here this way."

He settled back but discovered that relaxing wasn't as easy as it had once been. "Would you have come if I'd asked nice?"

Her lips curved briefly. "No. But that doesn't give you

the right to turn into a Cro-Magnon and haul me off by the hair."

The image of dragging Abra into a cave had a certain appeal at the moment, but she had a point. "It's not my usual style. Want an apology?"

"I think we've already passed around enough of those. You wanted to talk." She thought she was on firmer ground now. "Since I'm here, we'll talk."

"You look great in overalls, Red."

With a shake of her head, she started to rise. "If that's all—" But he held up a hand.

"I think it's fair to say that the plans we laid out about keeping our personal relationship impersonal are pretty well washed up."

Abra stared into the wine in her glass. When facts were facts, she wasn't one to evade them. "I guess that's fair."

She didn't look too thrilled by the admission, he thought, fumbling for a match. He nearly swore at his own clumsiness. Even when he dragged smoke into his lungs, all he could taste was her. "So, where do we go from here?"

She looked up then. Her eyes were calm again, calm and direct. Whatever fears were swirling inside her were carefully controlled. "You seem to have all the answers."

"Abra—" He stopped himself, knowing it would do no good to lose his temper again or to demand more than she was ready to give. "You'd like to keep things simple." He took a sip of his wine. "Do I have that right?"

Simple? she thought wildly. Things would never be simple again. Her fingers tightened on the stem of her glass, and she deliberately relaxed them. He looked so in control. "Yes. I can't imagine that either of us have time for complications at this point in our lives."

Complications. He nearly sprang out of the chair and

grabbed her to show her just how complicated things already were. She looked so composed. "Then we'll deal with the facts. Fact one, I want you." He saw something—passion, fear, hope—flicker in her eyes. "Fact two, you want me." He took a moment to crush out his cigarette. "Now, if we work with those two factors and add the information that neither of us are kids, that we're both responsible adults who are smart enough to approach a relationship intellectually, as well as emotionally, we should come up with, as you said, a simple answer."

She didn't want to be intellectual. She didn't want to be smart. It had taken his practical recitation of the facts to make her realize that she just wanted to open up her arms and her heart and take him in. The hell with facts and plans and simple answers.

That was Jessie talking, Abra reminded herself as she cooled her dry throat with the wine. What worked for Jessie was never going to work for her.

She looked at Cody over the rim of her glass. He seemed so relaxed, so at ease. She couldn't see the tension that had his muscles stretched and humming like wire. She only saw the faint amusement in his eyes and the easy way he sprawled in the chair.

"Want me to run through it again for you, Red?"

"No." She set the glass aside and folded her hands. "A simple answer. We have an affair."

He didn't like the cool way she said it, as though it meant no more than the letters it took to make up the word. Yet when you cut through to the core of it, wasn't that what he wanted? To be with her. Still, it hurt, and that amazed him.

"When do you want to get started?"

His curt response had her curling her fingers hard into her palms. She had opened the door, Abra reminded herself. Now it was time to face it. "I think it's best we understand each other first. We don't let our personal life interfere with the job."

"God forbid."

Taking a deep breath, she pressed on. "It's important that we go into this knowing there are no strings, no regrets, no long-term demands. In a few weeks you'll go back to Florida and I'll stay here. It won't do either of us any good to pretend otherwise, or to act as though what we're beginning isn't going to end."

"That's clear enough," he said, toying with the idea of strangling her for being so cool, so aloof, when all he wanted to do was make love with her until they both stopped breathing. "Obviously you've been through this before."

She didn't answer. She didn't have to. Before she lowered her eyes he saw them go bleak.

"What's this?" Rising, he moved over to crouch beside her. "Someone break your heart, Red?"

"I'm glad you're amused," she began, but he cut her off by touching a hand to her cheek.

"I'm not." He curled his fingers around hers before bringing them to his lips. "I don't expect to be the first man in your life, but I'm sorry someone hurt you. Was it bad?"

The last thing she'd expected from him was sensitivity. It brought tears to her eyes that had much less to do with the past than with the present. "I don't want to talk about it."

Some wounds scar over, he thought, and others fester. He intended to find out just how deep this one had cut, but he could wait. "All right. Let's try this. Have dinner with me."

She blinked back her tears and managed a smile. "I'm not dressed to go out to dinner."

"Who said anything about going out?" Leaning over, he

teased her lips with his. "Didn't you say something about liking hotels because you could order room service and eat dinner in bed?"

"Yeah." She laid a hand on his face and let herself drift with the kiss.

"I'll let you use my shower and drop the towels on the floor."

Her lips curved against his. It was going to be all right. She could almost believe it. "Sounds like a pretty good deal."

"You won't get a better one." Still holding her hand, he brought her to her feet. "You didn't mention anything about promises in your blueprints."

"I guess I missed that one."

"Then I get to make you one."

"Cody—"

He touched his lips to hers. It was his gentleness that stopped her words. It was her softness that made him speak. "Just one. I won't hurt you, Abra."

He meant it. She could see that clearly when she looked into his eyes. Too late, she thought, leaning her cheek against his. The heart she had tried so hard to hold on to was lost to him irrevocably. He was bound to hurt her now, though he would try not to. She could never let him know.

When the phone rang this time, they both heard it. Still holding Abra against him, Cody reached down for the receiver.

"Johnson." He listened a moment while he skimmed his lips over Abra's temple. "Lefkowitz, anyone ever tell you you're a pain in the neck?" Reluctantly he let Abra go and gave his attention to the phone. "You were put in charge there because we thought you could handle complications like that. You got the specs? Well, read them." Swearing, he shifted the phone to his other hand. "I hear what you're saying. Give me the number and I'll deal with it from here. Modify those blueprints and I'll break your fingers. Clear? Good. I'll take the first plane out."

When he hung up, Abra offered him his wine. "You're real smooth, Johnson."

"I leave tact and diplomacy to my partner, Nathan."

"Good thing." She toyed with her own glass and tried to be casual. "Taking a trip?"

"San Diego. Why we thought a pinhead like Lefkowitz could handle a job like that is beyond me. The man redefines the word *inept*." He moved to the closet and pulled out a small bag. "Some hotshot engineer's telling him he has to make changes in the design, and now a supplier's balking and he hasn't got the sense to bash their heads together and get on with it."

"Your design?" she asked, grinning.

"Mostly." He grabbed her braid and tugged hard enough to make her squeal. "Why don't you come with me, Wilson? You can point out all the reasons the engineer's right and I'm wrong, and then I can show you the ocean."

It was tempting—so tempting that she nearly said yes before she remembered she had a job to do. "I can't. There's no way both of us can leave the project." She turned away and tried not to show how much it mattered. "So, how long will you be gone?"

"A day or two—unless I murder Lefkowitz and stand trial. Abra." He put his hands on her shoulders and drew her gently back against him. "Is it against the rules for you to miss me?"

She turned around, covering one of his hands with hers. "I'll try to work it in."

He pulled her against him and kissed her until they were

both clinging. He had an image of sinking onto the bed with her and letting the night take care of itself but, like Abra, he understood responsibility too well.

"I have to toss a few things into a bag and get to the airport. I'll drop you back by your car."

"Sure."

When she stepped back, he kept his hands on her shoulders. It was funny, he thought. Never before in his life had he thought twice about hopping a plane or moving from place to place. Somehow, in the last few minutes, he'd grown roots. "I owe you a shower—and room service."

He wasn't going off to war, Abra reminded herself. It was a business trip. There would come a time when he would board a plane and fly out of her life. This wasn't it. "We'll settle accounts when you get back."

It took three days, and that infuriated him. The only thing that saved Lefkowitz was the fact that the resolutions took more time and trouble than Cody had anticipated. Now he was cooling his heels in another hotel room and waiting until it was time to catch his plane. His bag was packed, but there was one item he carried in his pocket—a choker he'd bought for Abra. Cody took it out now and studied it.

It had been a whim, a glance in a jeweler's window as he'd walked to an appointment. They weren't icy white diamonds, but delicate blue-green "fancy" stones the color of the sea. The moment he'd seen them, he'd thought of her.

Closing the lid, he dropped the box back into his pocket. He didn't suppose it was the kind of token two people involved in a casual affair exchanged. The problem for him—maybe for both of them—was that his feelings for Abra were anything but casual.

He hadn't been in love before, but he recognized the symptoms.

She wasn't ready to hear it, he mused. For that matter, he wasn't ready to say it. Words like *love* changed the scope of lives, the same way a single window could change the scope of a wall.

And it might pass. He knew people who fell in and out of love as if they were bobbing for apples. That wasn't for him. If it was true, and if it was real, he intended to make it last. He didn't design without making certain the building would stand the test of time. How could he do less with his own life?

With a glance at his watch, he noted that he had more than two hours before his flight. Dropping onto the bed, he plucked up the phone and called Abra. When he heard the connection click, he opened his mouth to speak. Her smooth recorded voice sounded in his ears.

"You've reached Abra Wilson. I'm sorry I can't take your call right now, but if you'll leave a message and the date and time you called, I'll get back to you as soon as possible. Thanks."

He was scowling at his watch and wondering why the hell she wasn't home when the recorder beeped. "Hi. You sound good, Red, but I'd rather talk to you in person. Listen, if you get in before seven, give me a call here at the hotel. I, ah... I hate these damn things. Don't get crazy or anything, but I missed you. A lot. Get home, will you?"

He hung up and, unsatisfied, dialed another number. The voice that answered was feminine—and real. "Hi, Jack. Cody."

"Cody. Did you get me the stuff I wanted on Monument Valley?"

"Nice to talk to you, too, Jack."

"Sorry." She laughed and changed her tone. "Cody, how the heck are you? It's great to hear from you."

"Thanks. By the way, I mailed off about ten pounds of pamphlets, pictures, souvenir books and assorted historical information on Arizona."

"My life for you. I'm halfway through the revisions on *Lawless* and I needed some more information. I do appreciate it."

"Anytime. I like being tight with a famous novelist."

"I'm not famous yet. Give me a few more months. The historical isn't coming out until May. How's Arizona?"

"It's fine, but right now I'm in San Diego."

"San Diego?" He heard the sound of pots clattering and envisioned her in the kitchen creating some exotic meal. "Oh, that's right, I forgot. Cody... I wonder if you could pick me up some—"

"Give me a break, Jackie. Are you fat yet?"

He could almost see her running a hand over her growing belly. "Getting there. Nathan went with me last week for my exam and heard the baby's heartbeat." She chuckled again, warmly. "He hasn't been the same since."

"Is he there?"

"You just missed him. I wanted some fresh dill for dinner. He had the idea that my going out and buying it would tire the baby, so he went himself."

"Nathan wouldn't know dill from dandelions."

"I know." There was a wealth of love in those two words. "Isn't it wonderful? When are you coming back?"

"I don't know. I'm, ah...considering staying out here until the project's finished."

"Really?" She paused a moment. "Cody, do I detect a purpose other than creative control?"

He hesitated. Stupid, he thought. He hadn't called to discuss the medical complex or the resort or any other project. He'd called to talk to a friend. "There's a woman."

"No! Just one?"

He had to smile. "Just one."

"Sounds serious."

"Could be."

Because she knew him, Jackie saw through his casual air. "When am I going to meet her? You know, give her the third degree, look her over, pick her apart? Is she another architect? Wait, I know. She's a graduate student moonlighting as a cocktail waitress."

"She's an engineer."

It was several seconds before Jackie could speak. "Are you kidding? You hate them more than Nathan does. Good grief, it must be love."

"Either that or sunstroke. Listen, Jack, I wanted to let Nathan know I'd cleaned things up here and I'm heading back to Phoenix."

"I'll let him know. Cody, are you happy?"

He paused a moment, discovering there wasn't a yes-or-no answer to that. "That's going to depend on the engineer. I'll give it to you straight. I'm crazy about her, but she's dragging her heels."

"If she messes with you, I'm going to fly out and break her slide rule."

"Thanks. That ought to keep her in line. I'll keep in touch."

"You do that. And, Cody, good luck."

It was nearly nine before Abra got in. She'd had a nice, long, talky meal with her mother. That sort of thing always left her of two minds. The first was amusement, pure and simple. Jessie was great company, funny, absurd and easy to be with. No one made a better friend.

The other was worry. Those same qualities made Jessie what she was, a free spirit, a take-it-as-it-comes woman who danced from man to man without collecting any bruises. Her newest partner was W. W. Barlow—or, as her mother had taken to calling him, Willie.

Jessie had been full of him during dinner. How sweet he was, how cute, how attentive. Abra knew the signs. Jessie Wilson Milton Peters was in for another run.

Rubbing the back of her neck, Abra tossed her purse aside and stepped out of her shoes as she crossed the living room. How was she supposed to keep a professional outlook on the job if her mother was having an affair with the owner? With a laugh, she scanned the mail she'd brought in with her, then tossed that aside, as well. How was she supposed to keep that same outlook if she herself was having an affair with the architect of record?

Life had gotten very complicated in a very short time.

She would back out if she could. One of the things she was best at was untangling herself from uncomfortable situations. The trouble was, she was almost sure she was in love with him. That made it more than a situation—it made it a crisis. She'd thought she was in love once before, but...

There were no buts, Abra told herself. Just because this was more intense than anything she'd ever known, just because she couldn't seem to go more than five minutes without thinking of him, that didn't make this any different from what had happened to her years before.

Except that this time she was older and smarter and better prepared.

No one was ever going to do to her what Jamie Frye had done. She was never going to feel that small or that useless again. If love was a crisis, she could deal with it the same way she dealt with any crisis on the job. Calmly, thoroughly, efficiently. It would be different with Cody, because they were meeting on equal terms, with the rules set out clearly for both of them to read. And he was different. That much she was sure of. He wasn't shallow and insensitive, as Jamie had proved himself to be. Hardheaded, maybe. Infuriating, certainly. But there was no cruelty in him. And, she believed, no dishonesty.

When he hurt her, which she had already accepted he would do, it would happen suddenly and without intent. Hurts healed; she knew that well. She would have no reason to look back on whatever time they had together with regret or self-recrimination.

Abra shook herself. She had to stop thinking about him, or she would work herself into the blues because he wasn't there. What she needed was a nice strong cup of coffee and an hour at the drawing board.

She changed into a basketball jersey for comfort, then settled down with the hot coffee, her mind open to ideas. It was then that she noticed the message light blinking on her answering machine.

Pressing the button, Abra bit into one of the stale cookies she'd dug out of a cupboard. The first call was from a college friend she hadn't seen for weeks. Abra made a note to return the call in the morning. The second was from Tim's secretary, setting a meeting for Monday morning. Grumbling a bit, Abra scrawled a reminder on her calender. Then she heard Cody's voice and forgot everything else.

"...if you get in before seven..."

Abra looked at her watch and sighed. It was well past that. He probably had late meetings. Even if she called the hotel she wouldn't reach him. Cupping her chin, she listened to his voice.

"...I missed you. A lot."

Ridiculously pleased, she rewound the tape and listened to the entire message again. Even though she called herself a fool, she rewound it a second time, then a third.

She worked a little and dreamed a lot during the next hour. Her coffee grew cold. Abra ran figures, then planned out how she would welcome Cody home. She'd have to go out and buy something wonderful. Tomorrow was Saturday. Surely he'd be home by the next evening, or by Sunday morning at the latest. That meant hours, and perhaps even an entire day, without the pressure of work to interfere.

She would stop by one of those fancy little boutiques the first thing in the morning and buy some glorious concoction of silk and lace. Something sexy and soft and irresistible. She'd go have a facial. Wasn't Jessie always touting the wonders of her beauty salon? Not just a facial, Abra decided. She'd go for the works. Hair, nails—what there were of them—skin, everything. When Cody got back, she'd look fantastic. Definitely black silk, she decided. A skimpy teddy or a sheer, elegant chemise.

She'd need some wine. What the devil was that brand he'd told her about? She'd have to throw herself on the mercy of the clerk in the wine shop around the corner. And flowers. Rising, Abra looked at her bedroom for the first time in days. Good God, she was going to have to clean up. Candles. She probably had candles somewhere. Caught up in her own fantasy, she began to gather up clothes and shoes. When a knock interrupted, she tossed an armful in the closet and slammed it closed.

"All right, I'm coming." Where in the hell was her robe?

She found it crumpled under the bed and struggled one arm into it as she ran to the door. "Who is it?"

"Three guesses."

"Cody?"

"Right the first time," he told her as she pulled at the security chain. She yanked open the door and stared at him. Grinning, he took a long, lazy look.

Her hair was tied back with a broken shoestring. The makeup she'd applied for dinner with her mother had long since been scrubbed off. Her robe dangled open, revealing the oversize basketball jersey, which skimmed her thighs.

"Hiya, Red. Wanna shoot some hoops?"

Chapter 7

Abra blinked, wondering if he was a mirage. "What are you doing here?"

"Standing in the hallway. Are you going to let me in?"

"Yes, but—" She stepped back, and he came in and dropped his flight bag on the floor. Mirages didn't look this good. Or smell this good. Confused, she glanced back toward the bedroom and the phone machine. "I just got your message. You didn't say you were back."

"I wasn't." Since she didn't seem to be in any hurry to do so, he shut the door himself. "Now I am."

She thought of the plans she had been making. Taking a quick look around her jumbled apartment, Abra ran a helpless hand through her hair. "You should have told me you were coming back tonight. I wasn't— I'm not ready."

"What's the matter, Wilson?" To please himself, he put his hands on her shoulders, then ran them slowly up and down her arms, gradually pushing her robe aside. She was definitely giving him a whole new perspective on athletic wear. "Got another man under the bed? In the closet?"

"Don't be stupid." Frustrated, she pulled back. She knew her face was scrubbed as clean as a baby's. And her hair—she didn't need a mirror to know that was hopeless. Then there was the green-and-white jersey. Hardly the sophisticated, seductive lingerie she'd envisioned. "Damn it, Cody, you should have let me know you were coming."

He checked an impulse to gather her up and shut her up. Maybe he'd let himself get carried away thinking she'd be as glad to see him as he was to see her. And maybe he shouldn't have assumed she'd be waiting patiently and alone for him to come back.

"I might have," he said slowly, "if I'd gotten you instead of a recording. Where were you?"

"When? Oh." Her mind still racing, she shook her head. "I was out to dinner."

"I see." He stuck his hand in his pocket, and it knocked against the jeweler's box. He didn't have any claims on her. *The hell he didn't.* "Anyone I know?"

"My mother," she said absently. "What are you grinning at?"

"Nothing."

Her chin came up as she snatched at the sleeve of her robe. "I know how I look, Johnson. If you'd given me any warning at all I could have done something about it. The place is a wreck."

"It's always a wreck," he pointed out. It was all beginning to seep in. She'd wanted to set the stage, and he'd come in ahead of his cue.

"I could have cleaned up a little." Scowling, she kicked a shoe aside. "I only have lousy wine."

"Well, in that case, I'd better go." He turned away, then

turned back as if he'd had a sudden thought. "Before I do, I have something to say about the way you look."

Abra folded her arms, and the glint was back in her eyes. "Watch your step."

"I guess there's only one way to handle this honestly." He stepped toward her and put a friendly hand on her shoulder. "You do want us to be honest with each other, don't you, Abra?"

"Maybe," she muttered. "Well, to a point."

"I've got to tell you something, and you should be tough enough to take it."

"I can take it." She started to shrug his hand away. "I wish you'd—"

Whatever she wished would have to wait. He jerked her forward and crushed her mouth with his. She tasted heat, waves of it that only increased when her lips parted on a half moan. In one quick movement he stripped the robe from her, then took his hands up and under the thin jersey to explore naked skin and subtle curves. Gasping, she strained against his rough hands. Then she was clinging, her knees buckling, as he sent her arrowing to the edge.

"Cody..."

"Shut up," he murmured before he pressed his lips to her throat.

"'Kay." She could manage no more than a moan as his fingers dug into her hips. Her head was spinning, but underneath the dazed pleasure was an urgency every bit as great as his. She tugged at his jacket as they began to work their way across the room. "I want you," she whispered, yanking his shirt up and over his head. In one quick, possessive stroke, she ran her hands up his chest. "Now."

Her desperate murmur triggered explosions inside him. He'd thought he'd be ready for them, but anticipation and reality were worlds apart. Desire became raw, impatient, primitive. For both, the bedroom was too far away. When they tumbled onto the couch he was still half dressed, with each of them fighting to free him. Her hands were wild, digging into him, dragging over him, while she reared up to keep her mouth fused with his. He could feel the heat radiating from her, driving him farther and farther from sanity.

With a sudden oath, he pulled the jersey down, yanking it to her waist so that he could bury his mouth at her breast. With an abandonment she'd never known before, she arched against him, pressing him closer, welcoming the dangerous scrape of teeth and tongue.

The lights burned around them. In the apartment overhead someone turned a stereo up loud, and the bass vibrated in a low, passionate rhythm. The delicate fragrance she'd splashed on an hour before mingled with the musky scent of desire.

She was going to drive him crazy. That was all Cody could think as he followed the trail of her jersey down, farther down the smooth, taut skin of her torso. Everywhere he touched, everywhere he tasted, she responded with a ripe, huge pleasure that astonished him. She pulled at his hair, and the shuddering breaths she drew in were nearly sobs.

They'd waited too long—a lifetime. Now they were together—no more evasions, no more excuses. Only impatience.

When clothing was finally stripped away, her long, graceful limbs twined around him. She could no longer think, nor did she wish to. She wanted only to feel. She wanted to murmur to him, something, anything that would tell him what was happening inside her. But the words wouldn't form. She had never wanted like this, never needed like this. Her body felt like a furnace that only he could stoke higher. There was a tremendous ache building. Instinctively she reached out, half in delight, half in defense. As if he understood, he drove her to a shuddering climax.

She gasped out his name and she felt herself falling, endlessly, weightlessly. Even as she spiraled down he caught her and sent her soaring again.

He could see her in the lamplight, her skin sheened with moisture, her eyes dazed and open. Her hair was spread out on the rug where they'd rolled. He tried to say her name, but the air in his lungs burned like fire, and the word flamed out like a curse when he crushed her lips one last time.

He watched her peak again, felt her fingers dig ruthlessly into his back. Driven to the limit, he plunged into her. She rose up to meet him with a speed that tore at his already-tattered control.

Fast, hard, hot, they raced together to a place neither of them had ever been.

Weakened, stunned, Cody collapsed onto her. He had neither the energy nor the clearheadedness to separate what had happened to him into individual actions, reactions, sensations. It was as though one huge bubble of emotion had enclosed him and then burst, leaving him drained.

She was as soft as water beneath him, her breathing slow and shallow. He felt her hand slide off his back and fall limply to the rug. Beneath his lips her heart beat quickly, and he closed his eyes and let himself drift with the sound and the rhythm.

They didn't speak. Even if words had been possible, he wouldn't have known which ones to use to tell her what she had done to him. Done for him. He only knew that she belonged to him now and that he would do whatever was necessary to keep her.

Was this what love did? she wondered. Did it fill you with wild energy, then leave you so fragile that you thought you would dissolve from your own breathing? Anything she had ever felt before paled to insignificance compared to what she had experienced with Cody.

Everything had been new and almost unbearably intense. She hadn't had to think or plan or decipher. She'd only had to act on her own needs—needs she had successfully ignored until the first time he'd touched her.

It seemed he understood and accepted that. Just as it seemed he understood and accepted her. No one else ever had—not like this.

Was it love, she asked herself, or just the most overpowering of desires? Did it matter? She felt his fingers tangle in her hair and closed her eyes. It mattered—too much. Just a touch and she was tempted to toss away everything she believed, everything she'd planned, if only he would touch her again.

There was no point in denying what she felt for him, and she didn't have the courage to think about what he might feel for her.

He pressed a kiss to her throat. "You okay?"

"I don't know." It was an honest answer, she thought as she dragged in a deep, greedy breath. "I think so." Clearing her throat, she opened her eyes again. They were on the floor, she realized, wondering how they'd managed it. "How about you?"

"Fine. As long as I don't have to move for the next week or two." He turned his head so that he could nuzzle lazily at her neck. "Still mad?"

"I wasn't mad." The trace of his tongue along her already-sensitized skin had her shifting beneath him. "I just wanted things to be set up."

"Set up?" He shifted lazily to her ear.

"Yes. I was planning…" She let her words trail off as he skimmed his fingertip over her nipple. She started to say his name, but the word ended on a sigh as his lips teased hers.

"Amazing," he murmured as her slow, sinuous movements had him hardening inside her. "Absolutely amazing."

She was as astonished as he when passion leaped out again and took control.

Sometime during the night they fell into the bed, but they didn't sleep. It was as though in the few weeks they had known each other a mountain of needs had built and tonight it had come tumbling down in an avalanche. There was no music, no flicker of candles, no seduction of silk and lace. They came together without frills, without illusions.

Energy fed on energy, desire on desire. In the darkest hour of the night they fell into an exhausted sleep, only to wake with the first light of dawn hungry for more. Passions, though satisfied again and again, remained raw until, in a tangle of limbs, they slept.

She awoke with the sun full on her face and the bed empty beside her. Groggy, she stroked a hand over the sheet, murmuring.

"Cody?" Sighing, she opened her eyes and saw that she was alone.

Abra sat straight up, looking quickly around the room. She couldn't have dreamed it, she thought. No one could have dreamed that. Rubbing her hands over her face, she tried to think.

Could he have left her? Sometime during the morning could he just have strolled out as easily as he'd strolled in? And what if he had? she asked herself as she leaned back against the headboard. They had said no strings, no commitments. Cody was free to come and go as he chose, just as she was.

If it hurt, if it left her feeling empty and miserable, it was no one's fault but her own. The trouble, Abra thought, was that she always wanted more than she had. Closing her eyes, she reminded herself that she had just been given a night no woman would ever forget. If it wasn't enough, the lack was in her.

"I was hoping you'd wake up with a smile on your face," Cody said from the doorway.

Abra's eyes flew open. In a nervous gesture she gathered the rumpled sheet to her breasts. "I thought you'd gone."

He walked over and, easing down on the mattress, offered her a cup of coffee. "Gone where?"

"I…" Feeling foolish, she sipped at the coffee and scalded her tongue. "Just gone."

His eyes darkened briefly, but then he shrugged. "You still have a very poor opinion of me."

"It's not that. I just thought you probably had things to do."

"Yeah." He shifted, sliding a leg onto the bed. He was damned if he could remember a night with a woman ever making him feel so light-headed. And awkward. Taking his time, he sipped. "Your coffee's stale, you know."

"I never seem to have time to make it in the morning." She drank again. Small talk. That seemed the best way out, and the safest. "I'd, ah, offer you breakfast, but—"

"I know. There's nothing in the kitchen but a banana and a bag of corn chips."

"There's cookies," she muttered.

"I thought they were rocks." Deliberately he put a hand under her chin. "You want to look at me?"

She did, while her free hand moved restlessly on the

sheets. "I'd have gotten a few things if I'd known you were coming back."

"I don't think bacon and eggs is the issue here. Why don't you tell me what the problem is, Red?"

"There's no problem." She struggled for a casual tone. She was an adult, she reminded herself. As such she should be able to handle the morning after. But what did you say to a man in the full light of day when he'd taken you to the darkest depths of your own passions? She could hardly tell him that there had been no one who had given her so much—or taken so much.

"Would you rather I'd gone?"

"No." She said it too quickly, and she swore silently. So much for small talk, she thought, and any pretense of sophistication. "Listen, I don't know what I'm supposed to do next, what I'm supposed to say or how I'm supposed to act. I haven't had a lot of practice at this kind of thing."

"No?" Thoughtful now, he took the coffee from her and set it aside. "How much have you had?" It wasn't a question he'd known he would ask. He'd told himself that her past life was just that—her life. But he wanted to know if there was anyone, anyone at all, who had shared what he had experienced during the night.

"I don't think this is a joke."

He grabbed her shoulders before she could roll out of bed. "Am I laughing? I get the feeling you're judging what's happening here by something that happened before. I don't like it."

"Sorry," she said stiffly.

"Not good enough." He kept his hold firm so that she couldn't yank away. "This guy, the one who bounced your heart around…tell me about him."

Angry color rose to her cheeks as she tried to push him away. "I don't see that that's any of your business."

"You see wrong. Nothing new."

She struggled with the temper she was very close to losing. "I haven't asked you about any of the women you've been involved with."

"No, but you could if you thought it was important. I think this is."

"Well, you're wrong. It's not important."

But it was important. He saw it in her eyes, heard it in her voice. Both tempted him to be gentle with her. If comfort had been the answer, he would have offered it. Sometimes life and love were tough.

"If that's true, why are you upset?"

"I'm not upset."

"I thought we said something about being honest."

"Maybe we did. We should also have said something about not poking around in past relationships."

"Fair enough." He gave her a long, level look. "Unless they seep over into this one. If I'm going to be compared to someone else, I want to know why."

"You want to hear about him? Fine." She pulled away, taking the sheet with her to wrap around her body. "He was an architect." She sent Cody a humorless smile.

"Is that your basis for comparison?"

"You're the one who says I'm comparing," she countered. "You could say I have a habit of tumbling into bed with architects. I was just out of college and working full-time at Thornway. I'd been given a shot as assistant to the engineer on a small project. James was the architect. He'd just moved from Philadelphia. He was very smooth, very smart." She moved her shoulders. "I wasn't."

It was hurting her, and he found he couldn't take it. Rising, he dipped his hands into the trousers he'd pulled on earlier. "All right. I get the picture."

"No." She pulled the sheet more securely around her as they faced each other over the bed. "You wanted to hear about it, and I'm going to tell you. We started seeing each other, and I got stars in my eyes. Looking back, I can't say he promised anything, but he let me believe what I wanted. I'd always wanted to be first with someone. You know, the person someone thinks about before they think about anyone or anything else."

"Yes, I know." He would have gone to her then if he'd thought she'd accept it.

Because he sounded as though he did, she calmed down a bit. "I was very young, and I still believed things like that happened, so when he told me how much he wanted me I was ready to take him on any terms. When I went to bed with him, I was smelling orange blossoms."

"And he wasn't."

"Oh, it was more than that." She laughed, pushing the hair back from her face. "I'd like to think if it was only a matter of me wanting more than I could have I'd have swallowed hard and gone on. I'm not a whiner, Cody."

"No." Anything but, he thought. "What happened?"

"I was packing to go on a weekend trip with him. It was going to be very romantic, very intimate. A ski weekend up north—snow, roaring fires, long nights. I was certain he was going to propose. I was already picturing white picket fences. Then I had a visitor. It's funny." Her voice quieted as she looked beyond him to something only she could see. "I was nearly out the door. I don't like to think what would have happened if I'd been a little quicker. The visitor turned out to be his wife, a wife he hadn't bothered to tell me existed."

Taking a deep breath, Abra sat down behind her drawing board. "The worst part was that she loved the bastard and was coming to see me to beg me to let him go. She was ready and willing to forgive him, if only I'd take pity on her and step aside."

Abra pressed her fingers to her eyes as the memory of that scene played back all too clearly in her head, and with it the shame, the hard, bitter shame. "I'm not the other-woman type, Cody. At first I thought she was lying. I was sure of it. But she wasn't lying. That became horribly clear."

She dropped her hands, folding them loosely together. "I just stood there and listened to her tell me about herself and the three-year-old boy they had and how she wanted to save her marriage more than anything. How they had moved out west to make a new start because there had been other incidents. Other women. I felt more horrid than I ever want to feel again. Not just used, not just betrayed, but vile, really ugly and vile. She cried and begged and I couldn't say anything at all. I'd been sleeping with her husband."

Cody eased down on the bed across from her. He had to choose his words carefully. "Would you...have become involved with him if you'd known?"

"No. I asked myself that a lot after it was all over. No, I wouldn't have...couldn't have."

"Then why are you blaming yourself for something you couldn't control? He deceived you every bit as much as he deceived his wife."

"It's not just blame. I got over that, or most of it, and I got over him." It wasn't easy, but she made herself look at him. "I've never been able to forget the fact that I opened myself up to what happened to me. I never asked him any questions. I never asked myself any questions. When you make that big a mistake once, you better be careful not to repeat it. So I concentrated on my career and left the romance to Jessie."

She hadn't been with anyone else, he realized with a kind of dull amazement. There had been no one else in her life, and when he'd come into it he'd rolled in like a bulldozer. He thought of the night. It had been wonderful, exciting, overwhelming, but he hadn't been gentle, he hadn't been tender. He hadn't shown her any of the romance she was claiming she had decided to live without.

"Abra, are you afraid you're making the same mistake with me?"

"You're not married."

"No, and there's no one else." He paused when she turned her head to look at him. "You're not a diversion or a convenience to me."

She could never explain how those words made her feel. How could she have known such a tiny flicker of hope could burn so brightly? "I'm not comparing you to James—or maybe I was, a little. It's me. I feel stupid because I don't know how to handle this kind of thing. My mother..."

"What about your mother?"

Abra rested her elbows on the drawing board and dipped her head into her hands. After a moment she straightened again. "All my life I've watched her swing from one man to another. It was always so easy for her, so light, so natural. It doesn't work for me."

He went to her to take her arm and lift her gently to her feet. "I don't want you to act any way that doesn't suit you, or be anything you're not." He brushed his lips over her brow, knowing that if he kissed her now he'd want her in the bed. She needed more than that now, whether she understood it or not. "Let's just take it from here, Red. A day at a time. I care about you. You can believe that."

"I do." She drew back. "I think I do."

He pulled her back to hug her in a way that made her eyes widen in surprise. There was something so sweet, so uncomplicated, about the gesture. "We've got the weekend ahead of us. Get dressed. I'll buy you some breakfast."

Abra was a little amazed at how easily Cody could change from the reckless lover to the casual friend. She was always surprised at how easy he made it for her to make the same transition. Breathing space, she decided as they shared a meal in a dusty diner Cody had unearthed along the highway.

She already knew his appetite—for food and other pleasures—so she barely lifted a brow when he packed away enough for two lumberjacks. It was the trip to the market, at his insistence, that left her reeling. When they returned to her apartment they were carrying what would have been for Abra a year's supply of groceries.

"What are we supposed to do with this stuff?" She dumped two bags on the counter in the kitchen, then stood back as Cody did the same.

"We eat it. At various times of the day." He began to pull out produce. "These are what's known as the basics."

"For a dormitory, maybe." She cast a dubious eye at the pile growing on the counter. "Do you cook?"

"No." He tossed her a bag of apples. "That's why you buy stuff that doesn't need it. Or..." He pulled out a can of chow mein and a frozen pizza. "Stuff that you heat and eat. As long as you have a can opener and an oven timer, you can live like a king."

She shoved a quart of milk, the apples and whatever else came to hand in the refrigerator. Cody watched her, decided she had other, more important qualities and offered her a box of corn flakes. She put those in, as well.

"Takeout's easier," she told him.

"You have to go out for takeout." He swung her around and rained kisses all over her face. A man had to love a woman who put corn flakes in the refrigerator. "You're not going anywhere until Monday morning."

Laughing, she pushed away and dug out a loaf of bread. "I was going to go buy a black silk teddy."

"Oh, yeah?" He grinned, then gripped the baggy waist of her sweats. "For me?"

"It's too late." After slapping his hand away, she tossed the bread in a drawer.

"Let's talk about this." He wrapped his arms around her waist and pulled her back against him. "I like the way you look in black silk. That's probably why I acted like a jealous maniac at Thornway's."

"Jealous?" She let out a peal of laughter. She was sure he was joking—until she turned and saw his face. "Jealous?" she repeated. "Of Mr. Barlow?"

"Don't rub it in."

"I thought you were just being insufferable and insulting."

He winced a little, then lowered his head to bite her neck. "Forget I said it."

"I don't think so," she murmured, even as she shifted to give him more access. "From where I was standing that night you seemed to be vastly entertained by Marci Thornway."

"Give me some credit." He slipped his hands under her sweatshirt to skim them up her sides. "I know a shark when I see one. No matter how pretty the teeth are, they still rip you up. Besides…" His fingers turned in to tease her breasts. "I'm not interested in cotton candy."

He had her backed against the refrigerator and was making her tremble. "As opposed to?"

"Just you, Red." He turned his head to give her a long, soul-stealing kiss. "Just you. Tell me—" he moved his hands down to mold her hips "—have you ever done anything constructive on this counter? Chopped vegetables, canned fruit, made love?"

"On the counter?" Her eyes went wide, then fluttered closed again when he ran his tongue behind her ear. "No. I haven't done any of those things."

He was moving too fast again. In a moment he wouldn't be able to pull back and give her the time and attention he wanted to. With an effort, he stepped back and brought only her hand to his lips. "We'll have to keep that in mind. I bought you something else."

"Something else?" Her breathing was almost level when she glanced around the kitchen. "What, a twenty-pound turkey?"

"No. Actually, I picked it up in San Diego."

She smiled as she took out a carton of eggs she hoped he didn't expect her to deal with. "You bought me something in San Diego? A souvenir?"

"Not exactly. Are we finished here?"

"I certainly hope so."

"Come on, then. I'll show you."

He took her by the hand to pull her out of the kitchen and into the bedroom, where his bag sat open on a chair. Reaching in, he took out a box and handed it to her.

"A present?" She felt foolishly shy as she ran a finger over the top of the box. "That was sweet of you."

"It could be an ashtray that says San Diego Padres."

"It would still be a present." She leaned over to touch her lips to his. "Thanks."

"That's the first time you've done that," he murmured.

"What?"

"Kissed me."

She laughed and would have drawn her hand away, but he reached up to hold it against his cheek. "You have a short memory."

"No." He uncurled her fingers to press his lips to her open palm. "That's the first time you've kissed me first, before I backed you into one of those corners. And you don't even know what I bought you."

"It doesn't matter. I like knowing you were thinking of me."

"Oh, I thought of you." He dipped his head to kiss her lightly, sweetly, and her lips parted in surprise. "I thought of you a lot." He checked himself again because he wanted nothing more than to gather her into his arms and show her. She needed space and time and more care than he'd bothered to show her. So instead he grinned and sat on the arm of the chair. "I would have given it to you last night, but you couldn't keep your hands off me."

She gave him an amused look before sitting on the arm beside him. "Better late than never." Then she opened the lid and sat staring and speechless.

She had expected some little token, some funny souvenir a friend might bring another after a quick trip. The gems glittered up at her, pale as water, smooth as satin. She didn't, as many women would have, recognize the glint of diamonds. What she saw were lovely stones that caught the late-afternoon light.

"It's beautiful." The amazement was still on her face

when she looked across at him. "Really beautiful. You bought this for me?"

"No, I bought it for Charlie." With a shake of his head, Cody lifted out the necklace and reached over to fasten it around her neck. "Think it'll look good on him?"

"I don't know what to say." She lifted a hand and ran it over the stones. "No one's ever given me anything so lovely."

"I guess I'll have to buy Charlie something else."

With a laugh, she sprang up to go to the mirror and look. "Oh, they are beautiful. They sparkle." Turning, she launched herself into his arms. "Thank you." She kissed him. "Thank you." And again. "Thank you."

"If I'd known it would only take a handful of glitters, I could have arranged this weeks ago."

"Laugh all you want." She pressed her cheek against his. "I really love it."

And I love you, he thought. Before too much longer, she was going to know it. "I want to see them on you," he murmured, and rose with her. With his eyes on hers, he slipped the shirt over her head. He saw the change in her face, and the invitation. He would take what she offered, but this time he would take it carefully.

"You're beautiful, Abra."

Now he saw the new change, the blank astonishment his words had brought to her. He cursed himself for a fool. Had he never bothered to tell her, or to make her believe it?

"I love the way you look in the sunlight. The first time I saw you I watched you in the sunlight."

With an easy tug he loosened the drawstring at her waist so that her pants slithered down over her hips. Now she wore only the necklace, shimmering like water around her throat. But he didn't touch her, not in any of the hot, hungry ways she'd come to expect. He framed her face as though it were made of glass and kissed her as softly as a dream.

Confused, moved to aching, she reached for him. "Come to bed."

"There's time." He kissed her again and again, lingering over it until she swayed. "This time." He peeled off his shirt so that she could feel the solid strength of his chest against her. But passion weakened now, where before it had streamed through her like fire. Her muscles trembled, then went lax. Her mind, so clear only moments before, blurred.

He only kissed her, and kissed her and kissed her.

"I don't…" Her head fell back as he deepened the kiss. "I can't…"

"You don't have to do anything. Let me show you." He swept her up, muffling her dazed protest with his lips until he lowered her to the bed.

His gentleness filled her until her limbs were too weighted to move. She would have clasped him to her and given him everything, but he linked his hands with hers and caressed her with his lips alone. Soft, moist, patient. Her mind began to float, then to soar with a pleasure far beyond the physical.

No one had ever treated her as though she were fragile, or delicate, or beautiful. He made love to her now in a way she hadn't known existed. In a way she would never forget. If the night had been flash and fire and the darkest of passions, this was quiet and cool and wonderfully light. She trembled over the first edge, then drifted like a feather in the softest of breezes.

She was exquisite. He'd seen the passion and the strength—felt them—but he hadn't seen, hadn't touched on, her fragility or her openness to love. Whatever he had felt before, in the heat of desire, was nothing compared to the intimacy of giving. Her body flowed like a river under his hands, warmed like a flower beneath his lips. When she murmured his name, the sound rippled over him, touching some deep hidden core. It was the only voice he ever wanted to hear.

He murmured to her. She heard him, responded, but she couldn't understand the words. Sensation layered over sensation, wrapping her in a cocoon of pleasure. There was the feel of his hands, the strength of them as they stroked over her skin. There was the taste of his mouth whenever he searched for hers, the warm, drugging taste of it. Over lids too heavy to lift, the sunlight beat so that vision, like her mind, was a red mist. Time spun out, inconsequential. For Abra, years might have passed without her noticing.

She felt the brush of his hair as he roamed over her, caught the scent of his skin as he skimmed over hers. If there were other things in the world, they had stopped being important. If night fell or the sun rose, it hardly mattered. Not as long as he was with her and showing her what there could be to love.

When he slipped inside her, she let out a long sigh of welcome. Still, he moved slowly, slowly, taking her gently up the wave, riding the crest. Trapped in the world he had opened up to her, she rose to meet him, matching rhythms, merging bodies.

Promises were made, though she didn't know it. A bond, solid and firm, was formed.

His own breath grew shallow as he dug for control. He'd thought she'd driven him wild in the night. And she had. Now, in surrender, she had taken him beyond even that. His muscles trembled, then steadied with a sweet, dark ache, and his pulse beat in hammer blows at the back of his neck.

He was driven to taste her again. Her breath whispered into his mouth as their lips met. Hers softened, opened, offered.

Then she opened her eyes, her lashes lifting in one long, languid movement. Though she couldn't know it, she had never been more beautiful than at that moment. Though she couldn't know it, from that moment on he was completely and irrevocably hers.

She spoke his name, and they slipped over the top together.

Chapter 8

It wasn't so hard, this being in love. Abra thought it through as she swung her car into the parking lot at Thornway. She didn't have to act differently, live differently, be different. She wasn't required to change her life so much as open it up. Perhaps she hadn't thought it was possible for her to do even that, but Cody had proved her wrong. For that, if only for that, she would always be grateful.

If she could love him without changing who she was, didn't that mean that when the time came for him to leave she could pick up and go on as she had before? She wanted to believe it. She had to believe it.

With her keys jingling in her hand and her step very light, she crossed the lot to the building. The sun wasn't really shining brighter this morning. She knew that. But in her heart it glowed more golden, more beautiful, than ever before.

It was all a matter of perspective, she told herself as she

passed through the lobby, heading toward the elevators. She knew all about perspective and planning and coming up with a workable structure.

A love affair could be engineered just like anything else. They cared about each other, enjoyed each other, respected each other. That was a solid foundation. They shared a common love of building. Even if they came at it from different angles, it was a base of sorts. From there it was a matter of adding the steel and the struts. After the weekend they had shared, Abra felt confident that progress had been made. Without the tension of work interfering, they had discovered pleasures in and out of bed.

She liked him. That seemed almost too elementary, but to her it was a revelation. It wasn't only a matter of need, attraction, falling in love. She liked who he was, how he thought, how he listened. Companionship wasn't something she'd looked for from him, any more than she'd looked for passion. In one weekend she'd discovered she could have both.

Abra pushed the button for the elevator and smiled as she remembered the way they had sprawled on her couch and watched a Cary Grant festival on television. Or the way they'd put together a meal of pizza and gingersnaps. Or the way they'd tumbled into her rumpled bed on Sunday afternoon with the radio playing jazz and the breakfast dishes neglected.

He'd made her happy. That in itself was more than she'd ever expected from a man. They were building a relationship, solid and strong. When it was time to walk away from it, she would be able to look back and remember something wonderful that had come into her life.

When the elevator doors opened, she stepped through, then felt hands encircle her waist.

"Going up?"

As the doors shut, Cody spun her around and captured her mouth with his. She held on the way he'd hoped she would. She answered the kiss the way he'd needed her to. It was hardly more than an hour since he'd left her to go back to his hotel and change for the meeting, but it seemed like days.

She'd gotten to him, he thought as he pressed her back against the side of the car. In all ways, in every way, she'd gotten to him. He was only just beginning to plan how to deal with the results.

"You taste good, Red." He lingered over her lips a moment, nibbling before he pulled back far enough to look at her. "And I like your face."

"Thanks." She lifted her hands to keep some sensible distance between them. "You were quick getting here."

"I only had to change. I could have done that at your place if you'd let me bring some things over."

She wasn't ready for that. If he lived there, really lived there over the next few weeks, the apartment would be much too empty when he left. She smiled and glanced up to check the progress of the car. They were still at lobby level. With a shake of her head she pushed the button both of them had forgotten.

"I'd hate for you to give up room service, and that neat little spa."

"Yeah." He knew she was evading him. No matter how intimate they became, she still refused to take the next step and close the final gap. He gave himself a moment to control his frustration, then pushed the button to stop the car between floors.

"What are you doing?"

"I want to ask you something before we go back to work.

It's personal." He trailed a finger from the base of her neck to her waist. "As I remember, one of the rules is no mixing business with pleasure."

"That's right."

"Have dinner with me."

With a long sigh, Abra reached out to start the elevator again. Cody circled her wrist before she could press the button. "Cody, you didn't have to trap me in an elevator to ask me to have dinner."

"So you will?"

"Unless I'm stuck between the fourth and fifth floors."

"At my hotel," he added, bringing her wrist to his lips. As always, it delighted him when her response came out in a rush. "And stay with me tonight."

The fact that he had asked rather than assumed made her smile. "I'd like that. What time?"

"The sooner the better."

She laughed as she pushed the button for Tim's floor. But her pulse would be hammering for some time to come. "Then we'd better get to work."

Tim was waiting for them with a tray of coffee and Danish, which Abra ignored. It took only moments for her to recognize the signs of stress, though Tim was as jovial and expansive as ever. She was forced to stem her own impatience as details of the plans were brought out and gone over yet again. If she wasn't on the site by ten, she would miss another inspection.

When Tim set up a flow chart that diagrammed the construction sequence and the estimated dates of completion, she settled back and gave up. She'd be lucky to be on the job by noon.

"As you can see," Tim continued, "the blasting and the

foundation were completed on schedule. Where we began to fall behind was on the roofing."

"There's no real problem there." Cody lit a cigarette as he studied the chart. "We were well within the usual grace period of twenty percent. In fact, it looks like we're no more off than five."

"We have another lag with the plumbing of the health club."

"No more than a day or two," Abra put in. "We'll be able to make it up with the cabanas. At this pace the resort will be built and operational within our time frame."

Tim was staring at the figures and projections. "It hasn't even been three months into construction and we're nearly ten percent behind." Tim held up a hand before Abra could speak. "Added to that is the budget. Unless we're able to take some cost-cutting methods, we're going to go over."

"The budget's not my province." Cody topped off his coffee, then filled Tim's cup. He'd seen the builder down three in the last half hour. Ulcers were made from less, he thought mildly. "And it's not Abra's. But I can tell you that from my own figures, and taking a look at the do list, you're going to come in as close to budget as it's possible."

"Cody's right. We've had no major hitches on this job. It's run more smoothly than any I've been involved with. The supplies have been delivered on time and in good order. If we've run over on a few things, such as the pool roof and the parallel windows in the main building, it's been minimal. I think that you—" She broke off when the phone rang.

"Excuse me." Tim picked up the receiver. "Julie, I want you to hold my calls until— Oh. Yes, of course." Tim pulled at the knot of his tie, then reached for his coffee. "Yes, Marci. Not yet. I'm in a meeting." He drew a long breath as he listened. "No, there hasn't been time. I know that."

He gulped more coffee. "I will. By this afternoon. Yes, yes, I promise. You…" He let his words trail off, rubbing the back of his neck. "Fine, that's fine. I'll look at them when I get home. By six. No, I won't forget. Bye."

He set down the phone. Abra thought his smile was a bit forced when he turned back to them.

"Sorry about the interruption. We're planning a little trip for next month and Marci's excited about it." He gave the chart an absent glance. "You were saying?"

"I was going to point out that I think you can be very pleased with the way this job's been going." Abra paused a moment, no longer sure Tim was listening.

"I'm sure you're right." After a long breath, Tim beamed at both of them. "I want to make sure I'm on top of things. I appreciate the input." He came around the desk. "I know I'm keeping you both from your work, so we won't drag this out any longer."

"Got any idea what that was all about?" Cody asked Abra as Tim closed the door behind them.

"I'm not sure." Thoughtfully she walked toward the elevators. "I guess he's entitled to be nervous. This is the first big job he's taken on solo. Everything else he's done was already in the works when his father died."

"Thornway has a good reputation," Cody commented as they stepped inside and started down. "What's your opinion of Thornway junior?"

"I don't like to say." Uneasy about the meeting, Abra stared at the wall of the elevator. "I was very close to his father. I really loved him. He knew the building trade inside out, every angle, every corner, and he was… It was personal with him, if you know what I mean."

"I do."

"Tim's not the man his father was, but they're big shoes to fill."

They crossed the lobby and started out to the parking lot together. "How tight do you figure he bid this job?"

"Close. Maybe too close." She narrowed her eyes against the sun as she thought the problem through. "But I can't believe he'd be reckless enough to risk taking a loss on something of this size. The penalty clause is a whopper, that I do know." She fished out her keys, frowning. "Enough to put the fear of God into anyone. It's offset by a bonus if the job comes through ahead of schedule."

"So maybe he's counting too heavily on the bonus." With a shrug, Cody leaned against Abra's car. "Seems to me his wife is an expensive tax deduction."

She gave a quick, unladylike snort. "That's a nice way to talk about a man's wife."

"Just an observation. That little dog collar she had on the other night would have set old Tim back five or six thousand."

"Thousand?" Her interest piqued, Abra stopped in the act of sliding into her car. "Was it real?"

Pulled back from his speculations, he grinned. "You're awfully cute, Red."

She almost snapped at him, but curiosity got the best of her. "Well, was it?"

"Women like that don't wear glass and paste."

"No, I suppose not," she murmured. But five thousand— she just couldn't conceive of it. That much money would go a long way toward buying a new car, or a piece of equipment, or—she could think of a dozen uses for five thousand dollars more reasonable than wasting it on something a woman wore around her neck.

"What are you thinking?"

"That he must be crazy." Then she moved her shoulders, dismissing it. "But the man's entitled to spend his money however he chooses."

"Maybe he considers it an investment." At Abra's puzzled look, Cody thought back to the night of the party and Marci's frank and unmistakable come-on. "You could say some women need a lot of incentive to stay with one man."

Because that thought made her think uncomfortably— and perhaps unfairly—of Jessie, Abra brushed it aside. "Well, it's certainly his problem. In any case, we don't have time to stand here gossiping about Tim and his wife."

"Just speculating." But he, too, brushed the subject aside. "Listen, I've got to make a stop on the way to the job. Can you follow me?"

She glanced at her watch. "Yeah, but why—?"

"There's something I have to pick up. I could use your help." He kissed her, then slid behind the wheel of his own car.

Ten minutes later, Abra drove in behind him at Jerry's Tire Warehouse. "What are you getting here?"

"A new suit. What do you think?" He pulled her out of the car and through the door. The place was a sea of tires— blackwalls, whitewalls, steel-belted radials. It smelled of rubber and grease. Behind a scarred counter piled with thick catalogs was a bald man wearing half glasses.

"Morning, folks," he shouted over the hissing and blowing of pumps and lifts. "What can I do for you?"

"See that?" Cody turned and pointed at Abra's car through the plate-glass window. "Tires, all around, and a spare."

"But I—" Before Abra could finish, the clerk was thumbing through the catalogs. He'd summed up Abra's car with one glance.

"We have some very nice budget products."

"I want the best," Cody told him, making the clerk's eyes gleam behind his dusty lenses.

"Cody, this is—"

"Well, well." Obviously seeing his commission soar, the clerk began to write out an invoice. "I have something in stock that should do very nicely."

Cody glanced down at the invoice, noted the brand and nodded. "Can you have it ready by five?"

The clerk looked at his watch and his daily list. "Just."

"Good." Plucking the keys out of Abra's hand, Cody tossed them. "We'll be back."

Before she could complete a sentence, Abra found herself being pulled back outside. "Just what do you think you're doing?"

"Buying you a birthday present."

"My birthday's in October."

"Then I'm covered."

She managed—barely—to dig in her heels. "Listen, Cody, you have absolutely no right making decisions like this for me. You can't just—just drag somebody into a tire warehouse, for God's sake, and order tires."

"Better here than the supermarket." He put his hands on either side of her head, resting them on the roof of his car. "And I didn't drag somebody in there. I dragged somebody important to me, somebody that I won't see driving around on four tires that gave up the last of their rubber six months ago. You want to fight about that?"

Because he'd taken the wind out of her sails, she only frowned. "No. But I would have taken care of it. I've been planning to take care of it."

"When?"

She shifted her feet. "Sometime."

"Now it's done. Happy birthday."

Giving up, she leaned forward and kissed him. "Thanks."

Abra came home that evening in a dead rush. She'd missed the inspector again, but the foundations for the first set of cabanas had passed without a hitch. She'd been able to see the sliding roof in operation, and at long last the elevators were riding smoothly.

The meeting with Tim had given her some problems, enough that she had made a point of checking the foremen's daily lists. Her description of Tim to Cody had made her feel guilty. To combat that, she had decided to take a personal interest in every facet of the job. The extra time had pushed the end of her workday to six, and then she'd eaten up nearly an hour more picking up her car.

"Never ready when they say they'll be ready," she mumbled as she sprinted up the stairs of her building. When she reached her landing, she saw one more delay at her door.

"Mom. I didn't know you were coming by."

"Oh, Abra." With a little laugh, Jessie dropped a piece of paper back in her purse. "I was just going to leave you a note. Running a bit late?"

"I feel like I've been running all day." She unlocked the door and pushed it open.

"Have I come at a bad time?"

"No— Yes. That is, I'm heading back out again in a few minutes."

"I won't be long, then." Jessie gave an automatic sigh at the sight of Abra's living room. "Were you held up at work?"

"First." Abra shot straight into the bedroom. She wasn't going to have dinner with Cody in work boots and dusty jeans. "Then I had to pick up my car."

Straightening up as she went, Jessie trailed behind her. "Did it break down again?"

"No, I was getting tires. Actually Co—a friend of mine bought me tires."

"Someone bought you tires—for a present?"

"Uh-huh." She pulled out a nile-green jumpsuit. "What do you think of this?"

"For a date? Lovely. You've always had a good sense of color. Do you have any gaudy earrings?"

"Maybe." Abra pulled open a drawer and began to search.

"Why did someone buy you tires?"

"Because mine were shot," Abra said absently as she pawed through cotton underwear and sweat socks. "And he was worried that I'd have an accident."

"He?" Jessie's ears perked up. She stopped tidying Abra's clothes and smiled. "Why, that's the most romantic thing I've ever heard of."

With a snort, Abra lifted out one silver earring with copper beading. "Tires are romantic?"

"He was worried about you and didn't want you to be hurt. What's more romantic than that?"

Abra dropped the earring back in her drawer as her lips pursed. "I didn't think about it that way."

"That's because you don't look on the romantic side of things often enough." Anticipating the reply, Jessie held up a hand. "I know, I know. I look on that side too often. That's the way I am, sweetheart. You're much more like your father was—practical, sensible, straightforward. Maybe if he hadn't died so young…" With a shrug of her slender shoulders, Jessie plumped the pillows on the bed. "That's water over the dam now, and I can't help being the kind of woman who enjoys and appreciates having a man in her life."

"Did you love him?" The moment she asked, Abra shook her head and began to search for an overnight bag. "I'm sorry. I didn't mean to ask you that."

"Why shouldn't you?" With a dreamy sigh, Jessie folded a discarded blouse. "I adored him. We were young and broke and totally in love. Sometimes I think I've never been happier, and I know it's a part of my life I'll never forget and will always be grateful for." Then the dreamy look was gone, and she set the blouse aside. "Your father spoiled me, Abra. He took care of me, cherished me in a way every woman needs to be cherished. I suppose I've looked for parts of him in every man I've ever been involved with. You were just a baby when he died, but I see him when I look at you."

Slowly Abra turned. "I never realized you felt that way about him."

"Because it's been so easy for me to form other relationships?" With competent movements, Jessie began to make the bed. "I don't like being alone. Being part of a couple is as necessary to me as your independence is to you. Flirting is like breathing to me. I'm still pretty." Smiling, she fluffed her hair as she bent to take a quick look in the mirror. "I like being pretty. I like knowing that men think I'm pretty. If your father had lived, things might have been different. The fact that I can be happy with someone else doesn't mean I didn't love him."

"It must have sounded as though I were criticizing. I'm sorry."

"No." Jessie smoothed the bedspread. "I know you don't understand me. The truth is, I don't always understand you. That doesn't mean I don't love you."

"I love you, too. I'd like you to be happy."

"Oh, I'm working on it." With a chuckle, Jessie moved

around the bed to set Abra's sneakers in the closet. "I'm always working on it. That's one of the reasons I came by. I wanted you to know I was going out of town for a couple of days."

"Oh? Where?"

"Vegas. Willie's going to show me how to play black-jack."

"You're going away with Mr. Barlow?"

"Don't get that look," Jessie said mildly. "Willie is one of the sweetest men I've ever met. In fact, he's fun, considerate and a complete gentleman. He's arranged for separate suites."

"Well." Abra tried hard to accept the news. "Have a nice time."

"I will. You know, honey, if you put away all these things on your dresser you'd be able to find them when you— Oh, my." Her eye fell unerringly on the necklace. "Where did you get this?"

"It was a present." Abra smiled as Jessie scooted in front of the mirror with the necklace held around her throat. "It's pretty, isn't it?"

"It's a great deal more than that."

"I really love it."

"I don't think you should leave it lying around."

"I've got the box around here somewhere." She rummaged. "I think I'll wear it tonight."

"If it were mine, I'd never take it off. You said a present." Jessie turned from the mirror. "From whom?"

"A friend."

"Come on, Abra."

Evading only made it into something that it wasn't, Abra reminded herself. She said lightly, "Cody picked it up for me when he went to San Diego."

"Well, well…" Jessie let the choker drip from one palm to the other like a stream of stars. "You know, sweetheart, this is the kind of gift a man gives his wife. Or his lover."

As her color rose, Abra made a production of brushing her hair. "It was a thoughtful token from a friend and associate."

"Associates don't give associates diamond chokers."

"Don't be silly. They're not real."

Jessie was silent for three heartbeats. "My only daughter, and she has such a huge gap in her education."

Amused, Abra glanced around. "Diamonds are white, these aren't. Anyway, it's ridiculous to think he'd bring me diamonds. It's a lovely necklace with beautiful colored stones."

"Abra, you're a very good engineer, but sometimes I worry about you." Picking up her bag, Jessie searched out her compact. "Glass," she said, holding up the mirror. "Diamonds." She scraped the stones across the mirror, then held it up.

"It's scratched," Abra said slowly.

"Of course it's scratched. Diamonds do that. And what you have here is about five carats. Not all diamonds are white, you know."

"Oh, my God."

"You're not supposed to look terrified." Abra stood stock-still, and Jessie hooked the choker around her neck. "You're supposed to look delighted. I know I am. Oh, my, they're stunning on you."

"They're real," she murmured. "I thought they were just pretty."

"Then I think you'd better finish getting ready so that you can go thank him properly." Jessie kissed her cheek.

"Believe me, sweetheart, it's just as easy to accept the real thing as it is a fake. I should know."

He was getting edgy waiting for her. He wasn't a man who kept his eye on time, but he'd looked at his watch over and over during the last ten minutes. It was after eight. The way he figured it, she should have been able to get home, toss a few things in a bag and be on his doorstep by 7:45.

So where was she?

You're getting crazy, he told himself, dropping into a chair to light a cigarette. Maybe this was normal behavior for a man in love. He'd like to think so. It was better than wondering whether he was the first and only one to go off the deep end.

He was doing this exactly the way she'd asked. While they'd been on the job he'd been completely professional. The fact that they'd nearly fallen into a shouting match twice should have reassured him. At least he hadn't lost his artistic perspective. He still thought of her as a damn annoying engineer once her hard hat was in place.

But they were off the clock now, and he was only thinking of Abra.

She looked beautiful while she slept. Soft, vulnerable, serene. He'd watched her Sunday morning until he'd been driven to touch her. He was even charmed—God help him—by the chaos of her apartment. He liked the way she walked, the way she sat, the way she got nose-to-nose with him when she started to shout.

All in all, Cody decided, he was sunk. So when she knocked he was up and at the door in three seconds flat.

"It was worth it." He relaxed the minute he saw her.

"What was?"

"The wait." Taking her arm, he drew her inside. Before

he could lower his head for a kiss he saw the look in her eyes. "Something wrong?"

"I'm not sure." Feeling her way carefully, Abra stepped past him. There was a table set near the terrace doors, with candles waiting to be lit and wine chilled and ready to be opened. "This is nice."

"We can order whenever you like." He took her bag and set it aside. "What's the problem, Red?"

"I don't know that there is— Well, yes, there is, but it's probably just for me. If I'd had any idea…but I don't know a lot about these things and didn't realize what it was at the time. Now that I do, I'm not sure how to deal with it."

"Uh-huh." He sat on the sofa and gestured for her to join him. "Why don't you run that through for me one more time, adding the details?"

She dropped down beside him, clasping her hands firmly in her lap. As beginnings went, that had been pitiful. "All right. It's this." She unlinked her hands long enough to touch the choker at her throat.

"The necklace?" With a frown, he reached out to trace it himself. "I thought you liked it."

"I did. I do." She was going to ramble again. To hold it off, she took a deep breath. "It's beautiful, but I thought it was glass or… I don't know, some of those man-made stones. My mother was by a little while ago. She's going to Las Vegas with Mr. Barlow."

Cody rubbed his temple, trying to keep up. "And that's the problem?"

"No, at least not this one. My mother said these were diamonds even though they aren't white."

"That jibes with what the jeweler said. So?"

"So?" She turned her head to stare at him. "Cody, you can't give me diamonds."

"Okay, give me a minute." He sat back, thinking it through. He remembered her reaction to the gift, her pleasure, her excitement. It made him smile, all the more now that he understood she had thought it only a glass trinket. "You're an interesting woman, Wilson. You were happy as a lark when you thought it was a dime-store special."

"I didn't think that, exactly. I just didn't think it was…" She let her words trail off, blowing out a long, frustrated breath. "I've never had diamonds," she told him, as if that explained it all.

"I like the idea that I gave you your first. Are you hungry?"

"Cody, you're not listening to me."

"I've done nothing but listen to you since you walked in. I'd rather nibble on your neck, but I've been restraining myself."

"I'm trying to tell you I don't know if it's right for me to keep this."

"Okay. I'll take it back." She sat there, frowning, while he reached around to the clasp.

"But I want it," she muttered.

"What?" It was hard to keep the smile from his voice, but he managed it. "Did you say something?"

"I said I want it." Disgusted, she sprang up and began to pace. "I'm supposed to give it back. I was going to. But I want to keep it." She paused long enough to frown at him. "It was a lousy thing for you to do, to put me in a position like this."

"You're right, Red." He rose, shaking his head. "Only a creep would go out and buy something like that and expect a woman to enjoy it."

"That's not what I meant and you know it." She paused again, this time to glare. "You're making me sound stupid."

"That's all right. It's no trouble."

She was nearly successful in stifling a giggle. "Don't be so smug. I've still got the necklace."

"Right you are. You win again."

Recognizing defeat, she turned and linked her hands around his neck. "It's beautiful."

"Sorry." He rested his hands on her hips. "Next time I'll try for cheap and tacky."

She tilted her head to study his face. He was amused, all right, she decided. It was hard not to admit he deserved to be. "I guess I should thank you for the tires, too."

He enjoyed the way her lips rubbed warm over his. "You probably should."

"My mother said they were a very romantic gift."

"I like your mother." He skimmed his hands up the length of her and down again as she traced the shape of his mouth with her tongue.

"Cody…"

"Hmm?" He lifted his hands to her face to frame it as he began to drift toward desire.

"Don't buy me any more presents, okay? They make me nervous."

"No problem. I'll let you buy dinner."

Her fingers were combing through his hair as she watched him through lowered lashes. "Are you really hungry?"

This time when she kissed him the punch of power all but brought him to his knees. "Depends," he managed.

"Let's eat later." She pressed closer.

Chapter 9

"Cody, will you get that?"

Abra sat on the side of the bed, pulling on her work boots. The knock at her door had her scowling at her watch. It wasn't often she had visitors at seven o'clock in the morning, and she was already cutting it close if she wanted to be on the site before eight.

Cody came out of the kitchen with a cup of coffee in one hand. His hair was still damp from the shower and his shirt only half buttoned when he opened the door to Abra's mother.

"Oh, hello." There was an awkward pause before Jessie smiled at him.

"Morning." Cody stepped back to let her in. "You're up early."

"Yes, I wanted to catch Abra before she left. Then I have a dozen things to do." Jessie cleared her throat as she pleated the strap of her purse. "Is she around?"

"In the other room." Cody wasn't quite sure how a man handled his lover's mother at 7:00 a.m. "Would you like some coffee?"

"Actually, I'd— Oh, there you are." She turned her nervous smile on Abra.

"Mom." The three of them stood there for a moment, forming an awkward triangle. Abra found that she didn't know what to do with her hands, so she stuck them in her pockets. "What are you doing out at this hour?"

"I wanted to see you before you left for the day." She hesitated again, then looked at Cody. "I would love a cup of coffee."

"Sure." Setting down his own, he stepped through to the kitchen.

"Abra, could we sit down a moment?"

Without a word, Abra took the chair across from the sofa. Certainly her mother wasn't going to lecture her about having a man in her apartment. "Is something wrong?"

"No, no, nothing's wrong." She took a deep breath, then accepted the cup Cody brought out to her.

"Why don't I leave you two alone?"

"No." Jessie spoke quickly, then managed a smile. Now that the initial discomfort had passed, she was glad, very glad, that her daughter had someone in her life. Someone, she thought as she studied his face, who obviously cared for her very much.

"Please, sit down, Cody. I'm sorry I've interrupted your morning, and I'm sure you both want to get to work. This won't take long." She drew a second, longer breath. "I've just gotten back from that trip with Willie."

Because she'd already resigned herself to that, Abra smiled. "Did you lose the family fortune at the craps table?"

"No." Perhaps it was going to be easier than she'd thought, Jessie decided. She plunged ahead. "I got married."

"You what?" The shock brought Abra straight up in her chair. "In Vegas? To whom?"

"Why, to Willie, of course."

Abra said nothing for ten humming seconds. When she spoke, she spoke slowly, spacing each word. "You married Mr. Barlow in Las Vegas?"

"Two days ago." She held out her hand to show off a twin set of diamonds. "When we decided it was what we wanted, there didn't seem any reason to wait. After all, neither of us are children."

Abra stared at the glittering rings, then back at her mother. "You—you hardly know him."

"I've gotten to know him very well over the last couple of weeks." No, it was going to be hard, Jessie realized as she watched Abra's face. Very hard. "He's a wonderful man, sweetheart, very strong and steady. I'll admit I didn't expect him to ask me, but when he did I said yes. We were right there, and there was this funny little chapel, so...we got married."

"You should be getting good at it by now."

Jessie's eyes flashed, but her voice remained mild. "I'd like you to be happy for me. I'm happy. But if you can't, at least I'd like you to accept it."

"I should be getting good at that, too."

The pleasure went out of Jessie's face. "Willie wanted to come with me this morning, but I thought it best that I told you myself. He's very fond of you, speaks very highly of you as a woman and as a professional. I hope you won't make this difficult for him."

"I like Mr. Barlow," Abra said stiffly. "And I suppose I shouldn't be surprised. I'll wish you luck."

An ache passed through Jessie's heart. "Well, that's something." She rose, worrying the rings on her finger. "I have to go in early and type up my resignation."

"You're quitting your job?"

"Yes, I'll be moving to Dallas. Willie's home is there."

"I see." Abra rose, as well. "How soon?"

"We're flying out this afternoon so I can meet his son. We'll be back in a few days to tie up details." She would have stepped toward her daughter, but she thought it best to give her time. "I'll call you when we get back."

"Fine." There was no affection in the word, only a brusque dismissal. "Have a nice trip."

Cody moved to the door to open it, then touched Jessie's arm before she could pass through. "Best wishes, Jessie."

"Thank you." Jessie was grateful the office would be empty when she arrived. She could have a good, healthy cry. "Take care of her, will you?" she murmured, and walked away.

Cody shut the door, then turned to see Abra standing in exactly the same spot. "A little rough on her, weren't you?"

"Stay out of it." She would have stormed into the bedroom, but he was quick enough to grab her arm.

"I don't think so." She was as rigid as ice, and just as cold. Except for her eyes. They boiled with emotion. "What's the problem here, Abra? Don't you figure your mother's free to marry whomever she chooses?"

"Absolutely. She's always been free. I want to finish getting ready for work."

"No." He kept his grip firm. "You're not going to work or anywhere until you get this out of your system."

"All right. You want me to get it out of my system? I'll get it out. She never changes." He heard the despair under the fury and gentled his hold. "It's the same pattern with her, over and over and over. First there was Jack, my father. He died before his twenty-fifth birthday." She pulled her arm free, then snatched a picture from the table. "He was the love of her life, to hear her tell it."

Feeling his way, he spoke carefully. "He's been gone a long time. She's entitled to go on living."

"Oh, she's gone right along. *Speeding* right along. It's been hard to keep up. Husband number two. Bob." She plucked up another picture. "I was, oh, about six when she decided she was free to marry him. That one lasted two, maybe three years. Hard to keep track." She dropped those pictures to grab another. "Then we have Jim. Let's not forget Jim, husband number three. Now before him, there were three or four others, but she never got around to marrying them. Jim managed a convenience store. They met over a carton of soft drinks and were married six months later. And that's about how long they were together afterward. Jessie doesn't really count Jim. She didn't bother to keep his name.

"Then there was Bud. Good old Bud Peters. I don't seem to have a picture of him, but this is Jessie on the day they were married."

Abra swooped it up, knocking several other photographs on their faces. "Bud sold shoes and liked to putter around the house. He wasn't a man to set the world on fire, but I liked him. I guess Jessie liked him, too, before they were together almost seven years. That's a record." She set the photo back. "Good old Bud Peters holds the record."

Cody took her shoulders, massaging them gently. "It's her life, Red."

"It was my life, too," she said passionately. "Damn it, it was my life, too. Do you have any idea what it's like never knowing what last name your mother's going to use, or wondering which 'uncle' is going to be your next step-father? What house or apartment you're going to live in? What school?"

"No." He thought of the steady and stable marriage of his parents, of the close-knit unit that was his family. "No, I don't. But you're a grown woman now. Your mother's marriage doesn't have to affect you."

"It's the same pattern, over and over. Don't you see? I've watched her fall in and out of love faster than a high-school cheerleader. And every time she gets married or divorced she says the same thing. This is going to be best for all of us. But it was never best, not for me. Now she comes here to tell me about this after it's already done. I always heard about these things after the die was cast."

He held her tighter. "If she's had poor judgment, Abra, it doesn't mean she doesn't love you."

"Oh, she loves me." Now that the venom was out, she felt hollow. Her voice sagged, and her resistance with it. "In her way. It was just never the way I needed. It's okay." She pulled back. The tears that had threatened were under control now, and so was she. "You're right. I'm overreacting. I'll talk to her, to them both, when they get back." She pushed her hands over her face and back into her hair. "I'm sorry, Cody. I took it out on you."

"No, you didn't. You just let it out."

"I guess I'm being stupid. And selfish."

"No, you're not. Just human." He stroked a hand over her cheek, wondering just how badly those early years had hurt her and how many hurts were left. "Come here." As he spoke, he pulled her into his arms and held her, just held her, until she relaxed against him. "I'm crazy about you."

He couldn't see the rush of emotions that came into her eyes. "Really?"

"Absolutely. I've been thinking that when things settle here you ought to come east—for a while," he added, not wanting to scare her off. "You can take a look at the house I'm building, give me a hard time about the design. Look at the ocean."

If she went east with him, would she ever be able to leave again? She didn't want to think about that, about endings and goodbyes. "I think I'd like that." With a sigh, she rested her head on his shoulder. "I'd like you to show me the ocean. I haven't had a chance to show you the desert yet."

"We could go AWOL today."

Her lips curved against his throat before she stepped back. He'd helped. By being there to lean on he'd helped her stand up again. "I don't think so. It wouldn't be right for me to neglect my mother's new husband's resort."

She was in a much better frame of mind by the time they reached the site. Without Cody—without his just being there—Abra knew she might have stayed depressed and angry for days. He was good for her. She wished she knew how to tell him *how* good without putting pressure on their relationship.

So far he seemed perfectly content to follow the blueprints she'd set up. There had been no promises, no talk of the future, no pretense about happy-ever-after. The invitation to visit back east had been casual enough that she felt safe in accepting.

Now, as so often happened on the site, he went his way and she hers. Later they would share the night.

She was coming to count on that, to depend on it, Abra thought as she made her way to the cabanas. It wasn't wise, it wasn't safe, but then there had to be some risks involved.

"Tunney." Abra nodded to the electrical foreman, then

stood, hands on hips, studying the framework of the cabanas. "How's it going?"

"Pretty good, Ms. Wilson." He rubbed the back of his
hand over his mouth. He was a big man who was running
to fat, and he was sweating freely. As he watched Abra he
took out a bandanna and wiped his face. "I thought you
were still busy at the health club."

"I wanted to check things here." She stepped closer. Tunney kept at her shoulder. "You think the wiring's going to
be done on schedule? Thornway's a little nervous."

"Yeah, sure. You might want to take a look at those units
over there." He gestured to a section across what would
be a courtyard. "The carpenters are really moving on it."

"Umm-hmm." Because she'd yet to find time to go
through a unit, she walked forward. "I haven't checked
with— Damn." She snagged her boot on a curled scrap of
wire. "These places need to be squared away. Safety inspector would slap our wrists for that."

She would have reached down for the wire herself, but
Tunney was ahead of her. "You gotta watch your step." He
tossed the scrap into a trash drum.

"Yeah. This delivery just come in?" Abra gestured to
three huge spools of wire. "As long as the suppliers keep
ahead of us, we'll be fine." Absently she leaned against
one of the spools.

She liked the look of the site, liked the ring of buttes
and mesas constructed by time and nature that cupped the
spreading growth conceived by man's imagination and
sweat. This was building to her. This was what had drawn
her. When a person could stand under the wide arch of sky
and see progress—the right kind of progress—it brought
hope, as well as satisfaction.

Though she hadn't told him yet, she'd begun to see and

understand Cody's vision. A little magic, a little fantasy, here in one of the harshest and most beautiful spots in the country. There were still coyotes in the hills, snakes in the rocks, but man belonged here. When the resort was finished, it wouldn't simply merge with the desert, it would celebrate it.

That was what he had seen. That was what she was coming to understand.

"It's going to be quite a place, isn't it?"

"Guess it is." He was shifting his weight from one foot to the other as he watched her.

"Ever take a weekend in one of these places, Tunney?"

"Nope." He wiped his face again.

"Me either." She smiled at him. "We just build them, right?"

"Guess so."

He wasn't the most expansive of men, and she sensed his impatience. "I'm keeping you from your work," she said. She tried to straighten, but the end of the wire caught at her jeans. "God, I'm a klutz today." She bent to free it before Tunney could reach her. Frowning, she pulled the length of wire out and ran it between her fingers. "Did you say this just came?"

"Right off the truck. Hour ago."

"Damn. Have you checked it?"

He looked down as she crouched to examine the wire. "No. Like I say, it was just off-loaded."

"Check it now." She waited while he bent beside her to take the cable in his hand.

"This ain't fourteen-gauge."

"No, it's not. I'd say twelve."

"Yes, ma'am." His face puckered as he straightened. "That'd be right."

Swearing, she walked over to the other reels. "These are all twelve, Tunney."

Breathing between his teeth, he pulled out his clipboard. "Fourteen-gauge on the order sheet, Ms. Wilson. Looks like somebody screwed up the delivery."

"I should have known it was too good to last." She straightened, wiping her palms on her thighs. "We can't use this, it's substandard. Call the supplier and see if they can deliver the fourteen-gauge right away. We don't want to fall behind."

"No, we sure don't. Easy mistake, though. Unit numbers almost match." He showed her the numbers on his invoice, then pointed to those stamped on the spool. "Can't tell twelve from fourteen by just looking."

"It's a good thing you can tell by feel, or else we might have had a mess on our hands." She shaded her eyes with her hands as she looked toward the cabanas. "Any chance some might have slipped by you?"

He balled the bandanna back in his pocket. "I've been in the business eighteen years."

"Right. Still, you might—" She broke off when she heard a crash of glass and a scream. "Oh, my God." She raced across the distance to the health club, following the sound of men shouting.

She was breathing hard by the time she reached it. Pushing her way through, she spotted Cody leaning over the bleeding body of one of the workers.

Her heart rose up to block her throat. "How bad?" She thought she recognized him vaguely. He was young, maybe twenty, with a long sweep of dark hair and a tough, tanned body.

"Can't tell." Cody's voice was curt. The only thing he

was sure of was that the kid was breathing. For now. "An ambulance is on the way."

"What happened?" Her boots crunched over vicious shards of broken glass as she moved to kneel beside him.

"Seems like he was on the scaffold inside, finishing some wiring. Lost his balance, took a bad step, I don't know. He went right through the window." Cody looked up, and his mouth was grim as fury and frustration ripped through him. "He fell a good twenty feet."

She wanted to do something, anything. "Can't we get him off this glass?"

"His back could be broken, or his neck. We can't move him."

Minutes later, when they heard the siren, Abra sprang into action. "Cody, get in touch with Tim. Let him know what happened. You men get back, give them room to do whatever they have to do." She wiped at the clammy skin of her brow. "What's his name?"

"It's Dave," somebody called out. "Dave Mendez."

When the ambulance pulled up, Abra waved the men back. "How about family?"

"He's got a wife." One of the men who'd seen the fall drew jerkily on a cigarette. What had happened to Mendez could have happened to any of them. "Her name's Carmen."

"I'll take care of it," Cody told her as they watched the paramedics strap Mendez to a backboard.

"Thanks. I'm going to follow the ambulance in. Somebody should be there." Because her stomach was rolling, Abra pressed a steadying hand to it. "As soon as I know anything, I'll be in touch." After a quick word to one of the ambulance attendants, she raced for her car.

Thirty minutes later she was in a waiting room, pacing uselessly.

There were other people scattered through the room. One woman waited patiently, almost placidly, with her nose in a paperback. Abra continued to pace and wondered how anyone could sit in a hospital without going slowly crazy.

She didn't even know Mendez, and yet she knew him very well. She worked with men like him every day of her professional life. It was men like him who made reality out of what she and Cody put on paper.

He wasn't family, and yet he was. As she paced the room she prayed for him.

"Abra."

"Cody." She turned, hurrying forward. "I didn't think I'd see you."

"I brought the kid's wife in. She's signing some papers."

"I feel so useless. They won't tell me much of anything." She dragged her hands through her already-tousled hair. "How's his wife?"

"Terrified. Confused. She's trying to hold on. God, I don't think she's more than eighteen."

With a nod, Abra went back to pacing. "I'll hang around with her. She shouldn't wait alone. Did you call Tim?"

"Yes. He's upset. He said to keep him posted."

Abra opened her mouth, then shut it again. In Thornway's day, if an employee was badly hurt, he came himself. "Maybe I could talk to the doctor now." She started out of the room just as a young, pregnant woman stepped in.

"Señor Johnson?"

Cody slipped an arm around her shoulders. She was trembling as he led her to a chair. "Abra, this is Carmen Mendez."

"Mrs. Mendez." Abra reached out to take both of her hands. They were very small, like a child's—and very cold. "I'm Abra Wilson, the engineer on the project. I'm going to stay with you, if you like. Is there anyone else you want me to call?"

"Mi madre." Tears flowed down her face as she spoke. "She lives in Sedona."

"Can you give me the number?" Abra asked gently.

"Sí." But she only sat there, weeping silently.

Moving to the couch, Abra put an arm around her and began to speak in low, fluent Spanish. Nodding and twisting a tattered tissue, Carmen answered. After a moment, Abra patted her shoulder, then gestured to Cody.

"They've been married less than a year," Abra said in an undertone as they moved to the corridor. "She's six months pregnant. She was too upset to really understand what the doctor told her, but they've taken Mendez to surgery."

"Want me to see what else I can find out?"

She leaned forward to kiss his cheek. "Thanks. Oh, her mother's number." Pulling a notebook from her pocket, she scribbled in it.

Abra went back to Carmen, sitting with her, offering what comfort she could. When Cody returned he brought little new information. They spent the next four hours waiting with a television murmuring in a wall bracket nearby.

Cody poured coffee from the pot kept on a warming plate in the waiting room, and Abra urged cups of tea on Carmen. "You should eat," she murmured, closing her hand over Carmen's before she could protest. "For the baby. Why don't I get you something?"

"After they come. Why don't they come?"

"It's hard to wait, I know." The words were hardly out of her mouth when she saw the doctor, still in his surgical scrubs. Carmen saw him, too, and her fingers tightened like a vise on Abra's.

"Mrs. Mendez?" He walked over to sit on the table in front of her. "Your husband's out of surgery."

In her fear she lost her English and sent out a stream of desperate Spanish.

"She wants to know how he is," Abra said. "If he's going to be all right."

"We've stabilized him. We had to remove his spleen, and there was some other internal damage, but he's very young and very strong. He's still critical, and he lost a considerable amount of blood from the internal injuries and the lacerations. His back was broken."

Carmen closed her eyes. She didn't understand about spleens and lacerations. She only understood that her David was hurt. "*Por favor*, is he going to die?"

"We're going to do everything we can for him. But his injuries are very serious. He's going to be with us for a while. We'll monitor him closely."

"I can see him?" Carmen asked. "I can see him now?"

"Soon. We'll come for you as soon as he's out of Recovery."

"Thank you." Carmen wiped her eyes. "Thank you. I will wait."

Abra caught the doctor before he stepped back into the corridor. "What are his chances?"

"To be candid, I would have said they were very poor when you brought him in. I had my doubts that he'd survive the surgery. But he did and, as I said, he's strong."

She would have to be content with that. "Will he walk?"

"It's early to say, but I have every hope." He flexed his fingers, which were obviously still cramped from surgery. "He'll need extensive therapy."

"We'll want him to have whatever he needs. I don't think

Mrs. Mendez understands about the insurance. Thornway has excellent coverage of medical expenses."

"Then I'll tell you frankly there'll be plenty of them. But with time and care he'll recover."

"That's what we want. Thank you, Doctor."

Abra leaned against the doorway and let her body go limp.

"You okay?"

She reached for Cody's hand. "Pretty good now. I was scared. He's so young."

"You were wonderful with her."

Abra glanced back to where Carmen sat on the couch composing herself. "She just needed someone to hold her hand. If I were in her position, I'd hate to wait alone. They're just kids." Weary, she rested her head on Cody's shoulder. "She was telling me how happy they were about the baby, how they were saving for furniture, how good it was that he had steady work."

"Don't." Cody brushed a tear from her lashes. "They're going to be fine."

"I felt so helpless. I hate feeling helpless."

"Let me take you home."

She shook her head, surprised by the sudden draining fatigue. "I don't want to leave her yet."

"We'll wait until her mother gets here."

"Thanks. Cody?"

"Yeah?"

"I'm glad you hung around."

He put his arms around her. "Red, sooner or later you're going to figure out that you can't get rid of me."

Later, when the sun was going down, Cody sat in a chair in her apartment and watched her as she curled up on the couch and slept. She'd exhausted herself. He hadn't known she could. He hadn't, he added as he lit a cigarette and let his own body relax, realized a good many things about her.

The explosion he'd witnessed after her mother's announcement that morning had told him a great deal. It hadn't been just the one incident, the one betrayal, that had made her so wary of relationships. It was her whole life.

How difficult would it be to trust yourself, to trust a man, after living in broken home after broken home? Damn near impossible, the way Cody figured. But she was with him. Maybe she still set up boundaries, but she was with him. That counted for something.

It was going to take time—more than he'd planned on—but he was going to see that she stayed with him.

Rising, he walked over to her and gathered her up in his arms.

"What?" Roused, she blinked her eyes open.

"You're worn out, Red. Let me tuck you in."

"I'm okay." She nuzzled her head in the curve of his shoulder. "I just needed a nap."

"You can finish it in bed." When he laid her down, she curled into almost the same position she'd been in on the couch. Sitting at the foot of the bed, Cody unlaced her shoes.

"I was dreaming," she murmured.

"About what?" He sat her shoes on the floor, then unbuttoned her jeans.

"I don't know exactly. But it was nice." She sighed, hoping she could find her way back to the dream. "Are you seducing me?"

He looked at the long line of her legs and at her narrow hips, which were bare but for a brief triangle of practical cotton. "Not at the moment."

She rubbed her cheek against the pillow, comfortably drowsy. "How come?"

"Mostly because I like seducing you when you're awake." He drew the sheet over her and bent to kiss the top of her head. He would have stepped back, but she reached for his hand.

"I'm awake." Her eyes were still closed, but her lips curved. "Almost."

He sat on the bed again, contenting himself with stroking her hair. "Is that a request?"

"Umm-hmm. I don't want you to go."

Cody pulled off his boots, then slipped into bed to hold her. "I'm not going anywhere."

Her arms curled around him as she settled her body against his. Then she lifted her lips to his. "Will you love me?"

"I do," he murmured, but she was already drifting with the kiss.

The light lowered, softened, glowed gold. She moved to him with the ease and familiarity of a longtime wife. Her fingers grazed him, exciting as the touch of a new lover. They didn't speak again, didn't need to.

Her lips were warm, softened by sleep, as they moved over his. Her taste was more than familiar now, it was a part of him, something he could draw in like his own breath. He lingered there, nibbling, then demanding, teasing, then taking, while she worked her way down the buttons of his shirt.

She wanted to touch him, to feel his strength beneath her hand. It was strange that she felt safe here, in his arms, when she'd never realized she needed safety. Protected, wanted, cared for, desired. He gave her all that, and she'd never had to ask. His heart beat fast and steady. The pulse of it against her was like an echo of her own.

This was what she had dreamed of—not just the pleasure, not only the excitement, but the simple security of
being with the man she loved.

Cradling his face in her hands, she tried to show him
what she was afraid to tell him.

She was overwhelming. Even though the loving was
slow, almost lazy, she took his breath away. There seemed
to be no bounds to her generosity. It flowed from her like
honey, warm and thick and sweet.

No hurry. No rush. The shadows washed the room until
the gold faded to a soft, soft gray. There was no sound but
his lover's sigh and the quiet shifting of her body over the
sheets. He looked at her as evening fell and the light faded.
Her eyes, aroused now, no longer sleepy, were like the shadows—darkening, deepening.

Very slowly, as though some part of him knew he would
need to remember this moment on some cold, lonely day,
he combed his fingers through her hair until her face was
unframed. Then he just looked and looked, while the breath
trembled through her parted lips. Slowly, almost painfully,
he lowered his head, his eyes on hers, watching, watching,
until their lips parted, separated and were drawn back together.

With a small, helpless sound she pulled him closer, almost afraid of what his tenderness was doing to her. But
the demand didn't come, only the gift. There were tears
in her eyes now, and an ache in her throat, as the beauty
weakened her. She spoke again, but only his name, as the
emotions that were flooding her poured out.

Then they were clinging together, as survivors of a storm
might cling to one another. It was as if they couldn't touch
enough, couldn't take enough. Wrapped tight, mouths
seeking, they rolled over the bed. Sheets tangled and were

ripped aside. Their tenderness was replaced by a greed that was every bit as devastating.

With their fingers locked, their needs fused, she rose over him, sliding down to take him into her. When he filled her she arched back, crying out. Not helplessly, but triumphantly.

Caught in the last light of day, they swept each other toward dusk and the welcoming night.

Chapter 10

"I appreciate you going with me."

Cody spared Abra a brief look as he stopped the car in front of the hotel where W. W. Barlow and his new wife were staying. "Don't be stupid."

"No, I mean it." She fiddled nervously with her choker as the valet hurried to open her door. "This is my problem. A family problem." After stepping out on the curb, she took a deep breath and waited for Cody to join her. "But I'd have hated to face this dinner alone."

It continued to surprise him to find these traces of insecurity in her. This same woman who was afraid to share a quiet dinner with her mother had once stepped carelessly between two angry construction workers with fists like cinder blocks. With a shake of his head he pocketed his parking stub, then took her arm to lead her into the lobby.

"You're not alone. Still, there's no reason to go into this believing it's going to be some sort of trial by fire."

"Then how come I can already feel the heat?" she mumbled as they crossed the lobby.

"You're not being interviewed by the State Department, Wilson. You're having dinner with your mother and her new husband."

She couldn't prevent a short laugh. "And I've had tons of experience." She paused again at the entrance to the dining room. "Sorry. No snide remarks, no sarcasm and no pouting."

He cupped her face, amused by the way she had straightened her shoulders and brought up her chin. "All right. But I had planned to pout at least through the appetizers."

She laughed again, and this time she meant it. "You're good for me."

His fingers tightened as he dipped his head to give her a hard, unexpected kiss. "Red, I'm the best for you."

"Good evening." The maître d' was all smiles. He evidently had a weakness for romance. "A table for two?"

"No." Cody let his hand slip down to take Abra's. "We're joining the Barlows."

"Of course, of course." That seemed to perk him up even more. "They've just been seated. If you'll follow me?"

It was early for dinner, so the restaurant was all but empty. Salmon-colored tablecloths and turquoise napkins were pressed and waiting for the patrons who would trickle in over the next two hours. A miniature fountain shaded by palms rose up in the center. The candles on the tables had yet to be lit, as the sun still filtered through the windows. As the maître d' had said, the newlyweds were already seated. They were holding hands. Barlow spotted them first and sprang out of his chair. Abra couldn't be sure, but she thought his smile seemed a bit sheepish.

"Right on time." He grabbed Cody's hand for a quick,

hearty shake. "Glad you could make it." He hesitated a moment before turning to Abra. He was wearing an obviously pricey Fioravanti suit, but he still looked like anyone's favorite uncle. "Am I allowed to kiss my new stepdaughter?"

"Of course you are." Trying not to wince at the term, she offered a cheek, but found herself gripped in a huge, hard bear hug. Instinctively at first, then with more feeling than she'd expected, she returned it.

"Always wanted a daughter," he mumbled, making a production of pulling out her chair. "Never expected to get one at my age."

Not certain what she should do next, Abra leaned over to kiss her mother's cheek. "You look wonderful. Did you enjoy your trip?"

"Yes." Jessie twisted the napkin in her lap. "I'm going to love Dallas as much as Willie does. I hope—we hope—you'll find time to visit us there."

"Always a room for you there." Barlow tugged at his tie, mangling the tidy Windsor knot. "Make it your home whenever you want."

Abra clasped and unclasped her purse. "That's kind of you."

"Not kind." Giving up his tie, Barlow smoothed what was left of his hair. "Family."

"You would like a drink before you order?" The maître d' hovered, clearly pleased to have one of the wealthiest men in the country at one of his tables.

"Champagne. Dom Perignon '71." Barlow laid a hand on Jessie's. "We're celebrating."

"Very good, sir."

Silence descended immediately, awkwardly. Cody had a quick flash of his own family meals, with everyone talking over everyone else. When Abra's hand found his under the table, he decided to give them all a little help. "I hope you'll be able to come by and check on the project before you go back to Dallas."

"Why, yes, yes. Planned to." Barlow gripped the life-line gratefully.

Sitting back, Cody began to steer the conversation over easy ground.

Why, they're nervous, too, Abra realized as all three of them struggled to hit the right tone, find the right words. Everyone could have walked on eggshells without causing a crack. Only Cody was relaxed, hooking an arm over the back of his chair and taking the reins the others gladly relinquished. Jessie continued to twist her napkin, though she managed the occasional forced smile. Barlow ran his finger under his collar constantly, clearing his throat and reaching out to touch Jessie's hand or arm or shoulder.

Reassuring each other, Abra thought. Because of her. It made her feel small and selfish and mean-spirited. Whatever happened between Barlow and her mother, they cared for each other now. Holding back her approval or acceptance helped nothing and hurt everyone. Including her.

There seemed almost a communal sigh of relief when the wine was served. The fussy little show began with the display of the label. The cork was removed with only a whisper of sound, and a swallow was offered to Barlow for tasting. Once it was approved, wine was poured in all the glasses.

"Well, now." Barlow sent his nervous smile around the table as bubbles raced to the surface.

"I'd like to propose a toast," Cody began.

"No, please." Abra stopped him with a hand on his arm. During the strained silence, Jessie linked fingers with Barlow. "I'd like to." She couldn't think of any clever words. She'd always been better with figures. "To your happiness," she said, wishing she could do better. She touched her glass to her mother's, then to Barlow's. "I hope you'll love my mother as much as I do. I'm glad you found each other."

"Thank you." Jessie sipped, struggled to compose herself, then gave up. "I must go powder my nose. Excuse me a minute."

She hurried off, leaving Barlow grinning and blinking his eyes. "That was nice. Real nice." He took Abra's hand, squeezing tightly. "I'm going to take good care of her, you know. Man doesn't often get a chance to start over at my age. Going to do it right."

Abra rose to move over and rest her cheek against his. "See that you do. I'll be back in a minute."

Barlow watched her take the same route as Jessie. "Guess if I were any prouder I'd bust my seams." He lifted his glass and took a long gulp. "Quite a pair, aren't they?"

"You could say that." He was feeling enormously proud himself.

"Ah, now that we've got a minute... Jessie tells me you and Abra are...close."

Cody lifted a brow. "Going to play papa, WW?"

Embarrassed, Barlow shifted in his chair. "Like I said, I never had a daughter before. Makes a man feel protective. I know Jessie would like to see that girl settled and happy. She thinks Abra's feelings might be serious. If yours aren't—"

"I love her." There. He'd said it out loud, and it felt wonderful. Cody savored it for a moment, finding it as rich and exciting as the wine. He hadn't expected it to feel good, hadn't expected the words to come so easily. As if experimenting, he said it again. "I love her. I want to marry her." The second part came as a surprise to him. It wasn't that he hadn't thought of the future, with her as a part of it. It wasn't that he hadn't thought of them spending their lives together. But marriage, the solidity of it, the absoluteness of it, came as a surprise. He found it a pleasant one.

"Well, well..." Doubly pleased, Barlow lifted his glass again. "Have you asked her?"

"No, I... When the time's right."

With a bray of laughter, Barlow slapped him on the back. "Nothing more foolish than a young man in love. Unless it's an old one. Let me tell you something, boy. You try to plan these things out—right time, right place, right mood—they never get done. Maybe you're not old enough to think about how precious time is, but take it from me, there's nothing worse than looking back and seeing how much you wasted. That girl...my daughter—" he puffed out his chest "—she's a prize. You'd better grab on before she slips away from you. Have another drink." He topped off Cody's glass. "Marriage proposals come easier if you're loose. Had to get damn near drunk to manage both of mine."

With an absent nod, Cody lifted his glass, and wondered.

Abra found Jessie in the ladies' lounge, sitting on an overstuffed white chair and sniffling into a hankie. Abra cast a helpless look around, then sat beside her.

"Did I say something wrong?"

Jessie shook her head and dabbed at her eyes. "No. You said everything right and made me so happy." She sobbed as she turned to throw her arms around Abra's neck. "I was so nervous about tonight, so afraid you'd sit there hating me."

"I've never hated you. I couldn't." Abra felt her own eyes filling. "I'm sorry. I'm sorry I made things so hard on you before."

"No, you didn't. You never have. You've always been the one thing in my life I could count on. I've always asked too much of you. I have," she insisted when Abra shook her head. "I know I've let you down, over and over again, and I regret it. But I can't go back and change it." She drew back, and her smooth cheeks were streaked with tears. "To be honest, I don't know if I would if I had the chance. I've made mistakes, sweetheart, and you've had to pay for them." She dried Abra's cheeks with her damp handkerchief. "I never thought of you first, and you have the right to resent me for that."

Sometimes she had, and sometimes the resentment had edged toward despair. Tonight wasn't the night to think of it. Instead, she smiled. "Do you remember the time, I was about ten or eleven and that boy up the street—Bob Hardy—pushed me off my bike? I came home with my knees all bloody and my shirt torn."

"That little bully." Jessie's pretty mouth thinned. "I wanted to give him a good smack."

The idea of Jessie smacking anyone, even a grubby delinquent, made Abra's smile widen. "You cleaned me all up, kissed all the scrapes and promised me a new shirt. Then you marched right off to Mrs. Hardy."

"I certainly did. When I— How do you know? You were supposed to be in your room."

"I followed you." Delighted with the memory, Abra grinned. "I hid in the bushes outside the door and listened."

Jessie's color was a bit heightened when she meticulously replaced the hankie in her purse. "You heard what I said to her? Everything?"

"And I was amazed." With a laugh, Abra took her mother's hand. "I didn't know you had even heard those kind of words, much less that you could use them so…effectively."

"She was a fat old witch." Jessie sniffed. "I wasn't going to let her get away with raising a mean, nasty boy who pushed my little girl around."

"By the time you'd finished with her she was eating out of your hand. That night she brought that mean, nasty boy to the door by his ear and made him apologize. I felt very special."

"I love you just as much now. More, really." Gently she brushed Abra's hair from her temples. "I never knew quite how to deal with a child. It's so much easier for me to talk to a woman."

Because she was beginning to understand, Abra kissed her cheek. "Your mascara's running."

"Oh, no." Jessie took one look in the mirror and shuddered. "What a mess. Willie will take one look and run for cover."

"I doubt that, but you'd better fix it before we miss out on that champagne." Abra settled back comfortably to wait.

"That wasn't so bad." Cody stripped off his tie the moment they stepped into Abra's apartment.

"No, it wasn't." She kicked off her shoes. She felt good, really good. Perhaps her mother's marriage would go the way of her others. Perhaps it wouldn't. But they had crossed a bridge tonight. "In fact, it was nice. Champagne, caviar, more champagne. I could get used to it." When he wandered to the window to look out, she frowned at his back. "You seem a little distracted. Cody?"

"What?" He turned back to stare at her. She was wearing a white sundress sashed at the waist with a vivid green scarf. She never failed to knock him out when she was wearing something slim and feminine. Who was he kidding? She knocked him out when she was wearing dirty overalls.

A little confused by the way he was staring, Abra tried a

smile. "I know I was pretty wrapped up in myself this evening, but I did notice how quiet you got. What's wrong?"

"Wrong? Nothing. I've...got some things on my mind, that's all."

"The project? Is there a problem?"

"It's not the project." Hands in his pockets, he crossed over to her. "And I don't know if it's a problem."

She felt her hands go cold. His eyes were very dark, very intense, very serious. He was going to end it, she thought, her heart trembling. He was going to end it now and go back east. Moistening her lips, she prepared herself. She'd promised herself that she would be strong when this moment came, that she wouldn't ruin what they'd had by clinging when it was over. Quite simply, she wanted to die.

"Do you want to talk about it?"

He glanced around the apartment. It was, as always, in chaos. There was no candlelight or mood music. He didn't have a rose or a diamond ring to give her. Then again, he was hardly the down-on-one-knee, hand-on-heart type. "Yeah. I think we should—"

The phone interrupted him, making him swear and Abra jolt. As if in a dream, she moved to answer. "Hello. I... Oh, yes. Yes, he's here." Her face blank, she offered Cody the receiver. "It's your mother."

A little skip of fear raced through him as he took the phone. "Mom? No, it's no problem. Is everything all right?"

Abra turned away. She heard snatches of his conversation, but they floated in and out of her head. If he was going to break it off, she had to be strong and accept it. As Cody had only minutes before, she walked to the window and stared out.

No, it was wrong. The whole idea was wrong and had always been wrong. She loved him. Why the hell did she have to accept that it was going to end? And why was she automatically assuming that he was going to leave? It was hateful, she thought, closing her eyes. Hateful to be so insecure over the only thing, the only person, who really mattered.

"Abra?"

"Yes?" She turned quickly, torn. "Is everything all right?"

"Everything's fine. I gave my family this number, as well as the one at the hotel."

"That's all right." Her smile was strained around the edges.

"My father had some trouble—heart trouble—a couple of months ago. It was touch and go for a while."

Compassion came instantly and wiped out her nerves. "Oh, I'm sorry. Is he okay now?"

"Looks like." He took out a cigarette, unsure how to balance his relief about his father with his nerves over Abra. "He went in for more tests today and got a clean bill of health. My mother just wanted to let me know."

"I'm so glad. It must be terrifying…" She let her words trail off as another thought sunk in. "A couple of months ago? About the time we were having our preliminary meetings?"

"That's right."

On a long breath, she shut her eyes. She could see herself perfectly, standing in the trailer on that first day and berating him for being too spoiled and lazy to leave his orange grove.

"You should have poured that beer over *my* head."

The grin helped. He walked over to tug on her hair. "I thought about it."

"You should have told me," she muttered.

"It wasn't any of your business—at the time." Taking her hand, he brought it to his lips. "Times change. Abra—"

This time the phone had him snarling.

"Yank that damn thing out of the wall, will you?"

Chuckling, she moved away to answer. "Hello. Yes, this is Abra Wilson. Mrs. Mendez? Yes, how is your husband? That's good. No, it wasn't any trouble at all. Mr. Johnson and I were glad to do it." She shifted the phone to her other ear as Cody moved behind her to nibble on her neck. "Tonight? Actually, I… No. No, of course not, not if it's important. We can be there in about twenty minutes. All right. Goodbye."

Puzzled, Abra replaced the receiver. "That was Carmen Mendez."

"So I gathered. Where can we be in about twenty minutes?"

"The hospital." Abra glanced around for the purse she'd tossed aside when they'd come in. "She sounded very strange, very nervous, yet she said that Mendez was out of Intensive Care and doing well enough. She said he needed to talk to us right away."

Since she was already putting on her shoes, Cody decided she'd made up her mind to go. "One condition."

"Which is?"

"When we get back we don't answer the phone."

They found Mendez flat on his back in a semiprivate room with his wife sitting beside him, clinging to his hand.

"It was good of you to come."

Cody noticed that Mendez's knuckles were white. The curtains between the beds were drawn. The other patient had the television on, and the squealing sounds of a car chase poured out.

"I'm glad you're doing better." Abra laid a hand on Carmen's shoulder, squeezing lightly as she studied the man in the bed. He was young, too young, for the lines of pain and trouble around his eyes. "Is there anything you need? Anything we can do for you?" She broke off, surprised and embarrassed to see his eyes fill with tears.

"No, *gracias.* Carmen told me how good you were, staying with her, taking care of all the papers and the questions."

Carmen leaned over him, murmuring in Spanish, but the words were too soft for Abra to hear.

"Sí." He moistened his lips, and though his back brace prevented him from moving, Abra thought he was set as if for a blow. "I thought I would die, and I could not die with sins on my soul. I told Carmen everything. We have talked." His eyes shifted so that he could see his wife and her nod of encouragement. "We have decided to tell you." He swallowed, closing his eyes for a moment. "It didn't seem so bad, and with the baby coming we needed the money. When Mr. Tunney asked me, I knew in my heart it was wrong, but I wanted good things for Carmen and the baby. And myself."

Uneasy, Abra moved closer to the bed. Across the prone body of Mendez, she and Cody exchanged one brief look.

Cody kept his voice calm. "What did Tunney ask you?"

"Only to look the other way, to pretend not to notice. Much of the wire we use on the project is not up to code."

Abra felt her stomach sink and her blood go cold. "Tunney offered to pay you to install substandard wire?"

"Sí. Not all, not everywhere. Not all of the men could be trusted—not to be trusted," he said lamely. "When a delivery would come, he would assign a few of us to work with the twelve-gauge. We would be paid in cash every week.

I know I can go to jail— We know. But we have decided to do what is right."

"David, this is a very serious accusation." But Abra was remembering the reels of wire she had examined herself. "That wiring was inspected."

"*Sí.* It was arranged to have the same inspector. He is paid, also. When he comes, you and Mr. Johnson are to be busy somewhere else in case you would notice something."

"How could Tunney arrange—" Abra closed her eyes. "David, was Tunney following orders?"

Mendez squeezed his wife's hand again. This was what he feared most. "*Sí,* he has orders. From Mr. Thornway." Murmuring, Carmen lifted a cup to his lips so that he could wet his dry lips.

"There is more than the wiring. I hear things. Some of the concrete, some of the steel, some of the rivets. Some," he explained. "Not all, you see? I think when I am asked that Mr. Thornway is a big builder. He is powerful, important, so this must be the way. When I tell Carmen, she is ashamed of me and says it is not our way."

"We will give back the money." Carmen spoke for the first time. Her eyes were as they had been on the day of the accident, very young and very afraid, but her voice was strong.

"I don't want you to worry about that now." Abra rubbed a hand over her temple. "Or anything else. You did the right thing. Mr. Johnson and I will take care of it. We may need to talk to you again, and you'll have to go to the police."

Carmen put an unsteady hand on her rounded stomach. "We will do what you say. *Por favor,* Señorita Wilson, my David is not a bad man."

"I know. Don't worry."

Abra stepped out of the room, feeling as though she had taken a long, nasty fall. "What are we going to do?"

"We're going to go see Tim." He put his hands on her shoulders. "I'm going to call Nathan. He needs to know about this."

She nodded, walking away as he headed to a bank of phones.

They didn't speak on the drive to Thornway's house. Abra could only think of the business Thornway had built, brick by brick, the reputation he had earned, the pride he had felt and had given her the chance to feel. In one flash the son he had handed it to had tossed it aside.

"I should have guessed," she murmured at length.

"How?" He was dealing with his own demons, and with the crumbling of his own dreams.

"The day Mendez was hurt. I was with Tunney. There had just been a delivery, and I happened to check it. It was twelve-gauge." She turned her head to look at him. "He spun me a tale about someone screwing up the invoice numbers. We were talking when the accident happened, and I never took it any further. Damn it, Cody, I never even thought of it again."

"You wouldn't have had any reason to suspect him. Or Thornway." He pulled up in front of Tim's house. "Why don't I handle this? You can wait here."

"No." She pushed open the car door. "I have to be there."

Moments later they were waiting in Tim's spacious foyer.

Elegant in a dinner jacket, Tim came down the steps. "Abra, Cody. This is a surprise. I'm afraid you just caught us. Marci and I are on our way out. She's still dressing."

"You'll have to be late," Cody said curtly. "This can't wait."

"Sounds serious." Tim checked his watch before gesturing them into his library. "I can always squeeze out a few minutes. Marci's never on time anyway." He went to a small ebony bar. "What can I get you?"

"An explanation." Abra took a step toward him, needing to see his eyes. "As to why you've been using substandard equipment on the Barlow project."

His hand shook once, and the whiskey spilled before he steadied it and poured. That was all she needed to be sure of the truth. "What in the world are you talking about?"

"I'm talking about materials that don't come up to code. I'm talking about payoffs and kickbacks and bribes." She grabbed his arm when he started to lift his drink, and her fingers dug in. "I'm talking about ruining a reputation your father spent his life building."

Whiskey in hand, Tim turned. Though the room was cool, there was already a light film of sweat beading above his mouth. "I have no idea what this is all about, but I don't appreciate being accused of any illegalities." He tossed back the whiskey, then poured another. "I realize my father had an affection for you, Abra, and that you feel a certain personal interest in my company. But that doesn't excuse this."

"Be careful." Cody's voice was too soft and too mild. "Be very careful what you say to her, or I may just decide to go with my instincts and break your arms."

The sweat was dripping now, hot and sticky down his back. "I don't have to stand here in my own house and be threatened."

Cody simply shifted in front of the door before Tim could storm out. "You're going to stand here and be a lot more than threatened. The game's up. We know about the materials, about the inspectors you bribed, about the laborers who were paid off to install and keep their mouths shut. Funny thing, Tim, it turns out that some of them have consciences."

"This is ridiculous. If someone's been skimming on the material, I intend to find out about it. You can be sure I'll initiate an investigation."

"Fine." Abra put a hand on his arm and looked him in the eye. "Call the building commissioner."

"I'll do just that."

"Do it now." Abra tightened her grip when he tried to pull away. "I imagine you have his home number. We can have a little meeting right here tonight."

Tim reached for his glass again. "I have no intention of disturbing the commissioner at home on a Saturday evening."

"I think he'd be very interested." Abra recognized the fear in his eyes and gave him one last push. "While you're at it, why don't you call Tunney, too? The commissioner's going to want to talk to him. Somehow I don't think Tunney's a man who'd be willing to take the fall alone."

Saying nothing, Tim sank into a chair. He drank again, this time in small sips, until the glass was empty. "We can work something out." He leaned forward, his hands braced on his knees. "It's business, you understand. I took a few shortcuts. Nothing that has to matter."

"Why?" She'd needed to hear him say it. Now that he had, her anger drained away. "Why would you risk everything for a few extra dollars?"

"A few?" With a laugh, he snatched the bottle from beside him and poured more whiskey. He'd already had too much and too quickly, but he badly needed more. "Thousands. It came to thousands. You skim here, cut through there, and before you know it there are thousands. I needed it." The liquor steadied his hand as he drank. "You don't know what it's like being the son, being expected to do things as well as they were always done. Then there's Marci." He glanced up as though he could see her in the room above his head. "She's beautiful, restless, and she wants. The more I give, the more she wants. I can't afford to lose her." He dropped his face into his hands. "I bid too low, way too low, on this project. I thought I could pull it off somehow. I had to. There are debts, debts to the wrong kind of people. Ever since I took over, things have been going wrong. I lost fifty thousand on the Lieterman project."

He glanced up when Abra said nothing. "It wasn't the first time. For the past nine months the business has been dropping into the red. I had to make it up. This was the best way. Cut a few corners, sweeten a few pots. If I brought this in under budget and on time I'd be in the black again."

"And when there was an electrical fire?" Cody put in. "Or the supports gave way? What then?"

"It didn't have to be that way. I had to take the chance. I had to. Marci expects to live a certain way. Am I supposed to tell her we can't go to Europe because the business is in trouble?"

Abra looked at him and felt only pity. "Yes. You're going to have to tell her a lot more than that now."

"Work isn't going to start again on Monday, Tim." Cody waited until he brought his head back up. "It's not going to start at all until after a full investigation. You bit this off, now you're going to have to swallow it. You can call the building commissioner, or we can."

Tim was getting drunk. It helped somehow. "You haven't told anyone?"

"Not yet," Abra said. "You're right that I felt close to your father and that I feel a responsibility to the business. I wanted you to have a chance to make this right yourself."

Make it right? Tim thought desperately. How in God's name could he make it right? One official inspection and everything would be over. "I'd like to speak with Marci first. Prepare her. Give me twenty-four hours."

Cody started to object, but Abra touched his arm. The wheels were already in motion, she thought. Another day wasn't going to stop what had begun. She could give him a day, because she'd cared for his father. "You'll set up a meeting at your office? For all of us?"

"What choice do I have?" His words were slurred now by drink and self-pity. "I'm going to lose everything, aren't I?"

"Maybe you'll get back your self-respect." Cody took Abra's hand. "I want to hear from you by nine tomorrow night, or we'll make that call."

Outside, Abra pressed her fingers to her eyes. "Oh, God, it's awful."

"It's not going to get better."

"No." She straightened and glanced back at the house. The light was still burning in the library. "This was going to be my last job for them. I never expected it to end like this."

"Let's go."

Tim heard their car start up and sat listening as the sound of the engine died away in the night. His wife, his beautiful, selfish wife, was primping upstairs. In a fit of rage, he hurled his glass across the room. He hated her. He adored her. Everything he'd done had been to make her happy. To keep her. And if she left him...

No, he couldn't bear to think of it. He couldn't bear to think of the scandal and the accusations. They would crucify him, and he would lose his business, his home, his status. His wife.

Maybe there was still a chance. There was always a chance. Stumbling to the phone, he dialed a number.

Chapter 11

Perhaps it was the strain of the evening, or the discomfort of witnessing another's despair and humiliation, but they needed each other. They fell into bed in a kind of fury, saying nothing, looking for what they could bring to each other to block out the lingering anger and disillusionment.

Together they had built something strong—or thought they had. Now they had learned that it had been built on lies and deceits. If they tangled together quickly, reaching, taking, it was to assure themselves that what they had built privately was no lie.

This was real, solid, honest. She could feel it as his mouth closed hungrily over hers, as their tongues met, as their bodies fitted together. If he needed to forget what existed outside this room, this bed, for just one night, she understood. She needed it, too, and so she gave herself utterly.

He wanted to comfort her. She had looked so stricken when Tim had collapsed into confession. It was personal with Abra, and he knew, though she had said nothing, that she was taking part of the failure as her own. He wouldn't have it. But the time for straight talk was in the morning, when her feelings weren't so raw. For now, for a few hours, he would give her release in passion.

Her scent. He remembered watching her dab it on before dinner, absently, as an afterthought. It had faded as the night had worn on, and now it was no more than a whisper along her skin, and all the more intimate for that. He drew it in as he let his mouth glide over her throat and down to where her skin became impossibly soft, impossibly delicate.

Her hair. She had taken a brush through it quickly, impatiently. She was never fully satisfied with the way it looked. He thought it glorious. Now, as he combed a hand through it, he could luxuriate in the wildness of it. When she rolled over, stretching her body over his as if she couldn't get enough of him, her hair streamed over her shoulders and dipped to his.

Her lips. She had added color to them, worried it off, then replaced it. They were naked now, smooth as silk, soft as rain. He had only to touch his to them for them to part in welcome. If he asked more, she gave more.

Now, with him trapped beneath the tangle of her hair and her agile body, she took her mouth over him, giving him pleasure, seeking her own. There was an excitement in having the freedom to explore the man she loved. To touch him and feel him tremble. To taste him and hear him sigh.

The light in the hallway was still burning, so she could see him, the lean lines, the firm muscles. And his eyes. She could see his eyes as she brought her lips back to his. They were so dark, so completely focused on her.

She could sense something different but was unable to understand it. One moment he was impatient, almost brutal, in his loving. The next he held her, kissed her, as if she were precious and fragile. However his hands took, however his lips demanded, she belonged to him. Passions layered so tightly with emotions that she couldn't separate desire from love. There was no need to.

When he filled her, she found both.

It was later, much later, when she woke, disturbed by some sound or some dream. Murmuring, she shifted, reaching out—and found him gone.

"Cody?"

"I'm right here."

She saw him then, standing by the window. The end of his cigarette glowed red in the dark. "What's wrong?"

"Nothing. Can't sleep."

Sitting up, she pushed her hair away from her face. The sheet slid down to pool at her waist. "You can come back to bed. We don't have to sleep."

He laughed and tapped out his cigarette. "I never thought I'd meet a woman who could wear me out."

She threw a pillow at him. "Is that supposed to be a compliment?"

"Just an observation." He came over to sit on the side of the bed. "You're the best, Red." He wasn't talking about sex. Because she understood that, she smiled and fumbled for something to say.

"I'm glad you think so." As her eyes adjusted to the dark, she frowned. "You're dressed."

"I was going to go for a drive. I didn't know whether or not to wake you."

"Of course you should have. Where were you going?"

He took her hand, carefully, as though weighing it. "I

have to see it, Abra. I might be able to get it out of my head for a few hours once I do."

Her fingers curled into his. "I'll go with you."

"You don't have to. It's late—early, I guess."

"I want to. Will you wait for me?"

"Sure." He brought her hand to his lips. "Thanks."

The air was cool and breathlessly clear. Overhead, the sky was a dark, calm sea pierced by stars. There was no traffic to dodge, only a long ribbon of road, banked first by houses and shops, then by nothing but acres of empty desert. With the windows down and the engine no more than a purr, Abra heard the lonesome call of a coyote.

"I've never driven through here at this time of night." Abra turned to look out the window at the distant buttes, which were no more than dark shadows rising and spreading. "It's so quiet. It makes you wonder."

"Wonder what?"

"That it's been this quiet, just this quiet, for centuries. I guess if we do it right it'll be just this quiet for centuries more."

"People in our business are supposed to see undeveloped land and think immediately of how it can be put to use."

She frowned a little and searched in her purse for a band or a string to tie back her hair. "Do you?"

He was silent for a moment, enjoying the drive, the quiet, the company. "There are places along the Intracoastal where the brush is so dense you can't see beyond the first foot. It's not quiet, because it's as thick with life as it is with leaves. The waterway cuts through—that's man's contribution—but some things are meant to stay as they are."

She was smiling again as she pulled her hair into a ponytail. "I like you, Johnson."

"Thanks, Wilson. I like you, too." He rested his arm on the back of the seat so that he could toy with the ends of her hair. "You said something before about the Barlow project being your last one with Thornway."

"Yeah. I've been thinking about it for a long time. After Tim took over I decided it was time to do more than think. I wish…" But it was no use wishing she had already cut her ties with the firm.

Because he understood, he massaged the tension at the back of her neck. "You got another offer?"

"No. I haven't exactly announced my resignation, but I'm not looking for another offer." She was afraid he would think her foolish, so she began to fiddle with the dial of the radio. Music poured out, as clear as the air. "I'm going to freelance, maybe start up my own business. A small one." She shut off the radio and shot him a look. "I've been putting money aside for a while now, to see me through the rough spots."

"Do you want out on your own or do you just want a change of scene?"

She considered for a moment, then shook her head. "Both, I guess. I owe a lot to Thornway. Thornway senior," she explained. "He gave me a chance, let me prove myself. Over the past year or so, things have changed. I didn't know…never had any idea Tim was into something like this, but I was never comfortable with the way he did business." Her eyes were drawn to the east, where the sky was just beginning to lighten. "He always looked at the ledger sheets instead of the overall project, the payroll instead of the men who were earning the wage. Nobody goes into business without the idea of making money, but when it's the only thing…"

"When it's the only thing you end up in a situation like the one we're in now."

"I still can't believe it," she murmured. "I thought I knew him, but this— Cody, how can a man risk everything, everything he's been given, to please a woman?"

"I'd say he loves her, obviously more than he should."

"Maybe she loves him. Maybe all the jewelry, the cars and the cruises didn't matter."

He ran a finger down the back of her neck. "They mattered, Red. With a woman like that, they always matter. It's a safe bet that when all this hits Marci Thornway takes the high road."

"That's cruel. She's still his wife."

"Remember the night of the party? She was his wife then, too, but she invited me to…let's say she invited me to spend an afternoon with her."

"Oh." Whatever sympathy she had felt for Marci Thornway vanished. "You turned her down?"

"It wasn't a hardship. Besides, I had other things on my mind. In any case, I don't think we can dump the whole mess in Marci's lap. Tim wanted too much too soon. Maybe he'd been given too much all along. Apparently he's been going after success in all the wrong ways."

"He mentioned owing money to the wrong kind of people," Abra said.

"He wouldn't be the first businessman to make a connection with organized crime. He won't be the first to lose because of it. What's this?" As they approached the turnoff for the site, he spotted another car. It hesitated at the crossroads, then swept to the right and sped away.

"I don't know." Abra frowned at the receding taillights. "Probably kids. A lot of times construction sites end up as lovers' lanes."

"Maybe, but it's late for teenagers to be out necking."
He slowed to negotiate the turn.

"Well, we're here to look around, anyway. If they were
vandals we'll find out soon enough."

He parked the car by the trailer. In silence they stepped
out of opposite sides and stood. The main building, with its
dome and spirals, was shadowed in the predawn light. Like
a sculpture, it rose up out of rock, a product of imagination.
The interior was rough, and the landscaping had yet to be
started, but Abra saw it now as Cody had.

In this very fragile light it looked more fanciful, yet
somehow more solid, than ever before. It didn't meld with
the rock and sand, nor did it harmonize. Rather, it stood
with and against and for—a celebration of man's ingenuity.

Standing apart, not yet connected by the flower-bordered
paths, was the health center. Castlelike, it grew out of the
thin, greedy soil, its arches and curves adding a richness,
even a defiance, to the stark strength of the landscape. The
early light struggled over the eastern rise and sprinkled on
the walls.

They stood, hands lightly linked, and scanned what they
had had a part in creating.

"It's going to have to come down," Cody murmured.
"All or most of it."

"That doesn't mean it can't be built again. We can build
it again."

"Maybe." He slipped an arm around her shoulders. The
sun had yet to rise, and the air held the clean-edged chill
of the desert night. "It's not going to be easy, and it's not
going to be quick."

"It doesn't have to be." She understood now, as she never
had, just how much of himself he had put into this. These
weren't just walls, weren't just beams and supports. This

was his imagination, his contribution and, though only one who built could feel it, his heart. She turned to put her arms around him. "I guess it's time I told you the truth."

He kissed her hair, and the scent was warm, sun-drenched, though the air was cool with dawn. "About what?"

"About this place." She tilted her head up but didn't smile. He saw that her eyes were gray, like the light in the east. "I was wrong and you were right."

He kissed her, taking his time about it. "That's nothing new, Red."

"Keep it up and I won't tell you what I really think."

"Fat chance. You always tell me what you think whether I want to hear it or not."

"This time you will. You may even be entitled to gloat."

"I can't wait."

She drew away to dip her hands into her pockets and turn a slow circle. "It's wonderful."

"What?" With a hint of a smile, he gripped her shoulder. "Must be the lack of sleep, Wilson. You're light-headed."

"I'm not joking." She pulled away to face him again. "And I'm not saying this to make you feel better—or worse, for that matter. I'm saying it because it's time I did. For the past few weeks I've been able to see what you envisioned here, what you wanted to say, how you wanted to say it. It's beautiful, Cody, and maybe it sounds overdone, but it's majestic. When it's finished—and it will be finished one day—it's going to be a work of art, the way only the best buildings can be."

He stared at her as the sun peeked over the ridges of rock and brought the first hints of daylight. "I know I'm supposed to gloat, but I can't seem to manage it."

"You can be proud of this." She rested her hands on his shoulders. "I'm proud of this, and of you."

"Abra…" He skimmed his knuckles over her cheek. "You leave me speechless."

"I'd like you to know that when it comes time to rebuild I want to be a part of it." Tilting her head, she smiled. "Not that there shouldn't be a few adjustments."

He laughed and yanked her close. He'd needed this. "There had to be that."

"Minor ones," she continued, holding on to him. "Reasonable ones."

"Naturally."

"We'll discuss them." She bit his ear. "Professionally."

"Sure we will. But I'm not changing anything."

"Cody…"

"I haven't told you that you're one of the best." Now it was her turn to look astonished. "As engineers go."

"Thanks a lot." She pulled back. "I feel better. How about you?"

"Yeah, I feel better." He ran a finger down her cheek. "Thanks."

"Let's take a look around, then. It's what we came for."

Arm in arm, they walked toward the main building. "The investigation's going to be rough," Cody began. It was easier to talk about it now. "It could mess up your plans to start your own business. At least for a while."

"I know. I guess I've been trying not to think about that. Not yet."

"You'll have Barlow behind you. And Powell and Johnson."

She smiled as he pulled open the door. "I appreciate that. I never asked you what Nathan said."

"He said he'd be on the first available plane." He paused just inside the door and looked.

The walls were up, the drywall smeared with compound and sanded smooth. Empty buckets were turned over, some of them bridged with boards to make casual seats. The elevators that had given Abra such grief were resting at ground level. The forms for the curving stairs were in place, the windows secured. Instead of the buzz and whine of tools, there was a silence, an echoing one that reached from the scarred subflooring to the brilliantly colored dome.

As they stood there she knew how he felt, even how he thought, because her own frustration at the futility of it all rose.

"It hurts, doesn't it?"

"Yeah." But he'd had to come and work his way through it. Minute by minute, it was becoming easier. "It'll pass, but I've got to say I don't want to watch when they start tearing it out."

"No, neither do I." She walked in a little farther and set her purse on a sawhorse. It did hurt. Maybe it would help for them to look beyond the immediate future to a more distant one. "You know, I've always wanted to come into a place like this as a patron." She turned with a smile because she felt they both needed it. "I'll make you a deal, Johnson. When it's done and your damn waterfalls are running, I'll treat you to a weekend."

"There's a resort I designed in Tampa that's already open."

She lifted a brow. "Does it have waterfalls?"

"A lagoon, in the center of the lobby."

"Figures. It's too dark to see much in here."

"I've got a flashlight in the car." He rocked back on his heels. "I'd like to take a closer look, make sure whoever was down here wasn't poking around where they shouldn't have been."

"Okay." She yawned once, hugely. "I can sleep tomorrow."

"I'll be right back."

She turned back into the room when he had gone. It was a waste, a terrible one, she thought, but it all hadn't been for nothing. Without this project, these buildings, she might never have met him. They said you didn't miss what you'd never had, but when she thought of Cody Abra was certain that was wrong. There would have been a hole in her life, always. She might not have known why, but she would have felt it.

Building had brought them together, and it would bring them together again. Maybe it was time she stopped sitting at the drawing board and planning out her personal life. With Cody, it might be possible to simply take, to simply act. With Cody, it might be possible to admit her feelings.

Scary, she thought, and with a nervous laugh she began to wander. She'd have to give the idea a lot of thought.

He cared for her. He might care enough to be glad if she told him she would relocate in Florida. They could go on there the way they had here. Until... She couldn't get beyond the *until*.

It didn't matter. She would deal with *until* when she got there. The one thing she was certain of was that she wasn't going to let him walk away.

With a shrug, she glanced up at the dome. The light was trickling through, thin but beautifully tinted by the glass. Pleased, she circled around. It was lovely the way it fell on the flooring, seeped into the corners. She could almost imagine the tinkling of the waterfall, the thick, cozy chairs circled around the clear pool.

They'd come back here one day, when the lobby was filled with people and light. When they did, they would remember how it had all started. His vision, and hers.

Daydreaming, she wandered toward the pipes that ran down the walls. Fanciful, yes, but certainly not foolish. In fact, she could— Her thoughts broke off as she stared down.

At first she wondered how the drywall finishers could have been so careless as to waste a trowelful of compound. And then not to clean it up, she thought as she crouched down to inspect it. A finger of light fell over it, making her look again, then look more closely and reach out to touch.

The moment she did, her heart froze. Scrambling up, she raced for the door, screaming for Cody.

He found the flashlight in the glove compartment, then tested it as a matter of course. It was probably useless to look around. It was probably just as useless to want to rip off a few panels of drywall and see for himself.

What did it matter if the place had been vandalized at this point? Correcting the wiring would have been difficult and time-consuming enough, but if the concrete and the steel were substandard, it all had to come down.

The anger bubbled up again, enough that he nearly tossed the flashlight back into the car. He'd come this far, he reminded himself. And Abra with him. They would look, and then they would leave. After the next day, what had once been his would be completely out of his hands.

His thoughts were running along the same lines as Abra's when he started back. Without the building—whatever Tim had done to sabotage it—he would never have met her. Whatever happened here, the moment the mess was turned over to the proper authorities he was going to tell her exactly what he wanted. Needed.

The hell with that, he decided, quickening his pace. He

was going to tell her now, right now, on the spot where it had all started. Maybe it was fitting, somehow, to ask her to marry him inside the half-finished building that had brought them together. The idea made him grin. What could be more fitting?

When he heard her scream the first time, his head whipped up. His heart stopped, but he was already running when she screamed again. He was close enough, when the explosion ripped, that the wall of hot air punched him like a fist and sent him flying in a rain of glass and rock and sheared metal.

The fall left him dazed—five seconds, ten. Then he was up and racing forward. He didn't feel the gash on his temple where something sharp and jagged had spun by close enough to tear his flesh. He didn't realize that the fall and those few seconds of numbness had saved his life.

All he saw were the flames licking greedily out of the windows the explosion had blown apart. Even as he reached what had been the doorway there were other explosions, one after another until the dawn echoed like a battlefield.

He was screaming for her, so strangled by fear that he couldn't hear his own voice, couldn't feel his own heart pumping out the panic. Something else blew, and a chunk of two-by-four shot out like a bullet, missing him by inches. The wall of heat drove him back once, searing his skin. Coughing, choking, he dropped to his knees and crawled inside.

There was more than fire here. Through the thick screen of smoke he could see where walls had crumbled, where huge chunks of ceiling had fallen in. As he fought his way in he could hear the sickening sound of steel breaking free and crashing down.

Blindly he heaved rubble aside, slicing his hand diagonally from one side of the palm to the other. Blood trickled into his eyes, which were already wet from the sting of smoke and fear.

Then he saw her hand, just her hand, almost covered by a pile of rubble. With a strength born of desperation, he began to heave and toss while the fire raged around him, roaring and belching and consuming. Over and over he called out her name, no longer aware of where he was, only that he had to get to her.

She was bleeding. In the turmoil of his mind he couldn't even form the prayer that she be alive. When he gathered her up, her body was weightless. For a moment, only a moment, he lost control enough to simply sit, rocking her. Slowly, with the terror clawing inside him, he began to drag her out.

Behind them was an inferno of unbearable heat and unspeakable greed. It was a matter of minutes, perhaps seconds, before what was still standing collapsed and buried them both. So he prayed, desperately, incoherently, while his shirt began to smoke.

He was ten feet beyond the building before he realized they were out. The ground around them was littered with steel and glass and still-smoldering wood. Every breath he took burned, but he fought his way to his feet, Abra in his arms, and managed another five yards before he collapsed with her.

Dimly, as if through a long, narrow tunnel, he heard the first sirens.

There was so much blood. Her hair was matted with it, and one arm of her shirt was soaked red. He kept calling to her as he wiped the worst of the grime and soot and blood from her face.

His hand was shaking as he reached out to touch the pulse in her throat. He never heard the last thundering crash behind him. But he felt the faint thready beat of her heart.

Chapter 12

"You need some attention, Mr. Johnson."

"That can wait." The panic was down to a grinding, deadly fear in the center of his gut. "Tell me about Abra. Where have you taken her?"

"Ms. Wilson is in the best of hands." The doctor was young, with wire-framed glasses and a shaggy head of dark hair. He'd been on the graveyard shift in the ER for a week, and he was looking forward to eight hours' sleep. "If you lose much more blood, you're going to pass out and save us all a lot of trouble."

Cody lifted him off his feet by the lapels of his coat and slammed him against the wall. "Tell me where she is."

"Mr. Johnson?"

Cody heard the voice behind him and ignored it as he stared into the eyes of the first-year resident. "Tell me where she is or you'll be bleeding."

The resident thought about calling for security, then decided against it. "She's being prepped for surgery. I don't know a great deal about her condition, but Dr. Bost is heading the surgical team, and he's the best."

Slowly Cody let him down, but he maintained the grip on his coat. "I want to see her."

"You can throw me up against the wall again," the young doctor said, though he sincerely hoped it wouldn't come to that, "but you're not going to be able to see her. She needs surgery. You're both lucky to be alive, Mr. Johnson. We're only trying to keep you that way."

"She's alive." Fear was burning his throat more than the smoke inhalation.

"She's alive." Cautiously the doctor reached up to remove Cody's hands. "Let me take care of you. As soon as she's out of surgery I'll come for you."

Cody looked down at his hands. Blood was already seeping through the bandage the ambulance attendant had fashioned. "Sorry."

"Don't mention it. From what the paramedics said, you've had a rough time. You've got a hole in your head, Mr. Johnson." He smiled, hoping charm would work. "I'll stitch it up for you."

"Excuse me." The man who had spoken earlier stepped forward and flashed a badge. "Lieutenant Asaro. I'd like to speak with you, Mr. Johnson."

"You want to speak with him while he's bleeding to death?" Feeling a bit more in control, the doctor pulled open a curtain and gestured toward an examining room. "Or would you like to wait until he's patched up?"

Asaro noticed a chair near the examining table. "Mind?"

"No." Cody sat on the table and peeled off what was left of his shirt. Both his torso and his back were lashed with burns and lacerations that made Asaro wince.

"Close call, I'd say."

Cody didn't respond as the doctor began to clean the gash at his temple.

"Mind telling me what you and Miss Wilson were doing out there at dawn?"

"Looking around." Cody sucked in his breath at the sting of the antiseptic. From a few rooms down came a high, keening scream. "She's the engineer on the job. I'm the architect."

"I got that much." Asaro opened his notebook. "Don't you figure you see enough of the place during the week?"

"We had our reasons for going tonight."

"I'm going to give you a shot," the doctor said, humming a little through his teeth as he worked. "Numb this up."

Cody merely nodded to the doctor. He didn't know if he could get any more numb. "Earlier this evening we were informed that there had been discrepancies on the job. Substandard materials used."

"I see. You were informed?"

"That's right." Cody divorced his mind from his body as the doctor competently stitched the wound. "I'm not going to name the source until I discuss it, but I'll tell you what I know."

Asaro set pencil to paper. "I'd appreciate it."

Cody went through it all—the discovery, the confrontation with Tim Thornway, the confession. His anger at the deception had faded. The only thing on his mind now was Abra. He continued, speaking of the car they had seen leaving the site, their assumption that it had been teenagers taking advantage of a lonely spot.

"You still think that?" Asaro asked.

"No." He felt the slight pull and tug on his hand as his flesh was sewed together. "I think somebody planted explosives in every building on that site and blew it all to hell. It's a lot tougher to identify substandard material when there's nothing much left of it."

"Are you making an accusation, Mr. Johnson?"

"I'm stating a fact, Lieutenant. Thornway panicked and had his project destroyed. He knew Abra and I were going to the building commissioner tomorrow if he didn't. Now we can bypass that."

"How so?"

"Because as soon as Abra's out of surgery I'm going to find him and I'm going to kill him." He flexed the fingers of his bandaged hand and was vaguely relieved when they moved. He spared the doctor a brief glance. "Finished?"

"Almost." The resident continued without breaking rhythm. "You've got some glass in your back and a few nice third-degree burns."

"That's an interesting story, Mr. Johnson." Asaro rose and pocketed his book. "I'm going to have it checked out. A little advice?" He didn't wait for Cody to answer. "You should be careful about making threats in front of a cop."

"Not a threat," Cody told him. He felt the sting as the resident removed another shard of glass. He welcomed it. "There's a woman upstairs who means more to me than anything in the world. You didn't see how she looked when we got her here." His stomach tightened, muscle by muscle. "You know her only crime, Lieutenant? Feeling sorry enough for that bastard to give him a few hours to explain all of this to his wife. Instead, he might have killed her."

"One more question. Did Thornway know you were going to visit the site?"

"What difference does it make?"

"Humor me."

"No. It wasn't planned. I was restless." He broke off to

press his fingers to his burning eyes. "I wanted to look at it, try to resign myself. Abra came with me."

"You ought to get yourself some rest, Mr. Johnson." Asaro nodded to the doctor. "I'll be in touch."

"We're going to check you in for a day or so, Mr. Johnson." The doctor wrapped the last burn before picking up a penlight to shine it in Cody's eyes. "I'll have the nurse give you something for the pain."

"No. I don't need a bed. I need to know what floor Abra's on."

"Take the bed, and I'll check on Miss Wilson." The look in Cody's eye had the resident holding up a hand. "Have it your way. You might not have noticed, but there are people around here who like my time and attention. Fifth-floor waiting room. Do yourself a favor," he said when Cody slid gingerly off the table. "Stop by the pharmacy." He scrawled a prescription on a pad, then ripped the sheet off. "Have this filled. Your being in pain's not going to help her."

"Thanks." Cody pocketed the prescription. "I mean it."

"I'd say anytime, but I'd be lying."

He didn't fill the prescription, not because the pain wasn't grim but because he was afraid that whatever he took might knock him out.

The waiting room was familiar. He'd spent hours there with Abra only days before, while David Mendez had been in surgery. Now it was Abra. He remembered how concerned she'd been, how kind. There was no one there now but himself.

Cody filled a large plastic cup with black coffee, scalded his already-raw throat with it and began to pace. If he could have risked leaving her alone for a time, he would have gone then to find Thornway, to pull him out of that nice white house and beat his face to a pulp on that well-groomed lawn.

For money, Cody thought as he downed the rest of the burning coffee. Abra was lying on an operating table fighting for her life, and the reason was money. Crushing the cup in his hand, he hurled it across the room. The pain that tore through his shoulder had him swearing in frustration.

She'd screamed for him. Cody dragged a hand over his face as the memory of the sound ripped through him every bit as savagely as the glass. She'd screamed for him, but he hadn't been fast enough.

Why had she been alone in there? Why hadn't he sent her back to the car? Why hadn't he simply taken her home?

Why? There were a dozen whys, but none of the answers changed the fact that Abra was hurt and he was—

"Cody." Her hair mussed and her face drawn, Jessie ran into the room. "Good God, Cody, what happened? What happened to Abra?" She took his hands, not noticing the bandage as she squeezed. "They said there was an accident at the site. But it's Sunday morning. Why would she be out there on Sunday morning?"

"Jessie." Barlow hurried in behind her to take her hand and lead her to a chair. "Give him a chance. You can see the boy's been hurt."

Jessie's lip was trembling, and she had to bite it to steady it. She saw the bandages and the burns, and she saw the look on his face, which spoke more clearly than words of shock and fear. "Dear Lord, Cody, what happened? They said she's in surgery."

"You sit, too." Taking charge, Barlow eased Cody into a chair. "I'm going to get us all some coffee here, and you take your time."

"I don't know how she is. They wouldn't let me see her." He was going to break down, he realized, if he didn't find something to hold on to. Reaction had taken its time seeping through, but now it struck like an iron fist. "She's alive," he said. It was almost a prayer. "When I pulled her out, she was alive."

"Pulled her out?" Jessie held the cup Barlow urged on her with both hands. Still, the coffee swayed and trembled. "Pulled her out of what?"

"I was outside, on my way back. Abra was in the building when it exploded."

"Exploded?" The coffee slipped out of her hands and onto the floor.

"The fire went up so fast." He could see it, he could feel it. As he sat in the chair, in his mind he was still back in the building, blinded by smoke and searching for her. "I got through, but I couldn't find her. The place was coming down. There must have been more than one charge. She was trapped under the rubble, but when I got her out she was alive."

Barlow put a hand on Jessie's arm to calm her, and to quiet her. "I want you to take it slow, Cody. Start at the beginning."

It was like a dream now. The pain did that, and the fear. He started with the call from Carmen Mendez and continued until they had wheeled Abra, unconscious, away from him.

"I should have pushed him," Cody murmured. "I should have picked up the phone and called the authorities myself. But he was drunk and pitiful and we wanted to give him a chance to salvage something. If I hadn't wanted to go out there, to look at it, to—I don't know, soothe my pride?—she wouldn't be hurt."

"You went in after her." Jessie rubbed the heels of her hands hard over her face. "You risked your life to save hers."

"I have no life without her."

The time for tears would have to wait. She rose to take his hand. "You know, most of us never find anyone who loves us that much. She's always needed it, and I always fell short. You're not going to lose her."

"I don't suppose you'd listen to an old man and stretch out on the couch over there?" When Cody shook his head, Barlow stood. "Thought not. Got to make a few phone calls. Won't be long."

So they waited. Cody watched the clock as the minutes ticked by. When Nathan and Jackie came in ahead of Barlow an hour later, he was too numb to be surprised.

"Oh, honey…" Jackie went to him immediately, her small, sharp-featured face alive with concern. "We heard almost as soon as the plane touched down. What can we do?"

He shook his head but held on. It helped somehow just to hold on to someone who knew him. "She's in surgery."

"I know. Mr. Barlow explained everything out in the hall. We won't talk about it now. We'll just wait."

Nathan dropped a hand on his shoulder. "I wish we could have gotten here sooner. If it helps any, Thornway's already been picked up."

Cody's eyes focused, then hardened. "How do you know?"

"Barlow did some checking. The police went by to question him. The minute he was told that you and Abra had been in the explosion he fell apart."

"It doesn't matter." Cody stood up and went to the window. It didn't matter whether Thornway was in jail or in hell. Abra was in surgery, and every second was an eternity.

Nathan started forward, but Jackie laid a hand on his arm. "Let me," she murmured. She stepped up quietly beside him, waiting for him to gather his control. "She's the engineer, isn't she?"

"Yeah. She's the engineer."

"And I don't have to ask if you love her."

"I haven't even told her." He laid his forehead on the glass because he was tempted to punch his fist through it. "It was never the right time or the right place. Jack, when I pulled her out—" He needed another minute to force himself to say it out loud. "When I pulled her out, I thought she was dead."

"She wasn't. She isn't." She laid a hand gently on his wrist. "I know I have this rotten optimism that can be annoying, but I don't believe you're going to lose her. When she's better, are you getting married?"

"Yeah. She doesn't know that, either. I have to talk her into it."

"You're a good talker, Cody." She touched his cheek, then turned his head so that she could study his face. He was deadly pale, with bruises under eyes that were still swollen and red-rimmed from smoke. "You look terrible. How many stitches?"

"Didn't count."

She turned over his hands, barely managing to suppress a shudder. "Did they give you something for the pain?"

"Some prescription." Absently he touched his pocket.

"Which you didn't fill." At least this was something she could do, Jackie decided, plucking it out of his pocket. "I'm going down to have it filled now, and when I bring it up you're going to take it."

"I don't want—"

"You don't want to mess with me," Jackie told him. She kissed his cheek before she strode out of the waiting room.

He took the pills to placate her, then drank the coffeepot dry to offset the drowsiness. Another hour passed, and then another. His pain dulled to a throb, and his fear sharpened.

He recognized the doctor as the same one who had operated on Mendez. Bost came in, swept a glance over the group huddled in chairs and couches and approached Jessie.

"You're Mrs. Barlow, Miss Wilson's mother?"

"Yes." She wanted to rise but found her legs wouldn't straighten. Instead she put one hand in her husband's and the other in Cody's. "Please, tell me."

"She's out of surgery. Your daughter hasn't regained consciousness yet, and she's lost a great deal of blood. We were able to stop the hemorrhaging. She has some broken ribs, but fortunately her lungs weren't damaged. Her arm was broken in two places, and she has a hairline fracture below the right knee."

Foolishly Jessie remembered kissing scraped elbows and knees to make them better. "But they'll heal?"

"Yes. Mrs. Barlow, we're going to do a series of X rays and a CAT scan."

"Brain damage?" Cody felt his blood dry up. "Are you saying she has brain damage?"

"She suffered a severe blow to the head. These tests are standard. I know they sound ominous, but they're our best defense against whatever other injuries she may have."

"When will you have the results?" Jessie asked.

"We'll run the tests this afternoon. They'll take a couple of hours."

"I want to see her." Cody stood, sending Jessie a brief, apologetic glance. "I have to see her."

"I know."

"She won't be awake," the doctor explained. "And you'll have to keep it brief."

"Just let me see her."

He wasn't sure what was worse—all those hours of speculation or the actuality of seeing her lying so still, so pale, with bruises standing out so harshly on her cheeks and the tubes hooking her to a line of impersonal machines.

He took her hand, and it was cool. But he could feel the pulse beating in her wrist, echoed by the monitors next to her.

There was no privacy here. She would hate that, he thought. Only a wall of glass separated her from the quiet movement of nurses and technicians in ICU. They'd given her a bed gown, something white with faded blue flowers. He resented the idea that dozens of others had worn it before.

She was so pale.

His mind kept leaping back to that, though he tried to fix it on other, inconsequential things. The faded gown, the beep of the monitors, the hush of crepe soles on the tiles beyond the glass.

Where was she? he wondered as he sat and kept her hand in his through the bars on the side of the bed. He didn't want her to get too far away. He didn't know what to say to bring her closer.

"They won't let me stay, Red, but I'll be hanging around in the waiting room until you wake up. Make it soon." He rubbed a hand absently over his chest as it tightened. "You came through okay. They want to take some more tests, but they don't amount to much. You've got a nasty bump on the head, that's all."

Please, God, let that be all.

He fell silent again, counting the monotonous beeps of the monitors.

"I was thinking we could take that trip back east once you're out of here. You can work on your tan and nag me about stress points." His fingers tightened uncontrollably on hers. "For God's sake, Abra, don't leave me."

He thought—or perhaps it was only a wish—that her fingers pressed just for an instant against his hand.

"You've got to get some rest, Cody."

He'd been staring at the same paragraph of the newspaper for twenty minutes. Now he looked up and saw Nathan. "What are you doing back here?"

"Putting my foot down with you." Nathan sat on the couch beside him. "I left Jack at the hotel. If I can't go back and tell her I convinced you to take a break, she's going to insist on coming out herself."

"I'm doing better than I look."

"You'd have to be to still be conscious."

"Be a pal, Nathan." He gave himself the luxury of sitting back and closing his eyes. "Don't push."

Nathan hesitated. He wasn't the kind of man who interfered in other people's lives. There had been a time when he'd chosen not to become involved at all. That had been before Jackie. "I remember saying almost the same thing to you once when I was confused and upset. You didn't listen, either."

"You were being too stubborn to admit your own feelings," Cody said. "I know what my feelings are."

"Let me buy you something to eat."

"I don't want to miss Bost."

"How about an update on Thornway?"

Cody opened his eyes. "Yeah."

"He made a full confession." Nathan waited while Cody lit a cigarette. The ashtray was already littered with them. "He admitted to substituting materials, the payoffs, the bribes. He claims he was drunk and in a state of panic after you and Abra confronted him. He made the call to arrange the arson with some kind of crazed idea that no one would be able to prove anything against him if the project was destroyed."

"Didn't he think there would be an investigation?" Cody expelled a quick stream of smoke. "Did he think we'd all just keep quiet about it?"

"Obviously he didn't think."

"No." Too drained even for anger, Cody stared across the room, where Jessie dozed on Barlow's shoulder. "And because he didn't think, Abra was almost killed. Even now she could be—" He couldn't say it. He couldn't even think it.

"He's going to spend a lot of years paying for it."

"No matter how many," Cody murmured, "no matter how much, it won't be enough."

"Still up and around, Mr. Johnson?" The young resident walked in, looking as though he'd slept in a packing crate. "I'm Dr. Mitchell," he explained to Nathan. "I patched your friend up, oh—" he glanced at his watch "—about eight hours ago." He looked back at Cody. "Hasn't anybody chained you to a bed yet?"

"No."

Mitchell sat and stretched out his legs. "I pulled a double shift, but I still don't feel as bad as you look."

"Thanks."

"That was a free medical opinion. I ran into Dr. Bost up in the lab." He looked longingly at Cody's cigarette, reminded himself he was a doctor and subdued the urge to ask for one. "He was just finishing up with the results of Miss Wilson's tests."

Cody said nothing, could say nothing. Very slowly he leaned forward and crushed out the cigarette.

"It looks good, Mr. Johnson."

His mouth was dry, too dry. He couldn't find the saliva to swallow. "Are you telling me she's all right?"

"We're moving her from critical to guarded condition. The scan and the X rays don't indicate brain damage. She's got one whopper of a concussion, to couch things in unprofessional terms. Bost should be down in a few minutes to give you the details, but I thought you could use a little good news. She came to briefly," he continued when Cody remained silent. "She recited her name and address, remembered who was president and asked for you."

"Where is she?"

"It's going to be a little while before you can see her. She's sedated."

"That's her mother." Cody rubbed a hand over his face. "Her mother's sitting over there. Will you tell her? I've got to take a walk."

"I've got a bed with your name on it," Mitchell said, rising with Cody. "The best way to stay close to your lady is to check into our little hotel. I can recommend the chicken surprise."

"I'll keep that in mind." Cody found his way out and walked.

Abra wanted to open her eyes. She could hear things, but the sounds ran through her mind like water. There was no pain. She felt as though she were floating, mind and body, inches off the ground.

She remembered. If she forced her mind to focus, she remembered. There was the sun shooting in red-and-gold fingers through the dome, and a sense of contentment, of purpose. Then came the fear.

Had she screamed for him? She thought she had, but that had been before that horrible noise had thundered around her. There was another memory, but it was unclear and dreamlike. She had gone flying— Something like a hot, invisible hand had scooped her up and hurled her through the air. Then there had been nothing.

Where was he?

She thought, was almost certain, that he'd been with her. Had she spoken to him, or was that a dream, too? It seemed to her that she'd opened her eyes and seen him sitting beside her. There had been a bandage on his face, and his face had been drawn and pale. They'd spoken. Hadn't they spoken? With the drugs clouding her mind, she struggled to remember and was frustrated.

Jessie. Her mother had been there, too. She'd been crying.

Then there were strangers' faces. They'd peered down at her, shone lights in her eyes, asked her foolish questions. Did she know her name? Of course she knew her name. She was Abra Wilson and she wanted to know what was happening to her.

Maybe she was dead.

She'd lost track of time, but so had Cody. He'd spent every minute he'd been permitted to, and as many more as he could fight for, beside her. Two days had crawled by. She'd been conscious off and on, but the medication had kept her drowsy and often incoherent.

By the third day he could see that she was struggling to focus.

"I can't stay awake." For the first time he heard petulance in her voice, and he was cheered by it. Until now she had accepted everything without complaint. "What are they giving me?"

"Something to help you rest."

"I don't want any more." She turned her head so that she could look at him. "Tell them not to give me any more."

"You need to rest."

"I need to think." Annoyed, she tried to shift. She saw

the cast on her arm and fought to remember. It was broken. They'd told her it was broken. There was a cast on her leg, too. She'd been confused at first, wondering if she'd been in a car accident. But it was becoming easier to remember now.

"The buildings. They're gone."

"They don't matter." He pressed his lips to her fingers. "You gave me a scare, Red."

"I know." She was beginning to feel now. Whenever she was awake for this long she began to feel. The pain reassured her. "You're hurt."

"Couple of scrapes. You're having pain." He was up immediately. "I'll get the nurse."

"I don't want any more medicine."

Patiently he leaned over and kissed her just below the bruise on her cheekbone. "Baby, I can't stand to watch you hurt."

"Kiss me again." She lifted a hand to his cheek. "It feels better when you do."

"Excuse me." The nurse bustled in, all business. "It's time for the doctor to examine you now, Miss Wilson." She shot Cody a look. He'd given her more than his share of aggravation over the past few days. "You'll have to wait outside."

"Yes, ma'am."

"I'm not taking any more medication," he heard Abra say. "If you've got any needles on you, you'd better lose them."

For the first time in days, he laughed. She was coming back.

In another week she was frantic to get out. The night nurse caught her trying to hobble into the corridor. Cody ignored her pleas to smuggle her into the elevators. The doctor scotched her compromise suggestion of outpatient care.

Abra found herself trapped, her arm covered with plaster, her leg in a cast to the knee. She'd gone through phases of anger and self-pity. Now she was just bored. Miserably bored.

When she awoke from a nap she'd taken in self-defense, she saw a woman in her room. She was small and obviously pregnant and had a wild mop of red hair. As Abra looked, she shifted around the arrangements of flowers and plants.

"Hello."

"Hi." Jackie turned and beamed a smile. "So you're awake. Now Cody's going to yell at me because I chased him downstairs to the cafeteria. He's gone from lean to skinny in a week. He'll be gaunt in another couple of days." She walked over to the bed and made herself comfortable beside it. "So how are you feeling?"

"Pretty good." It was easy to smile. "Who are you?"

"Oh, sorry. I'm Jack. Nathan's wife?" She glanced around. "Even with the flowers, hospitals are depressing, aren't they? Bored?"

"Stiff. It's nice of you to come, though."

"Cody's family. That makes you family, too."

Abra glanced toward the doorway. "How is he?"

"He gets better as you get better. We were worried about both of you for a while."

Abra glanced back and studied Jackie's face. She'd had a lot of time to study faces in the last week. This one was friendly and—thank God—cheerful. She'd spoken of Cody as family, and Abra was certain she'd meant it.

"Will you tell me something?" Abra began. "Straight?"

"I'll try."

"Will you tell me what happened? Every time I try to

talk to Cody about it he changes the subject, evades or gets angry. I can remember most of it, but it's patchy."

Jackie started to evade, as well, but then she looked into Abra's eyes. Eyes that strong, she decided, deserved the truth. "Why don't you tell me how much you remember?"

Satisfied, Abra relaxed. "We'd gone out to the site, then into the main building. It was still dark, so Cody went out to the car for a light. I was looking around. You know about the switch in materials?"

"Yes."

"When I was alone and looking around, I saw what I took at first for a bunch of drywall compound. It was plastic explosive. I ran for the door." She half lifted her casted arm. "I didn't get there."

Jackie realized she'd been right about the strength. It wasn't fear she saw but determination, laced with what she imagined was a healthy dose of frustration.

"Cody was still outside when the building went up. He managed to get through and find you. I don't know the details about that—he doesn't talk about it—but it must have been terrifying. He managed to drag you out. He told me he thought you were dead."

"It must have been horrible," Abra murmured. "Horrible for him."

"Abra, he's blaming himself for what happened to you."

"What?" She shifted, fought off a twinge of pain and struggled to sit up straighter. "Why should he?"

"He has the idea that if he had dropped the ax on Thornway straight off…if he hadn't wanted to go out there that night…if he hadn't left you alone in the building. If."

"That's stupid." She found the control button and brought the head of the bed up.

"What's stupid?"

Jackie glanced over as Cody walked in. She rose and moved over to pat his cheek. "You are, honey. I'll leave you two alone. Where's Nathan?"

"Took a side trip to the nursery."

She laughed and patted her belly. "I'll join him."

"I like her," Abra said when they were alone.

"Jack's hard not to like." He handed her a rose, careful, as he had been careful for days, not to touch her. "You've got a roomful of flowers, but I thought you might like to have one to hold."

"Thanks."

His eyes narrowed. "Something wrong?"

"Yes."

"I'll get the nurse."

"Sit down." She gestured impatiently toward the chair. "I wish you'd stop treating me like an invalid."

"Okay. Want to take a quick jog around the block?"

"You're a riot."

"Yeah." But he didn't sit. Restless, he roamed the room, stopping off by the table, which was loaded with flowers. "You got some new ones."

"Swaggart and Rodriguez. They called a truce long enough to bring me carnations. They were fighting when they left."

"Some things never change."

"And some things do. You used to be able to talk to me, and to look at me when you did."

He turned. "I'm talking to you now. I'm looking at you now."

"Are you angry with me?"

"Don't be ridiculous."

"I'm not being ridiculous." She pushed herself up, wincing. Cody's jaw tightened. "You come in here every day, every night."

"I must be furious to do that." He walked to her with some idea of helping her settle comfortably.

"Stop it." She took an ill-tempered swipe at his hand. "I can do it myself. A broken arm's not terminal."

He nearly snapped back at her before he bit down on temper. "Sorry."

"That's it. *That's it.* You won't even fight with me." She gestured with her cast, which was crisscrossed with signatures. "All you do is pat me on the head or hover over me or ask me if I need anything."

"You want to go a couple rounds, fine. We'll take it up when you're on your feet."

"We'll take it up now, damn it. Right now." She pounded a frustrated fist on the bed. She couldn't even get out of bed by herself and pace off the rage. "You've treated me like some kind of slow-witted child these last few days, and I've had enough. You won't even talk to me about what happened."

"What do you want?" The strain that had stretched his emotions to the breaking point finally snapped. "Do you want me to tell you what it was like to see that building go up and know you were inside? Do you want me to describe to you what it was like to crawl through what was left, looking for you? Then to find you half buried, bleeding and broken?" His voice rose as he strode toward her, and he gripped the rail along the side of the bed, his fingers white. "Do you want me to go over how I felt waiting in this damn place, not knowing if you were going to live or die?"

"How are we going to get beyond it if we don't?" She reached for his hand, but he snatched it away. "You were hurt, too." Her own temper and frustration broke free.

"Don't you know how it makes me feel to see your hand, your face, and know it happened because you went back for me? I want to talk about it, damn you. I can't stand lying here and trying to reconstruct it."

"Then stop." He waved his hand and sent a pitcher flying. There was some small satisfaction in hearing the plastic hit the wall. "It's over and it's done. When you get out of here we're not going to look back. You're never going to put me through anything like this again. Do you understand?" He whirled back to face her. "I can't stand it. I want you out of here. I want you back with me. I love you and I'm sick of lying in bed at night and sweating through what might have happened."

"What didn't happen," she shouted. "I'm here, I'm alive, because you saw to it. You didn't cause this, you jerk. You saved my life. I love you too much to sit here and watch this eat at you. It's going to stop, Johnson. I mean it. If you can't come in here and treat me normally, don't come at all."

"Stop this." A nurse hurried in. "We can hear you arguing all the way down—"

"Get out!" both of them shouted in unison.

She did, shutting the door behind her.

"You want me to leave, I'll leave." Cody stalked toward the bed again, this time sending the railing down with a crash. "But not before I have my say. Maybe I do blame myself for this. And that's my business. You're not going to sit there and tell me how I should feel or what I should feel. I've played along with your way of doing things too long already."

Abra set her chin. "I don't know what you're talking about."

"No strings, no commitment, no long-term plans. Isn't that the way you set things up?"

"We agreed—"

"I'm through agreeing, and I'm through waiting until the time's right, the place is right, the mood's right. Did you hear what I said a few minutes ago? I said I loved you."

"You didn't say it." Abra frowned down at her hands. "You yelled it."

"Okay, I yelled it." He sat beside her, barely controlling the urge to shout again. "Now I'm saying it, and I'm saying you're going to marry me. And that's the end of it."

"But—"

"Don't." His temper vanished so abruptly that he could only press his fingers to his eyes. "Don't push me now."

"Cody, I—"

"Just shut up, will you?" He dropped his hands, thinking—hoping—he'd regained control. "It wasn't supposed to be like this, a shouting match with you flat on your back. It seems whenever we plan things out it doesn't work. So here it is, Red—no plans, no design. I need you. I want you to marry me, to come back East and live your life with me."

She looked up and took a long breath. "Okay."

With a half laugh, he rubbed his hands over his face. "Okay? That's it?"

"Not exactly. Come here." She held out her arm and took him to her. For the first time in days he held her as if he meant it. "You probably heard what I said a little while ago, about being in love with you."

"You didn't say it." His lips curved with a combination of pleasure and relief as he pressed them to her neck. She was warm and very much alive, and she was with him. "You yelled it."

"It's still true." She eased him back so that she could look at his face. "I'm sorry."

"For what?"

"For putting you through all of this."

"It wasn't your fault," Cody told her.

"No, it wasn't." She smiled, curling the fingers at the end of her cast into the fingers at the end of his bandage. "It wasn't yours, either. It's not something I'd like to go through again, but it did push you to ask me to marry you."

"I might have done it anyway." He grinned and brushed his lips over her fingers. "Maybe."

She lifted a brow. They'd crushed the rose between them. Carefully Abra smoothed out the petals. "I have a confession. I was going to come East whether you wanted me or not."

He drew away to study her face. "Is that right?"

"I thought that if I got in your way often enough you'd get used to it. In my head I told myself I was going to let you walk away, but in my heart… I wasn't going to give you a chance."

He leaned closer to kiss her. "I wasn't going anywhere."

Epilogue

Cody scrawled the information on the registration form. Behind the desk, the slope of rock was dotted with cacti just beginning to bloom. Light streamed through the arch of glass. The clerk beamed at him.

"Enjoy your stay with us, Mr. Johnson."

"I intend to." He turned, pocketing the key.

People moved in and out of the lobby, many of them in tennis clothes. Some strolled down the wide, curving staircase, others glided up and down in the silent elevators. Overhead the dome let in the sun in a fantasy of color. He watched it spread over the tile floor. A waterfall tumbled musically into a small rock pool. Smiling, he walked over to it, and to the woman who stood watching the race of water.

"Any complaints?"

Abra turned, tilting her head to study his face. "I still remember how many feet of pipe we needed to give you your little whim."

He took her chin in his hand. "It makes a statement."

"So you always said." She'd tell him later how lovely she thought it was. "Anyway, thanks to me, it's functional." Resting her head on his shoulder, she turned back to watch the water.

"What's wrong?"

"You'll think I'm stupid."

"Red, I think you're stupid half the time." He sucked in air when her elbow connected with his ribs. "Tell me anyway."

"I miss the kids."

With a laugh he spun her around and kissed her. "That's not stupid. But I bet I can take your mind off them for a while—once we walk over to our cabana."

"Maybe." She smiled challengingly. "If you really work at it."

"I figure a second honeymoon should be even better than the first."

She linked her hands around his neck. "Then let's get started."

"In a minute." He drew her hands away to take them in his own. "Five years ago we stood in here at dawn. The place was empty, and neither of us could be sure it would ever be finished."

"Cody, it doesn't do any good to remember all that."

"It's something I'll never forget." He brought her hands to his lips. "But there's something I never told you. I was going to ask you to marry me here, that morning."

The surprise came first, even after nearly five years of marriage and partnership. Then came the pleasure and the sweetness. "I guess it's too late now. You're already stuck with me."

"Too late for that." Ignoring the people around them, he

gathered her close. They might have been alone, as they had been alone that morning years before. "It's not too late for me to tell you that you're the best part of my life. That I love you more now than I did five years ago."

"Cody." She pressed her lips to his. The feeling was as strong as ever, the taste as alluring. "I'm so happy to have you, to have the family. Coming back here now makes me realize how lucky I am." She traced the faint scar along his temple. "We could have lost everything. Instead, we have everything." For a moment she held him tight. Then, breaking away, she smiled. "And I like your waterfall."

"Praise indeed, from an engineer. Here." He took a coin out of his pocket. "Make a wish."

"I don't need wishes." She tossed it over her shoulder. "Just you." The coin sank slowly into the pool as they walked away together.

* * * * *